D0339918

02/2014

ACPL, Laramie, WY   11/2016
39092086613777
Kotecki, Nathan.
Pull down the night /
Suburban strange ;bk. 2
Pieces: 1

WITHDRAWN

BOOK TWO OF THE SUBURBAN STRANGE

pull down the night

NATHAN KOTECKI

HOUGHTON MIFFLIN HARCOURT

BOSTON   NEW YORK

Albany County
Public Library
Laramie, Wyoming

For Amanda, who only flies when
she thinks no one is watching.

Copyright © 2013 by Nathan Kotecki

All rights reserved. For information about permission to reproduce selections from this book, write to Permissions, Houghton Mifflin Harcourt Publishing Company, 215 Park Avenue South, New York, New York 10003.

Houghton Mifflin is an imprint of Houghton Mifflin Harcourt Publishing Company.
www.hmhbooks.com

The text of this book is set in Caslon Pro.

Library of Congress Cataloging-in-Publication Data
Kotecki, Nathan.
Pull down the night : book two of The Suburban strange / by Nathan Kotecki.
p. cm. — (The Suburban strange)
Summary: "Bruno and Sylvio transfer to Suburban High and find themselves entangled in its otherworldly mysteries and the uber chic clique known as the Rosary"
—Provided by publisher.
ISBN 978-0-547-73114-8
[1. High schools—Fiction. 2. Schools—Fiction. 3. Cliques (Sociology)—Fiction. 4. Supernatural—Fiction. 5. Brothers—Fiction. 6. Dating (Social customs)—Fiction.] I. Title.
PZ7.K8537Pul 2013
[Fic]—dc23
2013003938

Manufactured in the United States of America
DOC 10 9 8 7 6 5 4 3 2
4500450680

◉

We are fortunate to live in a world where we are not limited to experiencing only the things we understand. And as for whether things are possible, if they happen, does it matter whether or not they are possible?

◉

contents

1

a forest

BRUNO OPENED THE BACK door of his family's new house and stepped into the thickening air of dusk, having no idea he was about to fall in love. He left the flagstone patio and crossed the lawn to a high wall of cypress bordering the backyard. After passing through the hedge, he traversed a grassy alley and climbed two stone steps through another row of trees to the larger rear yard. There a neglected tennis court lay hidden under acorns and leaves, enclosed by more cypress and canopied by tall oaks. A picnic bench languished in the shadow of a tree. Fireflies blinked in the darkening corners.

Bruno went back to the grassy alley. At one end the peak of the garage roof loomed black against the purple sky. In the opposite direction the alley dead-ended in a copse of dogwoods and shrubs. Bruno figured the exact center of this neighborhood block must lie somewhere on the other side of those trees, surrounded by backyards. He walked to the copse, but it was too dense to see anything through it. A small flock of birds rose, whisking the sky, and resettled in the trees past the tennis court.

Cicadas thrummed around him. Bruno carefully stepped

into the tangle of greenery and near darkness, and just when he thought there was nothing to find, the overgrown area gave way and he emerged in a clearing.

Bruno found himself on a small square of freshly mown grass, enclosed by solid walls of bushes and trees on all sides. He couldn't see a roof in any direction. Well-tended clusters of white flowers grew in beds on each side of the clearing. An arched alcove sheltered a small fountain, its laughter echoing quietly off the marble. Turning back, Bruno couldn't see how he'd made it through the thicket.

The air in this unexpected place smelled of cloves, with a hint of the seashore. Bruno wondered what could be brining the air here, two hours' drive inland. He felt as though he had been transported to a remote sanctuary. The deep shadows held a chill.

There was a rustling that sounded too loud to be a bird, and he considered fleeing back into the trees, fearful of being caught trespassing. But before Bruno could move, a man emerged on the far side of the clearing, clad in a battered oilskin mackintosh, a dark work shirt and pants, and well-worn boots. His rugged face made it hard to guess his age; bits of dried leaves clung to his hair and the rake he carried.

"I thought I'd see you soon enough," the man said. He had a deep voice with a little gravel in it and an accent Bruno guessed was Australian. "How d'you do?"

"You did?" Bruno asked. "Are you our neighbor?"

"No, I don't live here."

"Are you the gardener?"

"That's about right," the man said, idly hefting the rake. "Are you Bruno, then?"

"How did you know?"

"It's my job to know. But not many folks come through here, so there aren't many others it could have been."

"Why don't people come through here?"

"Because they don't know how to find it. It's tucked in the middle of so many places, but most people don't even realize it's here." With the toe of his boot, the man pushed a loose piece of sod back into place at the edge of a flower bed.

Bruno approached the fountain and read the letters carved into the arch. "Ebentwine?"

"I don't know who named it. It's been called that as long as I've been here, and I've been here a long time." The gardener reached up to a branch and pulled it down slightly, inspecting it. "Where are you headed?"

It sounded like a suggestion that he be on his way. "Home, I guess." He turned to go but realized he had lost his bearings.

"Go this way." The gardener pointed to a hedge on one side.

"Thank you." Bruno carefully pushed through the hedge, expecting to reach the grassy alley behind his house. Instead he found himself in the far reaches of a lawn behind a house he didn't recognize. The scent of the clearing was gone, replaced by the more familiar suburban smells of pine trees and grass clippings. The shades of green around him seemed duller, perhaps because of the fading daylight.

Now he was sure he was trespassing. The gardener hadn't seen him come in; how could he have known which house was Bruno's? Then again, how had he known Bruno's name? Bruno turned to go, then stopped.

Music was playing somewhere—a song that tugged at him like a ghost. He scanned the house in front of him, looking for the source. In an open upstairs window, a slender girl stood in profile, pulling a brush through her shiny dark hair. Bruno stepped out from his cover among the trees, mesmerized by the sight. The music was faint, but wavering notes from an electric guitar reached him, and the low voice of a woman. The past and the future fell away.

He didn't pay much attention to girls usually, and when he did, he only compared them unfavorably with his older sister, Sophia. But now it was as if Bruno were seeing a girl for the first time. The air around her figure seemed to vibrate like heat above asphalt, and everything outside her window went out of focus.

She set her brush down and looked out over the trees. Bruno guessed she was a few years older than he was, and her pale face was more elegant than that of any teenager Bruno had ever seen. The song floated down to him over the wash of guitar, the lyrics unclear. All of it was so unexpected, so otherworldly; Bruno no longer cared that he didn't quite know where he was. He would have stood there all night watching her.

In the upstairs room, the shadow of another person slid across the ceiling, and the ethereal girl turned away from the window. She moved out of sight, and the spell on Bruno was broken. He became aware of the cicadas in the trees again, and he swatted at an insect by his ear. He waited, but after a minute the chill began to seep through his shirt. Picking through the wall of dark green, he found his way back to the clearing.

The gardener was still there. "Back so soon?"

"That's not my house," Bruno said.

"I know."

"Then why did you . . . I thought you said . . ."

"Come back whenever you like," the man told him, pointing to another place in the hedges.

"My house is that way?" Bruno couldn't tell if the nodding man was amused or annoyed. Bruno stepped carefully into the thicket, concerned he would wind up in yet another unknown place. But he emerged in the grassy alley and returned to his own backyard. In his mind he still saw the girl in the window. Who was she? He wondered how he might meet her. It felt like the easiest thing and the hardest thing in the world. He went inside his house.

His brother was calling his name as Bruno climbed the stairs, and the last bit of adventure faded from his mind. He shouted back, "What!"

"What time do we have to be there tomorrow?"

"I don't know." Bruno did know, but he liked holding out on his older brother. He went into his bedroom and over to his window. Across the trees the neighboring roof darkened as evening took hold. It was not the same roof he had seen on the other side of that strange little clearing named Ebentwine. Bruno must have gotten turned around; the girl must live on the other side of them.

He sat on his bed and considered the two sealed moving boxes huddled together in the middle of the wood floor. His bare dresser, empty desk, and lamp stood against the far wall.

"What did you say?" his brother called.

"I said I don't know!" Bruno went down the hall to his brother's bedroom. Sylvio was sitting at his computer, dressed in gray slacks and a black shirt, his black hair parted as if with a knife. Bruno wondered why he went to all that trouble when he hadn't left the house all day.

"We'd better find out."

Bruno pushed his hands down in his jeans pockets and

looked around his brother's room. After only two weeks it already looked as though he had been living there for years. Three walls were covered with the same posters and clippings that had decorated Sylvio's room in their old house. Dozens of wine crates were stacked on their sides against the fourth wall to make shelves that crowded the ceiling. All the same books, CDs, and notebooks were there. Bruno recognized the gloomy song that was playing on Sylvio's computer, though he didn't know its name or the name of the band. He wondered if Sylvio knew the song he had just heard in the beautiful girl's backyard, but there was no way he'd be able to describe it. "Do we have to make dinner?"

"Probably. They're out meeting people from the new parish. They didn't say when they'd be back."

Bruno wandered out into the hall. He had acclimated quickly to the dimensions of the new house. It was bigger than their last house, but older. The first bedroom at the top of the stairs had been put together as a guest room, which pained him a little, because it would have been their older sister's. But Sophia was off at college, and even farther, studying abroad. She had left for Argentina before she'd even had the chance to see this house. She wouldn't set foot in Whiterose until Christmas.

Later, Sylvio teased him as they ate the omelets Bruno had made. "So, are you going to start mowing all the lawns and walking all the dogs here, too?"

"Maybe. Who knows, maybe someone else has all the jobs already."

"I hope not; what would you *do* with all your time? Are you curious about high school?"

"Not really. Maybe a little."

"It sounds like Suburban is a lot bigger than Franklin High."

"That's not saying much."

"True. I may not see you very much at school. I remember when I was a first year and Sophia was a senior, we saw each other all the time. She kind of looked out for me. It's probably not going to be like that here."

"That's okay."

"Have you decided what you're going to wear?"

His brother was serious. "I haven't even thought about it."

"You kill me, you know that? It's the first impression you're going to make on everybody! You can't do that over."

"What are you going to wear?" Bruno already knew.

"White shirt, polka dot tie, black sweater vest, black velvet trousers. I know I'm breaking the rule, wearing velvet when it's not between Thanksgiving and New Year's. But this is a special occasion."

"And when you go out dancing."

"What?"

"You wear velvet when you go out dancing."

"Oh, yeah. But I don't know if there's anything like that around here. I had to drive forty minutes to get to Hermetica. Who knows; here I might have to drive a couple hours to find a club like that. I don't want to think about it."

Bruno thought only that his brother was going to be warm in velvet pants. The garage door motor churned on the other side of the mudroom door, and in a minute their parents came in.

"Oh, good, you ate!" Mr. Perilunas kissed them. "We met

some really lovely people tonight. I think this new parish is going to be fantastic."

"Mom, what time do we have to be at school tomorrow?" Sylvio asked.

Seven forty-five, Bruno thought.

"Seven forty-five," his mother said. "You must be so excited!"

After dinner, Bruno studied himself in the mirror in the upstairs bathroom. The edges of his sweatshirt were frayed, and his wavy brown hair bristled on his forehead as though he had toweled it dry and forgotten about it, which he had. He went back to his room and sat on the edge of his bed. Out the window the roof of the house next door was barely visible in the night sky. He went to the lonely moving boxes and pulled up the packing tape. He dug out a big burgundy book with *Maps of the World* written in gold on the spine and went back to his bed.

He opened the book at random, confident the cities he found would be familiar. "Pardubice," he said carefully, sounding out the letters on the map. He knew the names on these maps by sight, but not by sound. This was his favorite book, but during the move a different map had captured his attention: the full-scale one, where one mile equals one mile. His family had pulled up their pin from a place Bruno knew as well as the lines on his hand, and pushed it down again in a new place. He knew this new place decently well already—he had studied its map obsessively from the moment he had learned about the move—but the streets and corners of Whiterose waited for him to walk them or see them from a car window. There was a particular pleasure in proving a map right by going there in person, and that anticipated pleasure outweighed any sadness

Bruno had felt about what he was leaving behind. He was ready for the next thing.

"WELL, YOU LOOK ALL RIGHT, I guess," Sylvio said the next morning. Bruno looked down at his jeans and striped polo. He only felt self-conscious when his brother looked at him. But then, Bruno always thought Sylvio looked as if he was dressing for the movie he hoped to be cast in someday. "You ready?"

They went out to the garage and got into the old black car that had been purchased after forty-five minutes of negotiations between Bruno's brother and his father in a sales lot the previous week. Bruno liked the car. With rounded surfaces that would have been more sharply angled on a new car, it had the look some older cars do, as though it enjoyed its job of driving. Sylvio plugged his music player into the new stereo in the dashboard, and they coasted down the driveway.

His brother sang along with the opening lines of "Fascination Street." He looked over at Bruno. "You like this one, don't you?"

"Yeah," Bruno said.

"You know who it is, right?"

"Um, no," Bruno said, thinking, *The Cure.*

"C'mon—you do! The Cure!"

"Right," Bruno said. He was paying more attention to the world outside his window. He knew their street, populated by large houses with large lawns to keep them apart. He didn't see the house from the night before. *Where is it? How did I wind up somewhere else?* The first day of school might have intrigued him more if the girl he had glimpsed wasn't still vivid in his mind. There was nothing to be done about it now. He knew the next two turns, and then he mentally unfolded his map, predicting the street names and confirming them on the corner posts when they passed. "Why'd you go this way?" he asked when his brother turned.

"What do you mean?"

"You could have stayed straight and turned on King Street, and saved about half a mile."

"God, I forget how freaky you are," Sylvio muttered. "I can get there this way, though, can't I?"

"Sure," Bruno said. He watched Sylvio for a moment. "You're nervous."

"Yes, I am. You're not the one who's going to stick out like a sore thumb. I know it's a bigger school, but what if people don't really get my style here? At Franklin everyone was used to me. It could be a lot harder here."

"I like the stuff you like," Bruno said.

"No you don't, not really. But I'm glad to know that if I get pasted in the parking lot, you'll step in and get pasted with me." Sylvio grinned.

"I didn't say I would do that." Bruno grinned back at him. "I'm sure it'll be fine. There might even be some people like you."

As they approached Suburban High School, Bruno stared out the window at the imposing building that sprawled like a set of massive building blocks dumped out on the lawn. He was confused; something didn't match the pictures and plans of Suburban he'd seen on the Internet. "That wing is new," he said, pointing out the window.

"How do you know?" Sylvio's "Oh . . ." made it clear he had answered his own question.

Sylvio found a parking space. The morning was bright and

clear, and the white noise of hundreds of kids filled the air like ocean spray. The brothers got out of the car and looked at each other over the roof. "You ready?"

"Sure." They were about to head toward the building when Sylvio stopped. Bruno followed his brother's stare to a black sedan rolling sedately through the parking lot. It made a graceful arc into a space and stopped. Three doors opened, and out stepped two girls and a boy.

"They look like you," Bruno said, but his brother actually shushed him.

The girl who had driven wore a fitted black dress covered with tiny white polka dots. Her razor-sharp black bob shone like vinyl in the sunlight.

"Is she wearing driving gloves?" Bruno asked.

"Just shut up," Sylvio hissed.

The boy wore a light-gray suit with a gray shirt and a black vest. He pushed his curls back from his forehead, and what looked like the cross of a rosary on a beaded chain escaped from his shirt cuff. The second girl towered over the other two. She wore a charcoal suede skirt and a black sleeveless turtleneck, and her long, straight hair fell halfway down her back.

The three of them turned toward the building and caught sight of Bruno and Sylvio. As if someone had given an unheard command, they all stopped. They carefully bent their heads together to converse. Then the three strangers walked deliberately toward them. They reminded Bruno of slow-moving runway models, or one pack of lions approaching another on a wildlife television show.

"Hello," the boy said to Sylvio. "Are you new?"

"Yeah," Bruno's brother said. "We just moved here."

"I'm Marco." The boy extended his hand, and they shook.

"I'm Silver."

"Silver?"

"Well, my real name is Sylvio, but I've always gone by Silver." Bruno's brother looked at him for reinforcement, and Bruno remembered how desperately Sylvio had tried to get that nickname to stick in his old school. He nodded, wondering whether Sylvio would be any more successful here.

"Nice to meet you. This is Regine." Marco presented the girl in the polka dot dress, who smiled at Sylvio while her eyes devoured him. "And this is Celia."

"This is my brother, Bruno." Everyone shook hands, and Bruno felt like the sore thumb on a hand of elegant fingers. When it came time for him to shake hands with Celia, his discomfort became more acute. Her long, dark hair was shiny and impossibly straight. Her eyes were green and her skin was fair and smooth. She was almost a foot taller than Bruno in her heels. She smiled politely at him, and he was struck dumb —because Bruno was sure this was the girl he had seen in the window of the house next door—somewhere—the night before. In the darkness beneath her window he had found her captivating. Standing in front of her now, he was transfixed. Once again the rest of the world was a blur, and she was the only person he saw clearly.

"What year are you?" she was asking him.

"First year," he mumbled.

"I'm a junior. I can tell you all about this place." Celia smiled. "Do you need help finding your homeroom?"

Bruno had effortlessly memorized the floor plan of Suburban High and was sure he could find every room in the school, except those in the new wing. He had acquainted himself with the stairwells, the bathrooms, the cafeteria, the auditorium, the pool—even the janitor's closets—before he had packed his boxes to move. He looked up at Celia.

"Yes."

"Last year when I was new, Regine walked me to my homeroom," Celia said when they had parted with the other three in the lobby. Regine had volunteered to help Sylvio find his way, leaving Marco to smirk and watch them all go. "I had just met Marco and their other friends in the parking lot, like we did today. I was so nervous."

Bruno looked at her as they walked up the stairs. He waited for her to say more, but she didn't. He realized she was comfortable with silence, and if Bruno could have taken his heart out of his chest and handed it to her, he would have done it right there in the stairwell. She stopped for a moment on the landing between floors and pointed out the window. "These are my favorite trees. In another month they'll turn an amazing golden color." He looked out the window and then back at her. She carried a black bound sketchbook in one arm.

"So, are you into the same things as your brother?"

"Some things," Bruno said. "I like a lot of the music he likes."

"Really? That's great. But you don't dress like he does."

"No. I'm sorry."

"That's okay!" She laughed, and it was like a bell ringing. "You may not believe this, but a year ago I didn't have the first clue about style, or music, or anything, really."

"No, I don't believe it." Bruno couldn't imagine Celia in any other clothes. His brother's outfits always seemed affected, but Celia was something altogether different—sophisticated, effortless, beautiful.

An older boy passed them on the stairwell and said, "Hi, Celia." She gave him half a smile but didn't reply. She murmured to Bruno, "I don't think I've ever spoken to that guy."

In the first year hall Celia helped Bruno look through the lists posted by each of the homerooms. On the third one they found his name. "Well, here you are," she said. "God, I remember how petrified I was to walk in there!" She peered into the room, and pushed her hair back from her temple, flashing her delicate wrist. She turned back to him and saw he had been watching her. "Are you going to be okay?"

"Sure," Bruno said. "Can I ask you a question?"

"Of course."

"Where do you live?"

"Over on the east side, on Market Street," she said.

"Oh."

"Why do you ask?"

"I just . . . like to know where people live," he fumbled. "I like maps."

"You're funny." Celia smiled. For a few seconds she studied him, searching his face in an exquisite, terrifying way that made him feel she hadn't looked at him completely before then. "Maybe I'll see you at lunch. Good luck!"

"Thanks." Bruno watched her glide slowly down the hall. It was easy to keep her in sight even as she neared the far end. He turned and tried to walk into his homeroom with the same grace. In his beat-up sneakers he knew he wasn't pulling it off.

He sat down at the first free desk he saw, pondering what Celia had just told him. Bruno knew where Market Street was, and that had to be at least four miles away from his house. Was he mistaken? The girl in the window next door had looked exactly like Celia. He was sure he had seen her. It didn't make sense.

No matter. Before that day, Bruno would have scoffed at the idea of love at first sight. Now only one thing mattered: figuring out how, in less than twenty-four hours, he had fallen helplessly in love with two identical girls who lived on opposite sides of this new town.

BRUNO TOOK HIS TIME getting to his next class, looking in each doorway, examining the spaces that corresponded to the room numbers he already knew from the plan of Suburban High, half hoping he might catch a glimpse of Celia in one of them. He reached the intersection of the science wing and the main hall and noticed a girl stopped in the middle of cross traffic, studying her schedule. She looked in one direction and then the other, the ringlets in her blond ponytail flicking back and forth. Bruno thought she was a second or two away from tears.

"Where do you need to go?" he asked her.

"Um, two fifty-seven," she said. Her eyes were round and startled.

"Down there. It's the last door on the left." He pointed.

"Thank you!" She gave him a relieved smile as she rushed away.

High school was going to be a lot like eighth grade, he thought. Sit down and think about whatever it was the teacher wanted him to think about. Fifty minutes later, get up, go somewhere else, and think about something else. He liked the way his knowledge accumulated like water dripping in caves, gradually leaving long spikes of mineral deposits behind, hanging from the ceiling or rising from the floor, sometimes even meeting in the middle to make a column. Bruno couldn't think of any better use of his time. He didn't care much for making friends. If someone was nice to him, he was nice back. If someone was mean, he ignored them. A few times Bruno had surprised his middle school peers by stepping in to stop a fight. When it was over, he had walked away and put it out of his mind.

All morning Bruno thought about Celia. He had admired girls once or twice before, but he never had been entranced by one before. The dark style Sylvio liked, which to Bruno had seemed like some kind of pretend dress-up, Celia made seem natural. And she was beautiful—it always came back to that. Bruno felt like a fool, daydreaming about her, but he liked it.

At lunchtime he looked for her in the cafeteria, but it was Marco who stood up and waved across the room at him.

"Hey, Bruno! How's it going?"

"Good," Bruno said, setting his things down next to Marco. He was surprised to be acknowledged, much less called over.

"Go get food. I'll be here."

"Is Celia coming?"

"Um, I don't think she has lunch this period." Marco looked curiously at him. When Bruno returned with his lunch, Marco said, "I was sitting here with Brenden on the first day last year when Celia came in. I remember thinking she had no idea how beautiful she was. We kind of interrogated her, but she didn't seem to mind." Marco looked into the distance. "It seems so long ago. So much has changed. Our group used to be six, but three of them graduated, and they're all off at Metropolitan this year. And things were really crazy for a while when one of Celia's other friends died."

"Someone died here last year?"

"Yeah, she drowned in the pool. When we walked in here this morning I could still feel a sadness hanging around this place. Celia doesn't really talk about it. I wonder how she feels." Marco fell silent for a moment, and Bruno waited. "I remember at that first lunch we asked her for her favorite opening line of a song."

"Why did you do that?"

"We have those conversations a lot," Marco said. "Best cover version. Best black-and-white music video. This morning in the car we were listing our favorite couplets—you know, two lines from a song.

"When did they build the new wing?"

"The technology wing? This summer. They built the pool the year before last. This place was big and sprawling enough as it was, and now it's kind of ridiculous," Marco said. "Have you had any classes in the new wing yet?"

"No."

"There's a mosaic that last year's senior class donated. Celia designed it. Check it out when you go over there."

"Oh, okay." Bruno tried to look nonchalant.

"I know you have a total insta-crush on her." Marco grinned at him. "It was kind of obvious this morning." He saw the alarm on Bruno's face. "Don't worry! To start with, you have excellent taste. Even I've had a crush on her. I should tell you, though, she has a boyfriend."

"Oh, sure." The news was like a heavy door slamming. *Of course she's taken.*

"Tomasi. He's a senior at St. Dymphna's. I don't know him too well, but he's a good guy. And they're serious. Anyway, I just thought I should tell you. Might make it easier for you to let it go."

"Well, thanks," Bruno said.

"But she's one of the nicest people you'll ever meet," Marco continued. "So don't let a little crush stop you from getting to be friends with her."

"Why did you say even you had a crush on her?"

"Because I'm as queer as a Lewis Carroll story." Marco grinned at him. "My boyfriend, Brenden, was a senior here last year. He's at Metropolitan now. He only left a week ago, and I'm already jonesing for him. I'm going to visit in two weeks."

"That's cool. Do you have a picture of him?"

"I do!" Marco was thrilled to pull out his phone, and Bruno studied the photo carefully. "He reminds me of someone . . . I feel like I've seen a picture . . ."

"Maybe the Smiths? He looks a lot like the lead singer, Morrissey."

"Oh, yeah. My brother has a couple of his albums."

"Smiths, or his solo stuff?"

"Solo, I think."

"I'm not surprised Silver likes him, though the Smiths albums are even better than Morrissey's solo albums. So, what's your brother's deal, anyway? I mean, the way he dresses, he looks like he listens to the same music we do."

"Probably. But he didn't have any friends at our old school who liked that stuff. He went to a dance club every weekend, but it was thirty miles away."

"There's a great club here. Would you be into that scene, the music and everything?"

"I hear a lot of stuff he plays, and I like some of it. I don't look like it, though, do I?" Bruno said.

"Look like what?"

"Like you guys." Bruno wondered why that mattered to him, all of a sudden.

"Well, that's up to you. I have a feeling Regine will have sucked Silver into our group before the end of the day, judging from the way they hit it off this morning. All last year she was hung up on our friend Ivo—he's at Metropolitan this year, too—and I would have said she still hadn't gotten over him completely, until the moment she laid eyes on your brother in the parking lot." Marco chuckled. "Anyway, we tend to get a little serious with our clothes and our music and stuff. But it doesn't mean you have to."

"Okay." Bruno wondered what it would be like to take such things seriously.

"I kind of made it sound like we're a cult, didn't I? We're just friends who like the same things. If it turns out you do, too, well, we're not going anywhere—at least, not for a year. Don't take this personally, but if I could, I would leave now. I'm basically just waiting for this year to be over so I can go to Metropolitan and be with Brenden again. I'm almost finished with my application already."

Bruno looked aimlessly around the cafeteria, but he was thinking of the girl in the window from last night. If he had to get over his crush on Celia, how fortunate that there was another girl, who looked exactly like Celia, to whom he could devote his feelings. Bruno turned back and caught Marco studying him. "Well, maybe I could make you a shirt while you're thinking about it," he said.

• • •

BRUNO WENT TO HIS web design class, stopping on the way to check out the mosaic Celia had designed. It was pretty much what he had expected: a rectangular cobblestone patch from which kids in mortarboards, open books, and computers emerged. He imagined Celia laboring over the design in her sketchbook.

The computer lab was stark, with rows of laptops cabled to long tables and whiteboards on every wall, but Bruno's attention was caught by the teacher, who had wheeled around, obviously startled by his presence. Statuesque and imposing, her long wavy hair pulled loosely back, she wore a wide-legged pantsuit and a fitted blouse. "You surprised me!" Her deep voice was either nervous or defensive.

"I'm sorry . . . Is the web design class now?" He pulled his schedule out of his pocket.

"What's your name?" She took up her class list.

"Bruno Perilunas."

She located what he assumed was his name and put a mark next to it. A few other students arrived, and the tension dissipated. "Sit wherever you like."

The teacher wrote her name on one of the boards and started the class. "I'm Ms. Moreletii. One *t*. Two *i*'s, but only pronounce one of them. All right." She left the board and walked the aisles like a general reviewing her troops. "This is not a keyboarding class. This is not a class to learn to make cute presentations, or desktop publish, or create spreadsheets. You should have been doing all that since third grade or earlier, and if you haven't, God help you, but I'm not here to teach it to you. This is a programming class." Ms. Moreletii stopped at the end of a row and turned to face the table where Bruno sat among his classmates. "You are going to learn web design.

Sometimes we will use software that does the programming for us, but we also will be digging into the code and editing it directly. This class is an elective, but don't be fooled—it will not be easy.

"Because some of you may not have realized what you signed up for, I have a two-week grace period during which you can drop this class. Okay, your login ID is your first initial and the first seven letters of your last name. If your last name has six letters, use the first two letters of your first name, and so on. Your initial password is *Suburban* with a capital *S,* and you will be asked to change it the first time you log in." The class hesitated, and a hint of impatience crept into Ms. Moreletii's voice. "Well, go ahead!"

Bruno logged in, wondering whether he had made the right decision to take this class. *Welcome to high school,* he thought.

WHEN BRUNO MADE IT down to the lobby at the end of the day, he found his brother with the three kindred spirits. Celia smiled at Bruno, and he wondered whether Marco had told her anything about their conversation at lunch. "How was your day?" she asked Bruno.

"It was good. How was yours?"

"It was good, thanks," she said. She turned to talk to Marco, and Bruno waited patiently for his brother, who did not seem to have any sense of urgency about ending his conversation with Regine. Once again Bruno felt conspicuously out of place standing so close to this glamorous group of people. Sylvio managed to look as though he had known them for years. Bruno hung back from the four of them, but then something inside him rebelled and he stepped forward.

"This might be the best day of my life, and I never would

have guessed it," Sylvio said when they were finally in the car. "How'd you do?"

"Fine. They're nice."

"They are! And they're so cool, too! I can't believe it."

Sylvio gleefully tapped the steering wheel in time to the music. "Marco said he had lunch with you?"

"Yeah."

"I'm having a hard time picturing that."

"Did you get her phone number?"

"Who, Regine? Yes. She told me about a nightclub they go to on Fridays, Diaboliques. It sounds pretty awesome. Actually, I kind of wish we had moved here last year. She told me about three of their friends who were seniors last year. I guess they're all at Metropolitan now: a brother and sister, Ivo and Liz, and another guy, Marco's boyfriend. I forget his name . . ."

Brenden, Bruno said under his breath.

"The six of them call themselves the Rosary, and they did everything together. It must have been amazing. I guess I'm the newest member."

Bruno was a little stung that Sylvio already had placed himself with these intriguing new people. Sylvio's greatest wish had come true on their first day at Suburban.

"We're going to do what they did last year. Starting tomorrow we'll drive to Regine's house on the way to school, and then we'll make the rounds to pick up Celia and Marco so we can all arrive at school together. I'm so glad I got a black car!"

Bruno looked out the window, counting down the blocks until they got home.

WHEN THEY ARRIVED HOME, Bruno dropped his things and went back out the front door. He turned in the direction of the house next door—the house whose backyard he guessed he had visited the night before, even though from the front it looked nothing like that one. If that other girl—Celia's double—wasn't in this house, she had to live in one of the houses on his block, so he would work his way around until he found it. Bruno had intended to make the rounds in the neighborhood to offer his services, so he had an excuse to conduct his investigation.

This lawn was flat with only a few bushes. It would be an easy job to mow it, if they needed someone. The metal knocker sounded deep and important against the heavy wood door. Bruno stepped back and put his hands in his pockets and then pulled them out as a woman answered. She looked older than his parents, but not as old as his grandparents. Her curly hair was brown and gray, and in her long denim skirt and nubby sweater she reminded Bruno of a kindergarten teacher.

She gave him a friendly, curious smile. "Hello. Can I help you?"

"Hello, ma'am. My name is Bruno. My family moved in next door." Bruno motioned vaguely in the direction of his house.

"Oh, hello! It's nice to meet you, Bruno. I'm Alice Stein. I met your parents a couple of weeks ago when we were out walking. We've been meaning to invite you over for dinner." Alice turned when another woman came into view behind her. "Gertrude, this is Bruno—is it *Perilunas*?" She turned back to Bruno for confirmation, and he nodded.

"It's nice to meet you! I'm Gertrude Toklas." She extended her hand and Bruno shook it.

"I just wanted to let you know, I mowed lawns and walked dogs for people where we used to live, in case you need anything like that."

"You know, we might." Gertrude looked at Alice, who nodded. "We go out of town sometimes, and it'd be nice to have someone to bring in the mail and water the plants."

"Actually, I wouldn't mind having a break from mowing the lawn, too," Alice said. "Do you shovel walks when it snows?"

Bruno nodded. "We have a snowblower."

"Well, I think we definitely will be able to make use of your services. What are your rates?"

"For the lawn, the first time is free, and then I can give you a fair price."

The women raised their eyebrows at each other. "Very impressive. You are quite the businessman," Alice said. "I was going to mow the lawn this weekend. Would you like to do it?"

"Sure," Bruno said. "Do you mind if I take a quick look in the backyard?"

"Go right ahead. It's nice to meet you!" The women closed the door, and Bruno went off around the house.

There was a gazebo and a vegetable patch. No rock garden. The dense brush along the back side of the yard probably hid the Ebentwine clearing, but when Bruno looked up at the back of the house, there was no question: The windows were the wrong size, and in completely different places, and they had no shutters. This most definitely was not the yard in which Bruno had trespassed the night before.

He worked his way around the block and picked up two more yard jobs, but none of the other houses looked anything like the green-shuttered house in which he had seen the transfixing girl who looked so much like the transfixing Celia.

He returned to his own backyard and was heading through the hedgerow into the grassy alley when his mother poked her head out the back door. "There you are! Dinner will be ready in a little. Would you be a love and set the table?"

After dinner Sylvio got on the phone, and Bruno was sure he was talking to Regine. Ignoring his conscience, Bruno picked up a cordless extension, placed his thumb over the microphone, and carried it down the hall behind his back. He leaned around Sylvio's door frame to look in and said, "Are you on the phone?" When his brother angrily pulled his cordless away from his ear to snap that wasn't it obvious he was on the phone, Bruno turned on the phone behind his back. Feigning exasperation, he backed away from the door and retreated to his room to listen in.

"Tell me more about the Rosary," Sylvio was saying.

"Oh, it's the only thing that's kept me alive for the last three years," Regine said breathily. "My first year, I remember noticing Ivo and Liz immediately. Especially Ivo, because he was the first one who really started dressing the part and everything. I remember feeling so cool when they spoke to me—you remember your first year, when you felt lucky if anyone from the upper classes paid any attention to you? Bruno must have felt that way when we talked to him today. Marco didn't transfer in until the next year, so to start it was just the four of us. I don't remember how Ivo and Brenden met. The first year we were kind of in our own world, until Brenden got his license and we went to Diaboliques the first time, and then it all clicked." Regine's voice sounded dreamy and wistful. "By Halloween everything was in place. We were dressing up every day, and people started to recognize us the way they do now. The next year Marco got here, and he and Brenden started dating almost immediately. Then Celia joined us last year."

"How did you come up with the name?"

"It was Ivo's idea. And then we all wore rosaries for a while, which was funny since none of us is really religious."

"I thought it might have something to do with the Jesus and Mary Chain or something."

"Oh, I like that band! But no, not really, though I can see how it fits. Last year Marco made us the bracelets for First Night, and now that's our symbol."

"Do you think he'd make me one?"

"See, I don't know . . . The Rosary is a special group of people—it still is. Three of them are at Metropolitan now. I don't know if I have the right to say that you should join the group if three of the founding members haven't even met you."

"I suppose that makes sense," Sylvio said, trying not to sound disappointed.

"You'll meet them soon. I'm pretty sure they'll be back for fall break, and they'll definitely come back for Halloween. They'll like you—I'm positive." Regine was silent for a moment. When she spoke again it was clear she was trying to be as encouraging as she could. "I have no doubt when they meet you they'll be totally fine with making you a member. I already talked to Ivo today and told him all about you."

"You did?"

"Of course. So, who's your favorite band?" Regine asked.

"I don't know if I have one. The Cure, maybe."

"That's a good choice."

"But I love so much music, and a lot more obscure things than the Cure. Do you like Ikon?"

"Yes! Patrick plays them all the time. Do you like Faith and the Muse?"

" 'Shattered in Aspect' is a great song. Do you like Ghost Dance?" Sylvio asked.

"I don't know that song."

"Oh, no, it's a band."

"I—I don't think I've heard them."

"They're older. Most of their songs have never been released on CD, but they're really good. I'll make a disc for you." Bruno detected his brother's pleasure in knowing some music Regine didn't.

Bruno carefully put down the phone. He went downstairs, out into the backyard, and through the hedgerow. At the end of the grassy alley he passed through the trees and reached the strange clearing with the fountain marked EBENTWINE. Again the air was oddly perfumed with spice and brine, and the surrounding town might have vanished from beyond the perimeter. The gardener was there, working on one of the flower beds.

"Hello again."

"Hello." Bruno inhaled the different air. He half expected to hear the distant cry of a gull.

"Are you going to see her?"

"See who?"

"The one of whom you're so fond. What's her name?"

"I don't know."

"I thought you did."

"Do you know who that girl is, who lives in that house you sent me to?"

"I haven't met her, but I thought *you* did today."

"Do you mean Celia?" The gardener nodded. "It's not Celia."

The man laughed. "Of course it is." He lifted a plant from a wheelbarrow and set it into the hole he had dug.

"But it can't be. She told me she lives on Market Street, and that's at least four miles away." Confusion fuzzed around the edges of Bruno's brain.

"That's right. And you're almost there."

"To Market Street? That can't be right. It's all the way—" Bruno raised his arm, but he wasn't sure in which direction to point. His head felt light.

"No, no, her house is right through that hedge, just as it was last night. You can't stay here, so you'd better go see." The gardener moved to one side of the clearing and beckoned for Bruno to follow. Bruno went through the hedges, and when he reached the other side, he paused, waiting for his head to clear. He looked up at the window, and there she was.

She stood in profile, brushing her long, straight hair. She turned and looked out at the night sky, and there was no doubt. There had never been any doubt. It was Celia, even though Bruno had no idea how he had reached her backyard having barely left his own. There were mysteries to ponder, but for the moment he didn't care. He marveled at this perfect girl who stood in the open window above his head. The same ethereal song that had been playing the night before drifted down to him, but Bruno still couldn't hear the singer's words.

Once again Bruno felt the pull to her, and he wondered if this was what the moon felt, gazing on the earth. He was rooted in his spot, ready to stare up at Celia all night, when the back door of the house opened and an older woman came out into the yard, a phone to her ear. "Okay, I can talk now. I didn't want her to walk in on me," she said, and Bruno leapt back through the hedge.

The gardener looked disappointed. "That's it?"

"What do you mean?"

"I thought maybe you'd visit her for a while."

"How is it possible . . . I don't understand . . ."

"We are fortunate to live in a world where we are not limited to experiencing only the things we understand." The man's eyes were serious, and he spoke to Bruno like a child. "And as for whether things are possible, if they happen, does it matter whether or not they are possible?"

"I need to go home," Bruno said.

"All right then. It's just back that way." The gardener gestured, and Bruno ran in that direction, brushing past trees and hedges. The next thing he knew, he was pulling up short in front of his garage. The lights from his house waited on the other side of the hedge.

What just happened?

2

dance along the edge

THE NEXT MORNING, SYLVIO drove them to Regine's house and then they followed her car. Bruno's heart beat faster when they turned onto Market Street. They stopped in front of a house that had the same white siding and evergreen trees he had seen from behind for the past two nights, and Celia emerged. She waved at Sylvio and Bruno and got into Regine's passenger seat. They continued on to pick up Marco at his house before proceeding to school.

Bruno felt like a stowaway in a funeral procession. He had worn the only pair of dress pants he owned and a button-down shirt, but in the mirror he had looked rumpled and uncomfortable. When the five of them walked into school, Bruno fell back, watching Celia from behind. In twenty-four hours he had fallen in love twice. At least he knew now it had been with the same girl.

Celia looked around to see if he was there. She gave him the hint of a smile, then turned back. For the rest of the walk into school he studied the texture of her moss-green crushed-velvet jacket. She chatted with Marco, who looked like a proper companion for her. In the lobby she told Bruno, "You look nice," and he almost felt worse.

He thought about Celia all morning and wondered about her boyfriend, Tomasi. Sitting in geography class, he tried to guess what Tomasi looked like. Bruno supposed he must be tall, since Celia was tall, but trying to picture him was like peering into fog.

Bruno was distracted from his daydream by a girl in the hall outside the classroom door. She wore a sweater that was a riot of bright colors, and her hair was a vibrant mass of tight reddish-blond curls. He wondered how she could be wandering the school in the middle of a period without getting into trouble. She stopped, framed by the open classroom door, and looked curiously at Bruno.

"Excuse me?"

Bruno looked back at the front of the room to find the teacher, an Indian man with a British accent named Mr. Williams, regarding him with an expression of exaggerated patience. Everyone had turned to stare at Bruno, ready to savor the first mortification of the new year. "Am I boring you?"

"No," Bruno said, reddening.

"It's the second day of class. Am I to expect this level of inattention from you every day?"

"I don't know how to answer that."

"So much depends upon . . . I take it you are so well versed in European geography, I am wasting your time?"

Before Bruno knew it, he had said, "Probably." Around him students gasped.

Mr. Williams's shock shifted immediately to disdain. "Really? So you could list for me the European mountain ranges, then?"

Bruno looked inward, flipping his mental atlas to the appropriate page, and then he checked off the names as he wandered around the map. "Well, the Kjolens in Scandinavia, then the Pyrénées, Alps, Apennines, Dinaric Alps, Carpathians, and Balkans. Plus the Urals and the Caucasus Mountains, which separate Europe from Asia."

Mr. Williams gaped for a moment. "Pay attention in class," he snapped, and returned to the board. Bruno felt stares from all sides, but he kept his eyes forward. When the moment finally passed and he looked back out into the hall, the brightly colored girl was gone.

He didn't see her in the halls between classes, but he did find the timid blond girl from the day before, lost again, and pointed her to her next destination. This time she gave Bruno a longer look of gratitude, but he didn't dwell on it. It didn't matter how many mysterious girls there were around here; Bruno could only obsess about one.

WHEN HE ARRIVED IN the cafeteria for lunch, the vast room was already packed. He was heading to the lunch line when he saw her standing across the room. Her long, dark hair framed her pale face, and she raised her hand. Bruno froze as Celia mouthed the words *Come here.*

When he reached her, she said, "Hi! I didn't know you had lunch now. Let me see your schedule." He handed over his card and set down his books, marveling at the numbing rush that returned the moment he was near her.

"Do you want anything?" Bruno pointed at the lunch line.

"Oh, no, thank you!" She smiled again and turned her attention to his schedule. When he returned with a tray of food, Celia had a puzzled look. "Were you just in Spanish class?"

"Yes."

"That's all the way over in the Chancellor Wing. How did you get here so quickly?"

"It's not far." Bruno shrugged.

"Yes, it is! You have to go all the way through Chancellor and then down the main hall and through administration. It's almost the farthest point in the school from here. When I had Spanish before lunch, I used to get here ten minutes after the bell rang."

"I didn't go that way," Bruno said.

"What way did you go, then?" She looked incredulous.

"I went out the back door of Chancellor, across the grass, and in the back door of the technology wing. That's just down the hall from that side of the cafeteria." Bruno pointed over his shoulder.

Celia stared at him. "That's brilliant! And lucky; I can't believe that door was unlocked. I'll bet a lot of people start using your shortcut." For the second time she looked at him so directly, he thought she was seeing straight through to his heart, which sped up as she stared. *Why does she look at me that way?*

"I heard . . . Marco told me your friend died last year?"

"Oh." Her face fell, and Bruno hated himself for ambushing her. "Mariette. Yes. She was my best friend outside the Rosary. That's what we called ourselves last year. Did Marco tell you about that?" Bruno nodded. "It was crazy, in so many ways. She was such an amazing person, and I miss her every day." Celia pulled a chain out from under her blouse and showed Bruno an amulet hanging from it. "She made this."

The silence stretched out, and he felt obliged to fill it because he had dredged up unhappy memories. "I saw your mosaic."

Celia waved the idea away. "Oh, it's not my mosaic. I just

drew what the seniors wanted, and then the artisan did all the work."

"It's very nice," he said anyway.

"Well, thank you! So, Silver and Regine seem to have hit it off."

"Yeah, he was really happy to meet you guys. I hope I'm not ruining the impression you're trying to make."

It took her a moment to realize what he meant. "Oh, that doesn't matter." She gave a short laugh, and he liked that she didn't seem to take it all too seriously. "Who you are is more important than what you wear. That might not be what you'd expect me to say, considering how much time I spend thinking about what I wear."

"No, I get it." He met her gaze as long as he could.

They ate, and questions waited on his tongue, but what could he ask? Telling Celia he had been standing in the backyard of her house, watching her in her window, would only make him sound like a stalker. He decided to try something less specific. "There's a girl in my neighborhood who looks exactly like you."

"Seriously? What's her name?"

"I don't know. I've seen her a couple times. That's why I asked you where you lived yesterday."

"Oh, right. Well, that's wild. I wouldn't mind meeting my doppelgänger."

In his head he heard a distant echo of the plaintive, beautiful song that had reached him from Celia's window. If he could only find out what it was, he could ask Celia about it. If she didn't know it, he could go back to attempting to convince himself he had seen someone else.

• • •

BRUNO WAITED OUTSIDE SYLVIO'S room while he talked on the phone. He stayed far enough away so he couldn't hear the words, but he could tell Sylvio was flirting again. When he heard Sylvio hang up, Bruno walked in. "Were you listening?" Sylvio asked.

"No. Were you talking to Regine?"

"Yeah. She knows some music really well, and then other bands she's never heard of. She said most of what she knows is because of Brenden."

"Is that bad?"

"No, but it's weird. I mean, how can you love Siouxsie and the Banshees and not know that John Valentine Carruthers had been a member of Clock DVA?" Sylvio said it as though it were the most obvious thing in the world.

Bruno lingered in the doorway until his brother looked at him expectantly. "I'm trying to figure out the name of a song I heard."

"Where'd you hear it?"

"On a show." Bruno tried to think of anything he could compare to the mystery song he had heard through the mystery girl's window. "It's just a guitar—an electric guitar, but soft —and a woman's voice."

His brother made a halfhearted attempt to be helpful. "Do you remember any of the lyrics?"

Bruno shook his head. He scanned Sylvio's crates of CDs. As always, his brother had music playing. Now it was a simple song with strummed guitars and a steady snare drum, with a childlike woman's voice perched on top, lilting a wistful but pretty melody. "What are you listening to?"

"'Shining Road' by Cranes." Sylvio went to the wine-crate shelves and located the disc, which Bruno learned was called

Loved when Sylvio passed it to him. "What's with the sudden interest?"

Bruno shrugged, studying the pastel drawing of four women, perhaps ballet dancers, on the cover of the CD. "I like it."

"Well, that's cool."

Back in his own room, Bruno played the CD while he paged through the *Book of Maps*. He figured Celia probably liked Cranes, too. But this music wasn't the tantalizing, half-remembered song that was the muddled score of his fascination with Celia.

That night he stayed in his room listening to Cranes. Bruno wanted very badly to return to the mysterious clearing, and through it to the mysterious backyard. He wondered if this was what someone felt after trying a drug the first time. It was intoxicating, but something about it all—the too-perfect-to-be-real Ebentwine clearing, the gardener who seemingly worked twenty-four hours a day, the house whose location was both next door and four miles away—felt dangerous and forbidden.

The confusion, the violations of the laws of the universe, made him suspect that he'd do better to stay away from that place. It just didn't make sense. There was no way to draw a map that would show Bruno how he got to Celia's backyard. It was as disorienting as being awakened from a dream. Bruno went to bed early.

· · ·

THE NEXT DAY IN THE LIBRARY Regine looked up when Bruno approached the table where she sat with Sylvio and Marco. "Where did you come from?" Her eyes flicked over his flannel shirt and faded jeans, and he decided he didn't like her.

"What do you mean?"

"Were you in here? I didn't see you come in." Regine pointed to the library door directly across from where she sat.

"I came in the back door." Bruno hooked his thumb over his shoulder at the stacks.

"The back door?" Marco repeated. "There isn't a back door."

"Sure there is," Bruno said, confused. He didn't realize he had done something unusual.

"Show me," Regine said officiously, standing up.

Bruno turned and led the way back through the book-shelves. In a short wall between two sets of shelves, he pushed open a door, and they all looked out into a narrow hallway that led to the new wing.

"I had no idea this was here," Regine said.

"Me neither," Marco said. "This place is crazy." They went back to the table. "If we ever felt like stealing books, we could go out that door."

Regine was looking around. "Is it just me, or does the library seem larger than last year? I mean, they didn't do anything to it when they added the new wing, did they? I guess it's the same. Why does it feel bigger, somehow?"

"You shouldn't be surprised Bruno's figured this place out so quickly," Sylvio said. "He does it everywhere. We went to the shore on vacation when Bruno was seven. Last year we went back for the first time, and he remembered everything: street names, the way to get to the cottage we'd rented. It's crazy."

Marco smiled at Bruno. "I bet that comes in handy."

"Sometimes."

Regine turned back to Sylvio. "So, tell me about Hermetica."

"It's not as beautiful as Diaboliques sounds. It was kind of a hole, really—you know, brick walls painted black, that kind of thing. The owners spent all their money on the sound system and lights, and the rest of it was kind of falling apart. But the DJ, Pete, played the most amazing stuff. He loved to pull out tracks that you wouldn't hear anywhere else, like the Bollock Brothers, or Anne Clark."

"'Sleeper in Metropolis'? I love that song!" Regine squeaked, and clapped her hands. The librarian passed by with a disapproving look on her face. "What happened to the old librarian?" Regine asked Marco.

"I guess she retired," Marco said. "She was old enough." He turned to Bruno. "Did you ever go to Hermetica?"

"No."

"Why not?"

"I was too young. And I guess I didn't care," Bruno said. "Hey, would you help me buy some clothes?"

"Sure! How about this Saturday?"

THE GARDENER WAS STANDING there when Bruno pushed his way into the Ebentwine clearing. "Where have you been? Haven't seen you in a of couple days."

"Who do you work for? Who owns this place?"

"Ah, the time has come for questions. I shouldn't be surprised." The man put his rake down. "I don't work for anyone, really."

"But when I asked if you were the gardener, and you said you were . . ."

"It's because my name is Gardner, and you were pretty close, so I agreed."

"Your name is Gardner?"

"Well, Fredrick Calvert Gardner, but Gardner is good. What's important, though, is that there are things I can help you to do."

"How does this place work? How I can go through those trees and be across town?"

"That's a tough one. Not all questions have answers. My job is to keep this place presentable, or else it doesn't work so well."

"So you're in charge of maintaining a secret garden, which is some kind of shortcut between my backyard and Celia's?"

"*Shortcut* is such a plain word; in these parts it's called a *liminal*. Anyway, I suppose that's true, but it's not completely accurate."

"What is completely accurate, then?" Bruno took a step to the side, steadying himself as his vision faded for a moment.

"Feeling it, are you?"

"What is that?" Bruno waited for the dots of light to swim out of his eyes.

"There's going to come a day when you might be tempted to spend too much time here in Ebentwine. Other people certainly have tried. But this is a transitional place, here purely to help you get from one place to another by passing through. The dizziness, the disorientation, the enervation, the unconsciousness—it's the best way to make sure you don't stay too long."

"Unconsciousness?" Bruno felt a popping in his ears, as though the air pressure had changed suddenly.

"You don't want to try that. But don't worry yourself about it. You come, you let me know where you'd like to go, and I tell you how to get there. And it's time for you to go. Celia's? Or home?"

"Home," Bruno said, and staggered off into the trees in the direction Gardner pointed.

When he rounded the hedgerow into his backyard, his mother was there. "Bruno? Where were you? Didn't you hear me calling you?"

"I was . . ." He gestured vaguely behind him.

"Come and set the table for dinner."

He followed her into the house, firm in his resolve: *I will not go back to that crazy place.*

"IT WAS INCREDIBLE," Sylvio said wearily as noon approached on Saturday. "It's so much better than Hermetica. They have three dance floors, but the smallest room up on the top floor is just perfect. They know the DJ, and everything he played was fantastic. I heard a few things I'd never heard before."

"That's great," Bruno said, idly looking through the newspaper.

"And the people! Everyone looked amazing. If you asked me to describe my ideal nightclub, Patrick's room at Diaboliques would be it!"

"I'm glad you found a place to go."

"Regine is an amazing dancer. You should see her."

"Are you guys dating yet?"

"I think so." Sylvio smiled. "I like her, and I'm pretty sure she likes me."

Bruno wanted to say, *You think?* But he kept quiet.

"Speaking of liking someone, I met Celia's boyfriend, Tomasi." Sylvio looked disappointed when Bruno wasn't surprised. "You knew about him?" Bruno nodded. "I think you might have to let your feelings for Celia go."

"I don't have any feelings for Celia," Bruno said darkly.

Sylvio held up his hands. "Marco said he's taking you clothes shopping today. You don't want to go shopping with me?"

"Do you know where the stores are?"

"Well, no. Can I come along with you guys, then, to check it out?"

"How about next time?"

"Fine," Sylvio said. "So you're fast friends with Marco, then?"

"I don't know. Not as fast as you are with Regine."

"We have a lot in common. What about you two?"

The doorbell rang. Marco was there with a shirt on a hanger. "Hey, Bruno! I love this neighborhood. Hey, Silver! You have a good time last night?"

"I loved it! You guys are going shopping?"

"We are. I wanted Bruno to try this on before we go." Marco handed Bruno a short-sleeved shirt with a covered placket and a small collar, made of charcoal twill fabric. "I made a pair of pants out of this material last year, and I had just enough left over for this. I'm having a Jil Sander moment, I guess." Marco saw Bruno's blank look. "Fashion designer."

"You made this?" Bruno studied it. "It looks like it came from a store. I do like it—thank you! I'll go put it on?"

"Sure. And those trousers you had on the other day," Marco suggested. Bruno nodded and went upstairs to change while Marco reminisced about Diaboliques with Sylvio downstairs. The way the shirt fit him, it was clear Marco had sized him up as instinctively as Bruno read a map. Bruno also realized that if Marco was going to take him out in public, he didn't want him to look like a slob, and that made Bruno smile.

Marco nodded when Bruno came back down. "Nice! All

right, we're ready. See you later." Sylvio watched enviously as they left.

"You will never see this car in the morning procession," Marco said as they got into his gray sedan.

"Why's that?"

"It's not black!" Marco chuckled. "I don't mind. I never have to drive to school." He started the car and lunged for the volume knob on the stereo. "I also like to play music a lot louder than the others. You like the Screaming Blue Messiahs?"

"I don't think I've heard them."

"Well, you're going to now."

Bruno listened and looked out the window. Instead of checking off the street signs the way he normally did, Bruno thought about how he had never done anything like this before: have a friend come over, go shopping for clothes—go shopping for anything. Meanwhile the man on the stereo sang about looking down the barrel of a gun, just to see where the bullets come from. It felt like an adventure.

After the song ended Marco turned the volume down. "So, if I don't ask you questions, you probably won't say anything, right?"

"Probably not. I'm sorry."

"No, it's fine. God, you're just like Celia. I swear, the first half of last year the only time she spoke was if someone asked her a question. I'm a little chattier, if you haven't noticed. When we go out and we're being all serious and aloof, sometimes I have to fight the impulse to talk. So tell me, what are we looking for today?"

"Everything, kind of. I've never really shopped for clothes, at all."

"Okay, so we're starting from scratch. Have you seen things that you liked?"

"I like this shirt." Bruno looked down at himself.

"Good!" Marco laughed good-naturedly, and Bruno smiled. "Well, we're going to hit some of my favorite stores and try on clothes till you pass out."

Marco drove to the outskirts of downtown and parked in front of a sleek clothing store called Chris & Cosey. "This place has the best selection," he said as they walked inside. "Almost everything I wear that I didn't make myself, I got here."

Every wall was covered with built-in shelves and hang bars, like a massive walk-in closet. The store was bursting with unusual clothes. An elegant woman with black hair cut like Cleopatra's came out from the back, her asymmetrical skirt rustling. "Marco! So good to see you!" She kissed both of his cheeks. "Have you brought me anything?"

"You know I would love to make clothes for you." Marco beamed. "I'm just so used to designing with a specific person in mind; every time I think about making something without knowing who's going to wear it, I go blank. Oh, Cosey, this is my friend Bruno."

"Hi, Bruno." Cosey shook his hand. "I love your shirt."

"Marco made it," Bruno said.

"Just make me six of those!" she told Marco. "I could sell them in a heartbeat. Oh, I won't harass you. What are you guys looking for today?"

"Bruno needs to work on his wardrobe," Marco told her.

In a matter of minutes, Bruno found himself in a dressing room with a stack of things to try on. Every time he came out for inspection, Marco and Cosey had something else for him to consider. Each time he put on something new, he stood in front of the mirror and tried to decide if it was himself he was seeing.

"You *do* know what you want," Marco said after a little while, watching Bruno's yes pile grow. "You just don't know how to say it out loud."

"I think you're right." Bruno saw a style emerging in his selections: monochromatic, military influences, fitted shirts and sweaters that stopped at the hip. He handed back the rejects, and he and Marco reviewed his choices. "Do you like these?"

"I do. What matters, though, is whether *you* like them."

Bruno nodded. He wanted very badly to ask if Marco thought Celia would like his new look, but he knew that was foolish.

Marco had to help Bruno carry everything up to the register.

"This is going to cost a lot."

"I know." Bruno took out his battered leather wallet and pulled out several bills.

"I'm just curious," Marco said when they were outside. "Where did you come up with all that money?"

"I don't really buy anything," Bruno said simply. "Birthday money, lawn-mowing money, dog-walking money, allowance —I just keep it all."

"Wow. So why spend it now?"

"I needed to buy something."

Back at Bruno's house, Marco whistled when they walked into his empty bedroom. "When you said you don't buy anything, you really weren't kidding. Are you planning on putting anything on the walls?"

"Maybe. I kind of like it this way." He opened the first bag and put a new shirt on a hanger.

"That's cool. There were a couple things I want to tailor a little for you." Marco found them and put them aside. "Not everything fits perfectly off the rack, you know?"

"No, I don't," Bruno said. "But if you say so."

Sylvio showed up and looked around curiously. "My God, you got a lot of stuff! This is nice." He fingered a fitted black zippered sweater. "I'm going to have to go shopping with you, Marco."

"You really should make some things to sell at Chris and Cosey's," Bruno told Marco. "I mean, I think you should."

"Brenden has been after me about it for two years. I need someone to keep kicking my ass, or I'll never do it."

BRUNO SAT WITH SYLVIO and their mother in a pew at Wyndham Chapel for the first service his father would conduct as pastor—the whole reason they had transplanted their lives. As they had in their previous church, the Perilunas family sat in the second row on the left. Bruno caught sight of a few kids who went to Suburban. They looked curiously at him, and he understood: Just as in their old town, he never would be invisible here. The association with his father prevented that. *Everything is different and the same.*

Mr. Perilunas seemed to be thinking the same thing. After he had made his introductory remarks to the congregation, he said, "I believe there is something we already have in common, so it is an obvious choice for me to discuss today. An Italian author, Giuseppe Tomasi di Lampedusa, expressed the idea very well in his novel, *The Leopard,* when he wrote, 'If we want things to stay the same, they are going to have to change.' It's not a difficult idea to reason out, really. This world and our lives are formed in such a way that nothing stays the same.

Sure, the elements will always be there. Gravity will always pull us down. Yet think of how long an hour seemed to you when you were a child, but how quickly a week, a month, a year flies by now that you're an adult. I would bet even the way you know God has changed over your life, and will continue to change for as long as you live.

"Because everything changes, we inevitably make comparisons between then and now, now and what will come. And we make judgments: *This is better than it was before. This is worse. I love the way this is right now, and I wish it would stay this way forever. I can't wait for this to be over.* Making these kinds of comparisons is an essential part of being alive. And it has been an essential aspect of being human ever since we realized how drastically we could change our lives for the better by using the things we know to improve ourselves and the world around us.

"But change is not simply a matter of reasoning, is it? There are emotions to sort out, too, and the more important the change, the stronger the emotions, usually.

"You have lost a pastor here, and you have let go of all sorts of things associated with her. In order for one thing to stay the same—for this community of faith to persist—you had to accept a change. I have no idea how you feel about that, and I don't imagine all of you feel the same. You have hopes and maybe fears about what will happen next. And it is only realistic that at least some of you may be disappointed even if things turn out well, simply because they are different from before.

"All of these things you feel, I feel, too, in my own way. But if we want things to stay the same, they will have to change. Think of our church for the decades it has endured here, and the thousands of years it has endured in the world. Over that time, nearly everything about it has changed: the languages, the places, the people, even most of the rules. All these things have changed and evolved so the most essential things can stay the same: a community of people who experience God together, finding purpose in our lives and performing good works for ourselves and others. Those things must never change. Everything else can.

"I am so happy to be here, and I am so excited to meet all of you personally and learn how better to be your servant. All I ask is for you to remember that if we change—as we change—we do it so that the most important things can stay the same."

Bruno's father led the congregation in prayer. Instead of interlacing his fingers, he always cupped one open upturned palm in the other, as though waiting for something to be placed in his hands. It was familiar, and it reassured Bruno.

3

don't talk to me about love

BRUNO WAS ON HIS way to the library, thinking about Celia. His heart and lungs felt tangled up in his chest. He cursed himself for falling so hard, so quickly—it was completely unlike him.

He noticed the girl with the brilliant red hair and many-colored sweater at the far end of the hall. She always wore the same clothes, and she never seemed to be on her way anywhere. In the sunlight from the nearby window, she almost looked angelic. The hallway was clearing out, and the girl raised her hand in a hesitant wave at him. Bruno went through the back door into the library. *Sorry, I'm having enough trouble with girls.*

He nearly collided with the librarian when he turned into the aisle that led to the reading area. "Oh—you scared me!" she said, then quickly lowered her voice. "Where did you come from?"

"The back door." Bruno pointed over his shoulder.

"The back door?" Once again Bruno found himself leading someone to the door he had used. "I—I had no idea this was here! Are people walking in and out of my library without checking out books?" The librarian pushed the door open and glanced out, then pulled it closed and examined the handle.

"I don't think anyone else knows about it, either," Bruno said. "I've never seen anyone else use it."

"I'm going to have to get them to lock this door." She turned back to him, looking a little wilted. "This is so ridiculous to say, but I've been here for two weeks and I still haven't figured out where everything is!"

"It's a big building," he offered.

"Not even the building, just the library!" She waved one arm vaguely at the stacks. "I'll find a section, but when I go back to what I swear is the same place, it's not there! I feel like I'm losing my mind, but I'm far too young for that. At least, I hope I am."

"It is a little like a maze." Bruno looked around. The shelves loomed too high for him to see the far walls on either side of the great room.

"More like a labyrinth. If you can find Foreign Languages, I'll give you a hall pass. I'm serious."

"Isn't it over there?" Bruno walked off through the stacks, and she followed him. He turned one corner and then another, and found the aisle with the foreign language books.

"Oh, that is such a relief," she said. But her voice was thoughtful, not relieved. She looked at Bruno, looked away, then looked at him again. Finally she whispered. "Are you Kind?"

"Am I *kind?*" He stared at her. "I guess so. I try to be nice. Why do you ask? My dad's a minister—"

She cut him off. "I don't know why I said that. Of course you're kind; you helped me find this section. What's your name?"

"I'm Bruno Perilunas."

"I'm Lois Beggers-Jouré. Just call me Lois. Bruno, I have a

proposition for you. I need another library aide. I never thought a library would be a place where I'd have a particular need for people who can find places no one else seems to be able to, but hey, welcome to Suburban."

Lois's words reminded Bruno of the Ebentwine clearing. He hadn't gone back. Passing through that hidden place with its quixotic keeper, seeing and hearing things that made him think he'd been drugged . . . A small, nagging part of him was intrigued by Ebentwine. How crazy would it be if something like that were possible—passing through, what had the man called it, a liminal?—like poking a hole in a map and coming out the other side, somewhere else completely. But he was sure the clearing was a dangerous place, and just like the heartsickness he felt for Celia, the sooner he forgot about it, the better.

Lois was asking him, "Would you be interested?"

"Sure, I guess."

"That's great. It's not a huge commitment. In fact, I'm not going to call you a library aide, because I won't stick you behind the desk checking out books. Pretty much all I want is for you to help me find things around here, and not tell anyone I can't do it myself, okay?"

Lois's honesty made Bruno like her instantly. "I can do that."

"I know you've been studying here a lot. I've seen you and your friends a few times already. In fact, I think they're here." They went to the reading area and found Celia, Sylvio, and Regine sitting at a table.

"I'm going to be a library aide," Bruno told them.

"Nice!" Celia smiled up at the librarian. "He'll do a great job."

"He's already helped me." Lois patted Bruno's shoulder and headed back to her office.

"Great, someone to fetch books for us!" Bruno couldn't decide if Regine was trying to be encouraging or if she was mocking him.

"I really like this new style you have happening," Celia said to Bruno. "Marco said you got a lot of great stuff at Chris and Cosey's."

"I couldn't have done it without him," Bruno said, looking down at his clothes—Marco's shirt, a pair of dark wide-leg trousers, and black leather shoes with a rounded military toe. "You really like it?"

"I do." Every time Celia looked at him, Bruno felt like a little kid who might lose his balance and fall down even standing still. As he sat next to her, she noticed his drawing on the paper cover on his textbook. "You like Cranes?" She tapped the paper where he had attempted to copy the stylized letters that spelled out the band's name, and underneath it, in lowercase letters, the title of the album: *loved*.

"I do." He blushed, hating himself for it. "Do you?"

"I love that album. And the cover is so pretty." Celia's pen flitted around on the cover of Bruno's book and sketched in the cover illustration, four women adjusting their dresses on their bare shoulders, all from memory. Time slowed down, and Bruno watched, entranced. Celia caught herself. "I shouldn't be doodling on your book!"

"Oh, it's okay." Her artwork was nothing short of amazing.

"So, you like dream pop?"

"I—I think so. I haven't heard a lot." The mystery song played again in Bruno's head.

Celia went on. "I was just thinking my book covers were

missing literary quotes. Last year, our friend Liz was an endless supply of beautiful lines from books and poems. I guess we're going to have to look for them ourselves now."

"What was the one from *The Awakening*?" Regine asked. "'When I left her today, she put her arms around me and felt my shoulder blades, to see if my wings were strong, she said.'"

"Yes!" Celia's eyes shone. "But there's another one by Kate Chopin that I like even better: 'Perhaps it's better to wake up after all, even to suffer, rather than to remain a dupe to illusions all one's life.'"

BRUNO WAITED IMPATIENTLY for his turn to talk to Sophia. Finally his mother passed him the phone.

"Boono!" His sister still used his childhood nickname. "Tell me everything!"

"What do you want to know?" He drank in her voice, imagining her endless dark ringlets and bright eyes.

"How's the house? Do you like high school? Are you mowing all the lawns in the neighborhood yet?"

Bruno laughed. "The house is nice. School is big. I like it. I got a couple lawns so far."

"It's so good to hear your voice!" Sophia gushed.

"How's Buenos Aires?"

"It's beautiful! And I might actually be bilingual by the time I get back. My Spanish is really getting better. I wish you could be here to see everything!"

"I saw the pictures you sent," he said. "It looks . . . old."

"It reminds me of Paris, in a strange way," she said. "I've met some great people in my program."

"You sound really happy."

"I am! Are you? Are you getting along with Sylvio?"

"Yeah. He's excited because there are some people at school who dress like him, and they like all the same music."

"He must be over the moon. How about you? Have you made some friends?"

"I've been hanging out with them, too."

"Really? Am I going to come home and find you all goth and wearing black?" Even when she teased him, Bruno loved feeling like the center of Sophia's universe.

"I don't think so." He laughed with her. "Who knows, maybe."

"I can't believe you're in high school!"

"I can't believe you're in Argentina!"

"Check us out!" She laughed again. "Damn, I've been on the phone fifteen minutes already; this is going to cost a fortune. You know I would love to talk to you for hours, but I need to catch up with Sylvio, too, if he's around."

"He's here." Bruno looked up at his brother waiting in the doorway.

"I love you, mister. I miss you!"

"Miss you too. Love you." Bruno handed the phone to Sylvio.

Bruno went back to his room, thinking if there was anyone in the world who would believe his crazy story about the Ebentwine clearing, who wouldn't tease him if he told her he had fallen head over heels for a junior girl, who would spend hours helping him hunt for a song he could barely describe, it was Sophia.

THE NEXT MORNING, BRUNO woke up lonely. *What's the matter with me? I've never gotten lonely. Is this what love does to you —lets you feel great for a minute or two but then leaves you feeling worse than ever when you realize you can't have the one you want?* On the ride to school, he wondered what it would be like to slip his arm around a girl's waist, to feel her hand around his neck, her lips against his. Then he wondered if he was possessed. *You have got to snap out of it.* Outside his homeroom a guy with a bunch of flowers was approaching a girl by her locker, and Bruno was about to look away, when the girl turned and saw the guy there. She started to yell, snatching the flowers and crushing them into the boy's chest. Bruno raised his eyebrows and went into his classroom.

Toward the end of the first period, the web design class was dissolving into soft conversations, and Bruno listened to his classmates gossiping about the lovers' quarrel he'd witnessed. He was idly clicking around the web page he'd finished making when he felt a hand on his shoulder. Ms. Moreletii smiled down at him. "I need to talk to you for a minute."

He got up and followed her out into the hall, closing the door after them.

"I wanted to ask you if you've thought about dropping this class," she said gently. In her heels Ms. Moreletii was nearly as tall as Celia, but her effect on Bruno was very different. Looking up to Celia was like looking up to a queen. Looking up at Ms. Moreletii, he just felt short and awkward. And defensive.

"Drop the class? No, I haven't. Why? I finished the exercise." He pointed vaguely at the classroom door.

"I know. But things are going to get harder. Quickly. I've been teaching for a while. I can usually spot the students who are going to struggle very early on."

"You think I should drop the class?" He watched her nod, her face compassionate. He was silent, confused.

"Think about it. Don't ruin your GPA with a bad grade in a class you don't need to take."

He nodded as she opened the door for them to return inside. He watched Ms. Moreletii pull a girl out into the hallway and wondered if his classmate would feel as hollow and embarrassed as he did.

At lunch Bruno was about to ask Celia and Marco if they had taken a computer class with Ms. Moreletii when Regine arrived. "Did you hear what happened to Elsie?"

"Who's Elsie?" Sylvio asked her.

"I've pointed her out to you—that girl with the black hair who always wears that unfortunate headband."

"Oh, okay. What happened to her?"

"She saw the ghost! They say it's Mariette, but nobody's sure. I mean, a girl with curly strawberry-blond hair in a brightly colored sweater lurking around the science wing—who else could it be?"

Bruno perked up. *That girl was a ghost?*

"Plenty of people have said they've seen the ghost by now," Marco said quietly, looking at Celia.

"Yes, but how many of them have received a *note* from her?" Regine asked triumphantly. "Yesterday Mariette— the ghost—stopped Elsie in the stairwell of the science wing. She gave her a piece of paper, and when Elsie opened it, all it said was 'Chat Rouge—Wednesday—eight twenty-seven p.m.'"

"Chat Rouge—the restaurant?" Celia asked.

"Yes. And yesterday was Wednesday, of course. Elsie didn't know what it meant, but when she looked up, Mariette had *disappeared*"—Regine looked around to see what effect she was having—"so she couldn't ask her. The only thing she could do was to go to Chat Rouge and see what happened at eight twenty-seven."

"Does this sound completely insane to anyone else?" Marco looked around the table. "I realize some crazy stuff happened here last year, but nobody was seeing *ghosts*. Even if you believe that, though, do you believe in a ghost who passes notes?"

"You haven't even heard what happened!" Regine said. "Elsie went to the restaurant, and she was a little early, so she waited outside. At eight twenty-seven *exactly*, her boyfriend, Scott, came out of the restaurant with another girl! They didn't see Elsie there, and they started making out right in front of her on the sidewalk! Do you believe now?"

"Are you kidding? So a ghost told Elsie where to go to catch her boyfriend cheating on her?" Sylvio said, incredulous.

"Yes! How creepy is that!"

"That's pretty creepy," Celia said wearily.

"Okay," Marco said, "so Elsie caught her boyfriend cheating on her. But we're supposed to believe it was because she received a note from a ghost? I'm really having a hard time with that."

"And you're not the only one. Especially since Elsie doesn't have any proof. She swears the note disappeared out of her purse. No one else actually saw it."

"See!" Marco sat back.

"Why are you so skeptical? You *do* remember we had a curse on fifteen-year-old virgins here last year."

"What?" Sylvio asked, incredulous again.

"You haven't heard about that yet? No one ever really figured it out," Marco said wearily, glancing at Celia again. "Girls kept having bad things happen on the day before their sixteenth birthday. Broken leg, one girl had an epileptic seizure, another girl actually got electrocuted. They were always accidents, or something that couldn't have been caused by someone else. And the only girls who avoided it were the ones who had lost their virginity. It was freaky, to say the least."

"It's the reason Mariette died," Regine said. Marco made a disapproving noise in his throat, and Regine turned to Celia. "Well, wasn't it? She was helping the old chemistry teacher, who was also the swim coach, down by the pool, and she fell in and drowned. On the day before her birthday."

"Oh, my God," Sylvio said. "I've heard bits and pieces of that story, but I didn't . . . Did you know her?"

"Celia was her best friend," Regine said, and they all looked at Celia.

"Elsie must be devastated," Celia said, changing the subject.

"She's pissed! Scott even brought her flowers today, but I heard that she let him have it right in the middle of the hallway," Regine said. "I think it's safe to say that relationship is over."

Celia said, "I wonder if it's really Mariette."

"Would you want to see her?" Marco asked her.

"I would." Celia's expression was open and a little wounded. She chose her words carefully and kept her eyes on the table. "The last time I saw her, she was soaking wet and blue in the face. It's such a horrible way to remember her. If I accept that there is a ghost, and it's the ghost of Mariette, she sounds quite beautiful. I'd love to see her that way." Celia looked up and was a little taken aback that everyone was listening so intently to her. "I would tell her how much I miss her. And how chemistry is so much harder this year. But mostly that I miss her."

BRUNO'S GYM CLASS SPLIT into teams for flag football—not a favorite of Bruno's, but he was glad for the chance to stop thinking and blow off some steam. He was having a hard time ignoring the increasing number of mysterious things that had begun to happen since his family had arrived in Whiterose.

The gym teacher, a solid man just past his prime, had picked two seniors to quarterback. On the second play, a guy went down hard. Bruno didn't see what happened, but three seniors trotted away, laughing under their breath. The younger guy got up slowly.

The next time, Bruno saw it. One of the seniors clipped another guy just hard enough for him to fall. "Settle down, Van!" the teacher called. "I want to see flags, not hockey checks!" The guy who had fallen tried to shake it off, but he looked a little dazed.

They kept playing, and Bruno's quarterback connected with him. The second time Bruno caught the ball, he was running toward the goal when someone clipped him, and then the ground came up to batter his ribs on one side. Van turned away while one of Bruno's teammates offered him a hand.

It was just the excuse Bruno needed to vent his frustration. He jumped up, ran toward Van, and dove at his legs, taking him down. The gym teacher stepped in to break them up.

"Hey! You better stop right there, Van! I think we've had enough of you taking cheap shots at the underclassmen, so cut it out already!"

"I didn't hit anybody *that* hard!" Van protested.

"Cut it out! You got exactly what you deserved. Now"—the teacher looked around—"if I see any more contact from *anybody,* you will get detention, and those of you on the football team, you know there are repercussions for detention. Now play *flag football!*"

· · ·

STUDENTS WERE DISAPPEARING into classrooms when Bruno noticed a girl from his computer class tucked in a corner at the end of the hall. She pressed into the two walls as though she was trying to disappear, tears drpping from her eyes.

"Are you all right?" he asked as the bell rang.

"It doesn't matter," she said quietly. He stepped closer to hear her better, but she didn't say anything else.

"Did something happen?"

She made a halfhearted gesture. "Nothing happened." She sounded more confused than upset, but the tears kept coming. "All day it's just gotten worse, and I don't know why. I just . . . I just want to go to sleep and forget about everything."

"Are you sick?"

She shook her head. "I just don't care about anything. I've never felt like this before. Not even when my parents split up."

"Where are you supposed to be now?"

"English."

"C'mon, I'll walk you there." When Bruno slipped his arm around her shoulder to try to get her to move, the girl's slouched frame straightened up. She stared at him, relief in her eyes.

"I'm being foolish, aren't I? Why am I moping around like this? You are such a sweetheart." Before he knew it, she had hugged him.

"What are you doing?" he asked. He wouldn't have guessed his first hug from a girl would happen quite like this.

"I feel so much better. Thank you!" she said into his shoulder.

"You do?"

"I do! You're the nicest guy! I have to go to class, but thank you!" She gave him a peck on the cheek and took off down the hall, her bag swinging from her shoulder.

Bruno stared after her, wondering what had just happened.

4

anywhere out of the world

BRUNO WAS SITTING AT his desk in his room when Regine walked in with an imperious air. "My, you have a minimal style of decorating, don't you?"

Sylvio was behind her. "He's never had any stuff."

"But you're listening to My Bloody Valentine. Because Celia told you to?" She turned to Sylvio. "Did he ever listen to this music before?"

Sylvio was happy to join the attack. "Well, he hears a lot of stuff because I play it. But he never asked me for copies of anything before we moved here."

Regine's attention returned to Bruno. "I heard you have a thing for maps."

"I like them," Bruno said.

"I don't know — finding shortcuts and back doors at school, and making a fool of Mr. Williams in geography class — that sounds like more than just liking them."

"You heard about that?"

"Things like that get repeated," Regine said knowingly.

"Are you two coordinating outfits?" Bruno asked. Regine wore a deep-purple pleated dress over black tights, and Sylvio had on a purple cardigan.

"Of course," Regine said, as though it was the most obvious thing. "See you later." She led Sylvio out of the room.

Bruno went out into the hall and crept up to his brother's door to eavesdrop.

"Your room reminds me a little of Ivo's," Regine was saying. "Nothing is ever out of place. Look at all your CDs!"

"My most valuable possessions."

"Wow, you have Specimen's 'Wet Warm Cling-Film Red Velvelt Crush' on CD? That's rare."

"Cost me a fortune. But 'Kiss Kiss Bang Bang' is a classic. Do you like Kommunity FK?" She didn't respond, and Sylvio said, "'Something Inside Me Has Died'?" Another pause. "Oh my God, I'm going to play it for you right now."

Bruno was returning to his room when his father came into view, midway up the stairs. "Is your brother's door open?" Bruno nodded, and his father went back downstairs.

The bell rang as Bruno came out of the stairwell on his way to the home economics room to see Marco. Down at the far end of the emptying hall, the girl with curly red hair stood watching him. Her multicolored sweater practically glowed. She was, by all accounts, a ghost, and he shivered, wondering why this strange phenomenon didn't freak him out more—or anyone else at Suburban, come to think of it. Everything about Mariette unsettled him—to have died what sounded like a terrible death, and now to be haunting the school, wreaking havoc with the living . . . But the girl at the end of the hall, somehow always in a sunbeam, looking so wholesome and even happy, felt like a kindred spirit to Bruno.

"There you are! What are you doing?" Marco poked his head out of the classroom, a measuring tape draped around his neck. Bruno looked back down the hall, but Mariette was gone. He followed Marco into the home ec room and looked in amazement at the clusters of chattering girls hunched tentatively over sewing machines. Off in a corner, Marco had a workstation to himself.

"I know, it's a bit much. But it's the happiest time I have at school most days." He looked around at the girls. "They all want advice on their wrap skirts and aprons, and sometimes I give it to them, but they won't bother me while you're here."

"Why not?" Bruno asked.

Marco scoffed, "They know better than to interrupt me when I'm in a fitting. First let me get your proper measurements so I don't have to guess like I did on that shirt."

"You guessed perfectly."

"I'm usually pretty close." Marco wound the tape around Bruno's neck, then his shoulders, chest, waist, and hips. He jotted the measurements on a pad. "So, what are we making for you?"

"I don't know. It's up to you." Bruno wouldn't have presumed to ask Marco for anything.

"You could use a coat," Marco told him. "Something between a blazer and outerwear." He picked up a pencil and started sketching. "I'm thinking double-breasted, with a collar like a pea coat, but stopping at the hip instead of the traditional length. Fitted, but with enough room for a ribbed turtleneck underneath. You can wear it with those great trousers you got —the slim straight ones with the back pocket details."

Bruno studied the sketch. "You can make that?"

"Of course I can. I'll probably make one for Brenden, too, if you don't mind."

"Why would I mind? You have his measurements?"

"Oh, I know his measurements." Marco smiled mischievously. "Intimately. I can't wait for you to meet him. I've already told him about you. He's concerned I've found a new muse, which is why I have to make him one of these, too. I only have a week; I'm going to see him next weekend."

"Tell me about him."

"I think he'll be a great music critic. He just lives and breathes it. Sometimes I wonder why he doesn't make his own music. Over the past two years he did more for the Rosary than I think everyone realized. Ivo was kind of the leader, but Brenden shaped our taste in music, and that's a huge part of what the Rosary is about. Plus, he's the only one Ivo listens to, really. They're roommates at Metropolitan."

"You love him?" Bruno asked.

"I do."

"I didn't mean it like I doubted whether you did. I just wondered . . . what it feels like."

"How to describe it?" Marco pondered. "Everyone's so self-centered, you know? We're all so *me, me, me,* all the time. Even when you have a crush on someone else, it's always about how they complete *me,* how they make up for what is lacking in *me,* what they can do to make *me* feel better about myself. When you love someone, though"—Marco laid down his pencil and surveyed the chattering girls around them—"you forget about yourself. It's kind of a relief, really. You get to stop thinking about yourself all the time, and put someone else first. You get to delight in how good someone else is, how amazing it is that they are who they are. And if you're really lucky, they're doing the same thing about you. Then it turns out to be about you after all. Not because *you* wanted it to be about you—because someone else does. That's love." Marco smiled. "I'm just a hopeless romantic."

"I wonder if I am," Bruno said.

"A hopeless romantic? I don't know. I like to think everyone is. But that's what a hopeless romantic would say." Marco laughed at himself.

ON THE WAY TO THE LIBRARY that afternoon, Bruno compared Marco's description of love to the feelings for Celia that still churned in him. He couldn't be sure they were the same. That morning, when he had been near her, he hadn't thought of *anything*—not her, not himself. And when he had come away from her it was as though he was coming out of a trance, and then he spent the next half hour trying to remember everything she had said and done. He was just outside the library when Van suddenly stepped in front of him. "Where do you think you're going?"

"The library," Bruno said.

"I haven't forgotten about gym class," Van said. "Do you think I'm just going to let that slide?"

"I don't know." Bruno almost smiled, realizing he had actually forgotten about the fight he had picked with a senior.

"When are we going to settle this?" Van loomed over him, an order of magnitude larger than Bruno.

"Bruno, there you are!" It was a woman's voice, and Van stepped aside. Lois appeared in the doorway behind him. "I need your help." She looked curiously at Van, who slinked away, and she smiled at Bruno when he joined her.

"Okay, I have your first test," she said under her breath as they walked to the desk. "Mr. Dewey needs these books, and

I've looked three times. I swear the shelves rearrange themselves back there." Above the tall shelves of the main stacks, the ceiling grew darker and darker as it receded out of sight. Bruno couldn't tell if the back wall wasn't visible because it was too dark or too far away. "Will you take a look?"

"Sure." Bruno took the card from her and headed off into the stacks. Arnold Hauser's *Social History of Art*, volumes 1–4 — he had seen the art history section in the very first aisle just the other day. The section was right where he expected, and after a moment's scanning, he pulled the four slim volumes from the shelf. He turned to go back when his foot came in contact with a book on the floor. He stooped to pick it up.

"*You Are Here*? That's an odd title for a book." Bruno slipped the Hauser books under his arm. A torn strip of notebook paper marked a place in the middle of *You Are Here*, and when he opened it, Bruno found a map. He easily recognized North America, with a box drawn around the eastern half of the United States, and a note that read, *Bruno, see the detail in* You Are Here, *volume 2, in aisle 2.*

"Bruno?" He blinked, but there really was a message addressed to Bruno in this book. He wondered why the detail to the map would be in a different book, and why the second volume in a series wasn't shelved with the first one. He saw an empty space on the shelf above the place on the floor where volume 1 had been, so he slipped it back in and headed back down the row. At the main aisle, Bruno turned down the next row, which was marked with a large number 2 on its end cap. He slowly walked along the shelves, scanning for the book. Ahead of him a volume projected a few inches out from the row with *You Are Here, Volume 2* printed on its spine. Bruno pulled it out. Another bookmark, and when he opened the book, another map, this time of the northeastern United States. There was another detail box framing the state of Pennsylvania, and another note. *Bruno, see the detail in* You Are Here, *volume 3, in aisle 4.*

"You've gotta be kidding me," Bruno muttered, reshelving that book and returning to the main aisle. The library was eerily silent. He went two rows farther down. The sign with the number 4 on it was a little hard to see. "Why don't they have lights back here?" He walked down the row, wondering if another book would be sticking out, and sure enough, one was.

You Are Here, volume 3, was a little oversize. Back here the books all seemed to be a little larger than normal. Bruno couldn't guess why it would make sense to organize books by size. He opened volume 3 at its marker and found a map of Pennsylvania. There was a detail box around the south-central portion of the state, and the note read, *Bruno, see the detail in* You Are Here, *volume 4, in aisle 8.* "Aisle eight? Farther away this time," he mumbled, but he went off to find it.

In the eighth row of shelves the shadows were twice as deep. Once again, though, the volume he sought was protruding from a shelf just at eye level, and he pulled it out. It was the size of a phone book. "Show me the map of south-central Pennsylvania." He sighed. There it was, with a box around Whiterose. "It really knows where I am." Bruno marveled. "Aisle sixteen now? Seriously? It's going to be pitch-black."

He counted stacks as he went farther down the aisle in case he couldn't see the markers on the end caps. When he thought he had arrived, Bruno ran his fingers along the grooves of the plaque to feel the shape of the 6 next to the 1. "Here goes," he said at full volume, confident no one back in the reading area could hear him. He plunged into the darkness of the stacks. For a moment it felt as though he were passing through the darkness among the trees and hedges on his way to the Ebentwine clearing. Ahead Bruno saw a flickering light, which turned out to be a lantern resting on one of the shelves, a candle burning inside it. The aroma of cedar and olibanum greeted him as he approached. "Isn't fire dangerous in a library?" he asked the lantern. "Is the book here?" He lifted it by its handle and held it up to the shelves. *You Are Here, Volume 5* looked back at him, golden letters glinting in the candlelight. It was even larger than volume 4. "I'm guessing the box will be around Suburban High School."

He was correct. The scale of the map was large enough now for each house and building to have its own outline on the page. Inside this detail box Suburban looked less like a building than a maimed starfish, its bent limbs jutting out in all directions. *Bruno, see the detail in* You Are Here, *volume 6, in aisle 32.*

"*Thirty-two?* This is crazy," Bruno said. But he'd come so far, it didn't make sense to stop now. He picked up the Hauser books and the lantern and headed back to the aisle. Then he counted from seventeen up to thirty-two as he passed the dark stacks. Up ahead something moved in the darkness, and Bruno halted, suddenly afraid. He lifted the lantern and peered down the aisle, but no one was there. Behind him the reading area looked like a lonely rest stop on a nighttime highway. He shook off his fear and continued on his way to aisle 32.

The books were the size of fine art or photography monographs fit for coffee tables. Bruno had to find an empty space on the shelf to set down the lantern and the Hauser books before he could pull down *You Are Here,* volume 6. It opened to reveal a detailed plan of Suburban High School. Bruno was surprised the new wing was included in the drawing; the book looked far too old to document something so recent. On this page a box was drawn around the library, and he noticed immediately that on the plan, rather than four walls, the library had only three. The side of the room with these stacks, into which he had traveled so deeply, simply faded away. "Does it go on forever?" he asked the silent darkness around him. This time there was no detail box, but there was a note. *Bruno, see* You Are Here, *volume 6, page 1.*

The pattern was broken. Bruno turned back to the first page.

He found a heavily shaded drawing of two bookshelves viewed from the ceiling. The shelves extended all the way to either side of the page, so just a small stretch of the aisle was visible. In the middle were the head and shoulders of a boy viewed from above. The boy held a large book open in front of him. The only light in the picture came from a lantern on the shelf in front of the boy. The boy in the drawing was Bruno, as if someone on the ceiling had drawn a picture of him where he was, right there and then. Bruno looked up, but everything was black. For all he could tell, there might not have been a ceiling at all. He was so far from the reading area now; the library might as well have turned gradually into a cave.

On the page below the drawing there were twelve lines:

> *To earn your power, heed this poem*
> *Map the school with fine-tooth comb*
> *Find the one who sadly lives*
> *Inside a house where no one's home*

Go replant a family tree
Whose branches number only three
Wait until the moon is blue
Then what you seek is yours for free

Beware the walking crocodile
Who finds you guilty with no trial
Be sure to travel in short steps
What that one thinks will take a mile

Bruno didn't understand, but something in the pit of his stomach told him these words were not to be taken lightly. It was like finding an urn in a forgotten closet and being pretty sure someone's ashes were inside — it wasn't necessary to be sure, but it felt surreal, and serious, and slightly forbidden, all at the same time.

Bruno had to believe the poem was addressed to him, but he could barely make sense of any of the lines. He was supposed to be seeking power? He already had mapped the school "with fine-tooth comb" — he tended to do that wherever he was, without being told. How could someone live in a house where no one was home? And what to make of the warning? Who was the walking crocodile?

Bruno closed the book, but he didn't put it back on the shelf. He added it to the Hauser volumes and picked up the lantern so he could find his way back to the main aisle. He turned and walked toward the reading area, which glowed like a distant sunrise at the beginning of the stacks. When he reached aisle 16, where it was light enough, he set the lantern down. *Who knows — I may need it again.*

"Where have you been? I was starting to get worried!" Lois said when he made it back to the desk.

"Here they are," Bruno said, setting the Hauser volumes down.

"Thank you! So you had trouble finding them, too?"

"No, I found them right away. But I wound up looking for another book. That's what took so long." *You Are Here,* volume 6, looked even larger in the reading area, making a solid thump when he set it down on the counter.

"What is that? *You Are Here?* I've never heard of it."

"Neither had I. But apparently it's heard of me." Bruno opened to page 1 to show Lois the drawing of where he had been, but he was surprised to discover that now the illustration showed a bird's-eye view of his head and shoulders at a desk, facing a woman's head and shoulders on the other side. The Hauser volumes lay between them. Bruno looked up at the well-lit ceiling, but no one was there.

"Is that the two of us?" Lois looked down, and then up, and then at Bruno.

"It is. Except the first time I looked at it, it just showed just me where I was standing in the stacks. And this poem—I don't know what it means." Bruno turned the volume around so Lois could read it, and the color quickly drained out of her face.

"I need you to come into my office," she said in a strange voice, grabbing the big book with both hands. Inside her office, Bruno had only a moment to look around at the incredibly tidy space before Lois closed the door and turned to him. "I am going to tell you some things that may sound quite ridiculous, but I promise you, I am completely serious, and they are completely true."

"Isn't that, like, everything at high school?" Bruno asked.

"I guess it is, in a way. But this is different." Lois sat down at her desk. Bruno had a profound sense that something important was about to happen, and he only hoped it would explain at least some of the bizarre experiences he'd had since school had started. He didn't care whether it was good or bad. He had grown tired of all the mysteries, and he only wanted answers.

"Some people—very few—are given the opportunity to develop . . . powers that most people don't know are possible. Bruno, I'm pretty sure you are one of those people. I am one of those people, too." Lois looked around, then opened her desk drawer. As she concentrated, a handful of rusty paper clips floated up from the drawer and hovered like a flock of birds over the desk. Then the clips began to whirl around in space, now looking more like a swarm of mosquitoes. Glints of light began to leap out of the blur, and when the clips slowed down again and hung in the air, their metal was smooth and shiny.

"How did you do that?"

"It's not really important to know how. What's important is to realize it can be done." Lois eyed the clips back into the desk drawer and closed it.

Bruno put his head in his hands.

"What's wrong?"

I'm going crazy. He wasn't being dramatic; in that moment, all the inexplicable things from the past weeks became more than he could ignore, more than he could wish away. He felt the room spin. "I'm going crazy."

"No, you're not," Lois said brightly.

Bruno looked up at her. "I can't take any more . . . magic."

"What else has happened? What happened in the stacks?"

"I found volume one by the books you needed, and that sent me to volume two, which was in a completely different aisle, and then another, and I kept going farther into the stacks to find the next ones. It's so dark back there, someone left a lantern! And then I found this volume, which seems to know where I am at all times, and which has that poem that I think is for me, but I don't understand it.

"But that's not all; last week, I found a secret clearing behind my house, and when I went through it I was four and three-quarters miles away from my house in someone else's backyard."

"Four and three-quarters?"

"I'm good with maps," Bruno said.

"I should have guessed that, considering how well you find your way around here," Lois said. "Tell me about this clearing."

"It's called Ebentwine, and—"

"Ebentwine?" Her eyes widened. "Ebentwine?" She enunciated it slowly and watched him nod.

"What is it?"

"I should ask *you* that. I've never been there. There aren't many resources, and the legends I've found, the stories—it's hard to know what's true. Ebentwine is the source of the power, what you called magic. There are different ways to access it, but in its purest form it's far more concentrated than any person can stand. There are stories of people trying to access it directly and getting hurt pretty badly—or worse." Lois sat back, regarding him. "But that pretty much proves it. Bruno, if you've gone through the Ebentwine, you're one of the Kind."

"The Kind? Wait, is that why you asked me the other day if I was kind?"

"I wondered," Lois said. "We develop the ability to sense

one another, but I've met so few Kind myself, I wasn't sure what I was feeling with you. But I was right. You are Kind. That may be your main power, Bruno: finding your way around, finding hidden places. That may be why your admonition tells you to map the school."

"My admonition?"

"That's what this is." She put her finger on the poem. "I recognized it instantly. You've never seen something like this before?" He shook his head. "Then you are just starting on your path." She smiled brightly, trying to pull him back from the state of shock he knew was plain on his face. "I'm very excited for you! You are going to have some great adventures now."

"What's going to happen?"

"You must study your admonition carefully and try to decipher it. That won't be easy, but if you open yourself up to it, the answers will reveal themselves to you. You can't take too long, though; see here, there's a deadline. Find out when the next blue moon will happen. If you haven't fulfilled your admonition by then, you won't earn your power."

It was all too much; Bruno couldn't imagine doing such a thing. "What happens if I don't?"

"Nothing. You receive another admonition, probably completely different, and you try to fulfill that one."

"What's a blue moon? I thought it was just an expression."

"A blue moon is the second full moon in the same month. So they're kind of rare, which is where the figure of speech comes from. You need to find out when the next one will happen."

"Okay." Bruno scratched his head.

"But there are other things I must tell you. Very important things. You must keep all of this a secret. *All of it.* Don't tell anyone about the strange things that have happened, or may happen. When you figure out how to use your power, don't show anyone, and don't let anyone else catch you using it. Don't try to explain to anyone what I have explained to you."

Who would I tell? "Why?"

"Because people who are not Kind cannot know about us. In a world where everything must have an explanation, anything that can't be explained must be suspicious, evil. We are not evil, Bruno. You are not doing anything wrong; in fact, plenty of times we can help people without them even knowing it. We are just different. But it's better to keep this difference to yourself."

"Okay."

"That means you cannot tell anyone about me, either, okay? I will help you however I can, though in truth you will learn the most by yourself, in ways you won't expect. You'll receive messages from strange places, like this book. All you have to do is keep your eyes and your mind open. But if you have questions, I am always here."

Bruno just stared at her.

"You look so overwhelmed! It takes a while to settle in. Whatever you do, though, *please* don't tell anyone about me. It's the only thing I absolutely ask of you. You've heard of the Salem witch trials?" Bruno nodded. "That's what can happen when scared, superstitious people find out about us."

"I promise," Bruno said.

"Sleep on it, and I'm sure you'll have all kinds of questions in the morning." The bell rang. "Why don't you copy your admonition, and then why don't we keep the book here in my office so you don't have to go hunting in the dark for it again. Here's a hall pass." She wrote one out and tore it off her pad. "In case you ever need to come to me. I left the date off, so if someone asks, just pretend I'm scatterbrained. That won't be too hard." She laughed a little wistfully.

AS HE RODE HOME WITH Sylvio, Bruno thought about the new secret he carried—a secret so huge it seemed to be carrying him. He felt as though he'd found himself on an iceberg, its breadth and depth unfathomable to him, and the interests and intrigues of his social circle paled.

At home he sat on his bed and read his handwritten copy of the admonition for what felt like the hundredth time. Before today he had done his best to convince himself there was a reasonable explanation for all the strange things that had happened. But after the book, the maps, the admonition, the paper clips, the conversation with Lois, there was no point in denying it—everything was different, and instead of being a confused spectator, apparently he was right there in the middle of it. At least, Lois thought so. Bruno stared at the empty walls of his room; for the first time, they looked stark and unfriendly.

He read the admonition yet again. *The only thing I understand is to map the school with a fine-tooth comb. The rest, I have no idea.* Bruno sighed and went to his desk to dig out the plan of Suburban High School he had found online before his family moved. At least he could add on the new wing. Surprisingly, as much as he loved maps and plans, Bruno never had drawn one himself. His lines were timid and crooked, and even though he knew clearly what should be represented on the paper, it wasn't appearing there. He went downstairs to look for a ruler.

His father looked up when Bruno came into his study. "Hey there, what's going on?"

"Do you still have Grandpa's old drafting stuff from when he was an engineer?

"I think I do." His father opened a few drawers. "It's crazy how everything he did by hand on paper would just be done on a computer now. Wow, look at these. A scale, a couple triangles. What are you working on?"

"School project," Bruno said. He turned the scale over in his hand. It was triangular instead of flat, with a row of ruler-type markings along each edge. "How does this work?"

"I can't say I know exactly, but I think each side has a different size on it, like an inch equals a foot, or a centimeter equals a meter. You may have to do some research if you want to learn how to use it."

"Thanks, Dad."

"Sure. You can hold on to those as long as you like. I've never used them."

Back in his room, he turned the scale over and over to find the markings that might match the school plan. But the wing he wound up adding was too large in relation to the rest of the school. The drawing became cluttered and smudged with ink. He was going to have to draw his own plan from scratch, which seemed fair, since that was what his admonition instructed him to do.

Sylvio came in, and Bruno's first impulse was to try to hide what he had been doing. He stopped himself, remembering that Sylvio wouldn't find anything suspicious about Bruno with a map. *Is this what it's going to be like? Always trying to figure out if something I'm doing is going to reveal a secret I don't even understand myself?*

"Hey. Do you think I could borrow that zip cardigan you bought last week?" his brother asked.

"I haven't even worn it yet," Bruno said.

"Forget it."

STARTING THE NEXT DAY, Bruno paced off different areas of Suburban High School as unobtrusively as possible, jotting in his notebook the number of steps it took to traverse different hallways and rooms so he could convert them to feet and inches later. He had begun a new map on the inside back cover of the notebook; the challenge became an obsession. The ink had smeared in several places and his lines were wobbly, but he could see Suburban taking shape, and he was gaining a newfound respect for mapmakers and architects. Bruno spent time looking at architecture books in the library, and he did his best to copy the way doors, windows, and stairwells were represented on plans.

He stopped in the library to show Lois his progress. "Wow, that looks so complicated. Have you figured anything out?"

"No."

Lois hesitated. "There's something I need to tell you." She looked around them. "The book—*You Are Here*—disappeared from my office."

"Really? Did someone take it?"

"Maybe, but I don't think so. I've heard about books like that showing up to provide information, then slipping away."

"Wow."

"It makes me sad, because hey, I'm a librarian, you know?" Lois smiled weakly. "I've never had access to a primary source like that before. I've only been able to find obscure volumes filled with wild stories told by citizens who had no idea what they were talking about. And for a day, I had the real thing right there in my office."

"So you didn't look at the rest of it?"

"Well, I did take a quick look, right after you left. And apparently there was only one other thing the book wanted me to know."

"What's that?"

"When I opened it, the things you'd shown me were gone —the drawing on the first page, and your admonition. There was a drawing of Suburban, though, the floor plan. No words, just the walls and doors and stairs. Except right in the middle of a hallway, there was a drawing of a skull."

"A skull? What does that mean?"

"Who knows? I'd say it's probably not good."

"Like, someone is going to die here?"

"Perhaps. Or maybe it means there's a killer here."

"A *killer*?" The overwhelmed feeling started to come back.

Lois exhaled. "I don't know. I have no experience with these things. What else could it mean?"

"Which hall? Where was the skull drawn?"

"I don't remember," Lois said. "Nothing was labeled. It was . . . I'm really not sure."

If Bruno had seen it, he would have identified the hall immediately, but he reminded himself that not everyone had the same facility with maps and plans. Anyway, if Lois had seen the skull, he would let her worry about it.

With everything that was happening, he was having a hard time concentrating in class. Mr. Williams was the first to notice. "Mr. Perilunas, where are you now?"

"I'm here," Bruno said, prompting titters from his peers.

"Today we are discussing the Pacific Ring of Fire, the collection of active volcanoes that line both sides of the Pacific

Ocean. Mr. Perilunas"—Mr. Williams had turned back to the board and addressed Bruno without looking at him—"would you favor us with a list of the countries on the Ring of Fire?"

Bruno took a deep breath. The class waited expectantly, genuinely curious to see whether he could rise to this challenge. "Okay, well, Russia, Japan, Philippines, Indonesia, New Zealand, and then Canada, United States, Mexico, Costa Rica, Bolivia, and Chile?"

"You can include Antarctica, too," Mr. Williams said. Bruno flushed, but he didn't know why. He hadn't made a poor showing with his answer. He knew daydreaming in geography class was a bad idea, but he had answered Mr. Williams's pop quizzes correctly, and it still hadn't gotten the bull's-eye off his back.

He lingered after class and then went up to Mr. Williams's desk. "Yes?" the teacher said, once again not looking at him.

"I just wondered, why do you ask me those questions? You never ask anyone else."

"You're right, I wouldn't ask anyone else. Bruno, I need to remind you of something: I am here to teach you. And it became clear to me almost immediately that you are not learning anything in my class, because you already know what we're covering. If you don't learn anything, I am failing in my mission, don't you think?"

Give me a break. "I thought you'd be happy I know what you're teaching."

"That would be nice for you, wouldn't it? Then you'd have fifty minutes to space out every day. That doesn't work for me. Tomorrow I will receive from you two pages sharing with me some things about the Pacific Rim that you *don't* know right now. That means you have to come up with information I can believe you don't already have in that atlas in your brain."

"What? That's not fair," Bruno said weakly.

"I am well aware of that. Don't be late for your next class."

5
theft, and
wandering around lost

FOR A WHILE BRUNO became so focused on his map-drawing, he was almost able to forget the reason he had started the project. It was as though someone had realized that too much had been revealed to Bruno too quickly, and he needed a respite. One chilly morning near the end of September, Sylvio and Bruno pulled up in front of Regine's house, but instead of getting into her own car, she came over to theirs. Sylvio rolled his window down. "Celia's sick today. I never get to ride with you, so I thought maybe I'd join you this morning?"

"Sure," Sylvio said, clearly pleased by the idea.

Regine walked around to the passenger side and tapped on Bruno's window. When he rolled it down she said, "Would you mind if I sat in front?" There was an uncomfortable moment; then he shrugged and got out.

In the back seat Bruno tried to ignore their conversation, but they seemed to have forgotten he was there anyway. "Homecoming is a little dull. I went with Ivo last year. But I'd like to go with you, if you want."

"Sure," Sylvio said. "Do we dress . . ."

"Like Diaboliques? Absolutely. That's the whole point. Part of the fun of going to school dances is to point out to everyone how tiresome it is when no one has an original thought and everyone shares one brain. Plus, it's a good excuse for just the two of us to do something."

"Sounds great."

They arrived at Marco's house and he came out, looked confused for a moment, and walked to Sylvio's car. Regine was still talking. "Brenden and Marco were the power couple of the Rosary last year. I think someone has to take over that responsibility this year."

Marco got into the back seat next to Bruno. When Sylvio pulled out into the road, Marco looked over at Bruno and mouthed, *Did she make you get in the back?* Bruno nodded, and Marco rolled his eyes.

Bruno leaned over and Marco met him halfway. "She made him this little book of collages, with pictures and song lyrics," Bruno said under his breath.

"Of course she did," Marco whispered back.

In the front seat Regine was chatting away to Sylvio about their homecoming plans, and after a moment Marco said quietly to Bruno, "Before, we would have been making a list on some kind of music topic."

"They're in love," Bruno said.

"Sure, sure." Marco rolled his eyes. "What's your favorite song?"

Bruno tried to come up with something, but his thoughts kept returning to Celia's song that he couldn't identify. "I'm not sure if I have one. What's yours?"

"It is hard, isn't it? I love all the aggressive stuff—Screaming Blue Messiahs, Belfegore, the Blackouts—but my top song choice always seems to be something more delicate. Lately it's been 'Under the Ivy' by Kate Bush. It's short and simple, and it's not nearly as well known as her bigger songs, but I just love it."

"I haven't really listened to her."

"I'll make you a mix of her best stuff. She's amazing. Oh, I do like this song, though." Marco nodded at the front seat when "Other Voices" started playing on the stereo.

"The Cure is Silver's favorite band," Bruno said. "He plays them almost every morning."

They listened to the song and Regine and Sylvio's conversation, and Bruno wished he could ride with Marco every day.

THAT MORNING BRUNO'S GYM class played volleyball and Van was on the other team. He spent the class glowering at Bruno through the net and trying to spike the ball in his direction. It was clear he had put a target on Bruno, and his friends knew it, too. After gym, Van followed Bruno to his next class, and when Bruno ducked into a bathroom in hopes of evading him, Van came in after him. They stood there, the row of sinks on one side of them, the stall doors on the other side.

Van punched him so quickly that Bruno only saw the senior's arm retracting, leaving Bruno staggering back with a burning pressure in his chest. Van advanced on him, a hard, gleeful look in his eyes, and Bruno retreated to the window. Then Van stopped and looked around. "Is someone crying in here?"

They stood still and listened. In one of the stalls someone caught his breath, but Bruno had heard it, too.

"Who's in there?" Van barked. No answer. "How many sissies *are* there in this bathroom?"

It might have been simply the presence of a witness, or perhaps it was the crying, but Van seemed to lose his motivation. He looked at Bruno and said, "This isn't over. I will damage you wherever and whenever I feel like it, for as long as I feel like it." He walked out.

Bruno took a moment to let his heartbeat slow down, and in the meantime the crying resumed in the stall. "Are you okay?" He knocked on the door, which wasn't latched. When no one answered, Bruno pushed it open.

Wedged into the corner, a boy looked back at him, his eyes flooded, his face red.

"What happened?"

The guy said nothing for a moment, then managed, "Nothing. I just need to be alone." He was a little embarrassed, but he seemed too crushed to really care.

"Are you sure? Are you sick?"

The guy shook his head. "I don't even know why . . . I just . . . don't know why I'm here."

"In the bathroom?"

The guy shook his head again. "Anywhere. What . . . what's the point of being here? What good does it do?"

"Do you really feel that way?" The deadened look in the guy's eyes made Bruno uncomfortable. "Well, you can't just stay in there. Do you want me to go get someone for you to talk to?"

"Would you?"

"You'll stay here?" Bruno asked, and the guy nodded. "Okay, I'll be right back."

He left the bathroom and sprinted down to the nurse's office. The nurse looked at him suspiciously, but he accompanied Bruno back to the bathroom and enticed the boy out of the stall. The nurse thanked Bruno and told him to go to class as he put his arm around the boy's shoulders and escorted him out of the bathroom.

MARCO GOT UP FROM his stool when Bruno arrived at the home ec room. "Here you are. I think it turned out really well." He pulled a charcoal-gray jacket out of a garment bag and held it up behind Bruno so he could slip his arms inside. "It works best if it's buttoned." Marco watched him close it up. "What do you think?"

"It looks great! I can't believe you made this!"

Marco popped the wide collar so it wrapped around the nape of Bruno's neck. "With a turtleneck that'll look pretty cool."

"I really like it. Thank you very much!"

"You're welcome!"

"Can I ask you something?" Marco nodded. "What do you think about . . . I don't know . . . Do you believe in ghosts?"

"You mean Mariette? It is kind of strange that people aren't more freaked out, isn't it. I think it's because of the whole curse thing last year; there's just something about this place that makes stuff like that easier to believe. Compared to the way girls were getting hurt last year, the thing with Mariette's ghost and the cheating boyfriend is pretty mild. Did you hear she struck again?"

"No. What happened?"

"She gave a note with a place and date to a junior guy. Or at least, he says she did; he lost the note, or it disappeared, or there never was a note in the first place. Anyway, he caught his girlfriend making out with some guy from another school at the mall or something. They'd been going out for two years."

"Wow," Bruno said. "Why would Mariette do that?"

"I don't know. I don't remember her being mischievous or spiteful when she was alive. She seemed really nice, kind of all over the place, but always had a smile on her face. It would be just as easy to ask why people are cheating on their boyfriends and girlfriends, you know," Marco said.

"True." Bruno thought of the guy in the bathroom that morning and wondered whether it was the same guy.

"Either way, I hope Mariette cuts it out. It's starting to feel like last year, when everyone just waited to see who got hurt next."

One of the girls from the class came by. "Hey, Marco, is this your new boyfriend?" She was pleasant, but there was a gossipy undertone to her voice.

"No, I still have the old one," Marco told her. "Bruno is up for grabs."

The girl walked away, and Marco turned back to Bruno. "That's probably going to happen again if you keep hanging out with me. You okay with that?"

"I don't care," Bruno said. "I like hanging out with you."

"It might hurt your chances of getting a date. Then again, it might help you with some girls." Marco chuckled.

"I don't think I'll be getting a date anytime soon," Bruno said.

"You're still torqued for Celia, aren't you? That's not going to do you any good," Marco said. "I'm sorry to say it."

"That's okay. I'm fine with things the way they are." They were silent a moment. "You're driving up to Metropolitan tonight?"

"I am! Brenden said Ivo is clearing out of the room for the

weekend, so we'll have it to ourselves. I can't wait!" Marco bugged his eyes out at Bruno, who laughed.

"Have a great time. I'm sure they'll miss you at Diaboliques tonight."

"They'll be fine. You know, you should go with them. I think you'd like it."

"I'm waiting for Silver to ask me. I don't want to crash his party."

"Oh, it's not up to him. When I get back, you're going."

ON MONDAY, THE GHOST of Mariette struck again. Or at least, all the indications were that she had. By midday the story went around school that the German teacher had been seen crying to the trigonometry teacher outside the faculty lounge, and she had been overhead saying she had left her husband. A few students swore she had arrived late to class on Friday with a puzzled expression and a small piece of paper folded in her hand.

Then a senior boy caught his girlfriend cheating on him by stopping by her house at the appointed time on Mariette's note. The ghostliness of the notes—they always disappeared before the recipient could show anyone else—only made it easier to believe in the ghostliness of the source. In a matter of days there seemed to be no other topic of conversation at school.

"I think it's good," Sylvio said. "Everyone is going to think twice about cheating now."

"If this weren't a high school, I'd say you were right." Marco replied. "Teenagers are genetically wired to try to get away with as much as we can, even though we know perfectly well we're likely to get caught sooner or later."

"But what about how depressed it's making everyone?" Regine complained. "This morning a girl in my class just lost it. The teacher had to take her down to the nurse."

"Had she gotten a note from Mariette? Did all the depressed people get notes? Someone told me they didn't know why they were sad. It's not like they're distraught because they caught someone cheating on them," Marco said.

"So is that *another* thing, then?" Celia asked in a tired voice. "Last year it was the birthday curse, and now Mariette's kiss notes *and* the curse of the 'great depression'?"

Marco looked at her sympathetically. "I don't know, but it's all very strange, and last year no one ever really figured out what to do about it. It finally just stopped. Some people said it stopped because Mariette . . ."

"Are we going to have half the school wandering around under a black cloud because Mariette broke them up, or for no reason at all? That would be horrible."

"Why don't you ask Mariette? If she'd tell anyone, it would be you."

"I still haven't seen her. And who knows if she'd tell me anything. She sounds like a different person."

BRUNO NEVER WOULD HAVE guessed his first semester of high school would mess with his head so much. The real world was getting crowded out by another, stranger one, and while he could no longer pretend it didn't exist, he did his best to avoid it. Only one enjoyable thing had come out of the whole strange tangle of mysteries: drawing his plan of the school. He labored over the details—the spacing of windows, the direction each door swung—and he was impressed with his own work. But there had been no revelations; nothing had been out of place. If there was supposed to have been an epiphany, none had come. He remembered the paper clips whizzing around Lois's head —she had made it sound as though he'd gain the power to do something like that.

After Spanish class, Bruno went down the stairwell in the Chancellor Wing, en route to the cafeteria to meet Celia for lunch. He was going to take his shortcut across the side lawn, which had been adopted by plenty of other students, wearing a path in the grass. But before he exited the stairwell he looked at the stairs that led to the basement. He never had gone down there. He assumed the basement contained the usual mechanical rooms, perhaps the janitor's office. He left the stream of students and continued down the stairs.

The air grew warmer and drier as he descended, and at the bottom of the stairs Bruno's assumptions were confirmed: Double doors with small windows led to a dimly lit room with large metal boxes whose function he couldn't discern. A sign read KEEP OUT—NO ACCESS. Bruno sighed and turned to retrace his steps.

In the darkness under the stairs he was surprised to see another set of stairs rising behind the ones he had just descended. He walked around to where they began and could see up half a flight to a landing and a wall, lit by indirect daylight from above, just like the other set of stairs. He could hear the voices of students filtering down from somewhere above. Bruno went up these new stairs.

At the ground level the stairwell continued upward. Students were coming down from the upper floors and spilling out into a hallway. Bruno followed them and realized he was in the new wing, with the cafeteria just down the hall. As students brushed past him he was sure he looked completely lost.

"Hey, Bruno!" It was Celia. "Where are you coming from?"

"Spanish," he said before he had time to think.

"But you just came out of there." Celia pointed behind him, and Bruno actually turned around to look at the stairwell. "Wouldn't you take the shortcut across the back lawn from the Chancellor Wing?" The door from the back lawn was on the other end of the hall.

"Not today," he said.

"Then how did you wind up in that stairwell? You didn't . . . There's something you're not telling me," Celia said.

"No, there isn't." Bruno squirmed under Celia's stare, the one she had trained on him only a few times before—the one that felt like a scalpel and a healing balm at the same time.

She was silent for a moment. "Let's go have lunch." They got food and went to their usual table, where a few students were eating. "I'm really sorry, but we need this table," Celia told them. "Would you mind?" Bruno thought there was no way her request would be honored, but the kids got up and left, and he and Celia sat down. She looked at him. "Okay. I'm going to tell you something. Maybe if I go first, you'll be willing to go second." She collected her thoughts. "So you know about Mariette, my friend who died last year. The one everyone thinks is haunting the science wing."

"I do," Bruno said.

"Well, nobody else knows this, and I need you to promise you will never tell anyone. But Mariette had . . . powers. She could do things that were, I don't know, supernatural. When we did chemistry experiments, she didn't need to measure anything. She could tell how much of each substance was required, just by looking. She could bring dying flowers back to life by touching them. She could draw frost crystals on windows with the tip of her finger. All of her powers had to do with nature."

"Like, a witch?"

"No. Well, throughout history they've been called witches, but she, and others like her, are really called the Kind. The Kind only use their powers for good things. The ones who use their powers for evil are called the Unkind. So here's another part of the story no one else knows: Mariette died because the chemistry teacher here last year was Unkind, and all year he kept trying to kill fifteen-year-old girls on the day before their birthday, in order to gain more Unkind power. That's why everyone thought there was a curse. Mariette knew something was wrong, and she spent the whole year protecting all of us, but we couldn't figure out who it was until it was too late, and he got her. He never even realized he had killed one of his own."

So all of the secrets Lois had told him—Celia knew them, too? "The Kind and the Unkind?" he asked blankly.

"The way I understand it, they're two sides of the same coin. Good and bad, dark and light. So you know why I'm telling you this, don't you?"

"I think so." She stared at him expectantly, but Bruno labored to form a coherent question. "Are you one of the Kind?"

"No. For a little while I thought I might be, because a couple of my drawings caused things to happen to other people. I actually stripped the chemistry teacher of his powers. He had what's called an admonition—it's a twelve-line poem that tells one of the Kind, or the Unkind, how to increase his or her powers—and his admonition warned that he would lose his powers if I drew a portrait of him. It turns out that I am an

Ambassador: one of a small group of people who help the Kind interact with the rest of the world. In fact, I knew you were coming. Well, not *you*, but I knew *someone* was coming to Suburban this year. Someone who was just finding about being one of the Kind. I also fulfilled Tomasi's admonition by drawing him. Tomasi is Kind, too."

Bruno didn't think his eyes could open wider. "He is?"

"Yes. His powers have to do with books. He can read them when they're closed, and he can see the original text if a book has been translated or changed. He can also travel through books if they're open."

"Wow." Last week the revelations in the library had turned his world upside down. But Lois had led him to believe the Kind were so unusual, so isolated, the two of them might never encounter any others, and Celia had just blown that assumption away. Lois, Celia, Mariette, a teacher, Tomasi . . . Just as he had with Lois, Bruno needed to hear everything a second time, to make sure he hadn't imagined it. "So you gave him his powers, but you're not one of the Kind?"

"No. Ambassadors have limited powers that they can only use to help members of the Kind. Anyway"—Celia fixed her most penetrating gaze on Bruno again—"I'm not telling you all this because I thought it would be fun to reveal my deepest secrets to you. You seem to have a talent for navigating. For a while I just thought you had an incredible instinct for it, but now you seem to be taking shortcuts around here that don't really exist in this dimension. Bruno, I'm pretty sure you're one of the Kind, too.

"Have you ever had anything happen that you couldn't explain? I'm not talking about being able to find your old beach cottage five years later. Maybe something like starting out in one place and then finding yourself in another place and not being quite sure how you got there?"

Bruno squirmed again. She had hit so close to home, it was uncanny. He mentally retraced his steps from his back door to the Ebentwine clearing. Lois had reinforced his decision to stay away from it, but now Celia had unknowingly pointed out to him that the shortcut under the stairs here at Suburban was practically the same thing—just without the garden and the strange man named Gardner.

Celia sat across the table from him, waiting while he tried to figure out what to say. It was clear that in the space of ten minutes, her interest in Bruno had become much more intense —not romantic, but in a way that Bruno couldn't quite define.

Celia had made it clear that no one else knew the truth about Mariette, so Bruno figured Marco and Regine must not be privy to any of the things Celia had just told him. Instead, Celia had joined Bruno on the secret iceberg that drifted far away from the concerns of their friends.

He wanted to tell her everything so badly. But Celia hadn't mentioned Lois, and Lois hadn't mentioned Celia—was that for a reason? If there were Unkind as well as Kind, was someone lying to him? He tried to think of how he could play it safe. He wasn't going to squander this opportunity to bond with Celia, but Lois would have to be kept out of it for the time being.

"That has happened to me," he told her. "I went to the bottom of the stairwell in the Chancellor Wing, down to the basement, and when I went behind the stairs there was another staircase going up, and it came out in the stairwell of the new wing. It's like a wormhole or something in the school."

"That's fantastic!" Celia said. "I thought so! What did you think when you discovered it?"

"I didn't know what to think," Bruno said. "It doesn't make any sense. But it's happened another time, too." And he described the Ebentwine clearing, barely remembering to stop himself before he blurted out that the other place in which he had found himself—twice—was under her window in her backyard. "I wound up in another neighborhood, miles away."

"Ebentwine? I've never heard of it. But it sounds amazing." Celia's eyes shone with excitement for him. "I can help you make sense of all this. You have to meet Tomasi. You have to come to Diaboliques."

"Really?" Bruno couldn't help being curious about Tomasi. And Marco had already invited him to Diaboliques.

"There's a woman there you have to meet, another Ambassador. From what I understand, someone helps you get started, and then the whole world around you gives you instructions about the Kind. If Tomasi can't do it, Cassandra will know who can. Maybe she can do it, actually. Maybe I did just now, but I'm not sure, and I'd hate it if I screwed something up for you." Celia looked caringly at him, and Bruno realized he must have looked overwhelmed again. "Don't be scared. I know it's a lot to take in, but amazing things are going to happen to you. So, tell your brother I said you have to come to Diaboliques on Friday. I'll tell him myself."

"What if he asks why?"

"You've been listening to a lot of the music. I know you like Cranes now."

"And My Bloody Valentine," Bruno added.

"I think you know more of the music than you let on." Celia smiled. "It's about time for you to see what Diaboliques is like anyway. You should go just for the music. And now you have other reasons, too."

"So the others don't know about Tomasi being Kind?"

"No. They see him at Diaboliques, sometimes other places, but that's it. You have to keep that secret. All the secrets. About Tomasi, about Mariette, about me."

"I will."

"But I'm glad we figured this out," Celia said, and her eyes shone. "You're one of the Kind."

"I'm one of the Kind," Bruno repeated.

"I have to tell you some other things, though. Because even though I took care of the chemistry teacher, there might be someone else we have to be concerned about," Celia said. "Last year when I fought off Mr. Sumeletso—the teacher—there was someone else watching us. Mr. Sumeletso knew who it was, but he wouldn't tell me. That other Unkind was definitely powerful, though. I didn't get a good look at him, but I'm pretty sure he—or she—was part of the plot to kill Mariette. All summer I was scared he would come after me for vanquishing Mr. Sumeletso, but nothing's happened. If that Unkind person hasn't come back by now, there's probably nothing to worry about. I just wanted you to know everything, just in case. I've probably told you too much at once. I'm sorry!"

"It's all right." Bruno had no idea how he was going to concentrate in geography class that afternoon.

BRUNO WATCHED LOIS TRY to process everything he had just told her about what had gone on last year with Mariette and the chemistry teacher.

"How did you find out about this?" Lois was gravely serious.

"I . . . I can't tell you. You asked me to keep your secrets, and so did this other person. I didn't tell her about you, so I don't feel right telling you about her."

Lois thought. "It's Celia, isn't it?"

"What? How'd you know?"

Lois smiled. "I saw her writing in her sketchbook, and then other writing appeared on the page. She definitely has some kind of powers."

"Why didn't you say anything about that?"

"Honestly? I think Celia is Unkind, and I was trying to figure out how to tell you because I know you like her."

"She's not Unkind. She's an Ambassador." Bruno paused at Lois's alarmed look. "One of her drawings gave Tomasi his powers last year, and she made a drawing to defeat the Unkind teacher who killed Mariette."

"What makes you think she's an Ambassador?"

"She told me."

"Ambassadors are just as dangerous as the Unkind. Maybe more so. They trick the Kind into trusting them. You have to stay away from her!"

"What? She never said—"

"I'm surprised there's an Ambassador here; they're even rarer than we are. They aren't citizens because they have powers, but their power is completely dependent on the power of a Kind. They try to convince us they keep us strong, and they do little things to win our confidence. Often they serve as harbingers, providing important information to us at crucial times. But in the end, they drain our power away from us, and put us in danger."

Bruno had no idea what to say. "Have you ever . . . Did an Ambassador do that to you?"

"I've never met one, and I've never met anyone who's met one."

"Then how do you know? What makes you sure?"

"I'm not the most experienced with being Kind," Lois said gently. "But I've been doing this for fifteen years. You hear things. You learn things. There are so many stories—about admonitions, about the Ebentwine. But the one story everyone knows is that Ambassadors are like vampires—you certainly don't want to meet one, much less spend time with one. She just *told* you she was an Ambassador?"

"Yeah."

"What about her friends?"

"They're citizens. Marco and Regine don't know anything, and they're her closest friends, so I don't think she's told anyone."

"So, Celia told you Mariette was Kind, and killed by an Unkind? You have to be careful—she may not be telling you the truth. What does everyone else think happened?"

"They all think she drowned in the swimming pool. And now her ghost haunts the science wing. I've seen her. She has curly red hair, and apparently she's been making all kinds of trouble by passing notes to people, telling them where to catch their boyfriends or girlfriends cheating on them. And people say she sucks the motivation out of you, or that you get really depressed if you meet her. Several people have had to go on medication for it."

"All of this would just be so crazy, if it weren't really happening . . ." Lois smiled weakly. "I know you like Celia. But are you sure she's not the one who caused Mariette to drown? That sounds like something an Ambassador would do. She could be killing you with kindness so she can take advantage of you. I'm not trying to be mean! I'm just trying to help you protect yourself. Whether she's Unkind or an Ambassador, you have to stay away from Celia. You cannot trust her."

"I understand." Bruno got up. "I'll go shelve books."

"Okay. I know it's a lot, but you're doing well. You are." She watched him walk out of her office.

we came to dance

DOES SYLVIO FEEL LIKE you're horning in on his friends?" Bruno's dad asked him after dinner on Friday night.

"I think so. But we met them at the same time, and I hang out with them as much as he does. Regine's the only one he spends more time with."

Mr. Perilunas smiled. "I'm not saying you're doing anything wrong. Just try to be sensitive to how he feels, okay? So you want to go to Diaboliques? It's a great name, and I actually thought Hermetica was a pretty great name."

"Marco invited me. He thinks I'll like it."

"Then it's time for me to say the same thing to you that I said to Sylvio when he asked to go to Hermetica the first time." His father pointed to the armchairs in his office, and they sat down. "Everybody thinks if I'm a minister, I must be really strict with my children, but you know that's not true." Bruno nodded. "Sophia is off in Argentina taking care of herself, and Sylvio has a collection of music, some of which might not be sacrilegious but certainly flirts with it. It's not because I don't care, or I don't hope you grow up with my faith and my values. It's because your mother and I are fortunate enough to have three children who are all intelligent enough to understand the choices available to them. I might not always agree with each of your choices, but I have never seen any of you tilt so far into bad choices that I thought I had to intervene.

"What I said to Sylvio the first night he went to Hermetica was that people are defined not by the things they *don't* do but by the things they *do.* Parents and religions are prone to come out more strongly for the things we *shouldn't* do than the things we should, and while we do well to encourage people to avoid bad acts, we do even better to remember to encourage people in their good acts.

"What I mean is this: I want you to go, because I want you to experience the world, and the world is a never-ending series of choices I can't make for you. I'm not doing you any favors by keeping you from the world out there. That's just preventing you from becoming your own person by figuring out what your values are.

"Probably Diaboliques is far more harmless than it sounds —a little fury, signifying nothing. Maybe you'll be presented with some choices tonight, the kind that make parents and religions anxious. If you are, I have a feeling you'll do just fine. I'd love to hear about it when you get back."

RIDING WITH SYLVIO through the dark streets, following Regine's car to Diaboliques, Bruno was nervous. It didn't help that Sylvio was playing some menacing industrial song with a man growling the words *assimilate* and *annihilate* over and over.

"Why are we taking two cars now?" Bruno asked. "Is anyone going to see us?"

"That's not the point. I mean, sure, it's a great effect when people see it, but it's a lot more than that. When Regine explained it to me, it made complete sense. If you do something the easiest way, the most uncomplicated way, the normal way, it's only a matter of time before it becomes dull, something taken for granted. We do this for ourselves more than anyone else. These things remind us we're not like everyone else. We see the world differently. C'mon, it's like a movie!"

Bruno wasn't convinced, but it didn't really concern him. His nerves were up because he was going somewhere unfamiliar. And he was going to meet Tomasi.

If Tomasi were simply the other guy who shared this bizarre and fantastic secret life Bruno had just discovered, Bruno would have been desperate to meet him. Until recently, Bruno had resented Tomasi for being Celia's boyfriend, but now he wondered why Tomasi would risk that, if what Lois had said about Ambassadors was true. Everything was complicated.

At the club Celia climbed out of Regine's car, and Bruno felt that familiar rush: her snowy skin, her silky dark hair, her slender arms and breathtaking height. Her black tulip skirt and sheer black blouse worn over a camisole—Celia was a miracle every time she appeared. She might be dangerous, a wolf in a beautiful girl's clothing, but it was hopeless. Bruno had no chance of corralling his emotions. Things were just going to have to play out as they would—tonight and forever.

By a door in a brick wall they approached a hulking man, a cross between a biker and a crypt keeper, who turned out to be named Rufus. Bruno heard him call, "Twinkle, twinkle!" and the rest of them respond, "Release the bats!" It was only to be expected that Sylvio wouldn't have told him about this ritual in advance. Then they entered Diaboliques, up stairs and along corridors, while music thumped at them through the walls, as though the building itself had a heartbeat.

They entered a dark mezzanine that overlooked a dance floor flooded by searchlights, and he stared down over the balcony at the black-light circuslike performance going on below. They climbed more stairs and navigated a warren of halls and doors, while Bruno worked to keep his bearings. Finally they reached a velvet-lined inner sanctum, the third and smallest dance floor, presided over by a DJ named Patrick, who kissed Celia, Marco, and Regine hello, nodded at Sylvio, and shook Bruno's hand.

They took their places on one side of the dance floor, and Bruno remembered his brother's comment that all of this was somehow like a movie. A woman who looked like a cross between a vintage pinup girl and a dominatrix eyed him, and he wasn't sure if he should be flattered or concerned for his safety. A muscular man in a tight black shirt was dancing, metal goggles worn over his hair, dark shadow skillfully applied around his eyes. A host of other beautiful people stood around or sat on the velvet banquettes while the light from the wall sconces sparkled in the crystal beads that hung from them.

To Bruno, Diaboliques was the perfect frame for Celia. Perhaps it had to do with the darkness, but Celia almost glowed, and even in the light the rest of the exotic people around her somehow weren't as bright.

"Patrick does this every time!" Marco said when a new song began. "The moment we arrive, he puts on something he knows we love. Do you know this one?"

"No," Bruno said honestly.

"Christian Death, 'Church of No Return.' It's a classic!" Marco went out to join Regine and Sylvio on the dance floor.

From across the room a tall boy came over to Celia. He wore basic black. His short hair squared off his strong jaw. She slipped her arms around his neck and kissed him as a movie star should—with feeling and restraint at the same time. It was a kiss that suggested Celia saved more private kisses for when they were alone, and Bruno felt acid rise in his chest and stop in his throat. This was Tomasi.

Soon enough, it had to happen. Celia bent close to Bruno's ear so he could hear her over the music. "Bruno, this is Tomasi." Tomasi's steely eyes bored into Bruno, but he extended his hand.

"Celia says you're one of the Kind."

"I guess I am," Bruno said.

"You are. I can sense it in you. She says you've found a hidden passageway to get around Suburban." Bruno nodded. "It's a big school?" Bruno nodded again. "And you have a crush on Celia?"

"What?" Bruno looked up at him, startled.

"It's okay. Marco told me." Tomasi's mouth moved in a shape that Bruno thought might have been a smile. "I'm just giving you a hard time." Bruno realized that Tomasi, who was taller, stronger, and older, didn't regard him as a threat in the least. Though it stung, it made sense.

He was glad Celia hadn't been listening. Now she leaned in. "Does someone have to get him started?" she asked Tomasi. "The way your teacher did for you?"

"I don't know, really." Tomasi didn't look all that interested in helping.

"Well, I'm going to take him to meet Cassandra," Celia told him. "Come on, Bruno."

He received another cryptic half smile from Tomasi over Celia's shoulder, and Bruno followed her back down to the mezzanine. "Look for a plume of red hair. It's like a spiral on the top of her head," Celia told him on their way down the stairs.

Bruno peered around halfheartedly when they reached the mezzanine, wondering if two Ambassadors together would just suck whatever power he had out of him. It was dark until the lights from the lower dance floor swept across the space and blinded him for a moment. Celia pulled him toward one wall, and Bruno finally made out a couch where a regal woman with remarkable red hair sat by herself. She was smiling up at him and extending her hand, inviting him to sit down beside her.

"You lucky man! How do you know Celia?" she asked him. Celia perched on the edge of an ottoman across from them.

"From school," Bruno said. Cassandra took his left hand and grazed his palms with the tips of her long fingernails. The sensation ran through his body, and he was instantly aroused. *Oh, God. Did she do that? Is this what they do?*

Cassandra smiled at him. "That's okay. I have that effect on a lot of men, and some women." Bruno stared mutely back at her. She returned to his palm. "So, what do you need from me?"

"Nothing!"

Cassandra gave him an odd look. Celia leaned forward helpfully. "We just figured out Bruno is Kind a few days ago. I thought he needed someone to get him started. Someone did it for both Tomasi and Mariette."

"Someone already has."

"Did I do it? Can I do that?"

"You can, but in this case it wasn't you."

Surprised, Celia sat back. Cassandra turned to Bruno, speaking low so Celia wouldn't hear. "It's okay if you tell her the truth, but that is up to you."

"How do you know?" Bruno asked her.

Cassandra smiled indulgently at him. "I don't need a book called *You Are Here* to tell me about you. Celia is an exquisite woman, and you are going to be a bigger part of her life than either of you realizes. But not in the way you would like." She closed his fingers and tapped his wrist with her other hand, every touch sending a tingle through him. "I will tell you this: The one you are supposed to find, who lives in a house where no one's home? You will know her by the stranger she carries."

He stared again. "You know about that? Wait, the stranger she carries? What does that mean?"

"You are adorable," Cassandra said. "I would kiss you myself if you weren't so young."

"I . . . I don't know . . ." Everything was happening so fast, and these two women were pushing him along—was this what Lois had warned would happen? Bruno wished he felt more in control. Cassandra leaned even closer to his ear.

"What could I say to you to prove Celia and I won't harm you? You will be suspicious until you decide not to be. Not everything you've heard is true, but you will have to find that out for yourself."

"Thank you" was all Bruno could think to say. Cassandra let go of his hand—it felt like being left behind in a bathtub after the warm water had drained out—and she turned to Celia.

"And how are you, my dear?" she asked her. They bent their heads together, and Bruno politely looked away. After a minute Celia stood up and Bruno followed suit. Cassandra beckoned, and Bruno leaned down to hear her. "Don't be afraid of the Ebentwine. Follow its rules, but don't fear it." She smiled and sat back on the couch, her fiery red hair illuminated by a passing spotlight.

On the way back upstairs Celia said, "I've never met anyone like Cassandra."

"Neither have I," Bruno agreed. *Except you.*

"I wonder why she thinks someone already got you started? Do you remember meeting anyone like that?"

Bruno shook his head, uncomfortable lying. In five minutes Cassandra had given him a wealth of tantalizing information, and he wanted very badly to believe Lois was wrong about Ambassadors, because clearly Cassandra had an amazing gift. He needed to talk to Lois again.

"What else did she say?" Celia asked him on the way back upstairs. "Wait, I shouldn't ask you. It's none of my business."

Bruno leaned in close to her ear. Her hair brushed against his nose, holding the scent of cinnamon. He decided to trust her. "She gave me some really good advice. I can see why you like her."

She nodded happily at him, and again he felt like following her anywhere.

Near the end of the evening Bruno noticed Tomasi standing beside him; the two of them watched Celia dance. Eventually Tomasi said, "It's different for everyone. You'll have powers I don't have. All I can say is, do everything you can to keep it a secret—from your family, from your closest friends." Tomasi's warning sounded a lot like Lois's.

"Celia said your parents have been rough on you."

"That's putting it mildly. They think I'm the freaking Antichrist. They don't like Celia because they know I met her here, and they're convinced this place is some kind of devil worship club or something. If they only knew . . ." They looked around at Sylvio, Marco, Regine—a whole room full of beautiful people who had no idea who Tomasi and Bruno really were, or what Celia and Cassandra knew. "It makes me crazy that my parents don't like her, because she's the only reason I haven't run away from them again."

"I'm sorry to hear it."

Tomasi shrugged. "After this year I'll go to college, and then it'll be better. For now my parents and I just give each other as much space as we can."

"So, you can travel between places by going through books?"

"Not all books. I need some connection to the book I'm traveling to. I have to have a page or part of a page from it, and the book has to be open on the other side. Maybe when I get stronger I'll be able to do more with that power. Right now it's good for visiting Celia, though."

"And nobody else has that power?"

"I think some people do. Sometimes I see other people in there, in between the books. It goes by so fast, I can't make out a lot of details. But I think they're traveling the same way. Or maybe they do something else in that space. It's hard to see. It's more useful to be able to read what's in other people's books, or letters in their pockets. That's probably an important thing I should tell you: You have to be careful not to abuse your powers. It can really make a mess of things."

"I would think so. You could do a lot of illegal stuff with that power."

"Illegal is one thing. Harmful is another. Whatever you do, don't ever use your power at anyone else's expense. All it takes is one time, and you'll switch from the Kind to the Unkind. And from what I understand, it's hell getting back."

Bruno's searched Tomasi's serious expression. "Really? Just once?"

Tomasi nodded. "I've never met anyone of the Unkind,

although I saw the chemistry teacher the night Celia stripped him of his powers. But everyone knows the stories. Do not use your power to harm anyone. There is nothing to prevent you from doing it, but once you do, you cross over. Then your next admonition requires you to do bad things instead of good, and your powers grow darker and more destructive. You do not want to go down that road."

Bruno took a breath. "I thought Ambassadors were dangerous—that they got their power by taking it from Kind."

"What? Who told you that?"

"No one. I've just heard it . . ."

"I've never heard that. And it's definitely not true. Celia fulfilled my admonition and increased my power. She's only made me stronger, not weaker." Tomasi turned and walked away.

Bruno had barely spoken with Marco since they'd arrived. He went over to him, and Marco gave him a wistful smile. "There's always one point in the evening when one of us says something about it not feeling the same without Brenden and Ivo and Liz. All last year it was the six of us, and now three of us are missing. I can't get used to it."

"There are six of us here now," Bruno offered.

"Yeah—oh, I didn't mean to put you guys down. I'm really glad you finally came. But it's not like we've all been here together, you know? I have two years of memories with Brenden and Liz and Ivo in this place. It's just different." Marco's eyes shifted away, and Bruno turned to see what had gotten his attention.

A group of boys had entered Patrick's room in a tight pack. They were dressed elegantly in black shirts and suits. Some of them wore black ties. One had a black vest under his jacket. Another wore a black cummerbund. They looked authoritatively in every direction as they crossed the floor, their confident expressions saying *I might want to sleep with you, and aren't you lucky we're here?*

"Who are they?" Bruno asked Marco.

"I have no idea." Marco's face was crammed with fascination, defensiveness, confusion and envy. Meanwhile, the boys took a spot on the other side of the dance floor, clustering together like an elegant murder of crows. One of them slipped his arm over another's shoulder; two others linked arms.

Out on the dance floor Regine's whirling slowed and her steps became hesitant. Marco said, "Regine does not get upstaged very often when she's dancing." Bruno followed him into a huddle with Celia and Tomasi. "Have you ever seen those guys before?"

Celia shook her head. Tomasi said, "Not here, but I know who they are. They go to St. Dymphna's. I think they're all sophomores. I've never really talked to them. At school they're always together, big on dressing well and dark music. I'm kind of surprised they haven't come here before; maybe they didn't have a way to get here. They kind of remind me of your group —the Rosary. I think they try to be more provocative than you guys, though. There are rumors about how they're all bisexual and they've all slept with each other, but I think it's just a bunch of crap."

"They definitely know you," Celia said. From across the room, one of the boys saluted Tomasi by cupping his hand and touching his fingertips to his forehead.

"Um, I have no idea why," Tomasi said.

"Because you're a senior who wears all black and likes this music, and they look up to you?" Marco suggested.

In the car on the way home Sylvio wanted to talk, but Bruno was preoccupied with all the things he had learned. The world of the Kind was unfolding around him, with unexplored paths seeming to run off in every direction. Every answer only prompted more questions. Bruno decided his first priority had to be his admonition. If he didn't solve that mystery, the rest wouldn't really matter as much. *Who carries a stranger? What does that even mean?* Even though he couldn't be completely sure who to believe about Ambassadors, Cassandra had given him a clue, no less cryptic than everything else.

THE NEXT MORNING BRUNO stayed in bed for a while after he woke up. Something about the visit to Diaboliques had finally done him in; the world had become too complicated even for him to decide what to wonder about first. Lois had warned him about Ambassadors, but Cassandra had suggested Lois didn't know what she was talking about—none of which helped Bruno force down his attraction to Celia, with her dark beauty and her rare but delicious laughter. Tomasi stood between them, but Celia was kind—in the best way, with a small *k*—and he knew she liked him, which made him ache.

What did it really mean to be one of the Kind? It had just happened to him, like going to the doctor and finding out he had to have some kind of vaccination, and here comes a needle. Bruno still would have said yes, if someone had asked him today to be part of the Kind. But it wasn't easy, or simple, or without consequence.

He also needed to figure out the rest of his admonition. He had to find whoever was carrying a stranger and complete the inscrutable task of replanting a family tree. The next blue moon would happen in December; the first full moon would be on the second of the month, followed by another on New Year's Eve. That was still a few months away, but it stressed him out anyway, considering how unprepared he felt at the moment. In every class, every time he walked the halls, he was going to have to pay attention to the things his peers carried. What might someone carry that could be described as a stranger? Should he assume the person he sought was at Suburban?

7

isolation

"H ow's your day?" Lois asked when he arrived in the library.

"I just had a pop quiz in my web design class," Bruno told her. "The only reason I did okay was because it was about this diagram, a flow chart of operations, and I tend to remember things like that."

"Glad to hear it! Who teaches that class?"

"Ms. Moreletii. She's no joke."

"I don't think I've met her. I don't make it down to the teachers' lounge very often." Lois looked over his shoulder. "I don't know who this is, either."

Bruno turned. "That's Mr. Williams. He's no joke, either. I have him for geography."

Mr. Williams raised his eyebrows when he saw Bruno, but he spoke to Lois. "Do you have any volumes of Piranesi?"

Lois turned to the computer. "Giovanni Battista, or Francesco?"

"The father. Giovanni."

"We do. Would you track this down, Bruno?" Lois jotted the call number on a scrap of paper.

"Sure." Bruno went off and found the book, a sizeable collection of etchings. He glanced through it before he returned, and the drawings captivated him immediately. Some of them looked real: the Colosseum in Rome; ancient temples, plazas, and ruins. Other drawings showed foreboding cavernous spaces, and it was hard to tell if they were real or the product of Piranesi's imagination.

Back in the reading area, Mr. Williams thanked Bruno for the book and left.

"He seems nice," Lois said. "He complimented your knowledge of geography."

"That's a surprise—usually it seems to annoy him."

In the hall on his way to his next class, Bruno decided he was having a good day: He had dodged a bullet from Ms. Moreletii, and Mr. Williams might like him after all. Suddenly his books went flying out from under his arm and crashed to the floor.

Bruno turned and found Van retreating behind him, laughing with his buddies. Bruno sighed and dropped to his knees to gather up his things.

"Can I help?" The girl with the blond ponytail whom he had helped back at the beginning of the semester stooped next to him. "He's a jerk. He leaves miserable people behind, wherever he goes."

"Yeah, and he really doesn't like me."

"Why's that? You don't seem like the type of person someone would be mean to."

"I kind of gave him a reason," Bruno admitted.

"Oh. I'm sure it wasn't that bad."

"Thanks," Bruno said when she handed him the rest of his things.

"Sure," she said, smiling.

• • •

BRUNO NOW WORE DARK stylish clothing every day like his friends did, and listened to more alternative music. This was his surface life, which hummed along, untroubled by the supernatural riddles he labored to solve. That was the part no one remembered about having a secret identity, wasn't it? One's real, non-secret life still comprised the vast majority of one's day. Celia turned to him one morning. "Your hair's getting long," she observed pleasantly. Immediately he felt all wrong.

Between classes he studied himself in the bathroom mirror, brushing his bangs away from his eyes, consumed by the desire to fix this problem. At home after school he plotted every barbershop in Whiterose on the map, but none of them was close enough to reach on foot.

He went out his back door and made his way to the Ebentwine clearing. Once again, Gardner emerged from a corner. This time he carried a coil of hose. "Bruno, where've you been? It's been ages."

"I didn't realize it mattered to you."

"Were you avoiding this place?"

"I was," Bruno admitted. "It's a little crazy—no offense."

"None taken. So why are you back?"

"Because someone told me as long as I obey the rules, I shouldn't be scared of it."

"That's good advice."

"I was thinking about what you said about Ebentwine not just being a shortcut—liminal—between my backyard and Celia's. Does that mean it can go other places, too?"

"Yes indeed. Where are you headed, then?"

"I want to go to the barbershop on George Street."

"You need a haircut? I suppose you do. It's right through there." Gardner pointed.

"Thank you." Bruno headed off. Passing through the hedge, he stepped out of the trees onto a pedestrian path. A short way off was an intersection, and when he got there, he found the swirling barber pole easily.

While the kindly Italian man gave him the classic short cut he had chosen from the faded pictures on the walls, Bruno congratulated himself for finding another way to put his powerful secrets to good use. This is what being Kind was about —getting to places more easily, not needing a ride from his brother to get a haircut. He wondered how far the Ebentwine could take him. If he told Gardner he wanted to go to New York City, or Rome, would the man just point to a place in the hedges and send him on his way?

He strolled out of the barbershop and back down the pedestrian path, ducking through the bushes to return to the Ebentwine clearing.

"That's a good look for you," Gardner said.

"Thank you." Bruno had intended to return home, but paused. "Maybe I'll go by Celia's house."

Gardner nodded. "Sure. That way. But you know, she's not home."

"She's not?"

"No, she's at the bookstore. Where she works. She told you about that?"

"Oh, sure. Never mind, then."

"Well, why don't you go to the bookstore?" Gardner pointed to another side of the clearing.

Bruno followed his direction and stepped out of a privet hedge between two buildings onto a narrow street. He headed toward the main street about half a block away and found the bookstore on the far side. Bruno walked to the corner and stopped on the sidewalk across the street from the entrance. Through the window he saw Celia straightening books by the register. There was an older woman, too, with short white hair, arranging a display.

Two women walked up to the door. From across the street Bruno recognized his neighbors Alice and Gertrude. When they entered the bookstore, the other woman greeted them familiarly, and Celia came over to say hello. Then she went back to work and the three women huddled, instantly engrossed in conversation.

Bruno craned his neck to see Celia, feeling a bit like he had on those nights in her backyard, standing under her window. Even from this distance he felt her pull. He stepped into the street.

"Hey, Bruno, what are you doing here?"

It was Tomasi coming down the walk, looking as surprised as Bruno must have.

"I . . . was just taking a walk," Bruno said.

"Nice haircut," Tomasi said curtly, and Bruno realized with horror that it was almost an exact copy of Tomasi's. It hadn't occurred to him when he had chosen it. "Do you live around here?"

"Kind of. Not really," Bruno admitted. "Do you?"

"Yeah." Tomasi gestured behind him. "I was coming to pick up Celia from work and walk her home."

"Oh, okay."

"Were you going to go in and say hello to her?" Tomasi asked.

"No, I'll just see her tomorrow," Bruno said. "Goodbye." He turned and walked back down the narrow street toward the hedge. When Bruno looked back, Tomasi was standing there staring after him. Finally, Tomasi went into the bookstore.

Bruno crept back down the street toward the store. In the window Tomasi and Celia were talking by the front counter. She looked at him with a fondness Bruno had never seen on her face at school.

Bruno returned down the alley, back through the privet hedge and into the clearing. Gardner was waiting. "You don't visit very long, do you?"

"I couldn't. Her boyfriend was there."

"Her boyfriend? Who's that?"

"Tomasi," Bruno told him.

"Tomasi? Tomasi's her boyfriend," Gardner repeated to himself. "Well, that's a shame."

"Why is it a shame?"

"I thought you were her beau."

"Well, I'm not."

"And again, I say that's a shame. So you're the errant suitor who is content to gaze upon his lady, without any hope she'll ever reciprocate?"

"No, I'm just a fool," Bruno said.

"I don't think so," Gardner protested. "You have plenty going for you if you've found your way into this clearing."

"But Tomasi is Kind, too," Bruno said.

"Yes, I know. He travels differently, but he is Kind."

"And he's older, and taller, and stronger, and she loves him."

"What makes you sure she loves him?"

"I'm sure."

"How do you know?"

"Because she looks at him the way I look at her," Bruno said. "Can I ask you something?"

"Sure."

"You know Celia's an Ambassador?"

"Of course."

"Will she take my power?"

"You don't have much to take at this point. But no." Gardner looked at Bruno. "You don't know who to trust, do you? That's got to be rough." Bruno's head felt light. When he turned to look for the hedges that led home, some bright stars trailed in the corner of his vision. "You've been here too long. Off you go. That's the way."

"Good night," Bruno called as he stumbled through the hedge.

"Good night."

THE NEXT DAY BRUNO arrived at the library during his morning free period and was surprised to find Celia there, her head bent over her hands, her long hair draping down to the table.

"Hey, don't you have class?" Bruno asked her.

She looked up, and it was obvious she'd been crying. "I do. I just . . . I don't really care."

"What's wrong?" he asked, sitting down across from her.

"I saw her. Mariette, the ghost, whatever. It's really Mariette."

"Whoa." Bruno couldn't imagine how it felt to have a friend die, much less to see that friend's ghost. "Was it hard?"

Celia nodded. "She looks so beautiful. When she was alive her hair was always kind of a mess, and she didn't really pay much attention to the clothes she wore." Celia laughed despite herself. She shifted a piece of paper in her hands and pulled a compact out of her purse. "But now, when I saw her . . . I was walking through the science wing, and I happened to look into an empty classroom as I passed—and there she was, standing over by the window. I recognized her immediately. It's like she's almost completely there, but you can just barely see the sunlight shining through her." Celia looked at herself in the compact mirror and tsked at the way her makeup had run.

"But now her curls are beautiful, and she has this amazing sweater. I can't even describe the colors and the pattern. It's perfect for her."

Bruno watched Celia like a film. She had drifted away into her memories, and he was reluctant to tug her back. "Did you talk to her?" he asked quietly.

"Well, *I* talked. I don't think she can. She didn't say anything at all. I told her I had been hoping I would see her, and that she looked beautiful. I hugged her. I hugged a ghost!" Celia hiccupped a laugh that had a sob caught in it. "She was so warm and soft. I can't believe what I'm . . . Do you think I'm crazy?"

"No! Not at all," Bruno said. "I mean, I might have, before. I hope I get to meet her."

"Me too. You would have been friends; I'm sure of it." Celia smiled at him, and to Bruno it felt as though the sunlight she had described was passing through him. Then her eyes grew sad again. "But that's not even all. I started babbling about the old chemistry teacher, Mr. Sumeletso, and everything that had happened after she died, but she stopped me." Celia unfolded the small piece of paper she had been clutching. She handed it to Bruno.

He took it and read, *Stone Hill—Wednesday—7:49 p.m.*

"I've been holding it since she gave it to me because I was scared it would disappear, and I wanted to show it to you. It's her handwriting, just like when she was alive," Celia said. "She was gone when I looked up from reading it. I was standing by myself in an empty classroom."

"She gave this to you? I mean, it's *for* you?" Bruno asked.

"Yes. And it's pretty clear how I'm supposed to interpret it, after all the stories we've heard about other people's encounters with her."

"Tomasi . . . *someone* is going to cheat on you tonight at Stone Hill. What is Stone Hill?"

"It's a very fancy restaurant. I don't know how Tomasi could afford to take someone there," Celia said. Her voice had turned bitter.

"But you and Tomasi, you're—"

"I *thought* we were!" Celia's eyes blazed, even as they filled with tears. "Maybe I'm a fool, but I really think I love him, in whatever way a stupid teenage girl can be in love. And I really thought he loved me, too." She reached for her sketchbook. "Look, he even said he loved me when he denied it!" She opened to a page covered in handwriting and turned the book around, thrusting it across the table.

Bruno stared at the written transcript of a conversation in two different hands. "Is this how he writes in your notebook?"

"Yes. Read it."

Are you there? Mariette says you're going to cheat on me tonight. Care to explain?

What? She gave you one of those notes?

Yes! What are you doing tonight?

I thought I was seeing you! Do you think I would cheat on you?

Of course not, but what am I supposed to think now?

I will go with you wherever the note says you are supposed to go, and I will be with you the whole time. I love you and I would never cheat on you.

I'm really freaked out about this!

I understand. I'm sorry. Do you want me to come through?

You can't—I'm in school. You're in school.

Okay. I'll come after school. What time does the note say?

7:49 at Stone Hill.

The restaurant? I have better taste than I realized.

That's not funny!

I'm sorry! I will do anything to prove to you Mariette is wrong.

Thank you.

UM

UM

"What happened at the end?" Bruno pointed to the *UM*.

"Oh, that's how we say goodbye when we write," Celia said. "*UM* stands for 'understand me.' It's a Depeche Mode reference. Do you know the song 'Shake the Disease'?"

"No," Bruno said.

"If you hear the lyrics, you'll understand."

"So you'll be together," Bruno said.

"Yeah, but I'm still scared. Every one of Mariette's predictions has come true. Every person who has gone to the appointed place at the appointed time has caught the person they love kissing someone else. What if we get to the restaurant and some girl runs up and kisses him, and he has to admit he's been seeing her? What if it wasn't even a date, but she works there or something, and he would have been going to meet her if I hadn't told him about the note?"

"I don't know him that well, but he doesn't seem like the type of guy who would do that," Bruno said.

"No, he doesn't." Celia sighed.

Bruno thought for a moment. "Are you depressed? People say Mariette has that effect on some people."

"Not depressed, just freaked out about the note. I don't know what that depression thing is about. Hey, where did it go?" Celia looked around the table and lifted up her sketchbook. "Do you still have it?"

"No, I . . ." Bruno couldn't remember if he had handed the note back or set it down. They looked on the floor.

Celia sighed again. "Well, at least you got to see it before it disappeared."

"You know, I think it's good that you told him. Would you rather assume the worst and take the opportunity to try to bust Tomasi in the act, or assume the best about him and hope it's a misunderstanding? The first one doesn't sound like you."

"I guess you're right. Oh, I just want this day to be over."

"It will go faster if you go to class."

"True. It's almost time for history." Celia straightened her stack of books. "I'm sorry to unload on you like that. There isn't really anyone else I can talk to about a lot of this."

"I don't mind," Bruno said sincerely.

IT'S WRONG TO WISH BAD *things on other people.* Bruno repeated the idea over and over to himself. *He's good to her and he makes her happy.* What if it wasn't true, though? What if he was cheating on her, after all, and his offer to go with her was a bluff? She would break up with him, wouldn't she? And she would turn to Bruno to talk about it. Wouldn't she? He didn't know the first thing about love, but from all he had heard, he was pretty sure it wasn't selfish, and Bruno's desires felt incredibly selfish.

I don't deserve her, he thought. *Why is this whole thing a big knot that I can't untangle? If I loved her, I wouldn't want anything to cause her pain.* He checked the clock: 7:40. It was time.

He went out his back door and headed off down the grassy alley behind his house. Gardner was waiting for him in the Ebentwine clearing.

"I need to go to Stone Hill," Bruno told him.

"Who's there?"

"Celia and Tomasi should be, soon."

"Are you spying on them?"

"Kind of, but they're spying, too."

"Well, that makes it okay, then," Gardner said, only half sarcastically. "Turn down there."

Bruno thanked him and set off. Soon he emerged from the trees onto the grassy border of a parking lot. Stone Hill was on the far side, across the street; a man in a red jacket stood at the valet stand. Bruno crept behind a row of cars along the edge of the parking lot toward the restaurant. He caught sight of Celia and Tomasi approaching from the opposite side. They were moving as hesitantly as he was. From the shadow of a fence he barely could hear their hushed voices.

The front door of Stone Hill swung open, and Celia and Tomasi hid behind a large potted bush next to the awning. A man came out and gave a claim check to the valet, who loped across the street and into the parking lot without noticing Bruno.

Bruno looked at his watch: 7:48. And he had no idea how

Mariette's prediction could possibly be fulfilled. The restaurant door opened again, and a woman exited. She slipped into the arms of the man and accepted a kiss.

"Mom?" Celia had emerged from her hiding place, with Tomasi following her.

The woman reeled around in surprise. "Celia? What are you doing here?"

"We were taking a walk. What are *you* doing? Who is this?" Celia pointed at the man, who stared at her.

"This is Steven. Steven, this is my daughter, Celia, and her boyfriend, Tomasi, who have mysteriously chosen this neighborhood for a stroll, even though it's across town from where both of them live."

"Are you on a date?" Celia asked her.

"Yes, I am, and the funny thing is that at dinner tonight I had just been discussing with Steven how it was time for me to tell you about him."

"Mom, that's great! I'm very happy for you. You know I wanted you to start dating! I had no idea," Celia said, pivoting instantly to joy.

"Thank you. Seriously, what are you doing here?" Celia's mother looked at Tomasi.

"We just felt like going somewhere. We had no idea," Celia said.

"Well, my date isn't actually over yet. Could we talk about this when I get home? Assuming you've walked back there by then?"

"Oh, Tomasi drove. We'll be fine. I'm sorry for ruining the moment."

"It's okay." Her mother laughed, shaking her head.

"It was nice to meet you," Celia said to Steven, who said something Bruno couldn't hear. The valet pulled up with Steven's car, and Bruno slipped away.

A FEW DAYS LATER BRUNO forced himself to pay attention while he mowed Alice and Gertrude's lawn after school. Twice he'd come within inches of decimating the flowers at the edge of the grass. He was trying to figure out what a note from Mariette really meant. Up until Celia's, the pattern had seemed clear: Receive a note and go bust your love — boyfriend, girlfriend, husband, wife — cheating on you. It had set Suburban on edge; Mariette had pulled a curtain back, and things people might have suspected but never fully acknowledged suddenly were laid bare. Bruno wondered how often relationships in high school were based on love. There were class systems to be upheld, and there was social power to be wielded. There were superficial desires to gratify and insecurities to be manipulated. Perhaps that didn't change once high school was over.

And there were plenty of ways to respond, once a note from Mariette brought it all crashing down. Some people reserved their anger for the person who had betrayed them, but plenty of them had enough to spare for Mariette, even if they couldn't reach her. Other people, perhaps those who had believed their relationship was secure, joined the ranks of the brokenhearted, the shattered, the depressed — a small battalion that was growing each week. It was hard to imagine a high school in which more people were in therapy, on antidepressants, or just moping around aimlessly, shrunken inside their clothes. The anger from the others was strangely refreshing because at least it added some energy to the increasingly hushed Suburban halls.

But this note from Mariette had yielded a different result. And following her revelation to Celia, Mariette had sent a boy to a movie theater, where he had witnessed his sister kissing her girlfriend—news to him in two respects, but not a betrayal.

So what was the pattern, then? Bruno believed there had to be one. All of Mariette's notes had pointed to a kiss and a surprise. Someone kissed someone else, and it was a surprise to the person who witnessed it.

Was that it? Someone unexpected kissed someone unexpected?

ON FRIDAY AT DIABOLIQUES he waited for an opportunity to talk with Celia. Tomasi was never far. When he looked at Bruno now, there was suspicion in his eyes.

And while he might have protested, in his heart Bruno knew he deserved all of Tomasi's suspicion, and more. So Bruno avoided Tomasi, which only confused Celia, who clearly expected the two of them to have become friends, considering the secrets they shared.

Regine, Sylvio, and Marco danced, oblivious to the unspoken tensions among the other three. And across the floor the St. Dymphna boys posed and preened, turning the room into a chessboard with two sets of black pieces. They danced now and then, but they seemed more interested in observing the others and trading knowing looks.

Bruno decided to seek out Cassandra. He found the fortuneteller easily enough on the mezzanine and was relieved when she welcomed him, patting the sofa next to her.

"Don't let it affect your relationship with Celia," she said to him before he could speak. "She only wants the best for you."

Bruno fumbled to catch up with her. "I . . . I love her."

"Of course you do!" Her laugh made him feel justified and foolish at the same time. "And because of it, you will do things that will feel like turning a knife against yourself. But that is another time. There is something else you want to discuss now, isn't there?"

"I just feel . . . If Lois—she's the librarian, the one who" —Cassandra was nodding, so he skipped ahead—"if I could convince her Celia wasn't dangerous. I wish they would talk to each other. I'm not making any progress with my admonition."

"They can't help you with your admonition. If something is worth doing, it is usually difficult, and often you must do it by yourself. Your labyrinth keeper knows this, because she has been through it many times herself. Don't blame her for not understanding Ambassadors. Most of your Kind never meet one their entire lives."

"Why did you call her a labyrinth keeper?"

Cassandra stared at him, amusement in her eyes. "Think about it."

Bruno decided to puzzle over that description later. "So why have I met two of you? Two Ambassadors?"

"That is a good question, and possibly the best one you have asked me so far." Cassandra grew serious. "You have realized I don't always share everything I know. But in this case I don't have anything to keep secret. It is unusual enough that so many of you have gravitated toward your school recently —on both sides, good and evil, Kind and Unkind. And it is particularly unusual that an Ambassador was called to be in attendance there. Without knowing for sure, I believe this: A conflict has begun, one that will take on a size and a scale much greater than one person's admonition or another person's desire for power. It is very early, but our world is a sentient one, and it senses what is coming and works to maintain equilibrium."

"What does that mean?" Bruno braced for a quixotic answer.

"Last year at Suburban there was a Kind—Mariette— an Unkind—the crocodile teacher—and an Ambassador— Celia. A tidy balance, right? This year there are *two* Kinds —you and the labyrinth keeper—plus the specter of a Kind, and an Ambassador. If you have been assembled to maintain a balance, doesn't that suggest there is probably also *at least* one Unkind lurking around there?"

"Oh . . ." Bruno's eyes widened. "Of course." Unkind were hiding at Suburban! Who could they be?

"So you have two challenges, don't you? Actually, I think you have three. First, you must decipher your admonition and fulfill it, so you will grow stronger. Next, you must be very careful not to be surprised by an Unkind, and you must do whatever you can to discover who they are."

"And third?"

"You must work with *your* Ambassador, who is learning her role at the same time you are learning yours."

"You can't help us?"

"It is not a question of whether I *can* help you. It is a question of whether I *should*. If I was supposed to play that kind of role, I would have been summoned to Suburban myself. Since I haven't, I must be careful not to do things for you that you— and Celia—must rightfully do yourselves. Believe me, that was difficult enough for me with Celia last year.

"You should go. Patrick is about to play 'Everywhere' by

Cranes, and Celia will be dancing. You don't want to miss a moment like that, do you?" Cassandra put her hand over Bruno's on the couch between them, then laughed when Bruno shifted uncomfortably. "I'm sorry! I shouldn't have touched you!"

Bruno mumbled goodbye and made his way back to Patrick's room, but before he reached it, a figure stepped out of the darkness under the stairs.

"There you are." It was one of the St. Dymphna boys, broken away from the flock, looking exotic and slightly sinister. He was only a little taller than Bruno, and he made eye contact with Bruno in a way few boys did. In his black faux-horsehair pants, houndstooth check shirt, and closely cropped hair, he might have been Bruno's brother.

"What? Who are you?"

"Doesn't matter. We find you interesting, and when I saw you leave I thought it might be a good opportunity to talk to you alone."

"You're from St. Dymphna's?"

"Tomasi told you. I'm Turlington."

"Bruno." He felt awkward shaking Turlington's hand. "What do you want to talk about?"

"Anything, really. Do you know Tomasi well?"

"Kind of, yes. Don't you? You go to school with him."

"We do, but he keeps to himself. Barely talks to anyone. The stunning tall girl is his girlfriend, right?"

"Yes." Bruno hated saying it.

"That makes sense. We hoped he might be flexible, but it didn't seem likely."

"Flexible?"

"You know." Turlington put his hand on Bruno's shoulder and let it wander down his arm. "How about you? You're pretty friendly with the gay one."

"No, no. I mean, I am friendly with—How did you know he's gay?"

"C'mon, it's not that hard. There's nothing wrong with that. You *are* straight, aren't you?" Turlington's hand left Bruno's arm. "Well, we won't hold that against you. Several of us are more flexible on one side than the other. If you ever want to talk—if you ever want to freak your friends out—come over to our side. That other girl and boy don't seem to like you very much anyway."

"That's my brother," Bruno said.

Turlington shrugged. "See you around." He turned to the stairs and went back up.

As if this place isn't strange enough, Bruno thought, following Turlington at a safe distance. *And did he just come on to me?*

doubts even here

WHERE ARE WE, THEN? Just a continent will be fine." Geography class was the worst. If he paid attention, it was information he already knew. If he let his thoughts wander, it only provoked Mr. Williams.

Bruno hadn't been daydreaming that long. "South America."

"Are you as well versed in, say, the rivers of Chile as you are in European mountain ranges and the Pacific Rim?"

"You want to know the rivers in Chile? There are a lot . . . I don't know if I'll say them right, but there's the Baker, the Loa, Bio-Bio, Maipo—"

Mr. Williams cut him off. "So with all those rivers, Chile must have a very strong agricultural output, right?"

"Well, in the south, I think so, but the north is all desert —the Atacama."

"Mr. Perilunas, I thank you for bringing us up to date. If you had been paying attention, you would have heard me say exactly that, thirty seconds ago. See me after class."

Mr. Williams allowed the class their moment of amusement and then moved on. Bruno stewed in his seat. When the class was over, he went up to Mr. Williams's desk.

"I won't say that I'm not impressed with your knowledge of geography, but I've already told you I am not keen on you just being a warm body that doesn't pay attention in my class. What are we going to do about this?"

"I don't know. I don't mean to. I try to pay attention."

"You don't pay attention because this material isn't challenging you. My job as your teacher is to *teach* you something. If you already know this material, I'll teach you something else. Do you have any ideas?"

Bruno looked around, unsure what to say.

"My guess is it would have to be something that doesn't have to do with maps, since you seem to know those like the back of your hand," Mr. Williams offered. "Do you know how to draw buildings? Like, floor plans?"

"I've done some drafting. Perhaps something like urban planning, then? It's not exactly geography, but there's a connection."

"I'd like to learn about that," Bruno said.

"All right. Give me a couple days to come up with a lesson plan, and we'll do it. But you understand, you have to keep an A in geography, and this is over and above that."

This proposal from Mr. Williams was a surprise, and as Bruno headed to his next class, he got nervous. What was the warning in his admonition?

> *Beware the walking crocodile*
> *Who finds you guilty with no trial*
> *Be sure to travel in short steps*
> *What that one thinks will take a mile.*

Mr. Williams didn't quite fit that description, but ever since Cassandra had convinced Bruno that Unkind were hiding at

Suburban, he suspected everyone. Was he gaining a resource to help with his admonition, or was he straying into a trap he had been warned to avoid?

THE WAIL OF AN AMBULANCE disrupted second period, and by lunch everyone had heard how a girl had been found in the bathroom and taken to the hospital to have her stomach pumped. There were different stories about the pills, but the version Bruno believed was that she hadn't taken anything that would have killed her, only large quantities of things like aspirin and cold tablets. Everyone blamed Mariette, even though the depressed girl hadn't said anything about receiving a note from her.

Marco found him in the hall between classes. "Poor girl. It's sad, right?" He threw his arm around Bruno's shoulder. "Who knows if Mariette had anything to do with it. It's not like teenagers don't ever get depressed."

"How do you help someone like that?"

"I don't know. We could start by being happy ourselves. For example, we need to find you a girlfriend. C'mon, you're in high school!" Marco added when Bruno started to protest. "What's keeping you?"

"I'm just thinking about other things," Bruno said weakly.

"You're an adolescent male—there *is* nothing else! You're still hooked on Celia, aren't you? You have great taste, but dude, you have to let that go."

"I don't . . ." Bruno couldn't muster a defense.

"There's no one else around here? Just keep your eyes open, okay? Do you even talk to anyone in your class?"

"Sure," Bruno said, struggling to remember the last time he had. "Wait, do you talk to *your* classmates?"

"Well, I guess not," Marco admitted, laughing. "I'm friendly enough, but old habits die hard. Most days last year I only really talked to Brenden, Celia, Liz, Ivo, and Regine. Now Regine and Silver are always off whispering to each other. I do miss the way it used to be."

"Well, I don't know music like you guys do, but feel free to talk to me about it."

"Okay then, let's see . . . How about favorite alternative love song?"

"Hm." Bruno thought. "'Lovesong' by the Cure is too obvious, isn't it?"

"Yes!" Marco laughed. "Regine would say 'The Last Beat of My Heart' by Siouxsie and the Banshees. Brenden would say 'This Love' by Craig Armstrong and Elizabeth Fraser. What would I say? How about the Smiths' 'Please, Please, Please, Let Me Get What I Want.'"

"'Somebody' by Depeche Mode," Bruno said.

"Oh, yeah, good call. You've been listening to them?" Bruno nodded. "Their old stuff is absolutely brilliant. Have you heard 'Get the Balance Right!' yet?"

"No, I'll have to find that one."

"See, I miss this! This is why I don't bother to talk to other people around here. I can't have these conversations with anyone else."

"You don't seem unhappy."

"You don't seem unhappy, either. But it wouldn't hurt you to have a romantic life. How about at Diaboliques? Is there anyone there?"

"When did you turn into a matchmaker?" Bruno asked.

• • •

VAN WAS TRAILING BRUNO down the hall. No matter how firmly he'd resolved to not be intimidated by him, Bruno felt his internal organs rearrange. He broke into a run.

"Hey!" Van thundered behind him down the hall and into the stairwell. He was only half a flight back when Bruno turned down to the basement level and rounded the corner by the mechanical room. Van hurtled down the stairs after him, calling triumphantly, "There's nowhere to go down there!"

To Bruno's great relief, the mysterious second stairwell awaited him, and as he sprinted up it, he wondered what Van would see when he rounded the corner—a dark cul-de-sac of tiled walls? Bruno imagined him stopping short, probably swearing, then retreating, unsure of what had happened.

Bruno slowed his pace when he turned on the landing up to the ground floor, trying not to draw attention as he came up from the basement into the new wing. His heart still pounded and he made a beeline for the water fountain in the hall.

When he straightened up from the fountain, Van was there. They stared at each other. All Van's bluster was gone, and he looked at Bruno in shock.

Then Van walked away. He didn't go back into the stairwell. Bruno wondered where Van was supposed to be, and if it was on the other side of the school. *So anyone can use the supernatural shortcut? How am I supposed to keep that a secret, then? Couldn't anyone have wandered down to the basement and found it? Why hasn't anyone else found it before now? Like the janitor?*

IN THE LIBRARY BRUNO leaned in to Lois and said, "I need to talk to you." Celia would have been his first choice, but he wasn't sure how soon he'd be able to speak to her alone.

"What is it?" Lois asked him in her office.

"Something happened, and I think it's bad. I told you about the secret shortcut I found between the Chancellor Wing and the new wing, through the basement? Well, someone just followed me through it."

"Really?" Lois sat down.

"It's a senior guy who likes to pick on me. He was chasing me, so I went down the stairwell and through the secret passage to get away from him. But he came out the other side behind me."

"He saw you go through?"

"He was still coming down the stairs when I went through, and I figured when he turned the corner there wouldn't be anything there."

"So it's not like he was right next to you and you took him through." Bruno shook his head. "He went through by himself, then, separately. I'd say that means he's Kind. I don't think a citizen would be able to do that."

"You think he's Kind? I was thinking he was Unkind."

"Oh—that could be, too."

"I know you thought Celia was Unkind. Aren't you supposed to be able to sense them or something?"

Lois put up her hands. "Bruno, I have to tell you. You know I've been Kind for about fifteen years. I got started later than you, but it's been a while. And for fifteen years it's been a very quiet, very solitary experience. I haven't really known anyone else who was Kind. I've met one every once in a while, but I always had the sense that this was something people did by themselves. Everyone's power is so different, and there are so many risks of exposure. I'm not looking to do anything amazing with my powers; I just like that I can clean things, move things around, keep things organized more easily."

"That's it? Keep things organized? But then why do you have so much trouble finding things in the library?"

"If you figure that one out, please tell me!" Lois smiled helplessly. "Everywhere else I am completely on top of it. A place for everything and everything in its place. But that only illustrates what I'm trying to tell you, though: The moment I arrived at Suburban, my whole experience of being Kind began to change. And that's almost entirely because of you. Things are happening to you that have never happened to me in fifteen years. How to explain?" Lois looked around. "I had heard about the Ebentwine, Ambassadors, the Unkind, but after a while, when I hadn't come into contact with any of those things myself, I just figured they were myths, fantastic embellishments on something that was pretty fantastic in the first place. But you keep coming in here and telling me things . . . I believe you, but I'm having trouble. I can't be much help because you seem to know more than I do.

"It scares me a little. I've never been so nervous about being exposed. And being in this place, where I just feel *off* all the time . . ." Lois looked lonely and sad.

"I'm sorry," Bruno said.

"Oh, don't be. Whatever happens, I'm sure it will be interesting!" She managed a smile. "Just understand that it's different for me, okay? In some ways we live in the world with everyone else. In other ways, though, this world is not made for you and me. And the alternate worlds we inhabit, just a few degrees left or right of the real world, may be as different from each other as they are from the ordinary world of the citizens around us."

"I understand."

"I want you to keep telling me all these things, because it's fascinating, and I'm learning so much. And I do hope a time will come when I can help."

"You have helped me. If it weren't for you, I would have thought I was crazy." They grinned at each other.

"Well, good, then. Now, about the Unkind senior. I really don't know what the Unkind feels like, but I will pay attention. Who is it?"

"Van Mefferdy. You remember the day you found me outside the library and a guy was talking to me? That was Van."

"Vaguely. His name is Van?"

"Somebody told me it's actually Van Cliburn because his mother is a classical pianist or something. I don't know if that's true."

"And he's bullying you?"

"It's not that bad. It never even crossed my mind that he could be Unkind, until he followed me up the stairs."

"Maybe he isn't, then. But I can't imagine how he would follow you if he weren't Kind or Unkind. Be careful. I don't like this. I feel like I should do something."

"I think I can handle it. But I'll let you know if that changes."

IN THE CAR ON THE WAY home Sylvio put on Kraftwerk and excitedly tapped the steering wheel in time with the music. "Did you have coffee or something?" Bruno asked him.

"No. I'm just thinking about this weekend. It's fall break at Metropolitan, and Liz and Brenden are coming home. Ivo has to stay to work on a project or something. But Regine thinks after I meet Liz and Brenden, she'll be able to convince them to let me officially join the Rosary."

"Why does that matter so much to you?"

"What do you mean? I find the most amazing people I've ever met in my life, and you wonder why I want to be a part of their group?"

"Part of their group, yes. But a club? With members? You and Regine are the only ones who talk about it that way. Celia and Marco hardly ever mention the Rosary, unless they're reminiscing about last year."

"You wouldn't understand. This doesn't mean the same things to you. This isn't just a fun thing I'm doing to try to impress a girl, the way it is for you."

Bruno seethed, but Sylvio was too oblivious to notice.

"Anyway, on Friday at Diaboliques I finally get to meet them. And then Marco can make me one of those rosary bracelets. It's gonna be awesome."

ON FRIDAY NIGHT THE PROCESSION of black cars traveling to Diaboliques increased from two to three. "I feel like we're diplomats," Bruno said to Sylvio as they drove.

"I always think of a funeral. That's what Regine says."

Sylvio had taken an undue amount of care in dressing, and while his outfit was impressive, his desperation for approval was a little transparent. Regine had begun to hedge about the big Rosary decision, since Ivo hadn't come home. "We may have to wait until Halloween," Bruno had heard her tell Sylvio. "But that's only a couple more weeks."

Bruno liked Liz and Brenden on sight. They seemed more relaxed than the half of the Rosary that was still in high school.

Liz wore a leather biker jacket. Brenden's hair rose in the same Morrissey peak Bruno remembered from the photo Marco had shown him, and his charcoal suit bore telltale signs of Marco's handiwork. He held Marco's hand and looked at Bruno warmly. "It's great to meet you!" he was saying as Regine pulled Sylvio into their midst.

"Brenden, this is Silver. I feel like I've told you two so much about each other!" Brenden greeted Sylvio, but with not quite the same level of interest he'd shown in Bruno. Sylvio behaved as though he was on a job interview, shaking hands with Liz and Brenden and taking all his cues from Regine, who looked almost as eager for approval.

As they walked toward the club, Marco steered Bruno back over to Brenden. "Bruno's my best model when you're out of town."

"Thanks for keeping Marco company for me," Brenden said.

"No problem," Bruno said. "I'm surprised he wants to spend so much time with me."

"I'm not surprised." Brenden smiled.

Upstairs Liz chatted with Bruno when they had settled in. "I like your style," she said.

"Marco helped me a lot. How's college?"

"I love it. I highly recommend it." She smiled. "You like Suburban?"

"I do. I feel lucky we moved. The high school I would have gone to wasn't nearly as big."

"How's Celia doing? Last year was so crazy. Have you seen Mariette's ghost?"

Bruno nodded. "It's still crazy. But Mariette looks kind of nice."

"She was. I wonder why she's causing trouble now."

They took their usual spot at the edge of the dance floor. The Rosary had an easy authority in this space. Across the room, the St. Dymphna boys had taken notice of the additional faces.

"Who are they?" Brenden asked.

Marco told him what Tomasi had shared. "They seem a little desperate for attention, but I'm not going to lie — they're kind of hot."

"I can see that," Brenden said, taking Marco's hand again.

Bruno hadn't told anyone about his encounter with Turlington the previous week. Now from across the floor Turlington gave Bruno the odd salute, cupping his hand and touching the tips of his fingers to his forehead, the way the boys did to Tomasi.

Tomasi arrived, and Bruno was relieved when Celia and Tomasi and he separated from the rest of the group. "Regine really needs to calm down," Celia complained. "She's like a door-to-door salesperson over there, and her product is Silver."

"What's that about?" Tomasi asked.

"I don't know if she wants Silver to be officially part of the Rosary because she's in love with him, or if she's in love with him because he's such a good fit for the Rosary, but either way she is hell-bent on tying it all up in a nice bow. So it's the Silver show while Liz and Brenden are in town."

Changing the subject, Bruno said, "I think there's an Unkind at Suburban." That got their attention, but when Bruno explained what had happened with Van, they weren't convinced.

"So you've never seen him do anything else that would make you think he has powers?" Tomasi asked.

"No, just following me on those stairs."

"That is strange," Celia said. "But what does it mean? Last year with Mr. Sumeletso, he was doing horrible things to fulfill an admonition. Are we supposed to just go after Van because we assume that if he's Unkind, he must be up to something bad?"

"Well, he must have an admonition, too, right? So he probably has to do something bad to earn more Unkind power."

"I don't think all Unkind admonitions require you to kill someone, or even to hurt them," Tomasi said.

"Are you sure about that?" Bruno thought it was a legitimate question, but it seemed to annoy Tomasi.

"Who knows. I'm going to go dance." Tomasi stalked onto the dance floor as the ominous percussive notes of "Discotheque Necronomicon" began.

"I wish we had Van's admonition," Celia said. "Without that, we can't be sure about much."

"How do we find it?"

"I don't know. Last year Mariette found Mr. Sumeletso's admonition in some mysterious book she discovered in the public library. But she wasn't sure whose it was, so we had the opposite problem: We had the admonition but didn't know who we were trying to stop. Now we suspect we might have to stop Van, but we don't know what—if anything—he's doing or how he's supposed to do it."

"You said a mysterious book? I wonder if it's the same book I found in the library at school, which gave me my admonition. I'd have to go look for it again; it disappeared from Lois's office."

"Mariette said her book had vanished from the library

when she went back to find it again. There was no record of it, nothing. All these disappearing things . . ."

"I'll look on Monday," Bruno said. They watched Tomasi dance. "He doesn't like me."

"Oh, I don't think that's true . . ."

9

a girl in trouble is
a temporary thing

O**N SATURDAY EVENING BRUNO** got a call from Celia, summoning him to her house the next afternoon. "I don't think you and Tomasi got off on the right foot. The three of us have to stick together. Isn't that what's supposed to happen, when people like us find each other?"

Bruno thought of Lois. "I thought the Kind usually worked alone."

"Mariette said that, too. But doesn't it just seem obvious that you and Tomasi could do things together that you couldn't do separately?"

"You make it sound like we're superheroes," Bruno said, and was gratified by her laughter.

Upstairs in her room on Sunday, Celia said, "I told Mom I'm tutoring you in something or other." Bruno wasn't sure what to do. Being in Celia's bedroom felt privileged and illicit. He wanted to study her room like a map. He wanted to see what his place under the trees looked like from this vantage, but he thought she would find that strange, so he sat down on the chair by her desk.

The memory of the mystery song he'd heard her play all

those weeks ago flared up. "What are you listening to?" He pointed at the CD player on her dresser.

"Oh, it depends. Brenden's made us so many great mixes. I listen to them a lot."

"Marco's given me some of them."

"Sometimes I'll latch on to one album and listen to it over and over," Celia said. "This summer I must have listened to Tanita Tikaram's *Ancient Heart* album every day for a month."

"I don't know her."

"'Twist in My Sobriety' was her biggest hit, but the whole album is brilliant."

"Does Patrick play it at Diaboliques?"

"It's not really that kind of music," Celia said, smiling. "I *do* like some things that aren't part of that scene."

"Can I hear?" Bruno asked.

"Sure." Celia found the CD, and while the music was moody and beautiful, it wasn't the haunting song he remembered.

Celia looked at her open sketchbook on her bed. "I wonder where Tomasi is."

"He's going to come out of there?" Bruno asked.

"Yeah. I guess I'm used to it by now, but when you say it like that—it is rather odd, isn't it?" Celia kept her eyes on the page. "He always writes first, to make sure it's okay to come through. There he is."

Bruno could make out darkening marks that appeared on the page, like small stains seeping up from the underside. Celia took her pencil and jotted a word next to the newly formed letters, and then she went and stood by the closed bedroom door. When Bruno looked back at the book, a deep shadow was flowing out of the pages, across the bedspread, and up the far wall. It formed the silhouette of a tall, broad-shouldered boy. Then it moved, and as it turned around, Bruno saw that it was no longer Tomasi's shadow but had become Tomasi himself.

"Whoa," Bruno said.

When Tomasi saw Bruno, his expression was quite clear: *I am not okay with this.* "Hey," he mumbled, and Bruno heyed him back. Celia came over, and Tomasi accepted a kiss from her.

"You look serious," she said, and Bruno wondered how she could tell; Tomasi's expression was the same as always.

"It's weird. I felt like someone was following me," Tomasi told her.

"Where?"

"In there." Tomasi pointed at the sketchbook. "I see people in there sometimes, headed in another direction. It goes pretty fast, so I never get a good look at them or anything. But this time, I could swear there was somebody behind me. I can't really turn to look back. I have to stay focused on the exit. Maybe I was imagining it."

"Are the other people in there are doing what you're doing? Traveling in and out of books?" Celia asked.

"I don't know. I assume that's what they're doing."

Celia looked over at Bruno. "Well, I wanted you guys to come over so you could talk some more. It's hard to talk at Diaboliques, and I thought Bruno might have questions."

Tomasi sat down on the edge of the bed, facing Bruno. "Sure, what can I tell you?"

There were so many things Bruno wanted to ask, but he knew Tomasi really didn't want to play the role Celia was forcing on him, and Bruno didn't want to give Tomasi more reasons to resent him. But they couldn't sit there in silence. Two minutes earlier, this room had charmed him. Suddenly it was all so uncomfortable.

He had to ask something. "How old were you, when you found out?"

"Fourteen. If I think back, there were plenty of signs before then, but I didn't really understand anything until my reading teacher explained it to me."

"How many admonitions have you had?"

Tomasi silently counted up his fingers. "I'm on my seventh now. Some last a long time; others go more quickly. I have no idea how they work or where they come from."

"Have you ever missed one? Not finished it in time?"

"I missed the first five. The one last year was a close call, but Celia made it happen." Tomasi's eyes changed when he looked over at her. "For a long time I was only seeing the bad side of being Kind. My parents caught on that something was strange with me because the powers I had were making it harder for me to do some things, rather than easier, so I was doing my best to suppress it. I just ignored my admonitions and hoped it would all go away."

There was another moment of silence, and Celia prodded them on. "What else?"

"So your parents know about you?"

"Not really. They don't know the truth. They're scared of me because they've seen just enough to freak them out. If they knew, it would be easier—they could just burn me at the stake and be done with it." Tomasi looked bitter, resigned.

"I'm sorry."

"It's okay." His expression said *I don't want pity.* "Being Kind makes things harder, more complicated, but it does come with benefits. I see that now. Sometimes you have to look hard to find them, but they're there."

"Like being able to visit me any time of the day or night?" Celia said sweetly. Tomasi smiled just a little.

He turned back to Bruno. "So your powers are maps and stuff?" Bruno nodded. "You find shortcuts?"

"Have you ever heard of liminals?"

"No."

"Just wondering. I'm not really sure how I could use them. I mean, if people noticed . . ."

"Same here. I figure as I develop more, it will become clearer how to use the powers for more useful things. I want to go to college for dead languages or something like that, so I can work on translating ancient manuscripts. I figure I must have some kind of advantage, considering the way I see books."

"Maybe you'll be a city planner," Celia offered to Bruno. Then it was quiet, and she looked from one to the other. "Well, I really hope you guys can be friends. We are the only ones who know each other's secrets, and there might come a time when we need each other."

"Sure," Tomasi said coolly, his stare making Bruno uncomfortable.

"YOU HAVEN'T SEEN THE *You Are Here* book again, have you?" Bruno asked Lois.

"No." She shook her head. "I don't know when it disappeared, but I haven't seen it since the day you brought it to me. Are you looking for your admonition?"

"Not mine, Van's."

Bruno headed off to the stacks to see if he could find the

elusive book again. He easily found *The Social History of Art*, but he couldn't find *You Are Here* anywhere. He gave up and went to the next aisle, where the second volume had been. There was nothing there, either.

Why am I even going farther? he asked himself as he headed to aisle 4. *It's not going to be there.* When he turned into aisle 4, though, Bruno found a boy sitting on the floor, crying softly with his chin on his knees. Bruno had a few classes with this guy, but they had never spoken.

"Hey, David, what's wrong?"

David looked fearfully up at him, his glasses blurred by tears. "I think she got me. I just don't understand—I've never even seen the ghost."

"You're depressed?"

"I guess. Is this what being depressed feels like? It actually hurts—like something's pressing down on my heart."

On the floor, the David's notebook was covered with scribbled homework assignments, and Bruno wondered how he kept track of everything. "You'll feel better. It'll go away."

"It has to. I can't do this much longer."

Bruno sat down next to him. "What do you mean?"

"It hurts too much." Tears returned to his eyes.

"Did something happen?"

"*Nothing* happened. I was fine two days ago. Then I started feeling bad, and it just keeps getting worse and worse." David wrapped his arms around his knees.

"Where were you when you started feeling bad?"

"I don't know. In class, I think?"

"And you never saw Mariette . . . Can you remember anything that was strange, or unusual?"

"No. I just want it to stop. I'm scared if it doesn't stop soon, I'll do something to make it stop."

"What do you mean?"

"I've been thinking about ways I could do it . . . My mom has sleeping pills. That wouldn't hurt, would it?" David kept his eyes on his knees.

"You can't do that," Bruno said. "You have to promise me you won't do that. Why don't you go talk to the counselor?" He put his hand on David's shoulder.

David caught his breath. "How did you do that?"

"Do what?"

"With your hand. How did you do that?"

"I didn't do anything. I don't know." Bruno took his hand away.

"Wait! Do it again."

Bruno put his hand back on David's shoulder and watched his back unhunch and his fists unclench. "That's amazing." David wiped his eyes. "It's like you took the weight off."

"I'm not sure what I did. Maybe you just needed someone to listen to you."

"Well, thanks," David said.

"You're not going to hurt yourself?" Bruno asked.

"No. I promise. I feel a lot better."

"I still think you should talk to someone. If you feel bad again, you have to tell me, or tell someone, okay?"

"Sure." They stood up. "Is it just me, or is this library kind of creepy?" David asked.

"It's a strange place. But I like it."

BRUNO WAS LOST IN THOUGHT on his way to class when Van grabbed his arm. He hauled Bruno back into the stairwell and down the stairs, stopping by the mechanical room. "Don't you go running anywhere," Van grunted at him.

"What do you want?"

"We have something to discuss." Van pointed behind him at the light from the second staircase behind the stairs they had just used. "What's that all about? How'd you do that?" Bruno tried to leave, but the senior blocked his way.

"I didn't *do* it. I just found it."

"Cut the crap. I told you I'd damage you whenever I felt like it, and if you don't tell me what's going on I'll do it. I don't care who you are."

"What about you? Who are *you*?"

"I'm the one asking questions here," Van snapped.

They stared at each other. Van loomed over him, and Bruno wondered if there was any way to make a break for it.

"So, now we have *two* problems. First, you don't know how to act around seniors, and I still don't think you've learned your lesson."

"I'm sorry, okay? Can't you just forget about it?"

"I would, but my friends keep reminding me that I got tackled by a shrimp, so it's a little hard." Van advanced and Bruno braced himself for another punch. He put his finger square in Bruno's sternum and pressed hard. "But that's not all anymore. There's a freaky thing in the bottom of this stairwell, and clearly you knew it was here. How do you do it?"

"I don't have any control—I didn't do anything!" Bruno's head hit the wall behind him when Van shoved him.

"Bruno?" It was a girl's voice—Celia, looking down at them from the landing.

Van swore under his breath. "You're gonna get saved by a girl?" he taunted Bruno.

Celia came down the stairs and brushed past Van. "What's going on here?" She glared up at him.

"None of your business." But Van's voice had lost its menace. He stared strangely at Celia. "What are you doing with him, anyway? Don't you think you could do better?"

"You have no idea who you're threatening," Celia said. "If you're going to start trouble, you'll find that out very quickly. Let's go." Celia put her hand on Bruno's shoulder and guided him around Van.

"I'm not done with you!" Van followed them out of the stairwell.

Celia said to Bruno loudly, "You teach someone to use his words, and then he just won't shut up, will he?"

They left Van and went to the cafeteria, Bruno's adrenaline draining away. "So how did this start, again?" she asked him when they had settled in at a table.

"It's nothing. We have gym together, and he was picking on the first years, so I tackled him. Since then he's been a jerk, but he doesn't want to get in trouble and get kicked off the football team, so he's only hit me once."

"Ugh. Not all football players are like that," Celia said.

"But he has to be Unkind, right? He must know I'm Kind, but he didn't want to say it out loud, in case he's wrong and then he's revealed something he shouldn't have."

"We just don't know for sure," Celia said.

"He must be pretty new himself," Bruno said. "I don't think he understands half as much as we do."

"Sounds that way. And we barely understand anything!"

"But that's just another reason for him to come after me. If he does have any power, he's going to try to use it against me."

"I feel like I should be able to do something," Celia said. "I'm your Ambassador. I'm supposed to be helping you."

"I appreciate that, but how could you help? What is an Ambassador supposed to do in a situation like this?" Celia pulled out her sketchbook. "What are you doing?"

"I'm not sure. Every powerful thing I've done as an Ambassador has been with a drawing, so maybe I should try it. My drawing of Tomasi gave him his power to travel through books, and my drawing of the chemistry teacher stripped him of his Unkind powers. My drawing of Mariette would have given her powers, but she died before the eclipse, so she never received them."

"You're going to draw me?"

"Well, there's nothing in your admonition that makes it sound like I should draw you. I was thinking of drawing Van." Celia looked around the cafeteria and found Van, who sat on the far side of the room, scowling at them.

Celia's pencil flew around the page, and Bruno marveled at her skill. "What's it going to do?"

"I don't know. It might not do anything. I'm just guessing," Celia said, roughing in the students around Van, and adding tables, chairs, and the lights overhead. "When I drew Mr. Sumeletso, it froze him in the position I'd drawn him. And then when I threw the page out the window, he was sucked after it."

"Really?" Bruno looked across the room at the real Van. "It doesn't seem to be having any effect on him."

Celia paused to study her drawing and said, "That's funny. That kind of looks like you, doesn't it?"

Bruno leaned in to see the crowd of students surrounding Van in the sketch. One of the faces definitely looked like

Bruno. He looked up but couldn't find anyone in that position in real life. "You didn't do that on purpose?"

"No, I was just doing a background; I wasn't really looking at anyone else. But that one—it *is* you!" Celia was amazed.

"What does that mean?"

"I don't know."

"It's kind of creepy," Bruno said.

Celia turned her pencil over and erased the figure that resembled Bruno. Van remained, his face sketched rigid and mean-eyed. "Does he look any different?" They looked over where Van had been, but he was gone.

BRUNO WAS LATE GETTING to the parking lot after school, and the lobby was emptying out when he passed through. The girl with the blond ponytail stood by herself near the big front windows, looking even more lost than usual. She clutched her books and looked around as though someone had dropped her off ten miles outside of town.

"Are you okay?"

She jumped. "Oh, yeah, I'm fine."

Bruno noticed a folded piece of paper in her hand. "What's that?"

"Oh, nothing." She tucked it into her purse. "Why do you ask?"

"I thought it might be one of those kiss notes from the ghost."

"No, just a grocery list."

"Are you waiting for someone?" he asked her.

"Um, no, well, yes. I missed my bus," she told him.

"So is someone coming to pick you up?"

"Yeah, my mom. But . . . she's not done with work until five. I'll probably just walk home."

"C'mon, I'll get my brother to give you a ride."

"Oh, that's okay. I might live in the opposite direction from you."

"Where do you live?"

"Over on Mount Rose," she said reluctantly.

Bruno unrolled the map in his head. Mount Rose passed within a couple miles of their house. "It's barely out of the way," he told her. "C'mon."

"Are you sure? Do you want to ask your brother first?"

"He won't say no. What's your name? I'm Bruno."

"I'm Gwendolyn. You helped me find my way around," she said, as if convincing herself to trust him.

"It's a confusing place."

"You look different," Gwendolyn said as they went outside. "From the beginning of school. You've changed your style."

"I have. I didn't really have much of a style before."

"I like it."

"Thank you," he said, thinking he should return the compliment but unsure what to say. He wondered what her hair would look like if she ever took it out of the ponytail.

Out in the parking lot most of the cars were gone, and Bruno's group stood by the black cars, watching him cross the parking lot with Gwendolyn.

"Do you ride with them?" she asked, slowing down.

"The one on the right is my brother, Sylvio," Bruno said. "Why?"

"They scare me, a little."

"Do I scare you?"

"If you hadn't helped me before, yes."

"They're harmless. And the other three will be in the other car. Really, I promise."

Sylvio spoke first. "Who's this?"

"This is Gwendolyn. Gwendolyn, this is Sylvio, and Regine, Celia, and Marco."

"Hi, Gwendolyn," Celia said, looking at Bruno longer than she did at Gwendolyn.

"Hi." Gwendolyn stared at them.

"She missed her bus, and she lives on Mount Rose, so I told her we'd give her a ride home," Bruno said to Sylvio.

"Well, let's get going. It's late," Sylvio said indifferently. Bruno opened the back door of the car for Gwendolyn, and when she got in, a book fell from her backpack to the pavement. Bruno picked it up and handed it to her.

"What book is that?"

"*The Stranger* by Albert Camus. You know it?"

"No. What's it about?"

"Get in!" Sylvio shouted from the driver's seat.

As they drove off, Gwendolyn said, "It's kind of hard to explain. There's a man, and a bunch of things happen, but he never seems to know why he does anything, or if anything has a reason. I'm not sure if I like it. I'm only halfway through."

"Is it for school?"

"No. I like to read. I always have a book with me."

Bruno could tell Gwendolyn was confused by the slow pace at which they drove, and she watched curiously as they followed the other car, dropping off passengers one at a time. Eventually they headed in the direction of Gwendolyn's house, and she called out a few final turns to get them there.

They stopped in front of a sturdy two-story brick house

with a big front porch and peeling paint. "Thank you so much," Gwendolyn said, opening the car door and sliding out. "See you at school!" She ran up the walk.

"Wait," Bruno said, opening his door, too.

"What are you doing?" Sylvio asked, irritated.

Bruno pointed to the front of the house. "Why is one of your windows open when it's this cold? Is something wrong?"

"My mother must have opened it. I'm sure it's okay."

"Isn't she at work, though? Until five?" Something definitely was not right. It had less to do with the open window and more to do with Gwendolyn's agitated state. And there was also the small fact that she was carrying *The Stranger*. "I think I should come in and make sure everything's all right."

"You don't need to do that," she said quickly.

"What's going on?" They stared at each other. Bruno walked past her up her front steps to the door. She followed him.

She put her key in the lock. "The window is stuck. I haven't been able to get it down. We haven't been able to get it down."

"That's dangerous. Anyone could get in." Bruno followed her into the dark house. She switched on a lamp and he went into the living room to look at the window. It was jammed at a slight angle. He banged on one side of the sash as hard as he could until it slid down and closed.

"Thank you." She was watching him from the doorway.

"What's going on?" he asked her again. "You can tell me."

"I can't," she said. But she came into the room and sat on a chair.

"Your mom isn't going to be home at five, is she?"

"No," Gwendolyn said in a small voice.

"How about your dad?"

"No."

"Please tell me."

"They're getting a divorce." She looked up at him. "And I hate them both. They hate each other, and I hate them. He went off with the woman he was cheating on Mom with. Every time he called, she wouldn't talk to him, so I was stuck in the middle of all their conversations. And then Grandma needed help, and Mom went to go take care of her. She told me to tell Dad he had to come back because she was leaving, but I didn't want him to come back. So I told her he was coming, and she left. He doesn't ask to speak to her when he calls." Anger flashed in Gwendolyn's eyes. "He deposits money in the bank account each month, and I pay all the bills. The grocery store is two blocks away."

"How long has it been?"

"Two and a half months."

"And your mom hasn't come back? What if someone had come through that window in the middle of the night?"

"I lock my bedroom door every night. You can't tell anyone."

"But you need help! Your parents—"

"You can't tell anyone!" she repeated. "I don't want them to come back, either of them! I'm happier without them."

"But you're what, *fourteen?* Sooner or later someone else is going to find out."

"I've been okay so far. Promise me you won't tell anyone."

Sylvio's horn sounded, and Bruno looked out the window. "I can't promise that."

"It's none of your business!"

"It is now."

"Please." She began to cry.

"Okay! I'm not going to promise. But I will keep your secret for a while, if *you* promise me you'll figure out what you're going to do to fix this. You can't keep on this way."

She nodded, wiping her eyes.

"I have to go." Bruno noticed a pad of paper on the hall table by the phone. "I'll write down my phone number, and if you need anything, call me, okay? Anytime." He went to the table and saw two numbers written on the pad, one labeled *Mom,* the other *Dad.* He turned to the next page and wrote *Bruno* and his number.

"Are you going to tell your brother?" She followed him to the front door.

"I won't tell him. I'll see you tomorrow?" She nodded, and he went out the door. On the stairs he heard the click of the lock behind him.

"What the hell were you doing?" Sylvio asked him in the car.

"Just drive home," Bruno said.

"Do you like her?" Sylvio said half seriously.

"No." Bruno didn't even care if Sylvio was going to try to have fun at his expense. He was thinking of only one thing. He remembered Cassandra's words specifically now: The one he sought would be carrying *the* stranger. Finally he had found her. Sure enough, she sadly lived in a house where no one was home—Bruno was struck by the way the words of the admonition were gradually becoming clear. Just the day before, that line had been poetic nonsense. The realization of a single new line of his admonition gave Bruno a powerful rush. Something incredible was happening, and it was happening to him. Now, how was he supposed to replant Gwendolyn's family tree?

• • •

MR. WILLIAMS WAS SITTING at his desk in his empty classroom, eating plums. "Come in," he called to Bruno, who had stopped in the doorway. "They're much better when they're cold, straight out of the refrigerator," he said, throwing the pits into the trash and wiping his hands. "I appreciate you paying attention in class today. Was there anything you didn't already know?"

"You do talk about things that aren't on maps sometimes," Bruno said helpfully. "Like climate and some of the history of the people who live in the area. So yes."

"Well, that's a relief," Mr. Williams said drily. "I was thinking about how to structure what we're going to do. We have geographical maps"—he pointed at the classroom walls —"and there are city maps, and then there are architectural plans. All of these are representations of the world we inhabit, and it seems to me you have a, well, talent for understanding them and remembering them. Am I right?"

"I guess so," Bruno said.

"And instead of just reading them, you'd like to be able to draw them. Correct?"

"Yes," Bruno said.

"Have you ever tried?"

"I've been drawing the school." Bruno pulled out his notebook and opened it to the inside back cover. Mr. Williams studied the drawing of Suburban High School with interest. "It's kind of messy," Bruno said.

"Don't be self-deprecating. You've done a great job, considering you've never taken a drafting class or anything."

"I looked at a lot of plans to see how to do windows and doors."

"You must be using a scale," Mr. Williams observed.

"Yeah, my dad had one. My grandfather was an engineer."

"Most people do this type of thing on a computer these days. But it's great to learn to do it by hand. I think you internalize a place better when you draw it by hand." Bruno nodded, not sure what he meant. He had never had any trouble internalizing places, once he had seen the map or the plan. Mr. Williams put his finger down on the drawing. "What's going on in the library?"

Bruno had left the back wall of the library open because while he didn't know exactly where it was, he knew for sure it wasn't where the official plan of Suburban High School showed it to be. "I . . . I haven't finished that part."

"And what is this X?" Mr. Williams pointed to the mark in the stairwell of the Chancellor Wing.

"I don't remember why I put that there," Bruno lied.

"There's one over in this stairwell, too," Mr. Williams said, noticing the one by the cafeteria.

"I've been working on this since the beginning of school. I must have . . ." Bruno squinted at the drawing as though it would provide the lie he needed.

"No worries; I was just curious." Mr. Williams gave the notebook back to Bruno. "So tell me, are you more interested in drawing cities or buildings?"

"Buildings, probably," Bruno answered.

"Okay, this is your first assignment, then. I know you help out in the library. Go find a book of architectural drawings of great buildings. And then go to the art store and buy a roll of trace paper. I want you to spend some time tracing the floor plans of buildings. It's a great way to learn how the designer put the building together. How does that sound?"

"Sure," Bruno said.

"Next week you can show me what you've done."

BRUNO HADN'T SEEN VAN since Celia had drawn him in the cafeteria, and he'd wondered whether Celia's drawing had somehow made him disappear. But there he was in the locker room at their next gym class. The senior gave him a blank look. When they lined up for attendance in the gym, Bruno heard Van say to one of his friends, "Who? I've never seen that guy before. Is he new?"

They played flag football again, and the seniors kept the contact light under the teacher's watchful eye. But Van had no glares for Bruno, no threats delivered under his breath when he passed. He was more concerned about his friends, who now were calling him both a coward and an amnesiac. Bruno just concentrated on the game. *She really did something to him. It's like she erased me from his memory.*

∫houldn't have done that

C ELIA HAD BEEN ALARMED when Bruno told her about Van's apparent loss of memory. "I'm freaked out about it because last year Mariette fiddled with people's memories and made a colossal mess. I wouldn't have erased you if I'd known it would have that effect. Is he at least nicer to you?"

"When he looks at me now, it's almost like he's afraid."

"I'll call that an improvement, then." Celia smiled. She noticed Gwendolyn, who had seen the two of them and abruptly headed in the opposite direction. "Is she mad at you?"

"I don't know . . ." Bruno was grateful when Celia let it go.

Halloween was approaching, giving them less time to obsess about unsolved mysteries and moody girls. At least once a week there was a new story about someone at Suburban receiving a kiss note from Mariette and having to deal with the repercussions. It wasn't always a betrayal, but it was always a surprise. But Regine had typed up a Halloween itinerary for the group. First there were the perversely bright outfits they would wear to school on Halloween, then dressing up as Elizabethan ghosts to give out candy to trick-or-treaters at Brenden's house, and finally their costumes for the grand ball at Diaboliques the following night.

But the real occasion as far as Bruno could tell was that Ivo would be back from college this time, along with Liz and Brenden. For the first time since August, the entire Rosary would be reunited. And for Regine, the Halloween preparation was really to demonstrate to the other three—and to Ivo in particular—that she had been a faithful custodian of the Rosary's legacy at Suburban since they'd gone, and to position Sylvio to prove himself worthy of acceptance into the Rosary.

ON THE MORNING BEFORE Halloween, Bruno stared at the test questions on his computer screen in Ms. Moreletii's lab. He had come into this exam feeling well prepared, but the problems might as well have been in a foreign language. The ones he could decipher were asking him to design processes he was sure Ms. Moreletii never had discussed, much less taught. He started to panic, but the more he thought about it, the more certain he was that something was wrong.

Ms. Moreletii called to him, "Bruno, what's the problem?" The rest of the class looked up from their computer screens.

Bruno left his seat and approached her desk. He said in a low voice, "I think I have the wrong test."

"What do you mean? Of course you have the right test."

"I don't recognize any of the questions at all."

"Did you study?" she asked him, and he wanted to throw something. Instead, he nodded vigorously. "Then why aren't you prepared for the test?"

He turned to his classmates, who were watching with interest. "Don't say any answers! I just want to know if any of your questions are about a proof of concept." He scanned the room and saw only blank stares.

"Bruno," Ms. Moreletii warned from behind him.

"No answers. Just raise your hand if the words *proof of concept* are anywhere on your test—any question."

No one raised a hand. Bruno turned back to Ms. Moreletii. "I have a different test from everyone else."

"That's not possible." She stood up and went to his computer. There was a long minute when she didn't say anything. "This is the level two test. How did you wind up with this? Close out of that," she said, and returned to her own computer. In another moment she called to him, "Try again." He reopened the testing module.

This time the test that appeared on Bruno's screen had questions that were familiar to him. He nodded at Ms. Moreletii and only wished she had apologized for the mistake. He'd lost almost ten minutes.

"CAN YOU TAKE CARE of these?" Lois handed Bruno a small stack of books.

"Sure."

As he headed off to the stacks, Lois said, "Be careful."

"Why do you say that?"

"Two days ago one of my other aides couldn't find something, and yesterday someone actually started *yelling* because he couldn't find his way out of the stacks. It took me two minutes to get to him." Lois shook her head in disbelief at what she was saying.

"The labyrinth—it's getting worse," Bruno said.

"I think so. You've gone much farther into the stacks than I have. What was it like back there?"

"Just dark, really. And the books get larger the farther back you go. There was one point when I thought someone else was back there, but I couldn't see for sure. It might have been my imagination."

"You don't seem like the type to imagine things like that. But you weren't disoriented?"

"No."

"Well, keep an eye out, will you? I'm not the only one who's disoriented anymore. Maybe there's a gas leak or something."

"Sure." Bruno went off to the stacks.

Something was different. He couldn't say for sure, but as he worked his way through the stacks returning books, there were several times he thought a corner came too soon, or not soon enough. But eventually he found the rightful home of every book.

As he shelved the last one, he heard muffled voices a few aisles over.

"Stop! Just stop for a minute!" a girl hissed. "How do we get out of here?"

"What do you mean? Around that corner," a boy said.

"Are you sure? I could see the tables before. Where did they go?"

"They're around that corner. I'm sure. Come back here."

Bruno walked quickly back to the main aisle, down the next row, and around the corner to the section where he'd overheard the voices. Regine and Sylvio jumped apart.

"You guys all right?" Bruno asked.

"What do you mean?" Sylvio asked. "We're fine."

"Are you wearing lipstick?" Bruno leaned toward his brother, who rubbed at his mouth with his fingers.

"Don't you have books to shelve?" Regine asked scornfully.

"I did. I heard you whispering about being lost."

"Nobody's lost," Regine snapped. "You're a library aide, not a lifeguard."

"I'm sorry. I'll try to remember that." Bruno walked away. In another minute Regine and Sylvio returned to the table in the reading area where they had left their books. Neither of them looked at Bruno.

"GO AHEAD. I JUST NEED to ask Bruno something," Celia said to the others on their way to the cars after school. "Van talked to me today," she said as soon as the others were out of earshot.

"Really? About what?"

"He stopped me in the hall, and then he couldn't come up with an actual question. He kept starting to say things like, 'Is Bruno . . . I mean, does he . . .' And then he asked me how I knew you."

"You think he was trying to get up the nerve to ask you if I'm Kind, or something?"

"Maybe. But it gets weirder. The whole time, he was looking at me so strangely."

"Like he was angry?"

"No. He acted like he was shy, or nervous about being close to me. But the look in his eyes . . . I've seen it before, but I don't know what it means."

"You've seen it before with Van?"

"No. With Tomasi, actually. And with you, too. I think Van definitely is Kind or Unkind."

"What kind of look do I have in my eyes?"

"It's usually after we haven't seen each other for a while.

With Tomasi I used to think it was love. But I'm starting to think it has something to do with being Kind. Come to think of it, Mariette used to look at me that way, too."

"Strange," Bruno said. He felt bruised, somehow, but he couldn't figure out why.

AT SCHOOL HALLOWEEN MORNING, Bruno and Marco were dressed in matching blue seersucker suits. One of his classmates asked, "Are you guys dating?" hoping to embarrass Bruno.

"Would it bother you if we were?" Bruno replied, and the guy looked disappointed that his barb had missed its mark.

Bruno got plenty of attention for his costume. Even Gwendolyn, who had perfected the art of always being headed in the opposite direction from him, stopped short.

"What are you? You always wear black." It was the first time she had spoken to him in days. "Did you change your style?"

"It's Halloween!" he protested. "Have you talked to your parents?"

"Kind of," she said, and fled.

"I don't believe you!" he called after her.

He seemed to have caught Mariette's attention, too. All day he saw her at the end of hallways, her strawberry-blond hair flowing as though a breeze danced around her. He thought she was smiling at him, but she was always so far away, it was hard to tell.

After school, the five of them drove to Brenden's house to prepare for the trick-or-treaters. Ivo and Liz arrived soon after, and Bruno enjoyed watching the reunion of the Rosary. When the trick-or-treating started and they were all costumed and masked in the front yard, Bruno retreated to the far reaches of the fog machine's coverage to escape Sylvio's desperation. Marco and Brenden came to find him.

"Have you found any children to spook over here?" Brenden asked.

"Not really," Bruno said.

"So what's the deal with Silver? He's been trying to impress me with his music knowledge all night. Which is fine, but really, we're supposed to be having fun, you know?" Brenden said.

"He really wants to be a part of the Rosary," Bruno said. "That's all I know."

"It's pretty obvious. And it's pretty obvious Regine wants him to be, too."

"You don't seem as concerned about it," Marco said. "Why's that?"

"I don't know. I don't understand why it's so important to be a part of a club. I mean, is it a club?"

Brenden shook his head. "It's just a name."

"Would we be better friends if I joined—whatever it is?"

"No," Marco said. "It doesn't matter."

"So I don't see why it's important."

"Do you think you could convince Silver of that?" Brenden asked.

"I doubt it." The three of them smiled knowingly, then waded back into the fog.

THE FOLLOWING NIGHT, THERE were four black cars on the drive to Diaboliques instead of three: Sylvio and Bruno in front, followed by Regine and Celia, then Brenden and Marco, and finally Ivo and Liz. For their costumes, Marco had taken his inspiration from Edward Gorey's illustrations, so their eyes were lined with kohl, and each played a part in a forties murder: Ivo was the patriarch and Celia the matriarch; Liz was the starched maid. Brenden and Marco were detectives. Regine was the ingénue and Sylvio was the playboy. Bruno was the butler.

"How did we wind up being the help?" Liz smiled at him.

Everyone at Diaboliques had gone all out for Halloween, which didn't surprise Bruno. He took his place with his friends on the edge of the dance floor in Patrick's room. They barely had settled in when the boys from St. Dymphna's made their entrance. Each of them had dressed as a cross between a clergyman and a rock star: A priest in a black shirt and white collar with black leather pants. A cleric with a white stole and biker boots. An altar boy with aviator glasses.

"I like this place so much better than the club by Metropolitan," Brenden told Bruno, just as Patrick put on a new song. "'Wasteland' by the Mission UK—God, I love that man!" Everyone headed out to dance.

Later, Bruno went down to the mezzanine and found Cassandra on a couch by herself. She looked up at him expectantly. "Hello there!" She casually took his hand in hers, and immediately Bruno was aroused. Again he blushed, and again she gave him an amused look. "We Ambassadors make it . . . difficult for you, don't we?" she said, dipping her fingernails into his palm.

"I'm sorry to keep coming to you. I know I'm supposed to rely on Celia, but I found the girl who carries the stranger, and she lives in a house where no one's home."

"Good! It's okay if you come see me. I'm not in the habit of turning away handsome young men." Cassandra gave him a brilliant smile. "Just keep in mind, I may not give you the answers you seek."

"I'm supposed to replant her family tree," he said, trying not to make it sound like a question.

"And so you will," she said.

He gave up. "How do I do that?"

"You know. You know exactly, and you're hoping I'll tell you something different, because you'd rather not do it."

"You're right."

"Forget the admonition for a moment. If you had discovered that Wendy was a Lost Girl some other way—say, by accident—would you stand by without doing anything, allowing her to continue with her deception, knowing she's putting herself in danger?"

"No, I wouldn't," Bruno admitted.

"So how is this any different?" Cassandra closed his hand and wrapped her fingers around it. "It was good to see you."

"It was good to see you." He took her hand and kissed the back of it, and she laughed. "Go, you sweet boy, or I'll put you in my pocket and carry you around like a pet."

As the end of the night approached, Marco returned from the bathroom with a strange expression. Brenden was dancing, and Marco pulled Bruno aside. "One of those St. Dymphna guys just tried to talk to me. Or hit on me, actually."

"Really? Was it Turlington?"

"Turlington? No, he said his name was Evan. Turlington? Wait, did you talk to one of them, too?"

"A few weeks ago. I think he was trying to pick me up."

"Well, Evan was definitely trying to pick *me* up," Marco said.

They looked across the floor and caught a cupped hand salute from one of the St. Dymphna boys. "Is that Evan?"

"Yup. Which one's Turlington?"

"In the cassock with the neon-pink crucifix. What did you tell him?"

"That my boyfriend is hotter than the six of them put together," Marco said. "C'mon, let's dance."

fade to grey

BRUNO CORNERED GWENDOLYN at her locker on Monday morning. "What are you doing for Thanksgiving?"

"What?" She tried to finish collecting her books for morning classes. "Are you being mean?"

"No! So you *haven't* talked to your parents. Don't they want to see you for the holidays?"

"I hope not," she said scornfully.

"Do you mean that?"

"Yes." She looked straight at him, and her voice was firm but he saw doubt in her eyes.

"Well, you shouldn't spend it alone. Will you come to dinner with my family?"

"That's very nice. But I couldn't, I mean—"

"You won't be the only guest. My father's a minister, and every year he winds up inviting half a dozen people who have nowhere else to go for Thanksgiving. Think of it this way: At least I'll know you."

That got her to smile a little. "Can I think about it?"

"Sure. I'll tell my mom you're coming." This time he was the one to dash off before she could protest.

. . .

"MARIETTE GAVE LACIE A NOTE," Regine said at the lunch table.

"Omigod, who cares?" Marco said. "Maybe the truth will set you free, or whatever, but it all seems so mean-spirited."

"So you wouldn't want someone to tell you if Brenden was cheating on you?" Regine asked.

"Excuse me?" Marco looked at her sharply. "Why would you say something like that?"

Regine was only slightly cowed. "It's just a thought experiment. Would you rather not know, or would you rather suffer through someone being mean-spirited enough to tell you?"

"First, I don't think telling someone is what makes it mean-spirited—it's having some kind of ghostly access to all this information and making a hobby out of it. Next, what kind of relationship would I have if I didn't trust Brenden? So how am I supposed to do a thought experiment that is all about *not* trusting him?"

"Wow, touchy." Regine rolled her eyes.

"Would you want to know?" Celia asked Regine.

"Yes. If I'm going to have my heart broken, I'd rather get it over with than be the chump in a relationship that should have ended." She looked at Sylvio. "But I'm not suspicious or anything, okay? It's just a hypothetical."

"Sure." Sylvio nodded.

"How about you, Bruno?" Celia asked. "You've been quiet."

"Bruno doesn't have anyone to cheat on him," Sylvio said before Bruno could respond.

"Would you want to know if Gwendolyn was kissing someone else?" Regine asked.

"This is when I remember why I never liked having friends before," Bruno said.

"Ouch." Regine exchanged glances with Sylvio.

Bruno snapped, "Can't you just talk about music, or the books you're reading? At least that's interesting."

"You have a good point," Marco said. "I don't think anyone meant any harm, though."

"I'm sorry." Bruno sat back in his chair, aware that he had crashed the conversation. He looked around the cafeteria and caught Van staring at him. Van looked away quickly.

"The instruments of darkness tell us truths," Celia said quietly.

"What's that?" Regine asked.

"We're reading *Macbeth* in English, and I wrote down a quote: 'And oftentimes, to win us to our harms, / The instruments of darkness tell us truths; / Win us with honest trifles, to betray us / In deepest consequence.'"

"What does that mean?"

"I think it means we're more liable to believe a lie if there's some truth mixed in," Celia said.

"That's a lovely thought," Regine muttered.

"Yeah, but it's probably true," Marco said. "It's just hard to believe Mariette is an instrument of darkness." Celia gave him a grateful look.

WITH MR. WILLIAMS'S HELP, Bruno had nearly completed a new drawing of the plan of Suburban High School on a larger piece of paper, making better use of the scale. This time he had used a measuring tape in the halls and classrooms, quietly enjoying the intrigued looks from people around him. His lines were surer, and it was an even more satisfying project the second time around.

The missing back wall of the library challenged him every

time he looked at his plan, though. He could have taken the path of least resistance and penciled it in where it logically should have been, stopping in the same plane as the wall of the lobby below. But there was no doubt in Bruno's mind that he had walked much farther in that direction than he could have on the first floor. And the *You Are Here* drawing he had seen had left the wall out, too.

He set his things down on a table in the reading area and headed into the stacks. His measuring tape was nowhere near long enough to cover the distance he had traveled to the sixty-fourth aisle, but he figured the shelves must be evenly spaced, so he could always measure the span of ten rows along the aisle and then multiply to get the total length. But that still required finding the back wall.

He measured the distance from the first shelf to the tenth and set out, intent on walking until he reached the back wall of the library. The lantern was waiting for him at aisle 16, burning brightly, as though it had just been lit. Bruno didn't even waste time wondering how. He picked it up and kept going, and the darkness thickened beyond the glow from the candle. On either side the aisles of books faded into gray and then black, and in front of him the main aisle stretched out like a dark forest with nothing but night on the far side.

He passed aisle 32 and wondered if a volume of *You Are Here* was there now. He lifted the lantern to peer down the row, but the light from the candle dazed him for a moment, and when he lowered it, phosphenes trailed across his vision. He blinked and they were gone. A vague lightness began to haunt his head as he continued on. *Did I eat something bad for lunch? What's happening?* He kept walking.

The palpable silence he remembered from his first excursion back here was changing. Up ahead Bruno thought he could hear a sound that might have been wind, or a river, or a distant storm. Aisle 40, 45, 50 . . . He sensed a change in the air pressure, but he couldn't tell whether it was real or a by-product of his disorientation. He considered turning around, but he didn't want to admit defeat.

He had just passed aisle 64 when someone or something passed behind him, crossing the main aisle as it traveled down the row. He turned around but saw nothing besides shelves and shelves of oversize books. In the faint light they looked faded and forgotten. The lantern had grown heavy in his hand, and he could only lift it up by his shoulder for a few seconds. *This is a bad idea.* He continued walking, his steps unsteady.

The white noise grew louder but no more distinct, and Bruno thought he smelled sea air, but when he inhaled again he wasn't sure. Now things were moving in the distance in front of him. It might have been paper being blown by wind, or perhaps there were people rushing through the rows, crossing the aisle with a rustle of coats and the light tread of runners. Then he couldn't see anything, and he was unsure whether the blackness was around him or inside his head. A gust of air flowed from somewhere deep in the library and pushed against Bruno, and for a second he was scared a train was bearing down on him in this darkened tunnel. *What was I thinking? If someone is going to die at Suburban this year, this might be where it happens.* He lost his sense of the floor beneath him, and then he couldn't feel his legs.

HE AWOKE IN THE DARK with the sound of wind and water in his ears, unsure how long he had been unconscious. The lantern stood next to him on the floor, its candle still burning.

Bruno struggled to raise himself up on his hands, and he looked around for the distant light of the reading area. He pulled himself up and started back, leaving the lantern behind. His vision kept fading in and out, and he had to steady himself, letting go of one shelf and falling forward to catch the next one. When he willed himself to lift his head, the weak glow where the tables and Lois were didn't seem to be any closer.

He kept on, but it felt like hours before the light was finally strong enough for him to see the colors on the books he passed. The weakness wasn't leaving him. He couldn't hold up his head, and his legs lurched sideways without warning. If he allowed his eyes to close for too long, the lights that danced on his eyelids made him nauseous. He felt as though he hadn't eaten in weeks.

When he finally staggered out of the stacks and collapsed by the table where he had left his books, a figure swam into his vision as it bent over him. "Bruno! What happened?" she cried before he passed out again.

THERE HAD BEEN AN AMBULANCE, and a brief stay in the emergency room, where Bruno's family was told he was severely anemic. He was taken home and put to bed, and November was nothing but a fog that didn't seem to want to lift. His parents doted on him, and even Sylvio was kind, bringing him music and helping him with his schoolwork when he was able to resume it.

Being confined to his house was a worse torment than anything that had happened at Suburban. The long hours with nothing but home assignments gave him plenty of time to ponder, and to try to guess for what felt like the hundredth time what the library had done to him.

Marco came to see him every few days, which helped to break the monotony. "What the hell happened?" he asked on his first visit. "You had no idea you were anemic?"

"No," Bruno said honestly. "I never had any symptoms, anything. It just happened."

"I blame that library," Marco said, his eyes twinkling. "This is proof that too much learning is bad for your health."

"You don't believe that," Bruno said, catching Marco's dry humor.

"Probably not. Seriously, though, what is up with the library? The day after you bit it, some guys were in there testing it to see if there were high levels of carbon monoxide."

"Really?"

"I don't think they found anything, though. You're not missing much at Suburban. Actually, it seems like the depression curse might be over. Other than you, no one else has come down with a case of the sads in a couple weeks."

"Is Mariette still handing out kiss notes?"

"Yeah, she's still at it. Turns out I'm not the only gay senior. I'm just the only one who's not a closet case." Marco grinned. "So, are you feeling stronger?"

It was a good question, because even though his iron deficiency had been corrected, he wasn't. Sophia had called, offering to come home, and making him tell her over and over again it wasn't necessary. He made his family promise not to tell her when his doctor admitted it was taking far longer for him to recover than it should. The doctor ordered more tests.

Marco wasn't too concerned. "You'll be fine; just give it

some time. If you need anything Silver can't or won't bring you, let me know, okay? I miss you at school. You're the best company I have, and now I'm just wandering around cracking wise by myself."

"Sorry," Bruno said, smiling at the thought.

The first time Celia came to see him, she asked quietly, "What really happened?"

"I don't know. I went deep into the stacks again, but this time it was like it sucked the life out of me or something. I kept getting weaker, and I think I passed out for a minute. I had to turn around, and then by the time I got back, I was completely wiped out."

"What's it like, back there? Is it pitch-black?"

"Yeah. It gets windy, and it sounds like there's a storm really far back. Plus, I'm pretty sure there are other people back there. I kept glimpsing things, but I couldn't be sure."

"Really? And you didn't feel any of this the first time, when you found the book?"

"No."

"That's just so strange. I wonder why it was so different when you went back this time."

"Well, I have felt that way before, kind of."

"When?"

"In the Ebentwine clearing."

"But that didn't make you sick like this."

"I never stayed long enough. But within a minute or two I started to get lightheaded and see stars. Gardner would always shoo me out before it got worse."

"Do you think . . ."

"The Ebentwine is somehow in the back of the library, too?

It kind of seems that way. I smell the ocean when I'm in the clearing, and I smelled it when I was deep in the stacks, too."

"That's—" Celia stopped herself. "I was going to say 'That's crazy,' but that's not saying much, really, is it?" Celia's eyes smiled. She drove the torpor out of his bedroom, and he wanted her there forever. But too soon she said, "I wish I could stay longer, but I have to meet Tomasi." She squeezed his hand and then she was gone.

THERE WERE FAR TOO many hours in the day. The doctor ordered even more tests. His father brought him a copy of *The Stranger*. "It's been so long since I read this, I barely remember it," he said. "Why did you ask for it? Do you have to read it for school?"

"No, a friend was reading it, and I was just curious."

"Beware those existentialists. They'll make you question why you're here." Mr. Perilunas laughed and patted Bruno's forehead.

It might have been that his days already were somewhat surreal, being home sick, but *The Stranger* felt like a hallucination. It had the strange effect of making Bruno feel as though all the bizarre things that awaited him outside his house might not be so bizarre after all. It might just be a matter of changing the way he thought about them. That didn't make them less mysterious—only less extraordinary.

He gave the book to Marco when he was finished. "I don't know if you'll like it, but it kind of blew my mind."

"Cool. I'd love to read it. I'd bet Celia would, too. Oh, hey, I can't believe I forgot to tell you. One of those St. Dymphna guys talked to her at Diaboliques last week."

"Really?"

"She said his name was Moss. She even made him spell it. *Moss.*" Marco gave Bruno a moment to share in the absurdity. "But he cozied up to her just like Evan did with me, and what's-his-name—Turlington?—did with you. It's like they're looking for the weak link to recruit to the dark side or something."

"I bet Tomasi loved that."

"Ha, I wish I'd seen his reaction! I'll bet some words were spoken at St. Dymphna's on Monday."

Marco helped Bruno feel connected to the outside world, even more so than Sylvio, who seemed to think Bruno's illness was an opportunity to borrow his clothes. Yet as much as he enjoyed Marco's company, every time the doorbell rang, Bruno hoped it was Celia. She came once a week, and he had to be content with that.

On her third visit she brought her sketchbook. When Bruno admitted he still couldn't stand up for more than a few minutes, she shook her head with concern. "We both know this has something to do with the Ebentwine. I don't know if it'll help, but I want to try drawing you. I should have done that before now anyway. Do you mind?"

"No," Bruno said, immensely pleased as she sat down across from his bed.

"Gwendolyn asked about you," she said as she worked. "She told me you invited her for Thanksgiving. That's a really lovely thing for you to do. I never thought about the doctors and nurses who are on duty on Thanksgiving. It's too bad her mom has to work."

"Sure. Dad always invites parishioners who would be alone for the holidays. I just wish I was feeling better; it's the day after tomorrow." Suddenly Bruno began to feel a warmth in his limbs like he hadn't felt for weeks. "Are you drawing my arms?" She nodded. "I feel like I can tell where your pen is." She looked at him curiously, then went back to the drawing, and Bruno felt as if a ray of sun were dancing on his face. "Now you're drawing my left eyebrow."

"Are you serious? You can feel that?"

"I can. And it's amazing—I almost feel stronger."

"Do you think it's the drawing?"

Bruno nodded. "Keep going."

By the time Celia had finished, Bruno felt better than he had before his fateful trip into the library stacks. "Why didn't I do this weeks ago?" Celia marveled. "I never thought . . . I should have realized."

"How were you supposed to know?" Bruno wanted to hug her. Or go outside and run around. Mainly to hug her.

12

a person isn't safe anywhere these days

BRUNO'S RECOVERY MADE THANKSGIVING feel particularly meaningful. But Sylvio wasn't in a festive mood. He grumbled, "Funny how we move to a different state, and the first Thanksgiving, we already have a table full of strangers."

"I kind of like it," Bruno said. "It's our tradition."

"Yeah, you've even invited a stranger of your own." Sylvio stopped the car in front of Gwendolyn's house. Bruno got out, enjoying the crisp air. After being trapped in his house for so long, it still felt like a miracle every time he went outside. He had finally mowed one of his lawns the day before, and it had been a thrill.

Gwendolyn met him on the front walk. She wore a calico dress with a velvet blazer that made her look like a doll, and a ribbon tied in her ringlet ponytail.

"Hi," she said, hesitant but happy. "I'm so glad you're feeling better! Thank you for inviting me."

"Thanks for coming. I hope you enjoy it."

"I'm sure I will," she said. He opened the car door for her and felt like her date and her chauffeur at the same time. He hadn't intended to be either.

In the car Gwendolyn broke the silence. "So you've invited other . . ."

"Strays?" Sylvio said. "I think the table is set for eleven, so that means six other people. At least we *know* you. Bruno and I haven't even met these other people."

"Wow. Well, it's a very nice thing to do."

"I know, and I'm a horrible person for being a Grinch about it. I should be nicer."

"It's not wrong to want to do things just with your family," Gwendolyn said.

"Maybe that's it. Sometimes it feels like Dad takes more of an interest in his parishioners than in us."

"You know that's not true," Bruno said.

"I should just stop talking."

When they got back home, Bruno introduced Gwendolyn to his parents. His father welcomed her and introduced them to the rest of the guests: a widower, a mother and toddler, an elderly couple, and a foreign student at the local college. They started out shy and polite, but Bruno's father lured them into conversations with one another with the ease of a minister who had been turning roomfuls of people into friends for years.

Piano music floated in from the den, and the aromas of cider and roasting turkey wafted out of the kitchen. When it came time to be seated, Bruno motioned to Gwendolyn to take a place next to him. He was nervous because his parents clearly regarded Gwendolyn as his date, as did all the strangers, and of course Sylvio was doing everything he could to reinforce that impression. Bruno hadn't considered how easily people would make the assumption, and it bothered him. But there was nothing to be done about it now.

"This is the best Thanksgiving I've ever had," Gwendolyn

said to him quietly when they were eating pie. "It really feels like a family meal, and all these people just met each other today."

"It's weird how that happens," Bruno said. "I like Thanksgiving better than Christmas. It's all the good stuff: a break from school, lots of food, time with your family—and none of the hard things: what presents to get everyone, how to pretend you like a gift you don't like . . ."

Gwendolyn giggled. "I never thought about that."

He spoke softly, so no one else would hear. "What will you do for Christmas? I mean, won't you have to see at least one of your parents?"

"I don't know." Her eyes became distant. "I realize it can't go on like this forever; I'm kind of surprised it's gone on this long. I figured after a few weeks one of them would catch on. Or that Grandma wouldn't need Mom there constantly, and she would just come home. But I think she's using Grandma as an excuse to stay away, and now it's just as easy to leave things as they are."

"Don't you miss them? Either of them?"

"Sometimes." She searched his face. "When I have a bad day, or when something happens that I don't know how to deal with. There was a mouse in the basement. I missed them then."

He caught a flicker of longing in her eyes. She was regarding him as her hero, and he couldn't be surprised by it. But he looked away. He wondered if that was the look Celia had tried to describe—the look she said she received from Tomasi and him.

As night fell, Sylvio drove them back to her house. Gwendolyn was more relaxed, and she chatted with Bruno about school. "Have you seen the ghost?" she asked. "Everyone talks about it. Apparently it's some girl who died last year?"

"One of our friends knew her," Bruno said.

"Really? Have you seen her?"

"I have, but just down at the end of the hall a couple times. She hasn't given me anything."

"Do you have a girlfriend?"

"No, but he has a boyfriend," Sylvio joked.

"What? You're gay?"

"Sylvio's being stupid because I'm friends with Marco," Bruno said.

"Oh. That guy who makes clothes? He's nice. He smiles at me sometimes," she said. "Well, if you don't have a girlfriend, then the ghost can't give you a note about when to catch her cheating on you."

"I guess not," Bruno said.

"I don't have a boyfriend, so she doesn't have any reason to give me anything, either." Her voice was casual, but her meaning was clear. They were approaching her house. "Hey, why are all the lights on?"

"Someone's there," Bruno said. Sylvio stopped the car, and Bruno and Gwendolyn got out.

"That looks like my dad's car," Gwendolyn said. "If he's here—" The front door opened and a man and a woman came out onto the porch. "They're both here!" she said in despair.

"Gwen? Where have you been?" her mother called to her.

The three Winsomes met in the middle of the walk. Gwendolyn was in shock. "I went to have dinner at my friend's house. What are you doing here?"

"We both came home to surprise you, and it's a good thing

we did, since neither of us had any idea you were lying to us!" Her mother tried to be harsh, but her voice broke, and from the street Bruno could see she was crying. "Why would you do that?"

"Why do you think? I was miserable!" Gwendolyn began to cry, too. "I didn't want to see either of you!"

"Gwenny, we're sorry. We shouldn't have made it so hard on you," her father said. "Will you come inside?"

Gwendolyn turned back to Bruno instead. "Can I come with you?" she pleaded. "I don't want to go in there."

Bruno shook his head gently. "You have to give them the chance to fix it."

"Who is this?" Gwendolyn's father asked.

"It's my friend Bruno," Gwendolyn said. "When he found out I was alone for Thanksgiving, he invited me to his house."

"I think he did more than that," her father said, and he looked at Bruno. "You were the one who left us those messages, weren't you?"

"You did what?" Gwendolyn whirled back to Bruno. "You told on me?"

Bruno thought back to Halloween weekend, when he had waited for Gwendolyn to leave for the grocery store and gone in through the unlocked front window to copy her parents' phone numbers off the pad on the hall table. "No, I didn't. I told them you wanted them to come home. I didn't tell them you were alone."

"I'm glad he did," her mother said, coming down the walk. "Bruno, I wish we weren't meeting like this, but thank you for doing what you did." She shook Bruno's hand. He smiled politely at her, while he felt Gwendolyn's angry eyes bore into him.

"You said you would keep a secret," she said quietly.

"I'm sorry. But you know I'm right."

"No, you're not." Gwendolyn's voice was hard.

Her mother put her hands on Gwendolyn's shoulders. "Gwenny, please, let's talk. I think we can figure this out. We owe you an apology, that's for sure. We're not angry with you. And no one is going to leave until we sort this out. Okay? Please come inside."

Gwendolyn looked at Bruno, and he could tell she was struggling. "You should go. You can punch me on Monday," he said.

"I'm going to," she said, and went up the walk with her parents.

When Bruno got back into the car, Sylvio said, "What did you do?"

"Hopefully I've replanted a family tree." Bruno looked up at the Winsome house, every window brightly lit, as they drove away.

"What does that mean?"

"Never mind."

ON THE MONDAY AFTER THANKSGIVING, Bruno was sitting with his friends in the library when Gwendolyn approached the table. "Can I talk to you?"

"Sure." Bruno got up and went with Gwendolyn to another table.

"I'm not going to punch you," she said. "I was really mad, but I understand why you did it, and it turns out it was a good thing after all."

"What happened?"

"We talked for hours. They were really upset—they both

cried a lot. But they weren't as upset with me as they were with themselves, for being so caught up in how unhappy they were that they didn't even suspect the other one wasn't at home with me. They both got to the house really soon after you picked me up, and once they figured out that neither of them had been there for three months, they spent the rest of the time talking about everything. By the time I got home, they were so ashamed, they weren't really mad at me for lying to them anymore."

"That's good."

"Yeah. So they're still getting a divorce, but Dad's coming back home to live. He probably would have before. He was living with his girlfriend because he thought Mom was in the house, but I don't think that's working out."

"So that's good, right?"

"It is. They both apologized for everything. They apologized so much, eventually I had to ask them to stop. And now they're going to talk directly to each other instead of passing messages through me, so I'm not going to be able to fool them again." Gwendolyn smiled a little sheepishly. "They asked me to thank you."

"No problem," Bruno said. "It was the right thing to do."

"I know. So I want to say thank you, too."

"You don't have to. I'm glad I could help, even if I went behind your back."

"It wouldn't have worked any other way. I never would have let you, if you had asked me."

They sat for a moment, unsure what else to say. "So can we be friends, in school? I know I've avoided you, but I really wanted to talk to you."

"Sure," Bruno said. He was nervous he was agreeing to something else, but he didn't know how to avoid it.

"Good," she said, exhaling.

They got up and stood awkwardly. Then she hugged him, and Bruno helplessly put his arms around her.

"Thank you," she whispered. Then she gathered up her things and left.

Bruno returned to his friends to hear the expected comments.

"New girlfriend?" Regine asked.

"She's cute," Celia said sincerely.

"Does this mean you're going to drop us?" Marco asked.

"It's not like that," Bruno said.

"Silver told us about Thanksgiving dinner. It's okay," Regine said. "We'd love to meet her."

"It's not like that," he repeated.

"Okay," Sylvio said. "Sure it's not."

"It's not," Bruno said. "I have to go shelve books." He went off to help out, even though Lois wasn't expecting him.

"BRUNO! IT'S BEEN AGES! How've you been?" Gardner's happiness to see him surprised Bruno.

"I was sick for a while. I thought you might know about it."

"Because of the liminal in the library? I wondered if you realized what was going on there."

"Wait—the library is a liminal, too?"

"It's just a name for it. And that passage under the stairs. Glad you're well again. So, where are you off to?"

"The bookstore."

"And I'll see you back here in five minutes, then?" Gardner regarded Bruno half in amusement and half in exasperation.

"What do you mean?"

"Do you go inside? Do you even cross the street?"

"I just want to see her for a little." Bruno knew he sounded pathetic. He sometimes wished he could make it through this clearing without meeting Gardner, but that didn't seem possible.

"Are you ever going to make your case with her?"

"Not while she's dating Tomasi, I won't."

"Why's that?"

"Because it wouldn't be right!"

"Suit yourself." Gardner waved him through.

When he emerged from the alley across the street from the bookstore, Bruno looked for Celia in the front windows, but he only saw the petite woman with white hair at the front counter. He waited, but nothing changed. Wouldn't Gardner have told him if Celia wasn't there? Maybe it was time to go into the bookstore.

The tiny woman looked up when Bruno entered. The place was warm and dim, with a relaxing aroma of paper and spearmint. Piano music bubbled like a quiet brook. "Can I help you?"

"Is Celia here?"

"No. Are you one of her friends?"

"From school. I'm Bruno."

"You're Bruno? She's told me about you. She says you are quite extraordinary."

"She does?"

"I suppose I shouldn't be surprised. Everything in Celia's life is extraordinary, it seems." The woman's eyes crinkled when she smiled.

"Is this your bookstore?"

"It is. I'm Lippa."

"I've never been here before," Bruno said.

"Well, I've been waiting," the woman said. He looked at

her curiously. "That was a joke, my dear," she said, laughing. Bruno blushed.

The front door opened, and Lippa and Bruno turned to find Alice and Gertrude coming in.

"Bruno! What a lovely surprise!" Alice said.

"You know each other!" Lippa was delighted.

"Bruno is our neighbor." Alice beamed at him.

"It's so good to see you up and about again," Gertrude said. "He was sick for nearly a month," she explained to Lippa, then turned to Bruno. "You are not old enough to be all consumptive and bedridden." He nodded, wondering what *consumptive* meant.

"Have you been here before?" Alice asked, and Bruno shook his head. "You have found the best bookstore for miles around. Lippa is a peach."

"You flatter me." Lippa feigned modesty.

"And I do it with pleasure," Alice said.

Lippa changed the subject. "Bruno knows Celia."

"You do?" Gertrude said, "Of course, you go to Suburban, too! She is just a doll. So smart, so stylish, and *so* creative. Have you seen her drawings?"

"I have," Bruno said. "They are amazing."

"I'm sorry she isn't here," Lippa said.

"Well, I'll come back another time."

"Please do! It was so nice to meet you." Lippa pressed his hand.

Bruno was heading for the door when someone called his name. He turned to find Van standing by a table of books, looking completely out of his element and wearing a strange expression. "Van?"

"You feeling better?" Van asked.

"Yeah. What are you doing here?"

"Someone told me I should avoid this place, so I thought there might be some answers here." Van wasn't as imposing as Bruno remembered. "Hey, I'm sorry for being a jerk before. I tend to overreact to things."

"It's okay, I—"

"Are you an Ambassador?" Van blurted out.

"What? Am I a . . . what?"

It was as though Van's question had opened a floodgate in him. "I just can't figure out what happened, and it's the only thing that makes sense. Are you? An Ambassador?"

"No!" Bruno glanced around the bookstore. Over by the counter, Lippa, Alice, and Gertrude were staring oddly at them. "Come outside." He pushed Van out the door and around the corner. When they were alone on a dimly lit patch of sidewalk, Bruno said, "What are you talking about?"

Van wasn't dissuaded. "I lost my power, and all I know is that my admonition told me to beware an Ambassador. I have no idea who or what that is, but you're the only other powerful person I know, except . . . So if you took my powers, it means you're an Ambassador. Are you?"

"I am not an Ambassador. And you have to be careful— people could overhear you!"

"Why should I care? I've lost all my powers! What difference does it make?"

"Are you Unkind? Were you Unkind?"

"I *was*. I had just gotten started, and now it's over. Why did you do it?" Van seemed to be torn between fearing Bruno and wanting to beat him up again.

"I didn't do anything! I don't know what you're talking about."

"Well, you must be something. Are you Kind, then?"

"Yes, I'm Kind. And please, keep your voice down."

"You didn't draw me out? My admonition said to beware the Ambassador who would draw me out."

"Oh . . . no, I didn't draw you out. Listen, I'm sorry you lost your powers, but did you really want to be Unkind anyway? Would you really want to do worse and worse things, and get worse and worse, yourself?"

Van looked at the ground. "It changes you, being Unkind. It's like it shuts off parts of you, and then intimidating people was pretty much all I did. I could touch people and they'd lose their sense of purpose, like I'd just sucked the happy out of them. And it was awesome. Now, I don't know why I felt that way."

"You were doing that?"

"Yeah, and I should have realized there was something up with you earlier, because you didn't get all depressed when I punched you. That should have put you out of commission."

"How much do you know about all this?"

"Not a lot. I just started being Unkind at the beginning of the school year. How much do *you* know?"

"That's none of your business. Who got you started?"

"You really don't know? Right there at Suburban, and you have no idea."

"You have to tell me."

"Why should I? You're not the only one with powers."

"But *your* powers are gone, and while I didn't do it, there are things I *can* do."

"If I tell you, will you protect me?" Bruno nodded, hoping he wasn't promising something he couldn't deliver. "I can't be-lieve you really don't know. It's—"

Suddenly Van was gone, sucked up in the air as though pulled by a bungee cord. Bruno jumped back and heard Van yell in alarm. Bruno looked up to see where he had gone.

Van was suspended a few stories up, his head down and body limp. Next to him, a figure stood on thin air, holding Van by his shirt collar. Bruno gaped up at the two of them, but against the night sky he could make out only a silhouette of dark trousers, a dark cloak, and a head of Medusa-like wavy hair that hovered in tentacles around a shadowy face.

In that moment it became clear to Bruno that there was a lot more at stake than he had realized.

Then the cloaked figure shot up higher into the sky with Van in tow, disappearing like a comet. Bruno took off running across the street and down the alley, then crashed through the bushes.

"What happened?" Gardner asked.

"Who was that? The thing in the sky who took Van?"

"What are you talking about?"

"I have to go to Celia's house," Bruno said. "Which way?"

"There." Gardner pointed, staring at him.

Bruno ran through Celia's backyard and around to the front of her house. He rang the bell, and after a moment Mrs. Balaustine opened the door. "Bruno! How are you?"

"Hi, Mrs. Balaustine. Is Celia home?"

"Sure, would you like to come in?"

"Could I wait here?"

She looked at him oddly. "Sure." She turned to the stairs and called for Celia. "You're sure you don't want to step inside? It's cold out there."

"No, thank you."

Celia grabbed a coat and came out onto the front porch, closing the door behind her. "What is it?"

"The figure you told me about—the one who was there the night you fought the chemistry teacher? I just saw it!"

"What? Where?" Celia took Bruno's arm and pulled him farther away from the house.

"I was at the bookstore, and Van was there—"

"You were at Lippa's?"

"I . . . wanted to see where you worked. And to tell you I'm not interested in Gwendolyn."

"Okay . . . And Van was there?"

"He was, and he asked me if I was an Ambassador. He told me his admonition said an Ambassador would draw him out. When you drew him you stripped him of his powers!"

"Oh!"

"But he thought *I* was the Ambassador because he followed me up those hidden stairs, so he knew I had some kind of powers. He never realized you had anything to do with it. He just started being Unkind at the beginning of the school year. But there's *another* Unkind at Suburban, too!" Celia inhaled sharply. "He was just about to tell me who it was when he got sucked up off the sidewalk! When I looked up there was this other person holding him there, standing in the middle of the air. And then they just shot up into the sky like a rocket!"

"That's what happened last year in my backyard!" They both looked up nervously, and Bruno imagined Celia standing behind the house last year, watching the sky while a human spaceship flew away.

"What happened to Van?"

"I don't know! He's gone. He was the one making kids depressed — he could do it just by touching them."

"Whoever that figure is, I think he wants to make sure we don't find out about him. Was it a man or a woman?" Bruno shrugged. "Mr. Sumeletso was going to tell me something on the night I fought him off, but that figure prevented him from saying anything. Whatever Van was going to tell you, that person didn't want you to hear it."

"What do we do now?"

"I don't know. I don't think we're in danger. If whoever it is wanted to hurt us, wanted anything from us, it would have happened." Celia was quiet for a moment. "So you went to the bookstore to tell me you're not interested in Gwendolyn?"

"It just seemed like everyone assumed—"

"Bruno, we were just giving you a hard time. Why *don't* you ask her out?"

"I don't like her like that."

"She likes you, though — you realize that, don't you?" Celia saw his discomfort. "That's okay. It's hard when you realize someone likes you, and that person is really nice, and someone you really like . . . but you just don't feel the same way. It's a helpless feeling," Celia said carefully. They looked at each other for a moment.

"Well, I just wanted you to know," he said.

"I believe you." She smiled sadly. "I do think you should go out with someone, though. It doesn't have to be anything serious. Ask someone to a dance."

"It's okay. I don't think that's a good idea."

"I just remember, last year, I was so hung up on someone, I didn't date anyone all year, because I was hoping . . ."

"What happened?"

"Well, we started dating." She reddened. "Bruno, I know you like me."

"No, I don't."

"You're just saying that because you're a good guy and you have too much integrity to pursue someone who's in a relationship. And that makes me like you more," she said.

"I should go."

"Bruno . . ." she said, but he ignored her and went back around her house to the Ebentwine clearing.

"Did she help you?" Gardner asked.

"It doesn't matter," Bruno said, not slowing down.

"What happened?"

"It doesn't matter."

"Suit yourself. I'm on your side, you know. I want to see you get what you want."

Bruno stopped and turned back to him. "I'm not sure I believe you."

"You don't have to. You've fulfilled your admonition, and soon enough your power will grow. Who knows, maybe you don't need my help at all. You're getting stronger by yourself. They say becoming one of the Kind is a lonely thing. But you're never entirely alone, even if you feel you are. You can go it alone if you want, but I will always be here."

"I'm sorry. It's been a bad night."

"Nights always end."

AS IT HAPPENED, BRUNO almost wished his nights didn't end. Each morning brought school. Celia was kind, even tender to him, but on the first day back, he felt the boundaries separating them set in stone.

And Gwendolyn was there, staring hopefully at him. Rather than her usual colorful outfit, she wore a simple black dress. She appeared by his side with a flimsy excuse to talk to him. Later that day she hung back, seeming to hope he would be the one to close the distance between them. Every time he looked at her, she was looking at him.

Sylvio and Regine continued to find amusement in his love triangle. Knowing how each girl felt didn't make it any easier for Bruno, who couldn't think of how to change any of it.

"It's not like you're ever the bubbliest person, and believe me, I have no problem with that, but you look unhappy," Marco said to him as they walked down the hall in the middle of December.

"I guess I am," Bruno admitted.

"What's going on? I mean, I get that you don't like the one who likes you, and the one you like doesn't like you, but is that it?"

"That's a big part of it."

"Well, at least you know how the other two feel, right? Doesn't that help a little?"

"Not really," Bruno said. "Don't laugh at me."

"I'm not, I swear. I just want to give you a hug, is all. You look so forlorn!" Marco pulled Bruno into a headlock. Bruno struggled a little, but he liked knowing exactly where he stood with Marco.

Much to Bruno's surprise, Van was back in school. He had figured Van had met some kind of terrible end at the hands of his powerful abductor. He had envisioned him being dropped over a rock quarry from half a mile up. It had been a horrible feeling.

Instead, he was back, behaving exactly like the brutish jock everyone expected, though now he seemed to have lost interest in Bruno completely. What Celia had started with Van's memory, the figure in the sky had completed.

What to make of it all? With everything that had happened, Bruno knew only a little more than he had before. He had fulfilled his admonition and could expect new powers on New Year's Eve. Suburban had been freed from the threat of one Unkind—by either a powerful Kind who had stepped in to help or a powerful Unkind who wanted to protect the secrets Van was going to reveal. Meanwhile, the presence of the Ebentwine in the back of the library and its debilitating effects meant plenty of dangers remained.

Ms. Moreletii had made another play to get Bruno out of her class, since he hadn't had the software to do any of the assignments during his extended absence. She had gone as far as to notify the office that he had dropped the class, and it had taken a phone call from his father to have him readmitted. Bruno wasn't even that interested in website design, but he wasn't about to let someone bully him out of a race before he was done running it.

Mr. Williams welcomed Bruno back with an assignment to reproduce the plans of the Hoover Dam, thinking its balance between geography and engineering would interest Bruno. But Bruno was more interested in the drawings in the Piranesi book. He pored over it at home. The spaces in the drawings were so real—even the imaginary ones—they had personalities. Bruno wanted to visit a space like that, not a dam.

"IT'S CELIA."

Bruno took the phone from Sylvio, ignoring his mocking expression, and returned to his bedroom, where he closed the door.

"Hello?"

"Are you busy? Can you come over?"

"Now? Um, sure."

"The backyard?"

"I'll be there in three minutes."

Making sure no one was watching, Bruno went through the grassy alley and into the Ebentwine.

"Evening," Gardner greeted him. "Celia's?" Bruno nodded and went on his way.

"That is an awesome power," Celia said when he arrived. Then she got right to the point. "When you went to the bookstore, the night you saw Van there, you went inside, right?"

"Yes."

"And you met Lippa, and Alice and Gertrude?"

"Yes. Well, Alice and Gertrude are my neighbors, but I didn't know they knew Lippa. Or you."

"And Van was inside the bookstore?"

"Yes. Then we went outside to talk."

"What did Van say to you while you were still inside?"

"He asked me if I was an Ambassador. I told him to keep it down, and we went outside."

"Well, apparently he wasn't quiet enough. The women heard him."

"Oh. Did they tell you that?"

"Lippa did. She definitely heard him say *Ambassador*."

"So what, does she think I'm a diplomat or something?"

"I need to explain the Troika to you," Celia said. "Lippa, Alice, and Gertrude. They call themselves the Troika, and they are Kind and Unkind conspiracy theorists. They love the myths and urban legends. Most of the monster legends—vampires, werewolves, ghosts—grew out of someone getting a confusing glimpse of the Kind or Unkind. Someone witnesses a member of the Kind who has the ability to communicate with wolves, then next thing you know, the werewolf legend is started. That sort of thing.

"The Troika can't get enough of these stories, and they're always on the lookout for new information. They're particularly interested in the Unkind, but I think that's because monsters are usually bad, so most of the stories skew to the Unkind side. They've heard about Ambassadors, and they actually have a pretty good understanding of what that is—a person who is neither a citizen nor a Kind but who has one foot in both worlds. They don't suspect I'm one—at least, I don't think they do. Last year, when I didn't understand what was going on and my life was in danger, I actually tried to tell Lippa I thought I was Kind, but fortunately she thought I was an impressionable teenager who had heard too many of her stories.

"But whatever Van said—whatever they thought he said —it definitely got their attention. When I went to work tonight, Lippa interrogated me about you. And she remembered all the things I had told her last spring. I had to play dumb; I told them I didn't know you very well at all."

"Wow," Bruno said. "So this is bad."

"I'm not sure how bad it is. Those ladies are complete sweethearts, and they definitely prefer to read about their conspiracy theories in books and online, rather than going out in the real world where there might be real danger. I just wanted you to know, so the next time you're in the bookstore you'll understand if they ask you any questions. And you'll know how to answer them."

"Got it. I'm sorry—I had no idea."

"No, it's fine. Just wanted to let you know."

"I took him outside the moment he started talking."

"It's okay. How could you have known? I have to get back inside. I'll see you tomorrow, okay?"

"Sure. Good night." Bruno watched her go inside, then pushed through the hedge. The Ebentwine clearing always disarmed him. It was tranquil, its flower beds and fountain untroubled by the outside world, its light seeming to arrive from a different sun, different stars.

"Have you ever just put yourself out there, told her how you feel?" Gardner asked him.

"I didn't have to. She knows."

"I just think if you want her, you should fight for her."

"You mean fight Tomasi for her? Have you seen him? Anyway, I told you I'm not going to do that."

"But where does that leave you? Alone."

"I'm okay with that. I can sleep at night. Why do you even care?"

Gardner said nothing, and Bruno stormed off to his house.

faît accompli

ON THE LAST DAY of school before winter break, Bruno read Marco's acceptance letter from Metropolitan. Regine had been accepted, too. "I remember this day last year," Marco said. "I was miserable because it was the first time it really sank in that Brenden and I were going to be separated. Celia had to mop me up in the library."

"Well, it's awesome. Congratulations!" Bruno said.

"Thanks! It is kind of a bummer, since we've just become friends, and it's not like you'll be following me next year. I hope we'll stay in touch," Marco said seriously.

"I hope so, too. I still need advice on what to wear," Bruno said.

"No, you don't!" Marco laughed. "You figured that out very quickly. But you may get a new shirt in the mail now and then."

"When you're famous, I'll have the second-best collection of your clothes after Brenden," Bruno said. "You still haven't made anything to sell at Chris and Cosey's. Why won't you?"

"I know . . . There's just something so real about putting a price tag on something I've made. I've never had to deal with rejection."

"Maybe it would be good to try it before you get to college," Bruno said. "I really think you should."

"You're right. I will. I *will*!" Marco laughed at Bruno's incredulous look.

Later, Bruno and Celia went to the cafeteria instead of the library during their free period. "It's strange being down here," she said. "I wonder where Regine and Silver are. Are you excited about the power you're going to gain on New Year's Eve?"

"I guess so. It's like knowing you're going to receive an awesome present, but not having a clue what it will be."

"I'm sure it will be good. I guess you'll know by the time of the party at Ivo and Liz's. You have to tell me as soon as you figure it out! Is that the librarian?" Celia looked over Bruno's shoulder. "I've never seen her down here before." Lois headed their way. "She's looking for you, isn't she?" Celia said.

Sure enough, Lois stopped at their table. "Hi, Bruno. Hi, Celia. I'm sorry to bother you, but I'm hoping Bruno can come back with me to the library. There's a problem." Lois gave Celia an uncomfortable sidelong glance.

"What's wrong?" Bruno asked, gathering up his things.

"Someone is . . . lost."

"Lost? In the library?"

"Would you mind coming?" Lois looked pointedly at Bruno.

Celia gave him an encouraging look, and he told her, "I don't know if I'll be back right away."

"That's okay. Good luck."

As they walked away, Lois said quietly, "A girl is lost in the stacks. I can hear her, but she can't figure out how to get out, and I can't get to her. You're the only person I could think of."

"That's crazy."

"Bruno?" He turned back and saw Celia following them. He met her halfway.

"Put this on," she said, removing the chain with the amulet from her neck. "It was Mariette's. She made it to ward off evil."

"Thank you." Bruno ducked his head to let her reach around his neck with the chain.

"She knows about you, doesn't she?" Celia's soft voice, her head near his, her arms around his neck, almost made Bruno swoon. He held his breath. "She's one of the Kind." She studied Bruno's face while he tried to come up with something to say. "You don't have to tell me anything. Just be careful, okay?"

"She thinks Ambassadors take power from the Kind. She wouldn't let me tell you."

"She what?"

"I know it's not true. I just haven't been able to convince her."

"It's okay. We'll deal with that later." Celia stepped back, and Bruno reluctantly returned to Lois, putting the chain inside his sweater.

"What are you wearing?" Lois asked.

"It's a charm Mariette made last year. Celia thought it might help me."

"That's very sweet."

"She really is an Ambassador. I'm sure of it. When I was sick, she healed me by drawing me."

Lois didn't say anything. When they got to the library, she locked the door behind them. "She's over here. Hopefully she hasn't gone farther in." Bruno followed Lois to the stacks, nervous about entering them again. Lois called, "Gwendolyn, can you hear me?"

"It's Gwendolyn?"

He heard her voice from what sounded like a few aisles back. "I'm here! How do I get out?"

"Stay where you are," Lois called. "I have someone here who can help. He's going to come get you." She looked expectantly at Bruno.

He went into the stacks, heading in the direction of Gwendolyn's voice, but this time he had no doubt: The configuration of shelves had changed. He kept calling to her, and she responded, but the closest he could get was the opposite side of a row. On either side, the shelves turned at right angles, with no opening to the area where Gwendolyn stood.

He pulled a handful of books off the shelf at eye level, and on her side she did the same. "Bruno!"

"Hey. If we cleared off a shelf, could you fit through?" he asked.

"I don't think so." They sized up the gap between the shelves, which couldn't have been more than ten inches.

"I'll be right back," Bruno said, and returned to the reading area. "I wish we still had the *You Are Here* book," he told Lois. "Those maps would really come in handy."

"Do you think there's any point in checking my office again?" They went to look. "Wait—what is that? Did something fall behind the shelf?" Lois crouched down and pulled some books out. "How did that get back there?"

Bruno got down beside her. "It looks like it."

"Let's get it out." They stood up, and Bruno pressed his side against the bookshelf, intending to push it away from the wall. Lois put her hand on his shoulder. "Let me." He stood back, confused. Then the volume was sliding up the wall behind the books, rising from behind the shelf. It was covered in dust motes, but a small cyclone whisked them away from the book and carried them in a funnel-shaped cloud into the wastebasket.

"*You Are Here,*" he read when Lois floated the book into his hands. "It would be great if there's a chapter called 'Where She Is.'" He opened the first page and found the expected illustration of his head, seen from the ceiling. Lois's head was next to his, with the office furniture behind them. He turned the pages. The rest of the book contained the same floor plan of Suburban High School, over and over.

Lois pointed to a small but unmistakable skull, the only bit of ink that didn't represent an architectural detail. "That's what I saw before," Lois said.

"That's the technology wing."

"What does that mean?"

"I have no idea." Another mystery to be solved, but for now, Gwendolyn was waiting. He went back into the stacks and turned to the first page. Now the illustration showed the aisles where they both stood, with Gwendolyn's head on one side and Bruno's on the other. But the detail wasn't large enough to show a path to her. Bruno remembered the larger detail drawing that was the first thing he had found in the volume, before it directed him back to the first page. He flipped carefully through the pages of maps and skulls and was relieved to find the larger detail drawing that showed the map of the library.

"Are you coming?" Gwendolyn called.

"I'm on my way!" He went to the main aisle, heading deeper into the library, doing his best to ignore the nervous rocks in his stomach. He kept looking in the corners of his vision, but so far there were no flickering sparks, and he didn't feel any of the side effects of the Ebentwine. He followed the maze of shelves on the page, navigating the aisles to find Gwendolyn. A few times he closed and reopened the book to update his place on the page, but eventually he just kept his finger on the page, moving it through the drawing to keep track of where he was walking.

It felt like longer, but in a few minutes Bruno turned a corner and found Gwendolyn sitting on the floor. Her gray skirt flared around her legs, and she hugged herself across the front of her black twinset. "You found me!" She scrambled up and ran to him, her hug pinning his arms to his side. "How did you find me? How do we get out?"

"It's this way. What were you doing?"

"I was looking for some books to take home for the break. I swear I had only turned, like, two corners, but when I tried to go back, it wasn't the same. I must be crazy, but I swear the shelves moved."

"Don't worry about it," Bruno said. "It happens a lot." Now that he had navigated it, the way back wasn't all that complicated. He led her down another row and then turned into the main aisle. Gwendolyn shook her head at the sight of the reading area at the end.

"Why couldn't I do that?"

Lois was pacing by the tables. "There you are! This is insane." Gwendolyn sank into a chair. "I'm going to have to close the stacks, if people are going to get lost in there."

"I'm sorry!" Gwendolyn said.

"Oh, honey, it's not your fault. You didn't do anything wrong," Lois said comfortingly. "Are you late for a class? Do you need me to write you a note?" Gwendolyn nodded, and the two of them headed over to the desk.

"Am I crazy? It was like the shelves turned into a maze."

"It's a confusing place," Lois said brightly, and Bruno could read her mind. *Please don't ask questions I can't answer.*

He went to the table by his things and sat down, putting *You Are Here* to one side. He gave Gwendolyn his best reassuring smile. He could tell she wanted him to go with her, but when he didn't get up, she reluctantly left. Lois came and sat down across from him. "Were you disoriented again? I'm sorry I asked you to do that."

"No—I didn't have to go that far in. It was fine."

"What are we going to do?"

"I don't know."

"What do you think she'll say?"

"Probably not much. What could she say that wouldn't make her sound insane? 'I got lost in the library'?"

"I guess so." They sat in silence for a moment. "Celia knows about me, doesn't she?" Lois finally asked.

"She guessed. I didn't say anything. She's very observant."

"Well, I suppose it was bound to happen sooner or later. I just . . . don't know what to think. I wish there was some kind of user's manual for being Kind," Lois said in exasperation.

Bruno wasn't up for another discussion of Celia. "I should go to class, too."

Lois walked back to the counter where she had left her excuse pad. "Wait, the book—wasn't it just here? Where did it go now?"

They looked around, but the book was gone. "Are you really surprised?"

Lois gave a soft laugh that trailed off in a sigh.

On his way to class, Bruno stopped by his locker and remembered he was wearing Mariette's necklace. He wasn't sure what to do with it. Because Celia had fastened it around his neck herself, he wanted to continue wearing it. But it had been Mariette's, and he had no idea what power it possessed. He reached behind his neck, unclasped it, and set it carefully on the top shelf of his locker.

BRUNO RAN DOWNSTAIRS WHEN he heard his sister's voice. He had missed Sophia more than he realized. "Oh, you look so good!" She squeezed him, her long hair cold and fragrant with the familiar floral smell of her perfume. "You're all grown up!"

"I don't know . . ." Bruno looked down at the changes he knew Sophia was seeing, then back up to see the changes in his sister's face. Somewhere in Buenos Aires, she had crossed over from pretty to beautiful. She was admiring his clothes. Their parents had left them alone in the foyer

"Are you dressing like Sylvio now?" She took off her coat.

"Kind of. He told you about the kids we met at school?" She nodded. "I think he wishes he could have them to himself."

"He is a little possessive," she said. "Tell me everything. How is high school? Will you help me carry these up?"

Bruno hefted her larger suitcase. "It's good. It's harder. I like it."

"Do you see Sylvio a lot?"

"Yeah. We drive to school together. And the group studies together in the library, when we're free."

"Okay. Are you dating anyone? Girls? Boys?"

"Girls! But not really. There's someone I like, but she has a boyfriend."

"That sucks. I'm kind of in that place right now," Sophia said, looking around before she said in a stage whisper, *"Except he's married!"* She laughed at Bruno's shocked expression.

"I haven't *done* anything! It's just a crush." They set her things down in the guest room next to his room. "The house is really nice. Have you put anything in your room this time?"

"A couple things." Bruno grinned.

"So, what else?" She sat on the bed, and they smiled at each other the way they used to when their parents were out and she would let him stay up an extra fifteen minutes.

He wanted to tell her. More than that, he wanted to show her. It had been easy enough to keep his secrets from the rest of his family. But it was such a temptation, the thought of showing Sophia something that was all his own.

"We go to this club called Diaboliques," he said instead. "It's kind of like the one Sylvio used to go to, only bigger. They play all the music Sylvio likes. I like a lot of it, too."

"Nice! I haven't gone dancing like that in forever. I thought I would learn to tango, but so far that hasn't happened. I can't get over how good you look! I really missed you."

"Me too." Bruno was bothered now, thinking of all the things he wanted to share with her but couldn't. What was he supposed to say? *I'm Kind. I fulfilled my admonition, and in ten days I should receive new powers.*

"I should go be social. Mom and Dad asked a million questions in the car, and I'm sure they have a million more." Sophia pulled Bruno into another hug, and he hugged her back. "Let's go."

ON CHRISTMAS MORNING BRUNO sat in church with his family in their usual pew. Up in front, their father guided the congregation through the service, his voice as comforting as if he were reading them a bedtime story.

As usual, Bruno's thoughts slipped away. He fiddled with

the program while the pianist played a quiet meditation whose chords veered into dissonance, only to resolve even more beautifully on the other side. *Lux Aurumque*, he read, wondering what the Latin meant.

Bruno's father was fond of saying that when it came to understanding the world, science answered more and more questions every day, and whenever science could explain the world, it should be allowed to. "But there are things science will never be able to explain. And those instances, those unanswerable questions, are when religion is vital. After science has done everything it can, religion is what takes us the rest of the way—into the unknown, into the mysterious, into the sublime."

It made sense to Bruno, or at least it had, for a long time. Those questions that hung around the edge of his awareness and rattled him when he looked at them directly—*Why am I here? What is my purpose? What happens when I die?*—had always felt most manageable here, with a group of people around him also yearning for the answers.

And he supposed that still was true. But now there were new frightening questions, which seemed to have no place in this chapel. *What are these powers, these magic places I've found? Will they change me in ways I'll regret? Will the things I know about right and wrong, good and evil, that have gotten me this far, be enough to help me navigate this other world? I know what it means to believe in something I can't see or touch; what does it mean to see and touch things that are unbelievable? If I have to keep these things secret, does that mean they're bad, or wrong?*

Bruno looked at his father, who was seated now with his head down, his palms cupped one in the other in his lap, like a nest for his faith. What if his father was powerful, too? What if he was keeping amazing secrets from Bruno, only because he didn't realize Bruno knew them, also? Bruno glanced at his sister next to him, her head also down, one fist wrapped by her other hand. What if his sister was Kind? He had no reason to think she might be, other than that he loved her, and that made it easy to believe she was more spectacular than he ever could be.

THE FULL MOON ROSE. *It's not blue at all,* Bruno thought, though he knew there was no reason for it to be. All day he had been nervous. Over the past week he had pored over his admonition. Had he missed anything? Was there any chance he had misinterpreted something? Bruno couldn't remember anything in his life before this that felt so important, or that carried such a significant consequence. He didn't want to fail. He fully believed something incredible was about to happen. Somewhere between the paper clips flying around Lois's head and the way Cassandra had forecasted Gwendolyn with *The Stranger,* Bruno had let go of any doubt. But tonight was the ultimate proof. He had done everything he had been tasked to do, and tonight he would find out whether it had been worth it.

After ringing in the new year with his family, he stayed awake late into the night, scrutinizing every breath he inhaled and the smallest twinge or ache in his body. He studied his hands for any perceptible difference.

Nothing. Bruno wondered if he should go out into the Ebentwine clearing. Perhaps something was different there, and waiting for him to arrive. But the powers the others had seemed to be located in the people themselves, not in places outside them. Eventually he fell asleep, exhausted with disappointment.

THE NEXT NIGHT, BRUNO SAT on a sofa at the Fourads' home, Ivo and Liz's, after the First Night dinner. He watched Sylvio and Regine looking through another collage book she had made for him. On the other side of the room Marco and Brenden were trying not to kiss each other again in front of everyone; soon they sneaked out of the room. Celia was laughing with Liz. Ivo sat down next to Bruno on the couch.

"We barely got to talk at Halloween," Ivo said. "How was your first semester?"

"It was all right," Bruno said. "I don't think I'm as smart as you guys."

"Really? Celia says you're brilliant."

"She does?"

"She told us you're a human atlas, and about how the librarian depends on you to find books for her in her own library. That's pretty funny."

"I guess it is." Bruno grinned.

"Are you still in love with her?"

"I . . . I don't want to talk about it."

"Sorry." Ivo looked around the room. "I'm glad to see Regine has found someone. Last year was a little uncomfortable for me."

Bruno played dumb. "She liked you?"

"She did. It was difficult near the end, but we finally made peace with it, I think. She seems to have moved on, at least. Silver seems like a great match for her."

"I think so. How do you like college?"

"It's good. I'm still not sure if I want to be an architect, but

I have to say I love design. I love the ideas designers deal with. Every choice, the smallest detail, is important. Everything has meaning. Not just in a building—in every creative thing we do. In life."

Then Liz called to Ivo, and Celia came to take his place.

"You having a good time?" she asked him, and Bruno nodded. "I keep forgetting to ask you: Do you still have Mariette's necklace? I'd love to get it back."

"Oh! I left it at school!"

"That's okay! You put it in a safe place?"

"It's in my locker." As the others' conversations lulled, Bruno thought he heard a bell ring on the far side of the house. "What was that?"

"What?" she asked him.

"Did you hear a bell? It sounded like school."

"I didn't hear anything." Celia looked at him curiously.

Bruno looked toward the front hall and thought he heard the bell again, faintly, as though it were wrapped in cotton. He got up, and Celia followed him out into the hall. Bruno stopped by a door. "Is this a closet?"

"I think so." She pulled open the door. "Why?"

"I don't know." Bruno looked at the row of coats inside, confused. He had the oddest feeling Suburban High School was behind this closet, but he had no idea why. He reached through the coats to feel the wall behind them.

"What are you doing?" Celia asked.

"I feel like I'm supposed to go into the closet," he said.

"I thought you had to come out first," she said, then added, "That was a really stupid joke."

The feeling wouldn't go away. Bruno imagined what the Fourads' house would look like as an architectural drawing.

A pair of parallel lines would represent this hall, with a break on one side where the closet door was. The closet would be a small box alongside the hall, and a line with a row of hangers would represent the rod for the coats inside it. In his mind's eye Bruno saw another box, the same size as the closet, butting up against the back wall, with another door on the far side, and then another hallway that was larger and longer.

There was a pad of paper by the phone in the hallway. He took a mechanical pencil from the jar and drew what he had imagined. In a long rectangle he wrote *Fourad Hall,* and in the smaller adjacent box with a door he wrote *Closet.* On the back side of the box he drew another box with a door on the far side, and wrote *Janitor's Closet* in it. Then he drew another rectangle onto which the second closet opened, and labeled it *Suburban High School First Year Hall.* Celia watched. Bruno turned the pencil over and erased the line that separated the back walls of the two closets. Then he turned back to the real closet in the Fourad hallway.

He opened the door and reached through the coats again. Instead of a wall, this time his hand found a wooden stick. Bruno pushed his body through the coats and kicked something on the floor. He felt around and grasped something that felt like a broom handle. No, it was a mop. The bucket in which it rested rolled back and bumped his foot. Bruno let go of the mop and stepped carefully around the bucket. He found another door handle and pushed open the door, which opened out into a dark hallway. At the far ends exit signs glowed. He was in the first year hall at Suburban.

He crossed the hall to his locker, opened it, and retrieved Mariette's necklace from the shelf. Then he returned to the janitor's closet, pulling the door closed behind him, stepping around the mop bucket, passing through the coats, and re-emerging in the Fourads' front hall. Celia was still there, her eyes wide. He handed her the necklace.

"Did you just . . ." she said, gaping.

Bruno nodded. "I just made my own liminal." He said it as much to hear it himself.

"That's amazing! Is that your new power?" Bruno shrugged, but he couldn't help smiling. Celia kept looking at him while she put the necklace on. She squeezed his arm and whispered, "Congratulations!"

"We'd better go back," Bruno said.

In the living room, Regine was saying, "I was hoping you guys would want to make Silver an official member of the Rosary."

"If that's the case, then I nominate Bruno, too," Marco said. "He's as much a part of our group as Silver is." They all looked up at Bruno and Celia.

Regine exhaled. "Fine. I mean, you've had the chance to get to know them, and they do all the things with us that we used to do last year. We ride together in the mornings. We go to Diaboliques every week."

There was a long silence, and finally Ivo said, "I don't know." He looked from Sylvio to Bruno. "I like you guys a lot, and I'm really glad you've become friends with Regine and Marco and Celia. It's great that you're all keeping up the things we did. But I'm just not sure what the point is. I mean, at the end of this year Regine and Marco will graduate, and then they'll be at Metropolitan with us—all the founding members will be at Metropolitan. So do we say that the Rosary has moved to

Metropolitan then, or do we leave it behind at Suburban, and count on the younger members to keep it alive?"

"Or do we think of it as something that lasted three years, and is just . . . finished?" Brenden said. "I'm not trying to be mean, either. I really like you guys, too. But I kind of feel like the Rosary was certain people in a certain place at a certain time. If you change any of those things, I'm not sure it's the same."

He looked at Liz. "Listen," she said, exasperated. "The Rosary never felt like a *club* to me—something to which people applied for membership. It was just the name we gave ourselves because it amused us. When we met Celia, I don't remember us talking about it—it just happened, and we were all there, so it didn't feel like an event. This feels different. It feels forced. I kind of agree with Brenden that the Rosary is over. Maybe next year when Regine and Marco get to college, we'll call ourselves that again. But my hunch is we won't. Brenden's right: It has to do with Suburban as much as the group of us."

"Should we take a vote?" Regine asked.

"That definitely makes it sound like a club," Ivo said. "Is there going to be a secret password next?"

"I don't know if this makes a difference," Celia said. "But I haven't felt like the Rosary is at Suburban this year. I love what we're doing now, but we're doing it as a different group of people. It's just different."

"So should we have a different name, then?" Regine asked her.

"Why do we need a name? Isn't it enough that we're friends who like a lot of the same things, and do things together?"

Regine turned to Sylvio. "I'm sorry. This is definitely not how I thought this was going to go."

"It's okay. I understand," Sylvio said. To Bruno it was obvious his brother did not understand at all.

"I BET YOU'RE THE ONLY one who spends any time back here," Sophia said as they picked their way through the snowy alley and up the stone steps to the tennis court where drifts leaned into the sagging net and nearby the picnic table wore a white muff. They had gone out for a walk in the late afternoon, wanting just a little more time together before Sophia got back on a plane to Argentina.

"There's not enough grass to mow back here," Bruno said. "But I like it."

"You seem, I don't know—you seem more *alive*. I don't know how to describe it." Sophia looked at him in the winter light.

"I feel it," Bruno said, happy she'd noticed more changes in him than his clothes.

"What do you think it is?"

"I feel like I've learned a lot, these past months. I feel, I don't know . . . bigger."

"That's true. Learning expands you. Well, whatever it is, it looks good on you!"

The cold drove them back toward the house, but in the snowy alley Bruno turned away from the garage, toward the copse of trees, beyond which lay Ebentwine. *What if I don't tell her? What if we just stumble across it, the way I did the first time?* He supposed Gardner would be there, ready to take him to task for bringing a citizen to Ebentwine. But by then it would be too late—Sophia would have seen, and he would get to share it with her.

"Where are you going?" She had stopped behind him.

"I don't know. I've always wondered what's back there."

"And you want to find out now, in a foot of snow?" She laughed. "You haven't changed at all in some ways, have you?" But he heard her feet crunching the snow as she followed him.

He picked his way under the first trees, releasing small avalanches from the branches that clung to his hair and coat. It wasn't far; only five or six more steps and they would emerge in the clearing, pristine in the snow, the fountain likely reduced to a trickle over an ice-filled basin. Bruno's heart thumped. He was being reckless, and he didn't care.

"There's nothing back here, crazy!" Sophia called good-naturedly.

"I just want to look a little farther." Bruno said it as much to himself. He knew he would have arrived at Ebentwine by now if he had been alone. It was gone and he knew why: There was no place for citizens in Ebentwine. But he stubbornly pushed on until he tripped on a border stone and toppled into the back-yard of Alice and Gertrude.

"Are you okay?"

"Yeah." He struggled up and looked at the snowy gazebo before he turned back to his sister. "I guess I shouldn't be sur-prised it goes to the neighboring yard."

"Where did you think it would go—Narnia?" she asked, smiling. "C'mon, let's go inside."

IF I WERE BAD, WHAT *would I do?* Bruno opened his computer and searched for the world's biggest bank. Then he took a piece of paper, drew a large box, and labeled it *Bruno's Room.* Next, a smaller adjoining box he designated as his closet. Adjoining the back wall of his closet, Bruno drew a second small box, which he labeled *Vault*, and then a larger box on the far side, in which he wrote *BNP Paribas*.

Is this the type of thing that would turn me Unkind? Bruno figured if he had to ask, he knew the answer. He crumpled up the paper and threw it away.

What about someplace just to look? Bruno was itching to use his powers again. The discovery at the Fourads' had happened so quickly, he almost wondered whether it really *had* happened. He didn't want to go back to Suburban, though. There must be something more exciting to do.

He took another piece of paper and redrew his room and his closet, then added a small box against the back of the closet. This time Bruno wrote *Coatroom* in it, and *Louvre* on the far side. Then he broke the line from closet to coatroom.

"I'm just going to look," he said softly, opening his closet door.

Bruno pushed through his clothes and felt a tangle of empty metal hangers, some of which clattered to the floor. He stepped through them and caught a whiff of new air. *Is this what France smells like?* The coatroom was larger than he expected, and almost completely dark. He saw a faint light from a long window with a countertop on the far side of the room and made his way toward it.

He stopped for a moment, wondering what time it was. He hadn't thought about how many hours' difference it was between France and the United States. Just because it was night at his house didn't mean it was still night in Paris. But everything was quiet and still, so he figured it must be early morning. It would have been bad if he had shown up after the museum staff arrived.

As Bruno reached the counter, a beam of light swept across the far wall of the hallway outside the coatroom. *"Qui est là?"* a voice said, and without knowing what that meant, Bruno could tell the man who had said it was afraid.

Before Bruno could react, the man came into view and swung the flashlight directly into Bruno's eyes. Then there was yelling from both of them, and Bruno was charging back through the coatroom, knocking more hangers to the floor on the way back to his closet.

He closed the door behind him, returned to his desk, and redrew the line to close the French connection. Then he tried to stop grinning.

Fifteen minutes later, Bruno took his pencil and started over once again. Large box, small box, small box, large. This time Bruno wrote *Celia's Bedroom* in the larger box.

He knew nothing good could possibly come of it. It was bad enough that he had lurked in her backyard, hoping to see her in her bedroom window, and never told her. He would not do this. He would rob a bank before he did this.

Bruno went to his closet door and put his hand on the knob, then stood, unmoving, for a minute. His body felt light, ready to flee again. He imagined the darkness behind the door, the press of his clothes against his face, then the press of her clothes. What if she opened her closet door and caught him there? What if she was undressed? What if she wasn't alone?

He turned the knob, knowing it was wrong.

He opened the door just a crack. Nothing but blackness in the small space, and the faint sound of music. Bruno pushed his head into the closet, pulling the door as far closed as he could, as if that would somehow prevent the rest of his body from following. And there it was: the mysterious song he hadn't heard since before school. Bruno stepped into the closet and pulled the door closed behind him.

Her closet door must have been ajar; he could see a sliver of light beyond the bar filled with his clothes. He didn't need to go any farther; he could hear the song well enough now, and the lyrics felt like the sound track of his life.

Bruno retreated. Closing his closet door, he returned to his desk and tore up the map to Celia's bedroom. He went to his computer, and in a moment he had the answer: "Song to the Siren." The first version he found was sung by a man, but soon enough he found This Mortal Coil. A mystery he had stopped trying to solve was suddenly laid bare, and it stirred up the ache in him. He wondered if he was any better off now.

14

a time for fear (who's afraid?)

O N THE FIRST DAY back to school after the break, Bruno considered the janitor's closet across from his locker with new eyes. He hadn't tried his new power again since the night he had gone to Paris and Celia's bedroom closet. But he had thought about it plenty. He supposed he would never have to pay for a plane ticket if he traveled alone. But for now, his powers seemed best suited to stealing, or violating someone's privacy. What was he supposed to make of that? Was this strange new universe of the Kind trying to turn him into a jewel thief, or a spy? He closed his locker and looked down the hall as the rest of the students filtered into their homerooms.

Mariette stood at the far end, where the science wing adjoined the first year hall. She was looking at him, but like always, she was far enough away that he couldn't see her face clearly. She held up a piece of paper, and he thought she was beckoning to him. The bell rang, and Bruno crossed the hall to his homeroom.

Later that morning Bruno stopped by the library. Over the break Lois had had a gate installed at the mouth of the main aisle into the stacks. It wasn't really going to stop anyone; it was only four feet high, with a gap underneath like a saloon door, on a hinge with a spring so it swung back into place. There was no lock on it, but a sign read ONLY LIBRARY STAFF PAST THIS POINT. "I didn't know what else to do," she told him. "It's not like I can wall it off, but at least this way if someone else gets lost, I can say, 'I told you so.'"

"I think it's good," he said.

In her office, she said, "First, I should tell you that I haven't been able to find *You Are Here* again; it really did disappear."

"I thought so."

"I spent some time over the break going through some old books I have, which include some legends about the Kind. I never really took them very seriously; most of them are compendia of weird tales written back in the fifties and sixties, and the chapters on the Kind are next to stories about sea monsters and ectoplasm, so it's hard to tell how reliable the information is. But there are a few bits about Ambassadors. They receive only limited power themselves, but they make it easier for the Kind to coexist with everyone else, partially by keeping their secrets and partially by making connections that members of the Kind may not perceive themselves."

"Yes, exactly. Celia's done that for me," Bruno said.

"And Ambassadors are harbingers—they can glimpse the future and give the Kind vital information that helps them with their admonitions. Has Celia ever done that?"

Bruno thought of Cassandra, who demonstrated that power almost every time she opened her mouth. "I don't know. She hasn't for me."

"And, if the Kind become too involved with an Ambassador, the Ambassador may drain their power away. Wait"— Lois saw Bruno's irritation—"hear me out. Last year Celia was best friends with a girl who was Kind, and that girl died under mysterious circumstances. Celia says an Unkind killed her, but no one else was there. Do you understand why I'm concerned?"

"What about Tomasi? He trusts her."

"Not everyone obeys the rules. Bruno, I'm trying to look at this fairly. I don't want to just open the floodgates and risk making myself vulnerable to someone who, as well intentioned as she may be, might hurt me, or hurt someone I care about."

"But her drawing stripped Van of his memory *and* his powers. And her drawing healed me!"

"It seems like they did, doesn't it?"

"Would you just talk to her, please? She's done so much for me—more than you have!" Bruno stopped when he noticed Lois's eyes had grown watery. "What's wrong?"

"It's just, everything that's happening at Suburban—finding out there are other Kind and Unkind here, and something so severe happened last year that a student was killed . . . that the Ebentwine seems to have removed the back wall of the library, and is messing with my head and now everyone else's—it all makes me pretty sure something big is happening here. Something much bigger than anything I've ever known. And honestly, it scares the hell out of me. And if that figure, the one who abducted Van, shows up here, there'll be no doubt."

"I think you're right," Bruno said gently. "But we're here to *do* something about it. We have to be ready for it, whatever it is. Celia can help us."

"I've been looking for another job," Lois said. "I'm sorry. I just don't think I'm cut out for this."

"What? You're leaving?"

"I haven't found anything yet. But you need someone braver than I am. Someone stronger."

"If you leave, it's not like the next librarian is guaranteed to be Kind, too! Do you think they'll interview candidates about their library science degrees and oh, by the way, are you Kind, and have you ever dealt with Unkind and Ambassadors?" Bruno knew he was being harsh. He couldn't tell whether he felt more betrayed by Lois or sad for her.

"I know! I didn't want to tell you because I knew you'd be angry. But I'm in over my head here."

"You think I'm not?"

"I'm sorry . . . Can we just leave things as they are for the moment? I need to think about all this."

"Okay."

He lagged in the hall on his way to class, trying to come up with anything that might make it easier for Lois. He'd probably taught her more than he'd learned from her, but he didn't want to see her go. Bruno turned a corner and found Gwendolyn, acting as if she hadn't been waiting there for him. It was no longer a surprise to see her dressed all in black, a black ribbon on her ponytail. "Hi, Bruno! Where are you headed?" He almost wished she would go back to looking lost all the time.

AT LUNCH CELIA ASKED, "How do you like your new powers? Have you used them again?"

Bruno thought of the song floating to him through her bedroom closet. "I haven't figured out how to use them in a useful way."

"I guess so. You have to be on the lookout for your next admonition, too. You haven't received it yet?"

"No."

"It can come anywhere, at any time. I don't think you'll have to wait too long; the moment you get new powers, the process starts all over. I'm concerned about that mysterious floating person again. Something bad is happening, and we have to stop it. I mean, I don't know who else could."

"How do we do that?"

"I have no idea. The worst part is, Van probably knew all kinds of things that could have helped us, but between me erasing his memory of you and then whoever-it-is erasing the rest of it, there's no way he could help us now, even if we convinced him he should."

"Probably," Bruno agreed.

"Tell me everything he told you."

"He said he was new to being Unkind. He had just found out about all of it at the beginning of the school year, like I did. And he said there's someone else at Suburban, another Unkind who was helping him, the way you and Lois have been helping me."

"So we have an Unkind hiding at Suburban, and you've seen a map with a skull in the technology wing," Celia said. "I can't help but feel like those two things are connected."

"I thought the skull meant someone was going to die there. You think someone in the technology wing is the killer?"

"I don't know. But I would like to figure it out before it's too late," Celia said. The bell rang. "If you think of anything, let me know."

THE NEXT MORNING IN THE parking lot, Bruno was saying hello to Celia and Marco when Regine brushed by. She locked eyes with Bruno for a second and spat out, "What's wrong with your brother?" Then she stalked off toward the building, not waiting for anyone to follow her.

"Sorry?" Bruno asked, but she didn't turn back.

"What's going on?" Marco asked. "I could tell something was wrong in the car."

"I asked her before we got to your house," Celia added. "But she didn't want to talk."

"Do you know—" Marco started to ask Bruno, but then Sylvio was rushing away, too, and Marco put the pieces together. "Oh, God—they broke up."

"I bet you're right." Celia watched Sylvio go. "He didn't say anything to you?" she asked Bruno.

"No, but I think it happened last night. I heard him on the phone, and it sounded like a fight."

"Great." Marco sighed. "This is going to be fun."

"It's a shame," Celia mused. "I thought they were a good couple. I wonder what happened?"

"Two proud, insecure people? It could be anything. It could be *nothing*."

Bruno was struck by Marco's assessment. It was sad to realize other people could see Sylvio's faults that easily.

"ARE YOU OKAY?" Bruno asked his brother when he saw him later in the hall.

"What? Oh, yeah, I'm fine. I don't want to talk about it."

"Sure. It's none of my business."

Sylvio scowled at the floor. "I'm sure Celia and Marco will take her side."

"I don't think they will, actually," Bruno replied. "Especially if they don't know what happened."

"Regine will tell them."

"What will she tell them?"

"That I broke up with her!"

"Did she do anything wrong?"

"No—I mean . . . no, she didn't."

"Did you do anything wrong?"

"No. I just . . . No, I didn't do anything wrong."

"So why does anyone have to choose sides? It didn't work out, is all."

"Maybe. I guess we'll find out. See you later." Sylvio walked off, and Bruno tried to guess how his brother really felt. Relationships were like unexplored buildings—it was impossible to understand them from the outside.

"HOW WAS YOUR BREAK?" Mr. Williams asked Bruno at their first meeting of the new year.

"It was good. How was yours?"

"Quiet. But that's how I wanted it. I like the winter's desolate, dark weeks, even if it brings out the pessimist in me."

"Were you alone?" It was a question Bruno's father would ask.

"I saw some people. But I actually like spending time by myself. I think we're similar in that regard, don't you?" Bruno found himself nodding in agreement. "Did you receive anything good?"

"My parents gave me some drafting software."

"That's nice. I want you to work on your drawing skills, though. If you go into architecture or city planning or cartography, you'll do most of your work on the computer. But the ability to communicate with a pen and paper is a critical part of being a designer, and I'd say it's a critical part of who you are. So we want to develop those abilities, too."

"Sure." Bruno was struck again by the way Mr. Williams's descriptions matched up so well with the things about Bruno that he couldn't possibly know.

"MS. VONG WANTS THE HOME EC classes to do a fashion show," Marco blurted out as soon as they sat down in the library. "And she wants me to do a small collection for the finale!"

"That's perfect!" Celia said. "I bet you have a million ideas already."

"Yes! It's going to be so much work. I want to blow this school's mind. Oh, and you're both models," Marco said casually.

"What?" Bruno and Celia said in unison.

"I need all of you! Silver and Regine—I'll use Tomasi if he can get over here for it. I need so many models!"

"This is going to be insane," Celia said quietly to Bruno.

"I don't know how to model," Bruno said earnestly.

"Neither do I!"

"You have four months to practice!"

Celia gave Bruno a nudge, and he turned to see Lois hovering nearby.

When he went over to her, Lois pointed. "Can you deal with her?" Gwendolyn's dark figure stood on the far side of the gate to the library stacks, her ponytail flicking back and forth as she looked around.

Bruno walked up to Gwendolyn. "Are you looking for a book?"

"Why don't they put more lights back here?"

Bruno reached for a lie that felt plausible. "I heard it has something to do with the wiring. They didn't put enough circuits in, and now they can't add lights. No one reads most of these books anyway."

"That's a shame, isn't it? If someone printed them, they must be worth reading, right?"

"I guess so." They stood there at the beginning of the main aisle, the gate behind them, looking into the library, which Gwendolyn assumed stopped just beyond the darkness but which Bruno knew extended so much farther. "Did you like *The Stranger*? I read it when I was sick."

"I don't know. It's definitely not a book you read just to be entertained. I felt different when I finished it. I think it changed me a little. Is that weird?"

"No, not at all. I felt that way, too. That's a good way to put it."

"I used to think everyone had a reason for everything they did. Now I think sometimes people don't have a reason. Or maybe there is a reason, but they don't know what it is."

Bruno opened the gate so Gwendolyn would return to the reading area. He felt obligated to leave Celia and Marco and sit with her as some kind of reward for dropping her curiosity about the stacks, even if they just spent the rest of the period studying.

A LIGHT SNOWFALL LEFT a dusting on the walks, and Bruno went over to Alice and Gertrude's to sweep it off.

"Thank you, Bruno!" Alice opened the door as he was finishing the front steps. "Would you come in for some hot chocolate?"

Bruno hesitated, remembering Celia's warning about the Troika. But he was curious about what questions they might ask him. "Sure, thanks."

At their kitchen table it didn't take long. "That boy you

talked to at Lippa's, the night we saw you there—does he go to Suburban?"

"Van, yes, he's a senior. I don't know him very well."

"We couldn't help but overhear what he said to you before you went outside, about how he thought you were an Ambassador. That's what he said, wasn't it?"

"He did. I wasn't sure what he meant. Ambassadors go to other countries; why would he think I was an ambassador?" Bruno thought he didn't sound quite natural enough.

"That's what we wanted to talk to you about. Have you ever heard stories about the Unkind?" *Well, they just came right out with it.* "They're like stories about UFOs. Some people claim to have had encounters with people—humans—with strange powers, but there's very little proof, and for the most part the stories are dismissed as fiction."

Play dumb and say as little as possible. "No, I haven't heard about that. The Unkind?"

"Yes, and the stories about the Unkind also talk about Ambassadors—people who know about the Unkind and keep their secrets. The stories aren't well known, though, and the parts about Ambassadors even less so. If you haven't guessed, we find the stories fascinating, and we—the three of us, including Lippa—fancy ourselves experts on the subject. So we couldn't help but be curious whether you and Van were interested, too. The kids at school don't talk about the Unkind or anything like that?"

"No." Bruno wanted to find out what these women knew, but he didn't want to risk exposing himself. "So the Unkind have powers?"

"Yes, personal powers, which vary widely. Ambassadors

are even more fascinating. They have the privilege of knowing about the Unkind, and they become coconspirators in exchange for small powers of their own."

That didn't sound right to Bruno, and he reminded himself that these women were only repeating whatever strange things they'd read. He tried to be the devil's advocate. "What kind of powers? And what's the point in having powers if you have to keep them so secret, no one knows about them?"

"There's always a way to use them discreetly. I'm sure you have talents you don't share with everyone. Things you can do but don't do in front of most people because you're embarrassed, or because you don't want them to ask you to do it for their benefit, or because you like keeping it to yourself."

"I guess so. I don't understand how Ambassadors are different, though. They know the secrets, and they have powers. Isn't that the same?"

"Their powers aren't as strong. They are the gatekeepers between our world and the world of the Unkind. And they are even rarer."

"So how do they help each other, then? If they're so rare? How do they find each other?"

"The agon," Alice said knowingly.

"The agon?"

"It is the force that draws Unkind to Ambassadors. Ambassadors are almost irresistibly attractive to the Unkind. It's like a homing device, but it's also rather romantic. Unkind very commonly fall in love with Ambassadors."

"This just sounds crazy," Bruno said as nonchalantly as possible, while he felt as if his head were caving in. *Is that why I love her? If the agon affects the Unkind, it probably works for the Kind, too.*

"It does, doesn't it!" Gertrude smiled. "Most of the time, I don't know if we're standing just outside the door of some incredible world that's hidden in plain sight, or if there's no truth to it and we're making up the most amazing story ever written, but either way, it's completely fascinating."

"It sounds wild. But I'm pretty sure Van has never heard about any of it. I don't think he's much of a reader," Bruno said, trying to figure out how he could escape.

"We just wanted to check because it sounded like he had. If it turns out he is a conspiracy theorist, we'd love to meet him."

"Sure. I'll let you know."

"WHY DIDN'T YOU COME through my closet or something?" Celia asked Bruno after she'd let him in the front door of her house, and they'd gone up to her room.

"I . . . I . . . Wouldn't that creep you out?"

"Well, it would if you did it when I wasn't expecting you." She looked at him oddly.

"I would feel weird."

"I can understand that."

Tomasi came through the sketchbook, and Celia got straight to the point. "Tell him about the agon," she prompted Bruno.

"The Troika believe Ambassadors are irresistibly attractive to Unkind," Bruno said. "If it's true, they probably have the same effect on Kind."

Tomasi looked at Celia. "The women at the bookstore? Do they really know anything?"

"I don't know, but it makes sense if you think about it," Celia said. "Mariette fell in love with me. You fell in love with me. Bruno fell in love with me."

"Did Mr. Sumeletso fall in love with you?" Tomasi asked her.

"I . . . I don't know. Ew! But he wouldn't have told me anyway—he was a teacher! Now that you mention it, though, I do remember catching him looking at me once or twice . . ."

"Lois doesn't seem to have fallen in love with you," Bruno said.

"No, definitely not. Or is she avoiding me because she doesn't want to admit it? I can't believe I just said that."

They were silent for a minute, pondering it. Then Tomasi snapped his fingers. "Maybe that's the reason why every time I'm around Cassandra I, well . . ." He looked at Bruno.

"You too?" They sheepishly grinned at each other, and for the first time Bruno felt a genuine camaraderie with Tomasi.

"What?"

"Let's just say Cassandra must be a very strong Ambassador," Tomasi said, and Bruno nodded, laughing.

"I don't want to know." Celia smiled in spite of herself. "But if you're saying what I think you're saying, it goes along with the agon theory."

Tomasi turned to Bruno. "So you *are* in love with my girlfriend, but you can't help it."

"That's what it seems like," Bruno said.

"Dude, I'm sorry."

"It's okay."

"But wait, then," Celia said to Tomasi. "Are *you* in love with me only because of the agon? Or are you really in love with me?"

Tomasi reddened. "Of course I'm really in love with you! Maybe we should have that conversation when we're alone?"

"I can go," Bruno offered.

"Hold on. There are other things we need to talk about," Celia said. "Gwendolyn has been poking around the library, trying to figure out how she got lost in the stacks. Is that going to be a problem?"

"I don't think so. What could she say that anyone would believe?" Bruno said.

"I know how that feels," Celia said.

"So what is the Ebentwine, anyway?" Tomasi asked.

It was a strange moment, having Tomasi ask *him* about something in the realm of the Kind. Bruno tried to answer as coherently as he could. "At first I thought it was just this supernatural clearing behind my house that's some kind of shortcut between places. Gardner calls it a liminal. Remember that night you saw me go down the alley across the street from the bookstore? I can go through those hedges into the Ebentwine clearing, and when I go out the other side, I'm in my own backyard, four miles away."

"I get that. What's it doing in the library at Suburban, then?"

"I'm not sure. But the Ebentwine is back there, way in the back of the stacks. All those side effects I got when I went too far in were the same as what happens if I stay too long in the Ebentwine clearing—only worse."

"Our powers are really different," Tomasi said.

"Are they?" Celia asked. "You have a liminal to travel between spaces, too."

"Sure, but I don't hang out there. I can't."

"Still, I bet it's the same." They sat silent again.

"I wonder if Lois will leave," Bruno said. "She's Kind, but everything that's happened at Suburban has really freaked her out. She just seems completely overwhelmed."

"One of Mariette's admonitions told her to go to Suburban," Celia said. "And Cassandra said if we're there, it's for a reason. Lois just arrived this year, and that's probably not a coincidence. Everything seems to have a reason, even if it's not obvious right away. She may not know what her reason is yet, but I'd bet Lois is supposed to be at Suburban, so you should do everything you can to convince her to stay."

"What am I supposed to do?" Bruno asked.

"I don't know. You still haven't received your new admonition?"

"No."

After a long moment, Tomasi said to Bruno, "She always takes my hand. If she didn't touch me, I think I'd be okay."

"I know! Every time! I'm just glad it's dark there."

kiss kiss, bang bang

R EGINE AND SYLVIO HAD settled into an icy silence. They sat as far from each other as possible at lunch and in the library, using the others as a buffer. Bruno had wondered if Sylvio would give up on his dreams for the Rosary and start avoiding the group entirely, but he didn't seem to want to relinquish Celia and Marco. At Diaboliques the tension between Regine and Sylvio was easier to ignore, since they could distract themselves with the dancing. At least, it was that way for a few weeks.

"Well, this should be interesting," Marco said, subtly directing Celia and Bruno's attention to Sylvio, who had strayed from the group to talk to a girl who made regular appearances in Patrick's room. "Regine will lose her mind in five, four, three . . ." They watched Regine dancing, unsure whether she had noticed.

"I don't know which was worse. Last year she loved someone who didn't love her back. This year she loved a guy who broke up with her because she couldn't get him a membership in a club that doesn't exist." Celia sighed.

"She loved him?" Bruno asked.

"Oh, yeah, she told me all the time. She does an excellent job of covering it, but she's still heartbroken," Celia said.

"Is that why he broke up with her?"

"I don't know; I just assumed. It seems like the most obvious reason. Do you think it was something else?"

"No, I could totally see him being that way," Bruno said sadly.

Marco was looking across the room. "Can I change the subject for a minute? You know I need more models, right?"

"Yes?" Celia followed his gaze. "Them? Are you serious?"

"C'mon—I need guys, and right now I only have Silver, Bruno, and Tomasi. Those guys would be perfect. They clearly like the style, and they *are* hot. And there are six of them!" Marco turned to Celia. "What would Tomasi say?"

"Why don't you ask him?" Celia beckoned to Tomasi, who came over.

"Do you think they'd model for my show?" Marco asked him.

"They'd do it in a heartbeat. For some reason or another they are fascinated by all of you."

"Works for me." Marco strode across the dance floor, and the boys from St. Dymphna's clustered around him like nails to a magnet. In a moment he was back. "Six more guys! I'm going to do measurements with them tomorrow."

"It's never dull around here, is it?" Celia said to Bruno.

BRUNO TURNED AWAY from his locker and found a determined Gwendolyn standing there. "Hi. I wanted to ask you something." She shifted into a speech that sounded rehearsed, with a destination Bruno could have seen a mile away. "I like you, and it seems like you kind of like me. I thought maybe we could do something outside of school sometime. See a movie or go somewhere." She found his eyes and then looked down again. "You're really nice, and you've been so nice to me. And Valentine's Day is coming, so I thought maybe you'd want to be my valentine?"

Bruno should have been better prepared for this moment. All the signs had been there. Plenty of times he had wondered whether she would grow tired of waiting for him to make the first move. But he cursed himself for never having thought of what he should say if it happened.

"I . . . I haven't . . . thought about Valentine's Day at all," he stammered.

She looked at him again, then down. "Will you think about it?" she finally managed.

"Sure. I'll let you know." He watched her walk away, then turned back to his locker, wanting to bash his head into the metal door.

"THEY'RE AN ODD BUNCH," Marco said when they met in the cafeteria. "The six of them all play string instruments—violins, violas, cellos—and they have some kind of string sextet. Is that a thing? It sounds like they're serious musicians."

"The guys from St. Dymphna's?" Celia asked.

"Yeah. And they have the craziest names." Marco pulled out his notebook. "Moss, Turlington, Schiffer, Crawford, Campbell, and Evan, which is short for Evangelist. And yes, I asked, and they all swore to me they weren't made-up names."

"Well, I guess they're not any stranger than Ivo. Or Tomasi," Regine said.

"Or Regine." Celia smiled at her.

"But they're going to be great models. They definitely have

a flair for the dramatic," Marco said. "I know what I'm going to make for all of them."

"Is there a theme?" Sylvio asked.

"I have one, but it might change. I'll let you know. Don't worry—I won't put you in anything you wouldn't be happy to wear."

"How many models do you have?" Celia asked.

"Nine guys and the two of you." Marco nodded at Celia and Regine. "I'd love to find a third girl and make it an even dozen, but I'm not sure who to ask. Nobody at Diaboliques seems quite right."

They ate in silence for a moment; then Marco said, "Before, we would have been having some fantastic argument about music by now."

"Well, let's do it, then." Celia thought a moment. "Bands that are known for one great song, and nothing else they did comes close."

"Ooh, that's a good one!" Marco said.

"The Au Pairs, 'It's Obvious,'" Sylvio said.

"I don't know, I always liked 'Dear John,' too," Marco said.

"But does anyone ever play it?" Sylvio asked.

"How about 'Shadow Dance' by Eyes of the Nightmare Jungle?" Celia asked.

"I guess so. I'm not sure it's a great song, but if we're going to count that, I'd say 'Shirina' by Moonchild. Everything else they ever did is completely terrible," Regine said.

"'Underpass' by John Foxx," Marco said.

"But he was in Ultravox, and they had lots of great songs," Regine said.

"Technicality," Marco protested.

"What about Heaven 17?" Celia offered. "'Let Me Go!'?"

"But what about 'I'm Your Money' and 'Contenders'?" Sylvio countered.

"I've never heard them at Diaboliques."

"I'm going with 'A Way' by the Bolshoi," Sylvio said.

"*That* is the best answer yet," Marco said.

"What about you, Bruno?" Celia looked at him.

Bruno put his hands out in front of him. "I don't want to say anything wrong and have you all take my head off." They all laughed.

BRUNO WAS SURE MARIETTE'S ghost had him in her sights. He was seeing her at least once a day now, always in the vicinity of the science wing, and always with an expectant look on her face and a piece of paper in her hand. It confused him. He knew a piece of paper from Mariette could mean something other than a betrayal—and who would betray him anyway, since he was single? But it would no doubt involve an unsettling revelation. Perhaps he would have the pleasure of watching Tomasi stick his tongue down Celia's throat. That didn't quite fit the pattern—it wouldn't be a surprise—but Bruno preferred not to take the risk.

Now he stood at the end of the science wing, eyes locked with Mariette. He had to make it past her to get to his class. A girl in a black dress and black knee-high boots stopped next to him, and it took him a moment to recognize Gwendolyn. She had straightened her hair so it hung like a scarf around her shoulders. "Hi, Bruno."

"Hi, Gwendolyn. I've never seen you without a ponytail."

"You like it?"

"Sure."

"Have you been thinking about what I asked you?"

"Yeah. What made you decide to change your hair? And your style?"

"I don't know. You and your friends always look so nice, I thought I'd give it a try."

"I have to go to class." He was going to escape Gwendolyn by walking directly toward Mariette. For once the unknown was preferable to the known.

"I'm going this way. I'll walk with you."

"Did you do it—change your style—because of me?"

"I just said I admired you."

"I mean, are you doing it because you like me?" Up ahead, Mariette was waiting by the side of the hall.

"Is that such a surprise to you? But you know, if that was something people did—change their style to match the person they liked—did anyone ask you the same question at the beginning of the year, when *you* changed *your* style?" Gwendolyn tried to keep her tone light, but it cut into Bruno just as she must have hoped it would.

"They did, actually."

"So how did you answer that question?"

"I don't think I ever answered it," Bruno said. "If I had, I guess I would have said that maybe I had done it for that reason, but if it hadn't been something I liked, really for myself, I would have felt foolish and stopped."

"Are you hoping I'll feel foolish and stop?"

"No, you should do what feels right to you. I just—" Bruno lost his train of thought as they passed Mariette. She stepped backward into an empty classroom, the paper still in her hand. The light from the windows glowed faintly through her. Gwendolyn didn't seem to have noticed.

"What?"

"I hope you aren't disappointed," he said. "If things don't happen the way you want them to."

"Have you been disappointed?"

"In some ways, yes," he admitted.

"Well, it looks like you survived," Gwendolyn said bitterly.

"I'm sorry you're angry."

"You don't know how I feel. Actually, maybe you do."

Bruno watched her walk away as the bell rang. He tried to feel the way he knew she wanted. He knew how it felt to worship someone, but then again, that probably wasn't even love, but the inevitable attraction of a Kind to an Ambassador. *Would I even know real love if I felt it?*

DOWN IN THE CAFETERIA, Bruno was heading to the lunch line when Marco came in, wearing a shocked expression.

"What's wrong?"

Marco silently handed him a piece of paper that read, *Wednesday, Quincy Arch, 7:17 p.m.* "What's this? Did you get this from Mariette?"

Marco nodded. "I don't know where Quincy Arch is. I assume it's on the Metropolitan campus," he said softly.

"You don't think Brenden . . ." Bruno didn't want to finish his sentence.

"What else am I supposed to think?"

"Well, look what happened to Celia. When Mariette gave her one of these, it wasn't what she thought at all."

"Let's go to the library and find Quincy Arch. If it's at Metropolitan, I don't know how it could be anyone else."

"What about Ivo or Liz?"

"Why would I get a note about them?" Marco said sadly.

They went up to the library after they had eaten. "Even if

I left right after school, I wouldn't get there by seven o'clock," Marco said. They stared down at the book that lay open on the desk in front of them, its pages showing the buildings on the Metropolitan campus. Bruno had found Quincy Hall, which connected the central and eastern quadrangles with an arched passageway. The plan of the campus fascinated him.

"Why don't you call him? Don't accuse him of anything. Just talk to him. Ask him what his plans are for tonight."

"I don't want to be . . . I've never been the jealous boyfriend," Marco protested. "It's been almost two and a half years, and he's never given me a reason not to trust him. No, he calls me every night between ten and eleven. I'll just talk to him then."

Bruno tried again. "I'm sure it's not what you think."

"Yeah, it's just . . ." Marco put on a weak smile. "It's like missing the last stair and feeling like you're going to fall for a moment before your foot touches the floor. I just need to feel the floor under my feet again."

"You're right." Bruno knew neither of them was convinced. "Do you need a hug?"

"Yes." Marco stepped into Bruno's open arms and seemed better for it, for a moment, at least.

Bruno knew Celia would be passing through the new wing between classes, and he waited for her. "Marco got a note from Mariette."

"Really? Is it about Brenden? At Metropolitan?"

"The place in the note is at Metropolitan. Quincy Arch."

"Oh!" Celia was stricken. "What's he going to do?"

"Nothing. The time is seven seventeen tonight, and he can't get there by then."

"Oh, God! Is he okay?"

"He says he is, but he's worried. What I want to know is, should I go?"

"You can do that?"

"I'm pretty sure I can."

"I don't know. What would it accomplish? No matter what you saw, you wouldn't be able to tell Marco without explaining how you got there."

"I know. But if you had the chance to find out if someone was going to be betrayed, or if they had no reason to be worried, and even if you couldn't tell them, but maybe you could prepare them for when they did find out—if there is something to find out—would you do it?"

"So, should you find out, and then encourage him to have faith in Brenden, or encourage him to be skeptical?" Celia looked conflicted. "Bruno, I don't know. Is that overstepping your bounds?"

"Maybe it is. I'll do whatever you think is right."

"Oh, don't put this on me!" They pondered it for a moment, the hall gradually clearing around them as the next period approached. "I think you should go," she said finally.

"Why?"

"Because if I were in Marco's position, and someone could do for me what you can do for him, I would want you to do it."

"So, I should go."

"I think you should."

"Would you go with me?"

"Why?"

Bruno reached for an excuse. "Because I don't know if I'll recognize him. I've only met Brenden twice, and the one time was in the dark at Diaboliques."

"You don't remember him from First Night?"

"Kind of, but I'd feel better if you were there to be sure."

"You can take me with you?"

"If I can go, I can take you," Bruno said.

The bell rang. "Crap!" Celia said. "Where should I meet you?"

"Just be in your backyard at seven o'clock—I'll meet you there!" Bruno said, breaking into a run in the direction of his class.

BRUNO STEPPED THROUGH THE hedges into Celia's backyard at 7:01. "It's so bizarre to actually see you come through there."

"Well, we're going back that way," Bruno said, beckoning to her. He led her through the hedges into the Ebentwine clearing, where Gardner stood waiting.

"This is it? It's beautiful." Celia looked around in wonder.

"Thank you!" Gardner said. "And this is Celia?" he asked Bruno, who nodded. "You are exquisite. No wonder he's in love with you."

Celia looked at Bruno, who thought his head might explode. "I can't believe you just said that." He glared at Gardner.

"You deny it, then?"

"You know perfectly well why I feel the way I do. You've known all along. You at least could have told me."

"Forget it. We have to go," Celia said.

"Where to?" Gardner asked.

"Quincy Hall, on the Metropolitan campus," Bruno said. "Can we do that?"

"Finally, a trip worth passing through here. I thought you were never going to go farther than across town." Gardner clapped his gloved hands together. "All right, go down that way and stay to the right of the holly tree."

"Is he the one who got you started?" Celia asked him as she followed him into the trees. "Or was it Lois?"

"I don't know. Lois was the one who told me about the Kind. But I met Gardner first. He's always in the clearing to tell me which way to go."

"Is he . . . nice?"

"I'm not sure. Sometimes I think he likes to meddle in other people's business," Bruno said. He saw the holly tree and pushed past it to the right. The trees thinned, and light posts came into view over a path across the grass.

"Are we there?" Celia followed him out onto the path.

"Looks like it. This is my first time at Metropolitan." Bruno had spent only a moment with the campus map that afternoon in the library, but he unfolded it in his mind and fit the buildings in front of him to the shapes on the page. Across the quad lay a brick building with a passage through its lower level. A barrel lantern hung from the ceiling of the arched tunnel, dimly illuminating the passage. "There it is. With the arch, there." He pointed. "Quincy Hall."

"What time is it?" Celia asked.

"Ten after," Bruno said.

"I wish we knew which way they'll be coming," she said.

"They might already be there." Bruno squinted at two figures chatting under the lantern.

"Is that Brenden?" Celia began walking closer, and now Bruno followed her. Halfway across the quad she stopped and said, "You walk in front."

Bruno obeyed, and when they were fifty feet from the entry

to Quincy Arch, Celia put her hand on his shoulder and they stopped again. "It is. That's Brenden on the left."

"I recognize him now." Bruno felt her hand leave his shoulder and turned. "Where are you going?"

Celia was backing up. "I don't want to see this. I don't want to look at Marco and remember it. I'll be back by the trees."

Bruno watched her walk away for a moment, then turned back to the arch. Brenden and the other guy were in the same spot, still talking. They shifted their backpacks on their shoulders, and the other guy edged half a step closer to Brenden.

"Don't do it," Bruno whispered. "Don't do it."

Brenden looked around, and Bruno thought he had been spotted, but Brenden returned to his conversation. The other guy leaned slightly forward, while Brenden stood straight, his hands holding the straps of his backpack.

"Don't do it." Bruno thought about running over, interrupting the conversation, doing something, anything to prevent the two boys from kissing. But then Brenden would call Marco and ask him why the odd first year from Suburban had popped up midweek on Metropolitan's campus, and Marco would ask all sorts of questions Bruno couldn't answer.

Maybe if I threaten him, Bruno thought. *"I know what you were about to do, and I won't tell Marco if you never tell him I was here."* Bruno leapt forward just as the other guy leaned in to Brenden and kissed him. Bruno halted and watched the kiss continue. If Brenden had been unsure, he didn't look that way now.

Then Brenden pushed the other guy away, and even from a distance it was obvious he had marshaled every ounce of self-control he possessed to stop himself. Bruno fled back down the path to the trees.

"Celia?" She was nowhere to be seen. "Celia?" He walked all the way around the dense cluster of trees in the center of the quad. She was gone. He scanned the quad, but there was nothing but academic-looking buildings on all sides. What had happened? Metropolitan was a big campus next to a big city; did beautiful girls have to worry about being grabbed in the middle of darkened quads at night? The people walking alone on the paths didn't look that concerned.

Where was she? How long could he walk in a circle before someone noticed? But if he left, and Celia was still here, how would she get back? He couldn't leave her.

Maybe Gardner could help; he had known Celia's where-abouts before. Bruno stepped into the trees and made his way around the holly bush as quickly as he could to return to the Ebentwine clearing. He wondered if Gardner could leave the Ebentwine. He never spoke of going anywhere else. Bruno pushed the last branches aside and entered the clearing.

Celia stood facing Gardner. "There you are! I didn't know where you went! What's going on?"

Bruno seem to have interrupted a serious conversation, and Celia turned to him with a strange expression. "I'll tell you later. How do we get back?"

Gardner wore a tight smile. Bruno didn't wait for direc-tions but crossed the clearing and led Celia into her backyard.

"What happened? No, don't tell me." Celia studied Bruno's face in the dim light. "He did it, didn't he?"

"He regretted it immediately," Bruno said. "He stopped it."

"Oh, Marco! What are we going to do?"

"We're not going to do anything. We're going to be good friends to him, and try to comfort him if we can," Bruno said.

Celia was anguished. "When did everything get so difficult?

Regine and Silver were just a stupid high school romance, but Marco and Brenden were the one thing I thought was constant! Tomasi's being weird, saying people are following him all the time . . ." She looked up at him. "Bruno, I'm sorry you're in love with me."

"You don't have to be sorry for anything," he said angrily. "You've done nothing wrong."

"But you deserve to be in love," she said.

"What does that mean?"

"I don't know. If things were different . . ." She trailed off.

"Who's that in your room?" Bruno pointed up at her window, where he could see Tomasi. Celia turned to look, and Bruno clambered back through the hedges to the clearing beyond.

He walked straight up to Gardner. "What did you say to her?"

"Excuse me?"

"Before I came back. What did you talk about?"

Gardner put his rake down on the ground and rested his palm on the end of the handle. "I told her this was a strange place, halfway through the woods. And that it is in places like this, sometimes, that people leave you."

"What does that mean? I am never bringing her back here, that's for sure."

"Suit yourself."

Bruno stormed off, feeling Gardner's eyes on his back.

spellbound

D ID YOU TALK TO him?"

"Yeah," Marco said. "He said he missed me, and he asked if I could come visit him. I want to so badly, but I can't before he comes back for spring break."

"That doesn't sound like someone who kissed someone else under Quincy Arch last night," Bruno said, cringing inwardly.

"No, it doesn't. And I feel better. But Mariette's predictions have never been wrong before. Something must have happened last night. If it was Brenden, he's lying to me, and that would kill me. If it wasn't Brenden, it's someone else, and I can't imagine who, but someone I wouldn't have expected kissed someone I wouldn't expect under Quincy Arch."

"I'd say to forget about it, but I guess that's not really possible, is it?" They walked slowly down the middle of the hall, oblivious to the gusts of students on either side of them.

"I don't think so. But thanks for listening to me about it. You know, I almost called Liz and asked her to go to the arch last night, but I felt foolish when I thought about it."

"I guess so." Bruno gave silent thanks Marco hadn't acted on that idea.

"So, what if I find out he lied to me?"

"You're asking me?" Bruno scrambled for a response. "I don't have any experience with relationships . . . Well, what if he did it? What if Brenden came to you and said, 'I screwed up. Some guy kissed me, and I feel terrible about it.' What would you do?"

Marco studied the floor. "I'd be hurt, but I think I'd forgive him. I can see how that could happen to anyone."

"So, what if it did happen? I mean, I'm just guessing, but what if Brenden thought he was having a casual conversation with someone, maybe a classmate, last night under the Quincy Arch, and he thought he was being friendly, but the other guy thought it was something more."

"As long as he told me, I think I'd understand. He'd have to make it up to me, of course," Marco joked, and Bruno was relieved to see the cloud lift a little.

"I'm sure you know exactly how he could do that." They grinned at each other.

IT WAS BETWEEN THE SECOND and third periods of the day when Bruno first noticed something new was wrong at Suburban. He couldn't put a finger on it, but the energy in the halls was more subdued than usual. Most students were walking in silence, even with friends next to them.

After the next period it grew worse. Bruno passed a boy who stood by his open locker, looking aimlessly into space as though he had nowhere to go. That wouldn't have been so unusual last semester—it would have been Van's handiwork—but that had stopped when Van's slate was wiped clean. Even if it was the same malaise, now caused by the other, still unidentified Unkind, this time it wasn't affecting one person at a time. Bruno looked around the hallway. Instead of rushing, some kids were walking so slowly that at times they practically stopped. The lights on the ceiling seemed a little dimmer. It was as if Suburban was losing power.

After the next class it was even worse. Celia found Bruno in the hall and pulled him aside. "What's happening? Is that fog?" She pointed up at some kind of faint steam or smoke that was hovering overhead. "And am I crazy, or are a lot of people looking like they're sleepwalking? Or suicidal?"

Bruno heard crying among the subdued noises of the hallway. Everyone looked serious or confused as they passed. "I don't know. But if it gets much worse, are people just going to start curling up on the floor?"

"I just saw someone doing that in the Chancellor Wing," Celia said, and sighed.

"You don't feel it, though?" Bruno asked her. "Drained, sad, pointless?"

"No. Maybe I'm immune; I bet you are. But be careful. And if you notice anything—if you figure out anything that might be causing this—find me, okay?"

Bruno nodded. He wondered whether Lois had noticed it, too, but he didn't have time to stop by the library.

By lunch there were more people, students and teachers alike, who seemed to have caught the malaise. The mysterious fog had rolled across the ceiling in the hushed cafeteria. On all sides Bruno saw students attempting to console their friends, but the question on everyone's lips was *What's wrong?* and no one seemed to have an answer.

Marco was feeling it. "What the hell is happening?" he groaned, his head low as he pondered his lunch, untouched in front of him. "Why do I feel like going to bed, or just giving up? Do you feel it?"

"No," Bruno said. "Did anything happen?"

"Not that I remember. It just kind of crept up on me, all morning." Marco's eyes searched Bruno's face, hoping for some kind of answer.

"So nothing bad happened, you just feel . . ."

"Depressed. It sucks. I never get depressed."

"Are you free next, or do you have class?"

"I have calculus, but maybe I'll just skip it."

"C'mon, I'll walk you. I have web design. It's on the way."

Outside Marco's classroom Bruno asked him, "Is there anything I can do?"

"Could I have a hug?" Marco said, a little sheepishly.

"Sure." Bruno put his arms around him. He felt Marco's chin on his shoulder.

"It's silly, but it really does make me feel better," Marco said. "Is this weird for you?"

"A little," Bruno said. "Not the *you* part—the *hugging-any-one* part. But it's okay."

Marco let go and stepped back. "You should bottle that," Marco said, and the familiar gleam returned to his eye. "Thanks!"

"You're welcome! I'll see you later." Bruno headed to class.

Ms. Moreletii definitely was not feeling any malaise. She strode briskly around the room, ignoring clearly afflicted students who propped their chins in their hands in front of their computer screens. "I'm going to show you an important piece of code today. It's a little tricky because how it works depends on where you drop it in among other elements. The easiest way to get started is with a demonstration, so log in and then I'll run a short video."

The students did their best to focus. Ms. Moreletii watched

impatiently. Finally everyone was ready, and a media player appeared on everyone's screens. "This is the last big programming element we're going to learn before you start your final projects, so pay close attention."

The media player didn't expand to full size on the screen, and Bruno found himself leaning in close as he concentrated. Around him the classroom was silent, save for Ms. Moreletii's prerecorded voice on the video. She had finished introducing the code when there was a popping noise and a short flash from the screen before it went blank. Everyone jumped and then mumbled in confusion as the computers restarted.

Ms. Moreletii looked flustered. "There . . . there must have been a surge. Bruno, I need you to go to the building mechanic's office and tell her we're having electrical problems in the computer lab."

"Me?" Bruno stood up, wondering why she had chosen him. Had he looked too energetic? Most likely to actually complete the errand without giving up and lying down somewhere?

"Yes. We'll try it again, but if there's a problem, I need it to be fixed as soon as possible, or else we're going to fall behind schedule."

"But it'll take me ten minutes to get there!" Bruno suspected everything would be fine once the computers restarted, and then he would miss most of the lesson.

"Go as fast as you can." She turned to the class. "Is everyone's computer restarting?"

Bruno seethed as he left the classroom. He stood in the empty hallway, a current of charcoal fog blowing over his head. He pulled his assignment pad out of his pocket, drew a map, and stepped into the janitor's closet. In a few seconds he was pushing open the door into the mechanic's office.

"What are you doing here?" The woman looked up from her newspaper.

"Ms. Moreletii says there's a power surge or short or something in the computer lab. She wants you to fix it."

"I don't see how that's possible. That's brand-new wiring. The whole wing is less than a year old."

"She says if it happens again, she's going to fall behind schedule."

The woman didn't move from her chair. "Wait, again? What do you mean, again?"

"All the computers turned off and then restarted."

"Well, that's not a fuse, then, and all the computers are on surge protectors, so it's not the wiring. I'd say it's her server, and that's not my department." The woman leaned back in her chair.

Realizing she wasn't going to help him, Bruno gave up and ran back to the computer lab through the liminal he'd created. He had been gone for three or four minutes at the most.

He stopped short of the computer lab. A watery radiance drifted through the window in the door. Bruno crept closer and looked inside. The entire room was washed in a wavering, sickly light, reminding him of a large, fetid aquarium. In front of the computers his classmates hunched, slack-jawed, their eyes glued to the shimmering screens. They seemed to be held immobile by the eerie light that flooded their eyes.

Through the closed door Bruno could feel the malaise push out against him like a wind, and the realization hit him. *She's done this to every class she's had today! She's poisoning the school!* Ms. Moreletii was the crocodile, the Unkind one who Van had been on the verge of revealing to him. The growing malaise he and Celia had sensed all day was Ms. Moreletii's doing.

He backed away from the door. *How long have I been gone? As far as she knows, I haven't even made it down there yet.* Bruno wished he remembered what class Celia had now. Then he thought of Lois. He had ten minutes before Ms. Moreletii would expect him back. He loped down the hall toward the library.

"Bruno, what are—What's wrong?" Lois followed him into her office.

"Ms. Moreletii is the Unkind! She's been putting some kind of spell on all her classes today, some kind of negative energy. She must know about me, because she sent me on an errand to get me out of the way."

"I've been in here all day. Is that everywhere?" Lois pointed up at the tendrils of fog by the ceiling, and Bruno nodded. "I knew something was very wrong, but I didn't know how widespread it was. What did she do?"

"She's doing something through the computer screens. But the computers crashed, and she sent me to the mechanical room to get help. She thought it would take me fifteen or twenty minutes to get down there and back, but I drew a shortcut and came back quickly, and I saw it through the door."

"Your Kind energy must have counteracted what she was doing the first time, just by being in the room." Lois was excited to have figured something out. "She's probably known about you since the beginning of the year, and she's been counting on you being a novice, since you didn't detect her."

"I didn't do anything to counteract . . . I didn't know what was happening until it was too late!"

"It doesn't matter. She had to get you out of the room for it to work."

"What's happening? You must have noticed how everyone's been acting."

"I started noticing it this morning. Students have been coming in here looking like they were ready to crawl into a hole. And it's been getting worse all day. The malaise probably spreads, too, so students who weren't in her classes are catching it from the students who were. I bet plenty of the teachers have gotten it, too. I wish I had sensed the Unkind here," Lois said, berating herself. "I should have felt her. I've just never had any experience with Unkind."

"What can we do?" Bruno asked her.

"That I do know. We'll have to get all this out of here." Lois pointed at the ceiling again.

"What is that? Don't we have to help the people?"

"Sure, but I don't think this is about the students at all. Bruno, I think this is about Suburban."

"What?"

"I'll explain later. Have you done anything to reveal to Ms. Moreletii that you know what she's doing?" Bruno shook his head. "Good. You'll have to go back to class and not let on that you know what happened, or else she'll be suspicious. Do you have any free periods before the end of the day?" Bruno shook his head again. "All right, is there any way you can get here tonight, say, eight o'clock? I know what to do to clean up the school, but we have to figure out what to do about Ms. Moreletii, and we have to do it fast. If she gets here tomorrow and the malaise is gone, she'll know someone has counteracted her. Just because I didn't know about her doesn't mean she doesn't know about me. But she definitely knows about you, so if things don't go the way she wants, she'll probably take it out on you."

"She's the skull in the technology wing!" Bruno said.

"I forgot about that! You're right. Be careful. If she does anything threatening, get out of there immediately."

Bruno nodded nervously. "I'll come back tonight. Is there anything I can do for my friends?"

"I think touching them probably will help. Your Kind energy should be strong enough to do it for one person at a time, though who knows, you may start to feel lightheaded if you do it for too many people."

"Okay. I'll see you at eight."

Bruno went back to the computer lab. All the students were now slouched in their chairs, their faces listless and tired. No one had escaped the malaise. Ms. Moreletii stood lecturing to herself by the wipe-off board.

"Well, where is the mechanic?" she asked.

"She said it can't be a fuse, since the power came back, and all the computers are on surge protectors, so it's probably a short in your server," Bruno said carefully. "She wouldn't come with me."

Ms. Moreletii sighed dramatically. "Fine, I'll check the server. We'll try this again next class," she announced, but no one seemed to care.

Bruno went to his workstation and collected his things as the rest of the students hoisted themselves out of their chairs. He kept his eyes away from Ms. Moreletii.

BRUNO CAUGHT SIGHT OF CELIA down the hall, standing to the side, immobilized and staring into space. In the midst of the shuffling crowds of what he could only think of as zombies, she looked as if she had become one of them. There were small lightning flashes in the clouds above her head, and he wondered whether it really might rain in the middle of the hall. He threaded his way through the zombies to get to her.

"Are you okay?" She nodded and pointed into an empty classroom. The lights were off, but a silhouette stood at the windows on the far side, facing out. "Is that—?"

Celia nodded. "I just happened to notice when I was passing by. I think he's talking." They went into the classroom and approached the windows.

Van's eyes looked as if they were seeing something a hundred miles away. His hands hung at his sides, and his lips moved just enough for his soft, monotone words to escape.

"There are. There are things that are. There are things that are important—beyond this violin, this violence. You said, in the senses . . . you said, innocence is uneven."

"What did he say?" Bruno whispered. Celia's eyes were fixed on Van.

"When did my hands grasp? When did my eyes dilate? When did my hair rise? My shadow is long. Is longing too late? Why am I not useful?"

Celia whispered, "What does it mean?"

"I have no idea."

Van's eyes were locked straight ahead, his expression a death mask. "Did we stop admiring the things we don't understand? My visions are bleeding into one. I am a bat, watching everything upside down. Unsafe here. Are those elephants, pushing? Wild horses? Sleepless wolves under the trees? No, they are crocodiles."

Celia caught her breath. "Your admonition says to beware

the crocodile. Cassandra used to call Mr. Sumeletso the crocodile."

"I know who the crocodile is," Bruno said. "Ms. Moreletii. She's the one causing all this. She's the crocodile." Celia looked sharply at him. "I just figured it out last period."

"Ms. Moreletii is the one who . . . She was here last year, but I never . . . Mariette never . . ."

"She's the one."

Van was still speaking. "The truth flows through me. It runs down my spine. It pulls through my veins. This imaginary garden has real lizards in it. Unsafe here. They were interested in me, once . . . Smile into these memories. The sand washes over me."

Celia spoke in a calm but authoritative tone. "Van, do you remember what happened to you?" Van didn't reply. "How do we stop this?" she asked him.

"There are things that are," Van said. "There are things that are important. Why am I not useful? The truth flows through me."

"We have to help him," Celia said. "He's gone. We have to get him back."

"How? Should you draw him again?"

"Maybe." Celia pulled her sketchbook out of her bag and opened it. She started drawing Van's face in the blank corner of a page.

"My visions are bleeding into one," Van said, tears escaping from his eyes. "Unsafe here."

"His eyes closed!" Bruno told Celia, who rushed to finish her sketch. Then Van turned away from the window and opened his eyes to look at them.

"What . . . what's going on?" The life returned to his limbs, and his voice was the familiar Van, gruff and confident even as he wiped his face with the back of his hand and tried to orient himself. "What the hell are you doing here?"

"Are you okay?" Celia asked him.

"Of course. Why are we in this room?" Van stepped away from them with a look of disdain that only partially masked his confusion. "I'm getting out of here."

Bruno and Celia watched him walk quickly out the door. "Did your drawing . . ." he began, unsure what he was asking.

"I don't know," she said. "It may have been a coincidence. I think there's something lingering in him, some of his Unkind self left somewhere deep inside, and it came to the surface for a few minutes."

"But what he said didn't make any sense. Other than the part about crocodiles, did you understand any of it?"

Celia shook her head. "I'm not sure if there's anything to understand. He was totally gone. I feel bad, but he's not going to be able to tell us anything."

"I told Lois about Ms. Moreletii. She thinks all of this has something to do with Suburban."

"The school?"

"She didn't explain. But she wants to do something here tonight, after everyone's gone. I'm coming back to help her."

"Is there anything I can do?" Celia asked.

"I don't know. I'm not even sure what I can do. I think she's just scared to be here by herself."

"Okay. But be careful. If someone is going to die at Suburban, this seems like the kind of day when it would happen."

• • •

THEY WERE SUCH A SAD LOT, waiting listlessly by the cars at the end of the day. Regine must have cried recently, and Sylvio leaned against the car, his chin on his chest. They still stood as far away from each other as possible, as they had done ever since the breakup. Bruno saw that Celia's Ambassador status had not made her immune to the malaise; sometime after their encounter with Van in the empty classroom, it had gotten even her. Her shoulders caved forward over the books in her arms, and she stared at the asphalt.

Marco was still the biggest shock to see. His spirit was so constant; Bruno realized now how much he had taken that for granted. The cloud Bruno thought he had cleared away from Marco after lunch had returned, making him look forlorn and lost.

"What's wrong?" Bruno asked them all.

"Today just sucked," Marco said, and Celia nodded.

"Come here," Bruno said, and opened his arms for a second time to Marco, who willingly accepted his hug.

"Seriously? Do you guys need a room?" Sylvio grimaced.

"C'mon, it's sweet," Celia said.

Bruno released Marco and saw how quickly his Kind energy had affected Marco again. "I have no idea how you do it, but I really needed that." Marco smiled gratefully. He turned to Celia. "You should get a magic hug from Bruno."

"Can I have a hug?" Celia asked Bruno. Her body was slim but strong in his arms, and as expected, she straightened up in his embrace. "You're right," he heard her murmur over his shoulder to Marco. "That was just what I needed."

Bruno stepped back and she gave him a smile. "Thanks!" She turned to Regine. "You should really take a Bruno hug."

"Seriously?" Regine tried to scoff. "Are we really doing this?"

"I just want to help," Bruno said. He opened his arms and waited.

"Fine," she said, and walked into them. Bruno hugged her close and rubbed his hand across her back just once. "Wow," he heard her say. "You should have a hugging booth or something." When he released her, her entire countenance had changed. "I never would have believed it, but I really do feel better. You're a sweetheart."

Sylvio gave him a look. "Don't even think about it," he grumbled. Bruno shrugged and said goodbye to the others.

In the car, Sylvio brooded. "What was that about?"

"I don't know. It felt like the right thing to do," Bruno said. He was trying to decide: Should he let Sylvio stew in his own malaise or do the right thing and lift the invisible weight off him? When they got out of the car at home, Bruno grabbed Sylvio from behind and hugged him.

"What are you—" Sylvio didn't finish. Bruno felt his brother relax in his awkward grip. "Okay, let go of me!" Sylvio gave him a confused look, but by the time they got into the house he had begun to ramble about the strange day, and how out of it everyone had been.

AT EIGHT O'CLOCK BRUNO emerged from the janitor's closet in the hall at Suburban. There wasn't a closet in the library, so the janitor's closet was the closest space he knew that he could use as a liminal. He ducked his head when there was a flash. Lightning darted about almost continuously in the thick clouds that obscured the ceiling. The floor was damp and slick, but he couldn't tell whether it was condensation from the foggy air or if it had rained since he had left that afternoon. He carefully made his way to the library. Lois was there already.

"All right, this is going to be quite the experience for you, and I'm only sure of that because it's going to be quite the experience for me!" Lois sounded a little nervous but excited. "For the life of me, I had no idea what 'push back the storm' meant until today. Crazy admonitions . . . I swear to you, I have spent my entire Kind life doing quiet, private things with my powers —nothing like this!"

"What do we do first?"

"I have to get started, but that's kind of the easy part. We need to be thinking about Tina Moreletii." It was the first time Bruno had heard her first name.

"Do you have any ideas?"

"I don't think we're supposed to kill her, or even strip her of her powers. That would have been in at least one of our admonitions. But we have to prevent her from doing this again, and we have to be prepared if she retaliates against us. If we could just weaken her somehow . . . at least to give us time to come up with a plan."

Bruno tried to think of something. "What if we got her to go into the Ebentwine?" He pointed at the swinging gate and the dark aisle that hurtled into blackness between the rows of shelves.

"That's an interesting idea. If we could trap her there long enough, presumably the same thing would happen to her that happened to you."

"Something like that," Bruno said. "If we get her to go in there, I think I could redraw the shelves to trap her."

"How would we get her here? She's never come into the

library, as far as I know." Lois yelped, and Bruno turned to see what had surprised her. "Who are you?"

"That's Mariette," Bruno said, smiling shyly at the girl with the halo of curly red hair and the sweater of many colors. She smiled back at him.

"What is she doing here now?" Lois asked.

"I'm pretty sure she has a good reason. She's a ghost." Bruno waited for Mariette to do something.

"That's the ghost? I've heard things here and there, but . . . wow."

Mariette stepped forward and said, "The crocodile will be here in eleven minutes."

"Tina Moreletii?" Lois asked.

Mariette nodded. "Unless she gets here earlier."

"Why is she coming here?"

"Because I gave her a note that said *Suburban Library, aisle 242 — Wednesday — eight fifteen p.m.*"

"Why did you do that?" Lois asked.

"So she would come." Mariette looked to Bruno to explain.

"How have you not heard about the kiss notes? All year Mariette's been giving people notes with the place and time to find someone kissing someone unexpected." Bruno looked at Mariette for confirmation, and she nodded.

"God, I guess I should start eating my lunch in the teachers' lounge. Maybe I would have known about this. Maybe I would have picked up on Tina. So, you gave her a note, and she thinks she's going to find someone here kissing someone else? Is that true? Who else is coming?"

"No one. I just figured it was a good way to get her here," Mariette said, smiling conspiratorially.

"So she'll be here any minute. All we have to do is wait until she's far enough into the stacks, and then I'll draw the shelves closed. I wish we had *You Are Here*—it would make this so much easier."

"Do you think it's back in the stacks?" Lois asked him.

"It's on the shelf in your office," Mariette said.

They went to look, and sure enough, the book was there. "Should we leave the lights on?" Bruno asked, looking out the window in the office door.

"Maybe just a couple. I'll put this flashlight on the table by the gate." Lois hurried out. Bruno turned to talk to Mariette, but she had disappeared.

He crouched with Lois in the dark office, waiting. Soon they heard the library door opening.

"Oh, is *that* what Unkind feels like?" Lois whispered. "I've felt that before—it's like the change in the air when a storm is coming."

"I can't feel it."

"There was a student who used to come into the library who felt like that, but not nearly as strong."

"That must have been Van. He's been harmless since Ms. Moreletii stripped him of his powers, but it really messed him up." Bruno said. "Won't she know we're here? She's really powerful—I've seen her fly, and she erased Van's memory like a whiteboard."

"If she does, we have a serious problem. But it's too late now."

Bruno opened *You Are Here* to the map of the library. Now three people could be seen on the map: two in the library office and one in the reading area near the gate into the stacks.

Through the window from the office to the reading area, Bruno and Lois saw a flashlight beam travel across the room, and then the gate into the stacks squeaked open.

"She's going in!" Lois whispered. Bruno closed and reopened the book. The third figure had moved four rows down the main aisle into the stacks.

"We have to wait," Bruno whispered. He kept closing the book and reopening it, tracking Tina's progress deeper and deeper into the stacks.

"Seal her in now!" Lois handed him a pencil.

"The Ebentwine effect won't be strong enough unless she goes a lot farther." Bruno waited and then opened the book again. "She's only twenty rows in."

"How far do we need her to go?"

"I'd say at least past the sixty-fourth aisle. She's a lot stronger; I bet that's why Mariette sent her to aisle two forty-two."

"Check again."

Bruno reopened the book. Ms. Moreletii was even deeper into the stacks.

"If she notices she's getting dizzy, she might turn around," Lois said.

Bruno closed and opened the book yet again. "She's gone at least sixty rows."

"Do it!"

"Let her go farther!" Bruno protested.

"Close off sixty. If she goes farther, you can close off more shelves."

"Okay." Bruno used the pencil to connect the shelves across the aisle, isolating the person in the drawing in the depths of the library. When he reopened the book, the aisle was closed, and the figure had continued on. "I don't think she noticed."

When Ms. Moreletii had traveled another twenty rows, Bruno drew the stacks closed behind her again. And in twenty more rows he did it a third time. "There's no way she's getting out of there now," he said. "Unless she flies."

"Don't say that!"

When Bruno opened the book again the figure hadn't moved from its position just beyond the third barrier.

"She noticed. She knows something's wrong," Lois said.

"I hope that's far enough. If she really needed to go to aisle two forty-two for the Ebentwine to be strong enough to overcome her, we have a problem."

"Or maybe it'll just take longer to work?"

"I don't know."

"I wonder if we can hear her."

They went out into the reading area and stood by the gate. A voice called from the distance. "What did she say?"

"I can't hear." Bruno pushed through the gate, and Lois followed him into the stacks.

Tina was saying the same thing over and over: a single word she called out like a name. "What is she saying?"

"Orland?" Bruno repeated.

"Something like that." They crept along, waiting for Ms. Moreletii to call out again.

The next time it was clear. "Orland! *Or*-land!"

"What is Orland?" Lois asked. "Who is Orland?"

"I have no idea. But if she's getting weak, she won't be able to yell like that for long."

For several more minutes Ms. Moreletii kept calling the

name, sounding frustrated and then desperate. Soon, though, her voice began to fade. When her calls were too soft to be heard clearly, Bruno and Lois returned to the reading area.

"How long do we leave her in there?"

"I have no idea," Bruno said. "If we let her out too soon, it's going to be bad."

"But if we leave her in too long, could she . . ."

"I don't know."

"Well, let's take care of the school, and we'll just have to make a decision at some point."

Bruno followed her out to the hall. "What are we going to do?"

"You're just keeping me company for this part," Lois said. He accompanied her to the end of the hall, and when she cranked open one of the windows, he opened the other one. Then they went back down the hall, and Lois raised her hands, her palms facing the open windows on the far end. "Here goes," she said, and a wind rose up in front of her and pushed the stagnant clouds across the ceiling ahead of it. The storm was gradually forced out the open windows, leaving a clear hallway.

"Ha!" Lois clapped her hands in triumph. When Bruno started down the hall, she stopped him. "Wait, I want to try it from here." As they watched, the windows at the end closed and latched.

"I'm really glad you didn't leave," Bruno said.

"You know, so am I! Now we just need to do it all over again in all the halls in this crazy school." They went upstairs.

"I still don't understand what this is about," Bruno said. "Van was putting the malaise on people one at a time, and Tina was doing it to a lot of people at once, and it seemed like it was spreading. What were they doing to the school?"

"The same thing. Buildings take on the energy of the people inside them. If a family is happy, the house is happy. Once enough people at Suburban had the Unkind malaise, it contaminated the building. Then it becomes a vicious circle; the people infect the building, and the building infects more people."

"And that's what they wanted?"

"Seems like it."

"But why?"

"That's where I run out of answers," Lois said. "C'mon, the storm is only the first part. You can help with the next part. We should charge each of the doors."

"Charge the doors?"

"If I clean the malaise out of the school, but everyone who was here today is still carrying it, they'll just bring it back in, and by noon tomorrow everything will be back to the same bad place. So we have to clean the malaise out of the people, too. And doorways are good for that." Lois went to the first set of doors in the front lobby. She pressed her palm against the door frame and waited a moment. "I wonder if you can do it, too. Try it. You can feel when it's done."

Bruno went to the next door and put his hand up to the frame. For a moment he felt nothing; then the metal pulsed twice against his hand, like a single heartbeat. "Wow!"

"You felt it? When someone walks through these doors now, it will pull the malaise out of them, just like a hug. How'd that go, by the way—touching people?" Lois asked Bruno.

"It totally worked. It was so drastic; I was surprised that they weren't suspicious. Their moods changed like night to day."

"They were just relieved to not feel like that anymore. One of the nice things about citizens is that they will write you as many excuses as *they* need. If something they can't explain happens, but it's good, ninety-nine times out of a hundred they won't question it. God bless human nature."

They worked their way through the building. In each hallway Lois pushed the storms on the ceiling out the nearest windows. And they charged every exterior door they could find, so that no matter how people entered the school in the morning, they would pass through a cleansing door. In a few hours they were finished. Suburban slumbered in a familiar, benign stillness, without a cloud in sight.

Back in the library, Bruno erased the lines he'd added to the plan in the first page of *You Are Here,* unblocking the main aisle. He and Lois reentered the stacks, pushing into the darkness. "Tina?" Lois called. "Tina?" She looked around as the darkness loomed. "Now I wish I hadn't given her the flashlight."

"There's usually a lantern up here," Bruno said. He looked into the rows on each side, and soon he spotted it on the floor, glowing like usual.

"Well, that's a pleasant surprise. We have to be quick, or the Ebentwine will affect us, too, right? Tina!" Lois continued calling as they hurried into the darkness of the stacks, wondering what awaited them. "I can feel it," she said, slightly out of breath. "Lights around the edge of my vision." It wasn't until they were almost to the hundredth row that they heard anything. Lois stopped short and caught Bruno's arm. "What was that?"

Bruno listened and heard a faint voice. "It sounds like Ms. Moreletti."

"She's weak. That's good."

They found her slumped on the floor right where Bruno

had closed off the aisle the last time. Bruno stared down at her, fighting the lightheadedness that washed across his brain every time he moved his head.

"You tricked me," Ms. Moreletii whispered up at them, her eyes dull and defeated.

"Yes, *we're* the Unkind ones here," Lois said. "Can you stand?"

"No," Ms. Moreletii said from the floor. But then she began to rise, as though someone very tall had grabbed her underneath each arm and hoisted her up until her feet barely grazed the ground. Her head was too heavy for her to hold it up, and she hung there like a marionette.

"Are you doing that?" Bruno asked Lois, who nodded.

"We'd better get back," she said. "I'm not going to last much longer back here, myself." They hurried toward the reading area, with Tina Moreletii floating between them.

"Hopefully it'll go away pretty quickly as we get farther out," Bruno offered. "Other than the one time I stayed too long, it's always gone away as soon as I got out." He couldn't be sure whether his own exhaustion was the effect of the Ebentwine or his body's natural comedown after the adrenaline rush of the past hours. He wondered what time it was.

When they reached the reading area, Lois turned to Ms. Moreletii. "Do you think you can stand?" Lois lowered her down and she sank into a chair.

"What are you going to do to me?" Her voice was low but stronger. She looked a little more alert.

"Nothing. I don't know about the Unkind, but we're Kind; we can't harm you," Lois told her. "The malaise is gone, and now you have to go, too. If you come back and try something like this again, or anything that hurts people at Suburban, I wouldn't be surprised if we got an admonition to strip you of your powers for good."

Tina shook her head. "It's not that simple."

"Maybe not, but it's a start. I know you're quite powerful, or at least, you will be once your strength returns. But we know who you are now, and we'll be ready for you."

"You have no idea." The teacher's eyes filled with tears, and Bruno and Lois exchanged a curious look. *This is how a powerful Unkind reacts when she's beaten?*

The clock on the wall had its hands up to midnight. "I need to go home," Bruno said.

"We all need to go home," Lois agreed. "We should make sure she gets to her car, though."

They walked her out of the library, down the stairs, and out to the parking lot. Tina moved like someone twice her age, and a few times she had to stop and rest. She seemed defeated, and Bruno was tempted to feel sorry for her. "You knew I was Kind?" he asked her when they were outside.

"Of course I did. And I knew you'd be a problem, which is why I kept trying to get you to drop the class. I also knew you had an Ambassador, which made things harder."

"And you were working with Van?"

"Of course. That fool was supposed to be my project, but he was useless. It was a relief when he got taken out of the picture."

"Did you turn him Unkind?" Lois asked.

"I may have supplied the right temptation, but the choice was his." Tina said wearily. "And Van didn't need a push; he jumped over to the Unkind side."

"Why did you do this? Why would you try to make everyone lose hope?"

"Why do you think? It was in my admonition. But it's so much bigger than that." Her face came alive with defiance.

"Who is Orland?" he asked her.

Her eyes widened. "You know what, why should I keep any secrets? If Orland couldn't be bothered to help me in there, it's pretty clear how little I mean to that—" She straightened up to her full height for the first time. "I was prepared to be loyal, but it seems I've been abandoned, now that I've failed." She looked around angrily. "I was ready to go into exile, and try to get back to the Kind side, before this. And I see now that I should have."

Bruno asked again. "Who is Orland?"

Ms. Moreletii fixed her eyes on him and then Lois. She paused, as if to make it clear she was about to tell them something more important than anything she had ever said out loud. "Orland is—"

There was a blinding flash and a sickening crack. Bruno threw up his hands. When he lowered them, Tina Moreletii lay in a heap on the pavement in front of them. An acrid smell hovered in the air, and a charge lingered, like a science experiment gone terribly wrong.

"Was she struck by lightning?" Lois clutched at Bruno's arm. "Who is that?" she asked under her breath.

Bruno looked up. The night was full of stars, and the nearly full moon cast a cold light on everything. There were no clouds to be seen. Instead, there was a figure in the middle of the open air above them—standing calmly as if on a glass platform five stories up.

"I thought . . . I have no idea," Bruno whispered. The school was too far away for them to run for cover. He and Lois huddled together as though they might somehow make themselves a more difficult target for the next lightning bolt. Bruno braced himself and held his breath.

Then the figure rose higher into the sky and shot across the curved night, disappearing over the trees on the far side of the school. A cool wind pushed down against them, and for a minute they didn't move.

Lois spoke first. "That was Orland? The one Tina said betrayed her?"

"I guess so," Bruno said. "When I found out she was Unkind, I thought she was the one who took Van. I didn't realize that was who she meant when she said Orland. Why didn't he strike us with lightning, too?"

"Was it a man? I thought it was a woman. Who knows." Lois looked down again at Ms. Moreletii's body. "Is she alive?" Bruno knelt down and carefully pressed his fingers under her chin, hoping to find some breath, some life in her form, but there was nothing. He shook his head and Lois gasped. "I never would have asked you to come here tonight if I'd thought—"

"It's okay." He was in shock.

"We can't leave her here."

"If we call someone, we'll have to explain what we were doing here at one in the morning." He stood up. "Lock me in the school and I'll pull the fire alarm before I go, so they'll come and find her."

"Okay," Lois said. They hurried back to the door. "Well, at least we took care of the school," she said. "I never thought she would die. I'm sorry you saw that."

"What does Orland want?"

She sighed. "Not us, and that's all I can think about tonight."

"Go quickly, so the fire trucks don't see you when they get here."

He went back up to the main hall and pulled the alarm before he ducked into the janitor's closet and returned home. He was standing in his bedroom, redrawing the line to close the link between his closet and Suburban, when there was a soft rap on his bedroom door. His father looked in, eyes sleepy and hair askew.

"Did you hear a fire alarm?" he asked, and Bruno did his best to look confused by the question. "I must have been dreaming. Why are you up and dressed, anyway?"

"I couldn't sleep. I was thinking of going for a walk," Bruno said.

"Don't go far. It makes me nervous to think of you out there alone in the dark. Anything could happen."

"I won't go far."

"Good night."

"Good night."

Bruno went downstairs to the front door and pressed his hand against the frame until it pulsed from his Kind charge. He went to the back door and did the same. Back upstairs, he sat on his bed in his clothes. His body was exhausted, but his mind wasn't ready to let go of everything that had happened. He had made peace with the truth that being Kind made some things easier and other things harder. And he had made his choice — to take his place in the world of the Kind, and not back away from it.

17

heartbreak beat

WHAT'S GOING ON?" CELIA whispered to Bruno in the hall the next morning. "What happened? Do you know why there's an assembly?"

Bruno thought it might be easier to tell her what *hadn't* happened. "Ms. Moreletii's dead."

"*What?* She's *dead*?"

Bruno nodded. "Last night. Or this morning. I don't know; it's all kind of a blur. She came back to school because Mariette gave her a fake kiss note, and Lois and I trapped her in the Ebentwine in the library to weaken her. Lois cleared the malaise out of the halls, and then we let Tina—Ms. Moreletii —out. She wasn't as bad off as I was, but she could barely stand up. We took her out in the parking lot, and that floating figure struck her with lightning, right in front of us."

"Wait—the floating figure wasn't Ms. Moreletii?"

"No—I thought that, too!"

"You could have been killed! What did you do?"

"Nothing. It wasn't interested in us. It zapped her, and then it flew off. But there's more. She knew its name: Orland."

"Orland? Did you see . . . him?"

"Not really. Orland stayed up in the air, just like before."

"So the assembly must be about that. And then there'll be grief counselors, just like last year with Mariette . . ." Celia sighed. "So they think she was struck by lightning?"

"Probably. I guess we'll find out."

"Even if everyone thinks it was a freak accident, that's still two deaths in two years at the school. People are going to start wondering what's going on here."

"What do the Unkind want? What does Orland want? It seems like they're trying to take over Suburban, but why? But if Orland is Unkind, why kill another Unkind?"

"If Orland is Kind, why stand by watching while an Unkind tried to kill me last year?"

"So what does Orland want?"

"All I know is, finding out might be the most important thing we ever do."

They went off to their homerooms and then down to the auditorium, where Mr. Spennicut broke the news.

After school, Celia met Bruno at a table in the reading area of the library. "Do you think Lois will leave now?" she asked quietly while they waited for the others to arrive.

"I don't know. She can't say she has nothing to offer anymore. She's the reason Ms. Moreletii's malaise is gone from the school."

"I wish I could have been there," Celia said. "It must have been scary, but now that it's over and you're safe, it sounds exciting, too."

"It was plenty of both."

"And now we have a name. Orland." Celia waved as Marco came into the library. "He's still stressed about Mariette's note."

"This fashion show is the perfect thing to distract him. Is that Gwendolyn?"

"Sure is. What's she doing here after school?" They watched her walk up to Marco to say hello. "Did he ask her to model, so he could have three girls? It sure looks like it."

"Why didn't he tell me?" Bruno said.

"Because you would have told him not to do it!" Celia laughed in spite of herself. "Don't worry about it. She has a crush on you, and you're not interested, and now you're going to be in Marco's fashion show together. That's it."

"I just . . . I know how it feels," Bruno said.

"Oh," Celia said. "I won't give you advice, then. Just try not to make it tense, for Marco's sake, okay?"

"I won't." They went to join the others.

Sylvio and Regine arrived and took their now customary seats on opposite sides of the reading area. Marco gave them a pained look and said, "I guess we're just waiting for the St. Dymphna contingent, then."

As if on cue, the group of boys entered. Tomasi wore an annoyed expression, as though fully aware that he and the six sophomores looked like a tall black shepherd with six black sheep.

There were introductions and compliments, and then Marco laid out his plans for the fashion show. Bruno was distracted by the St. Dymphna boys, who always seemed to be staring at Celia. When the planning session was over, the six of them fanned out to talk to everyone else, and Bruno wondered if they'd coordinated their targets in advance.

"How've you been?" Turlington asked Bruno.

"Good. Thanks for doing this. It means a lot to Marco."

"We were thrilled to be asked. So this is Suburban High.

I've never been here before." Turlington looked curiously at the stacks that receded into darkness. "If half the stories I've heard are true, this is a pretty crazy school."

"What stories have you heard?"

"Didn't a teacher just die here last night? And we heard about the curse on sophomore virgins last year, and the girl who died then. Does she really haunt the science wing?"

"Some people say they've seen her," Bruno said cagily.

"Giving out kiss notes?"

"You've heard about all this?"

"If a story is juicy, it travels," Turlington said. "So, have you received a kiss note?"

"No. I'm not dating anyone, so . . ."

Turlington's eyebrow went up. "Oh? Would you like to change that?"

"I'm good, thanks," Bruno said.

Turlington looked over at one of his friends monopolizing Celia, and Bruno tried to remember whether that was Schiffer or Crawford. "Celia is amazing. We're all kind of in love with her."

"I'm sure she'd be flattered if you told her" was all Bruno could think to say.

"Well, I guess I'll see you at Diaboliques!" Turlington went to join the conversation with Celia.

Bruno found Tomasi. "Are they Unkind?" he asked him.

"What makes you think that?" Tomasi asked.

"They're all in love with her." The two of them watched the boys collected around Celia, hanging on her words. "Is it the agon?"

"Oh. I don't know. They kind of act like that with every-one."

"Are you sure?"

"No."

"MR. PERILUNAS HAS BEEN researching the cartographers of the fifteenth century," Mr. Williams told the class. "Mr. Perilunas, would you care to explain to the class how early maps of the east coast of the Americas were distorted by the agendas of the explorers?"

Bruno was no longer surprised by these requests from Mr. Williams. As he tried to make a quick, coherent summary so he could sit down again, Bruno remembered the times he had wondered whether the warning in his admonition had been about Mr. Williams.

Once again, he waited after class.

"What is it, Mr. Perilunas?"

"I just want to know why you've given me all this extra stuff to do. It's more work for me, but it's also been more work for you. You could have just done enough to keep me on my toes so I'd pay attention in class, but you've done a lot more than that."

Mr. Williams was silent for a moment. "When I was younger, it was plain to me I must make something of myself. I guess the short answer is that I see a lot of myself in you, Bruno." It was the first time Mr. Williams had called him by his first name. "Sometimes we need someone to push us, to help us be as great as we can be. But being good at something doesn't necessarily mean we have it easier than others. Sometimes it makes things harder." He looked out the window.

"I'm glad you did. Thank you. I've learned a lot."

"You have. And I'm glad. I hope you'll stay in touch next year, even if we don't have a class together."

Bruno never had thought about being friends with a teacher, but then he had to admit he thought of Lois as a friend, too. "I will," he said, and was pleased to shake Mr. Williams's hand.

"Then again, the year is far from over. I have a feeling you have quite a bit left to learn. In this class and elsewhere. I'll see you tomorrow."

BRUNO WAS WALKING PAST the science wing on his way down the main hall when one of his books slipped from his arm and fell to the floor. The assignment he had tucked inside the front cover skittered through the doorway into the empty classroom. He picked up the book and then went after the paper. When he stood up, Mariette was there.

"You are impossible," she said, but her face was contagiously happy, and he found himself smiling like someone who's just lost a game of assassin. She held a folded piece of paper in her hand. "I've been trying to give you this forever."

"I hoped the date would expire and then you wouldn't have any reason to give it to me."

"That's not how it works, and you know it," she said. "I wanted to meet you for other reasons, though. We barely got to talk in the library."

"Why?" He thought a moment. "Celia?"

"We have a lot in common. Pining away for that girl."

"Is that why you're still here?"

"In a way. Not exactly, but it has something to do with it."

"She said you didn't talk. Why didn't you talk to her?"

Mariette shrugged. "There wasn't any reason to speak. What would I have said?"

"How did you make peace with it—knowing she wouldn't

love you back? Even now, when Tomasi understands the whole agon thing, he still acts like he thinks I'm going to try to steal her from him."

"He doesn't hate you. He's doing what anyone would do if he knew another guy was in love with his girlfriend. He could have beaten you to a pulp by now."

"I don't want it to be that way. I really don't want to break them up. It's my problem. I get that completely."

"When you're in high school and you fall in love, it's so easy to believe it's the most important thing in the world. But you know it's not, so you enjoy the ache when you can, and remind yourself you aren't completely in control when you can't."

"That's your advice?"

"That, and I will give you this, finally." Mariette put the paper in Bruno's hand.

"What's it like, being a ghost?"

"What's it like, being alive?" she asked him. "It's nice to meet you."

"You too," he said.

They looked at each other, and she said, "Well, read it!"

Bruno braced himself for a date and time, but when he opened the paper he found an admonition instead:

> *Gain your power; learn your purpose*
> *Find what lies beneath the surface*
> *Do all this before the last*
> *New moon before the summer solstice*
>
> *The one you think you've long opposed*
> *Will be the one who needs you close*
> *Find new spaces in between*

And kiss the one who means the most

Beware the one with much to tend
With more than one means to an end
Who sometimes masquerades as foe
But likes to masquerade as friend

Bruno shook his head. *Here we go again.* He folded the paper and slipped it into his pocket. He was heading toward the classroom door when his books flew out of his arm and scattered on the floor. "Really, Mariette?" He laughed, turning around.

But it wasn't Mariette who stood behind him. Her skirt and jacket glowed as the sun shone faintly through her. Her wavy hair cascaded around her shoulders, and her eyes held the glint of a gentle crazy person who might shriek with sadness at any provocation. Tina Moreletii backed away from him, her fingers wiggling in his direction. Then she turned and walked out the door.

"Oh, God. Now we have two ghosts?"

BRUNO LOOKED AT THE CLOCK. It was nearly three in the morning, but he hadn't slept yet. He must have listened to "Song to the Siren" on his headphones at least fifty times.

Just as before, his new admonition was a tossed salad of words whose meaning eluded him no matter how many times he read it. But just as with the first admonition, one line stuck out: *Kiss the one who means the most.* Who wrote these admonitions? Was there any other possible way to interpret that line? With seven words Bruno's oldest dilemma had changed yet again. The same unknown forces that dictated the bizarre laws of this alternate universe, in which he was uncontrollably in love with a girl he couldn't have, had told him to kiss her anyway. Why had he spent the last six months wrestling with his will, putting honor above all, if in the end he was going to be ordered to throw it all to the wind?

He got up and went to his desk. One click turned on the lamp. One piece of paper and one pencil. In less than a minute Bruno had drawn the liminal between his bedroom closet and hers.

He opened the closet door and leaned in. There was no light, no sound on the other side. Carefully he picked his way through the hanging clothes on his bar, and then hers, until he put his hand on the back of Celia's closet door.

He opened the door and waited for his eyes to adjust. The window admitted enough moonlight so that eventually he could see. She lay asleep in her bed, her slender arm across her body on top of the duvet. In four soft steps he was standing over her bedside.

You were creepy when you went to the bookstore to watch her through the window. You were even creepier when you stood in her backyard watching her through her window. What the hell are you doing now?

Bruno tried to rationalize it. *If you do it while she's asleep and she doesn't wake up, she'll never know. You can fulfill that part of your admonition and still have a shred of integrity left.* In sleep she was even more beautiful, pale skin washed by the moonlight, dark straight hair fanning out around her face.

He stood there. Her breathing was light and slow, and her chest rose and fell gently.

He crept back to her closet and silently closed the door behind him. Back in his room he tore the paper with the terrible shortcut into smaller and smaller bits. He got back into bed and put his headphones back on. "Song to the Siren" was still playing.

"LIKE THIS?" BRUNO LOOKED around from the desk in Marco's bedroom.

Marco put down his pins and came over to see. Bruno couldn't even guess what part of a garment Marco had him cutting. "Yes, perfect." Marco went back to the tailoring dummy where he was fitting a jacket, but he didn't seem to be getting much done.

"You're nervous," Bruno said.

"Hell yeah, I'm nervous! He's going to be home in a few hours. I just won't be sure everything's okay until I see him. What if he's waiting to break up with me in person?"

"Do you really think that's likely?"

"I don't know. Maybe?" Marco exhaled, looking around the room at the unfinished garments on every surface. "Probably not. But part of me keeps wondering." He paced around the room. As Bruno turned back to his cutting, the doorbell rang. "Who's that?" Marco left to go downstairs, and in a moment Bruno heard him shout in surprise. "What are you doing here?"

"I couldn't wait!"

Bruno went out into the upstairs hall and looked down over the foyer, where Marco and Brenden were locked in an embrace. Then Brenden started crying.

"What's wrong?" Marco pulled back and held his shoulders.

"I couldn't tell you on the phone." Brenden wiped his eyes and tried to pull himself together. "I've felt so guilty. This guy kissed me, and I made him stop—I don't like him at all, I swear! I never meant, I never wanted—" He started crying again.

"Hey, it's okay. Tell me what happened." Marco put his arms around Brenden.

"This guy in my writing class, he's really cool and we hit it off, and I kind of suspected he liked me. But I told him about you, and I made it clear I wasn't interested. I wasn't even tempted. He's too tall." They laughed. "But one night we were walking back to the dorms, and there's this archway under a building on campus. There are all these stories about if you kiss someone under the arch, you'll marry them. All the sorority girls take their dates there.

"So, we're walking under the arch and he stops, and tells me he likes me, and I'm trying to be kind, because I know it sucks to like someone and have them not like you back. And then he just kisses me! I stopped him, but I've felt so guilty ever since." Brenden's voice broke. "I almost felt like you knew, the way you sounded on the phone that night. Something in your voice—it was like you had guessed, somehow. But I wanted to tell you the whole thing in person, so I could swear to you that nothing else happened, and I'm completely in love with you, and I don't talk to that guy anymore."

"It's okay! I believe you!" Marco kissed him. "Have you been beating yourself up about this for a month and a half?" Brenden nodded. "You crazy man."

They kissed again until Marco pulled away and said, "Bruno's here."

"What?"

"He's been helping me with the collection. And trying to keep me from going insane until you got home."

"Really?" Brenden arched an eyebrow.

"Oh, please! You've just come clean about making out with some guy at college. Are you really going to get suspicious of me and Bruno?" They laughed. Upstairs Bruno went back into Marco's bedroom to get his coat.

He said hello and goodbye on his way out. There was a dense patch of trees between the houses across the street, and on impulse he crossed over and walked into it. He had a nervous moment, worried he would stumble into a stranger's backyard and have to try to explain what he was doing there, but sure enough, he found himself in the familiar clearing.

It took Gardner a moment to appear. "Well, I'm impressed!"

"So am I." Bruno grinned.

"THEY'RE ALMOST FINISHED," the student stage manager said to Marco. The rest of the home economics students had taken turns walking the runway in their simple A-line skirts and square-cut Windbreakers, to polite applause from the audience of students and parents. Marco's collection would close the show.

"Good, good." Marco turned back to the line of his models, scrutinizing them for the hundredth time. Bruno marveled once more at the black silk blazer Marco had made for him, paired with a gray shirt with French cuffs and lightweight wool trousers. All the models wore black leather gloves.

Turlington stood in front of Bruno. "He shouldn't be nervous. This is going to be awesome!"

Then the lights went out in the auditorium, and Marco's models shuffled from the wings toward the opening in the middle of the curtain, which gave way to the catwalk that stretched out halfway into the first section of seats. The eerie opening notes of "Stranger" by Clan of Xymox played in the darkness, and Bruno turned to Gwendolyn, in line behind him. She didn't look as scared as he expected. "You look great," he told her.

"So do you," she said, but her smile looked polite and nothing more.

"Thank you for doing this for Marco. I know he really appreciates it," Bruno said.

"I did it for you, too," she said. "Or at least, when I said I would do it, it was for you, too."

"Well, thank you." Bruno looked awkwardly away.

Tomasi took his place in the darkened opening. His gray silk suit, accessorized with top hat and the gloves, foreshadowed the rest of the collection. When the drumbeat of the song kicked in, the spotlight opened on him and he strode out onto the catwalk. Soon the stage manager beckoned, and Campbell stepped closer to the opening. When Tomasi returned to the top of the catwalk, he turned around so the two of them could walk together. When they returned, Tomasi exited and Turlington joined Campbell for his second walk.

Bruno was next. At the stage manager's cue he stepped into the light, joining Turlington as Campbell exited. Bruno was concentrating so hard on all the pointers Marco had given them — keep his chin up, shoulders back, don't walk too fast, don't swing his arms — he was at the end of the runway before he noticed the audience. They were quiet and almost motionless. Here and there a camera flash went off. Bruno and Turlington turned around and went back.

When Gwendolyn stepped out to walk with Bruno, the audience applauded for the first time. She wore a gown that gave the illusion of a fitted jacket over a full skirt, all made from the same charcoal raw silk, elaborately trimmed with black gros-grain ribbon, and in the spotlight, with her hair swept up in a chignon, she looked like a movie star. She gave Bruno a quick smile, excited this time, and then they were walking again. Now Bruno relaxed a little and was able to enjoy the thrill of doing yet another thing he never would have predicted he'd do before he arrived at Suburban. Too soon they returned to the top of the catwalk, and Bruno's work was done until the final parade.

Marco pulled Bruno over. "What's the audience like?"

"I think they're blown away," Bruno said honestly. "This is like a real show."

"I hope so!" Marco beamed. "I couldn't have done it with-out you."

"What do you mean? I barely helped you. You did all this yourself."

"Still, I knew you had my back. It meant a lot."

"Sure." They watched the rest of the models go out for their walks.

Celia closed the show in a full gray gown laced from the bodice to the floor with grosgrain ribbon, and drew the most applause yet. Then Marco joined her, and Bruno and the rest of the models followed the two of them down the catwalk and back, clapping along with the audience, which roared its ap-proval.

"I can't believe it!" Marco said when it was over. "I can't believe that just happened!" He hugged everyone within reach.

Within minutes Chris and Cosey had found their way backstage. Cosey gushed, kissing Marco on both cheeks. "I want all of it! I knew you were talented, but you just blew my mind! You *must* come by this weekend, and we'll place an order for as much as you can make!"

"Thank you!" Marco said. "Thank you so much!"

Bruno got back into his own clothes and went out to find his parents. "Here's one of the models!" Mr. Perilunas pulled him close. "You looked great! You all did! Your friend is an extraordinary tailor."

"He is."

Bruno's mother kissed him. "Alice and Gertrude are here. Did you know they were coming?"

"I'm not surprised. They're friends with Lippa, Celia's boss at the bookstore." Bruno looked around the crowd and saw the Troika in a cluster.

"Go say hello. We'll keep an eye out for Sylvio."

Bruno went over to the women, who greeted him warmly. He thanked them for coming.

"We wouldn't have missed it," Lippa said. "Your friend is incredibly talented, and you all did a great job. But we were almost as curious to see this school as the show."

"Really?"

"Did Celia tell you about her friend Mariette, and what happened here last year? Well, at the time Celia thought Mariette was one of the Kind, and I thought I had just put too many ideas in her head. But after that boy found you at the store that night and asked you about being an Ambassador, I remembered it. Now we wonder if she wasn't on to something." Lippa looked at Alice and Gertrude, who nodded knowingly.

"You think . . . you really think?" Bruno looked from one to the next.

"I don't know what I think, but I am definitely intrigued," Lippa said. "How crazy would it be if Suburban was a hot spot of Unkind activity, and no one had any idea? Maybe we could tell you and Celia what to look for, and you could let us know if you see anything unusual."

"Nothing very interesting happens here." Bruno said.

Marco appeared in the lobby, hand in hand with Celia, who hadn't changed out of her gown. She made the rounds with him, beaming as he received his well-deserved accolades. Every time Bruno looked at her, he thought only of the new moon that was coming soon, and the power he was about to squander by failing to meet his admonition—it made his attraction to her all the more vibrant, more desperate. But his head held his heart at bay. Even in the strange world of the Kind, if something felt wrong, he was determined not to do it. There would be another admonition after this one expired. One with terms he hoped he could accept.

SYLVIO HANDED THE PHONE to Bruno and lingered to hear what he said. "Hello?"

"Bruno? It's Celia. Something's wrong."

"What happened?"

"It's Tomasi. He was supposed to come to me last night, through my sketchbook. He never came, and I was bothered by it, but only in the annoyed girlfriend kind of way."

"Okay . . ."

"But this morning his parents called me, wondering if I knew where he was. They must be really concerned, because they've never been crazy about me."

"So he's not at home, and—" Bruno looked at Sylvio standing over him. "You know, let me come over."

"Would you? Please!"

Bruno hung up, and Sylvio said, "What's going on?"

"I don't know," Bruno said honestly. He had a bad feeling. "I have to go."

"To Celia's? Do you need a ride?"

"That would be great."

"Sure. That's how cool I am. You can be all mysterious and I'll still give you a ride." Sylvio went to get his keys.

At Celia's house Bruno traded polite greetings with Mrs. Balaustine before he went upstairs with Celia. Bruno still felt strange being in her bedroom and hoped Tomasi wouldn't suddenly reappear.

Closing the door behind them, Celia said, "All I can think is that he went into the book in his house, but didn't make it to my sketchbook. Have you figured out anything about how he travels?"

"Not really. Did he ever tell you what it was like in there?"

"He says it's like jumping out the window of a plane and then hurtling through space like a skydiver toward another window." Celia fell silent.

"And he thought someone was following him."

Celia nodded. "But he never actually saw anyone because it goes by so quickly."

Bruno didn't know what to do. "I wonder if Gardner knows."

"Gardner?"

"He seemed to know about Tomasi. One time he said something about how Tomasi traveled differently, and I didn't understand what he meant, but I bet Gardner is familiar with that space, too. Of course—it's a liminal, so it's another form of Ebentwine!"

"Would you ask him?"

"I'll go right now." Bruno got up, and Celia did, too.

"Can I go with you?"

"Would you mind if I went alone? I have a feeling he might tell me more if you're not there." Bruno felt bad about leaving her because he could tell she was scared. But he had a hunch he wasn't going to like what Gardner had to say.

He went out into the backyard and glanced around before stepping into the bushes behind Celia's house. In a moment he reached Ebentwine, where Gardner was waiting.

"You know where Tomasi is, don't you?"

"Well, hello to you." When Bruno didn't speak, Gardner added, "Yes, I know where he is."

"What have you done to him?"

"Why do you care? If Tomasi is out of the way, you can console Celia, be a shoulder for her to cry on. You never know where that might lead."

"Why would you say that? The way he travels—that's the Ebentwine, too, isn't it? Is he trapped in the Ebentwine?"

"I don't know if I would say trapped, but he's there," Gardner said. "And I suppose you're going to try to get him out now."

"I have to."

"No, you don't. You could go back and tell her there's nothing you can do. There are other people she could ask for help, you know."

"Is what happened to me, and Ms. Moreletii, happening to him?"

"What do you mean? The lightheadedness? The blurred vision? Disorientation and loss of strength? Unconsciousness?" Gardner watched Bruno, who already could feel the first symptoms encroaching on him.

"You shouldn't have done this!" Bruno said, and stumbled back through the bushes to Celia's house.

She was waiting in the backyard. "What did he say?"

"Tomasi is trapped in the Ebentwine, and I have to go get him out."

"He's in the clearing?"

"The Ebentwine isn't just the clearing. It's all the places inbetween. When Tomasi travels between books, he uses the Ebentwine, the way I use the clearing."

"How can we get to him?"

"I don't know. I don't know how to get to his Ebentwine."

"Please, think. Anything!" Celia pleaded with him.

"My in between is a shortcut between places. His in between is a shortcut between books . . . The library! I think the school library might be the way."

"I'll come with you," she said, but he stopped her.

"If he . . . I think you should stay here. Please, trust me," Bruno said. Celia looked ready to cry. "I have to go. If he's been in there that long . . ." Bruno reached out to touch her but stopped halfway, not sure if he should. "Can I use a piece of paper?"

She pulled a sheet out of her sketchbook and watched as he quickly sketched her bedroom and closet, connecting them to the janitor's closet and the hallway at Suburban. Then he went into the closet, pushed past her clothes, and felt for the mop bucket behind them. In a moment he was in the first year hallway. Bruno took off running for the library. *What if it's locked?* He tried to think of a closet in the library he could use to pass through. But it was no matter—when he got there, the library doors were open and the lights were on.

"Bruno! What are you doing here?" Lois looked up in surprise.

"Tomasi is trapped in the Ebentwine," Bruno said, panting. "I have to get him out."

"Here? How will you—in the stacks?" He nodded. "Do you know what you're doing?" He shook his head. "Are you sure this is a good idea?"

"No." Bruno ran through the gate that protected the stacks, sending it swinging. He charged down the aisle and paused to pick up the lantern. *One, two, four, eight, sixteen, thirty-two, sixty-four. That means if there's another volume of* You Are Here, *it's in aisle one hundred twenty-eight.* Bruno ran as fast as he could down the main aisle until it was as black as a cave. He slowed down every now and then to raise the lantern and check the aisle number. The air began to change, turning hollow and gusty, as though a storm were brewing. Pockets of wind blew out of the side aisles, buffeting him as he passed. There was a rustling, a distant roar that grew, and then the first scrap of paper brushed across his face like a giant moth, flapping away in the darkness.

When he reached aisle 128, the lights had begun to flit around the corners of his vision. He scanned down the aisle until he found *You Are Here.* This volume was so large, he had to put the lantern down and lift it with both hands. He opened it and found a twelve-line poem.

"An admonition? I don't need an admonition!" Bruno turned the page and found another admonition. "Help me out!" He kept turning pages, and each one flapped away from his hand in the wind.

Halfway through the book he found an illustration. Bits of graphite streaked across the page, making it look like a blurry sheet of newsprint. The edges of the drawing were dark, but in a corner a silhouette was visible, looking like a drunken man crumpled on a park bench. "Tomasi!" Bruno called as loudly as he could into the gusts that blew off the page from the space in the drawing, mixing with the tormented air in the library. The figure lifted its head. Bruno put his hand to the page and was surprised when it went straight through. Bits of paper brushed against his arm as he strained to reach as far as he could, but Tomasi was too far from the surface of the page.

"Tomasi! Can you reach for me?" Bruno stretched as far as he could into the drawing, but Tomasi barely moved his head. Bruno yelled in frustration and pulled his arm out of the book. He pounded his head, trying to figure out what to do.

What's next? One twenty-eight . . . two fifty-six? Bruno left the book on the floor, scooped up the lantern, and headed back to the main aisle. He took off running again, and now the wind grew louder, like a storm coming in off the sea on a night with no moon. The pressure in his ears kept changing, and once he slipped and crashed into the end of a row of shelves. Now and then someone rushed across his path, but he ignored them. He kept going, checking the aisle numbers, and slowed down a little as his destination approached. Ahead of him a figure loomed in the darkness. It was Gardner, standing by aisle 256.

"You shouldn't be here," Gardner said.

"I have to save Tomasi," Bruno said, gasping.

"No, you don't. Go be happy with Celia."

"I can't do that. Are you going to stop me?"

"I can't stop you." Gardner stepped aside, and Bruno entered the aisle, feeling as though he might faint.

The books were nearly as tall as he was. He hoped the volume he needed was on the bottom shelf, because he didn't know how he would get a book down from the top. *You Are Here* jutted out from the bottom, and he set down the lantern and tugged at it, blacking out for a moment. He shook his head and his vision returned, and he labored to prop the huge book against the shelf so he could heft the cover open.

This time the drawing was on the first page: graphite images of papers streaking across the page. Some of them flew out of the drawing, whipping around him like headless birds before they drifted to the floor. Tomasi was there, too, hunched in the same place as before. But now he was twice as close to the surface of the page, and when Bruno reached through, he could grasp Tomasi's arm. "Come on!" he called. Tomasi's head lolled to the side. Bruno pushed his other arm through the page and pulled on Tomasi with all his might. Tomasi struggled up and lurched toward Bruno. He fell, but his hand caught on to the bottom of the book as though it were a windowsill, and Bruno pulled him back up, hoisting his upper body over the threshold. "Tomasi, you have to lift your legs!" Bruno reached into the drawing and dragged one of Tomasi's legs up over the bottom of the page. Then he pulled him as hard as he could, and Tomasi toppled out onto the library floor. Bruno closed the book.

"Can you hear me?" he asked Tomasi, who weakly lifted his head and looked up at Bruno. "We have to get back!"

Tomasi tried to speak, and Bruno bent close to hear him. "How did you find me?"

"I got lucky," Bruno said. He helped Tomasi roll onto his hands and knees and somehow managed to get him on his feet.

"Where are we?" Tomasi croaked.

"In the library at Suburban."

"Don't they have lights?"

"Not back here," Bruno said. He picked up the lantern and pulled Tomasi's arm around his shoulders to support him. "This way. We have to get out of here."

"I can do it," Tomasi groaned, but he sagged into Bruno and they went down. "I'm sorry!"

"I've been back here too long, too," Bruno said, willing his quivering legs to hold him up while he hauled Tomasi back onto his feet. They knocked back and forth between the shelves, groping their way to the main aisle.

Gardner stood waiting. Tomasi bristled at the sight of him. "What are you doing here?"

"It makes far more sense for me to be here than you," Gardner told him.

"You trapped me here!" Tomasi said weakly.

Gardner chuckled. "That doesn't change what I said."

"Come on!" Bruno tried to take more of Tomasi's weight against his shoulders, but he nearly went down again. He looked at Gardner once more. "I will deal with you later."

"Oh, you will, will you?" Gardner walked into the darkness, deeper into the Ebentwine, as Bruno and Tomasi started back toward the tiny light that looked miles away.

"I don't think I can . . ." Tomasi pulled them over to the end of a shelf, and they leaned there.

"You have to," Bruno said, trying to convince himself of the same thing.

They made it another few rows, and then their legs tangled and they went down again. Bruno wasn't sure if he lost consciousness for a moment, but Tomasi was out cold. "Help!" he yelled, sure no one could hear him. "Help!" He looked down the aisle toward the reading area and thought he saw a flashlight. Then he passed out for good.

WHEN BRUNO CAME TO, he was sprawled on a table in the reading room, and someone was stroking his hair. He tried to sit up but collapsed back onto the hard surface. Mariette looked down over him. "Give it another minute."

"Oh, good!" Lois exclaimed, coming over.

"Did you get us out?" Bruno asked, rubbing his head.

"The two of you are heavier than my sofa at home," she said. "I'm pretty worn out myself."

When Bruno was able to get up, he saw Tomasi on his back on the next table, eyes closed, unmoving. "Is he . . ."

"Celia's working on him."

There she was, off to the side, her face ashen as she labored over her sketchbook.

"How did you get here?" Bruno jumped off the table, but his legs failed him and he fell onto the floor. Lois helped him up.

"Did you think I was going to just wait in my room, when you left the closet door open?" Celia said without looking up.

"It's a good thing she did," Lois added. "I can't do what she's doing."

They fell silent, watching Celia. She stopped drawing, looked at Tomasi, and said, "C'mon! I finished! I guess I'll draw him again?" She turned the page and started another portrait. After a minute, Tomasi's eyelids fluttered and he inhaled deeply. Soon he put his hand to his head and then rolled onto his side. "Where . . . What happened?" He saw Celia and tried to roll toward her. She set down her sketchbook and went to put her arms around him.

"Bruno got you out," she said, kissing his forehead. "I should keep drawing you, to help you get more of your strength back." She kissed Tomasi again and returned to her sketchbook.

"Why did he do that? That man?" Tomasi asked Bruno. He saw Lois and gave her a small, confused wave.

"Gardner. He seems to be in charge of the Ebentwine."

"Why would he do that to me? Did I do something wrong?" Tomasi asked. He noticed Mariette, who was standing away from the rest of them. "Is that . . . I heard you were around."

"Hi!" Mariette smiled.

Lois stepped closer to Tomasi. "In a strange way, you have done something wrong. But I don't think you could guess what it is." She paused, looking at Celia. "As I'm sure Bruno has told you, I wasn't very familiar with Ambassadors. I've never met one before Celia. I'm sorry I didn't trust you. I hope you didn't take it personally." Celia shook her head. "It's just that there is as much bad folklore about Ambassadors as there is good, and I didn't know what to believe."

"This is about Celia?" Tomasi asked.

"It's about you *and* Celia. I never would have believed this was true before, but I think you've heard about the agon between Ambassadors and our Kind. We are invariably attracted to Ambassadors if we meet them. We have amazing chemistry with them, and we tend to fall in love with them. You fell in love with Celia," Lois said to Tomasi. She turned to Bruno. "And so did you."

Celia added, "And Mariette." Mariette nodded silently.

"So, are you in love with Celia, too?" Tomasi asked Lois.

"No, but I'm pretty sure that's only because I'm straight. If I ever meet a male Ambassador, I will inevitably have very strong feelings for him."

"We don't have a choice." Tomasi looked at Bruno.

"Do we ever choose who we love?" Lois asked.

"I guess not. But I think you should start drawing Bruno," Tomasi said. "He looks pretty bad."

Bruno had been trying to hold himself up, but he sat down hard in the chair behind him, and Celia quickly turned the page in her sketchbook. "I'm so sorry! You were in there, too!" She started drawing him, and immediately Bruno felt the lines of warmth spreading across his face.

"Here's the problem," Lois continued. "This agon between an Ambassador and someone of the Kind is very destabilizing. In small doses it is good: It connects us with people who understand us and help us. It motivates us to follow through on admonitions, and makes us stronger. But if it becomes too deep, too serious, too lasting, it's bad. If an Ambassador becomes too attached to one Kind, she's less able to fulfill her duties to the other Kind around her. I think your relationship must have become too serious," Lois told them. "And the forces of the Kind were bound to try to stop it."

"What are you thinking?" Celia asked Tomasi, who wore a strange expression.

"She told me. Cassandra told me. The first time you took me to meet her. Remember? You asked me, and I told you she said I was to be good to you? What she really said was that my love would be my greatest strength and my greatest weakness. And I must learn to love you from a distance. At the time, I just thought she was warning me not to pressure you, to, you know . . . But she must have meant this."

"Oh, God," Celia said, her eyes wide.

"So that's why Gardner ambushed you," Bruno said. "I thought it was because he wanted me to have a chance with Celia."

"Well, he probably did want you to go after Celia," Lois said. "If you had succeeded in breaking up Tomasi and Celia, it would have served the same purpose. But if you and Celia had become a couple, eventually Gardner would have done something to break you two up, as well."

"But I don't want to stop dating Celia." Tomasi turned to her. "I love you."

Celia put down her sketchbook again and went to him. "I love you, too," she said in a voice Bruno wished he hadn't heard.

"I don't know what to tell you," Lois said. "Now that we're pretty sure these stories are true, they would suggest that bad things will continue to happen if the two of you stay together."

"Will Gardner stop me again if I travel between books?"

"If your relationship with Celia hasn't changed, he might."

"What am I going to do?" Tomasi asked Celia.

Lois said, "The other thing to keep in mind is that something could happen to Celia, too—anything that would separate you."

"I can't believe this," Tomasi said.

"I'm sorry, you guys." Bruno didn't feel completely well, but he wasn't going to ask Celia to return to drawing him now.

Celia asked Lois, "What happens now?"

"I wish I could be more helpful."

"You have been, though—no one else could have gotten Bruno and Tomasi out of there. I know you were thinking of leaving, and I'm so glad you stayed!" Celia said to Tomasi, "I think we should go back to my house. I can walk you home from there." Tomasi nodded and stood up carefully.

Celia turned to Mariette. "This is so crazy—I've barely talked to you! I didn't realize you could talk at all! Can we . . . sometime?"

"Sure," Mariette said. She hugged Celia and turned to Bruno. "Let's walk them to the liminal."

"Thank you so much," Celia said to Lois, and was echoed by Tomasi and Bruno.

"You're welcome. Please forgive me for not—for not be-lieving Bruno sooner."

"It's okay. I'll come to see you; we have a lot of catching up to do, if I'm going to be your Ambassador. I really hope you'll stay here."

"I think I have to, now." Lois smiled.

"I'll be back," Bruno told Lois, and he went with Celia, Tomasi, and Mariette down the hall to the janitor's closet.

Celia embraced Bruno, kissing him on the cheek. "Thank you, Bruno," she said softly.

"You're welcome." They smiled at each other in a new way.

Bruno and Tomasi looked at each other, and then Tomasi stepped in awkwardly and hugged him. "I owe you."

"No you don't," Bruno said.

"There were a couple times I really wanted to deck you."

"I probably deserved it."

Tomasi and Celia went into the closet and were gone. Bruno glimpsed the light from Celia's bedroom through the mops; then he heard her door close on the other side. He closed the door. Mariette glowed faintly in the darkened hall-way.

"You are a hero. A tragic hero, but a hero all the same."

"I don't feel like one."

"Here, take this," she said, and without thinking he held out his hand. "As if you haven't had enough for one night."

"Really?" Bruno looked down at the piece of paper she had given him. When he looked back up, Mariette was gone.

Lois was waiting for him back in the library. "Why were you here tonight?" Bruno asked her.

"My admonition told me to come," she said. "But I had no idea . . ."

"You and me both," he said. "I just fulfilled two-thirds of my admonition."

"What's that?" Lois pointed to the paper in Bruno's hand. He opened it and read, *Perilunas tennis court, Tuesday, 8:00 p.m.*

BRUNO'S HEART BEAT FASTER as he approached the clearing. Gardner was waiting for him. "There you are," said the man in the mackintosh, as though nothing had happened.

Bruno knew he couldn't stay long. "What you did was wrong."

"That's like saying the moon coming up is wrong," Gardner said plainly. "It doesn't matter if you think it was wrong or not."

"I don't trust you."

"I have never lied to you, and you know I have no motivation to do anything other than to keep this place — this world — in order."

Bruno stared at him. "It's wrong to try to kill someone."

"Yes, it is. But it is not wrong to go about your life knowing it may be dangerous at times. In fact, it is the right thing to do."

"Are you saying you knew Tomasi wouldn't die?"

"That is not what I said. He *will* die someday, you realize. If it's not now, it will come. But that's no reason to flee from anything that is difficult, or anything that's worth struggling to attain." Gardner looked at Bruno in a way that reminded him of Cassandra. "Tomasi wouldn't have died. I would have pushed him out before that happened."

"I don't believe you."

"That's up to you. Are you on your way somewhere?" Gardner seemed to know when the light spots began to swim around in the corners of Bruno's vision.

"No." Bruno turned and went back home.

18

watching you without me

REGINE SAT DOWN WITH Bruno and Marco in the cafeteria, and Bruno noticed that Marco didn't make a sarcastic comment about her decision to grace them with her presence. Her eyes flicked in Marco's direction, but when she spoke, it was to Bruno.

"I feel like I owe you an apology," she said quietly. "At the beginning of the year, I could tell Silver wanted to have this group to himself, and I took his side. I didn't really give you a chance."

"It's okay," Bruno said.

"But . . . things haven't turned out the way I thought they would, and I know that's not a surprise to the rest of you. I just really wanted . . . I shouldn't have been mean to you."

"It's okay," Bruno said again. "I'm sorry about Silver."

Regine looked at the ceiling. "I think about it, and I try to figure out what I should have done differently. And I guess I shouldn't have tried so hard. But would it have been so crazy? Why shouldn't there have been a Rosary this year? We did all the same things. We were the same kind of group."

When Marco spoke he sounded sad but earnest. "You still don't understand, do you? Everyone has a Rosary, whether they call it that or not. The Rosary is the group of people who keep you alive in high school. That's what matters."

Regine slowly breathed out and looked at Bruno. "What does it mean if your Rosary keeps you alive but beats you up along the way?" Bruno thought she could have been talking about him, too.

Marco spoke more gently than Bruno ever had heard him. "So you haven't been lucky in love. That doesn't mean your Rosary hasn't been one of the best things in your life so far."

"It's just so hard to separate those things, you know?" Regine looked at him, her façade gone. "It's all one complicated mess."

"Well, everything's about to change again, in a month or so. And then it will keep on changing. When you leave Suburban, you can leave behind whatever you'd like. I just hope you'll keep the good memories."

Regine nodded. "I can't wait to get out of here."

"IF YOU KNEW SOMETHING about Regine, you'd tell me, wouldn't you?" Sylvio asked in the car on the way to Diaboliques.

"What do you mean?"

"Like, if she's going out with somebody."

"Is she? Wait, why would you care? You broke up with her months ago."

"I know." Sylvio sounded irritated. "But I didn't think we'd *stay* broken up."

"Are you serious?"

"Forget it," Sylvio said.

"Were you just dating her so you could get a Rosary bracelet?"

"No!" Sylvio sounded even more irritated. "No. I mean, I

really wanted it to be the way they all described it last year. I guess it's a little late now. But I do like her. I did like her."

"You still like her," Bruno said, and Sylvio didn't bother to reply. "And now you wonder if she's moved on. Well, I haven't heard anything."

When they were parking outside the club, Sylvio said, "Don't tell Marco it's my fault, okay? It's humiliating enough as it is."

"Why do you think I would tell Marco?"

"C'mon, you two tell each other everything."

"That's not true. Anyway, I don't think Marco cares."

"Or Celia."

"Celia either. She thought you were a nice couple."

"And I screwed it up." Sylvio opened the car door.

But that night the issue wasn't going to go away quietly. They arrived upstairs in Patrick's room to find the St. Dymphna boys already there. The six of them saluted from across the dance floor. Then without saying anything, Regine crossed over to them, and they clustered around her like courtiers around their queen. As if on cue, Patrick put on "Over the Shoulder," and Regine and her new admirers stepped out onto the floor, where they danced in weaving patterns around her as she pinwheeled her arms.

"What's going on there?" Marco was at Bruno's side.

"I don't know," Bruno confessed.

"They invited her to one of their performances—their string sextet, or whatever it is," Celia said. "She said it was amazing."

"They only invited her?" Marco asked, and Celia nodded. "Is Silver going to be okay with this?"

"I don't see what it has to do with him."

Bruno empathized with his brother; he knew what it was like to watch an object of affection being happy with someone else. But Sylvio had made his choice, and now he had to accept the consequences.

Later in the night, Celia bent close to Bruno's ear. "I'm going to say hello to Cassandra. Do you want to come?"

"I think I'll stay," Bruno said. "I think it's better for you to be my only Ambassador."

She nodded, obviously pleased, and went out of the room.

"WHEN YOU GOT THE NOTE, what was the first thing you thought?" Marco stepped up onto the bench and sat down on the top of the picnic table, looking around the tennis court. Dried leaves from winter still clustered around the net. It was Tuesday, and it was nearly time.

"All I could think was that somehow Celia and Tomasi would wind up here." Bruno sat down next to him.

"Well, I can't imagine they would come over to your backyard to make out."

"And it wouldn't fit the pattern of Mariette's predictions, anyway. Other than them being here for no reason, there wouldn't be anything unexpected about it."

"So you think it's going to be more like what happened with Celia's mom? Not someone you're romantically involved with?"

"Well, I'm not romantically involved with anyone, so, yeah, probably."

"If it's here in your backyard, it's probably someone in your family." On the far side of the court the color was draining out of the tall bushes as the sun dipped low. "You don't really use this place, do you?"

"We haven't used it once since we moved in."

"I can't imagine you'd suspect your parents of cheating. Your dad's a minister."

"Well, if you watch the news, ministers seem to cheat more than the average population," Bruno joked. "But no, I'd be very surprised."

"Your family is close. I like that. I'm closer to my mom than my dad, but I guess we're all pretty close."

"How is it, being an only child?" Bruno asked him.

"I don't know any different. But I guess you become more self-sufficient. How about you? What's it like being the youngest?"

"Well, Sophia's pretty much gone all the time now. Sylvio, I don't know. I think in some ways I've felt like I was supposed to catch up with them, and since I couldn't, I kept going in the other direction."

"I could see it being difficult, having him as an older brother," Marco said. "But as much as you guys like to squabble, I think you're closer than you let on. He's only a jerk now and then, isn't he? Or is he worse when we aren't around?"

"Not really. He thought I was changing who I was just to fit in with you guys."

"Which was only slightly inaccurate. You were changing who you were in hopes of getting Celia to like you." Marco playfully punched Bruno's shoulder. "I'm giving you a hard time. I know you well enough to be sure you're better than that."

"So why did I do it, then? Buy all those clothes and start going to Diaboliques?"

"I'd say it was the right thing at the right time. I think everyone hits a point—in middle school, in high school, maybe in college—where you start taking control of your life. You realize you can make your own decisions and start to become your own person, whoever that is. Maybe you try a few different options before you settle on the truth. Maybe it takes years to figure out. But that's what it looked like to me. Your tastes might be influenced by your brother, and by us, too, but hey, we all have influences, right? And I can see where your tastes differ from Silver's, too. What time is it?"

Bruno looked at his watch. "Two minutes."

They stared around the tennis court, waiting. Marco said, "I knew Gwendolyn was pretty, but she was stunning at the fashion show. And it's obvious she likes you."

"I know. I just don't feel that way about her."

"So you're ending the year at a net zero—your love is unrequited, and you are *unrequiting* someone else's love. Such a tragedy. All this love lost."

"I think we'll all survive," Bruno said.

"I am glad you've become friends with Celia, though, everything else aside. I would have felt bad about leaving her alone at Suburban next year. Now at least I know she'll have you."

"And Sylvio."

"Sure. But she's closer with you."

"We'll miss you next year."

"Yeah. I wish we'd overlapped more than just one year. When I think about it, I've spent more time with you this year than with Celia or Regine."

"I didn't think you'd want to spend so much time with me, just a first year."

"Maybe it's a guy thing. Don't tell Brenden I said this, but you've been my best friend at Suburban this year."

"You know, I'd say the same thing about you." It was the first time Bruno had considered it, but it was absolutely true.

"Not Celia? Forget the romance. You two have gotten pretty close in other ways."

"I guess we have. It's weird, though. I mean, Celia and I are friends, but it almost feels like something else."

"What, like you're business partners?" Marco chuckled.

"Maybe the right way to say it is that we're still figuring out what kind of friends we are. It's been a little complicated."

"I can see that."

"You and I—it's never been complicated."

"Not even when people think we're dating?"

"That's complicated for them, not for me," Bruno said. His mind was stuck on one thought, a thought that had been repeating itself since the moment he'd agreed Marco had been his best friend. It was so obvious, Bruno couldn't believe he hadn't realized it sooner.

He turned to Marco, who looked at him curiously. Bruno leaned in and touched his lips to Marco's. Then he sat back and looked down at his watch. Eight o'clock on the dot.

"You're a sweet guy," Marco said quietly. "That really means a lot to me."

"I'm not—"

"Of course you're not. That's why it's so sweet."

They sat in silence for a while. Then Marco spoke again. "Well, if it's not Celia and it's not Gwendolyn, who's it going to be? You're too good-looking not to be dating someone, and everyone else in this group is either in a relationship or still climbing out of the wreckage of one."

"I guess I've had other things to worry about." They got up from the picnic table.

"Well, that was definitely unexpected."

OUTSIDE BRUNO'S BEDROOM WINDOW the light was fading and the air was fragrant with blossoms. He went downstairs to pick up the phone on the eighth ring, wondering where everyone else was. "Hello?"

"Bruno?"

He recognized Sophia's voice instantly, and just as quickly he could tell she was crying. "What's wrong?"

"I'm so glad it's you," she said, her voice breaking. "I hoped it would be you." She paused. "You remember that married man I told you about when I was home? Well, I've managed to break my own heart, and it's nobody's fault but my own."

"I'm sorry. What happened?"

"I'm such a fool . . ." She sobbed. "I'm so embarrassed to tell you."

"You don't have to tell me," he said. "Are you okay?"

"I'll be okay," she said. "I just wish I could get a hug from you right now."

Bruno thought about what he could do with a piece of paper and a pencil. About how easily he could connect his closet to Sophia's, somewhere in Buenos Aires. How badly he wanted to put his powers to use, to comfort his sister. It made him crazy. Instead, he said, "Me too. I wish I could."

"How are you?" she asked.

"I'm good. I was in a fashion show."

"You were? Really?"

"I told you about Marco, and how he makes clothes. Well,

he got to do a fashion show at school, and—Do you really want to hear about this?"

"I would love to hear about it," Sophia said. "Tell me everything, and I'll try to imagine I was there."

"There are pictures somewhere. I'll send them to you."

"You have to!"

Bruno did his best to describe the show to his sister, the clothes everyone wore, what it had felt like to walk on a runway in front of everyone. But his heart kept pushing against his chest, willing him to use his power, while his head reminded him that was impossible. He thought the tug of war might pull him apart, and he hated it. So he concentrated on his story, and listened for the life that slowly returned to Sophia's voice.

"When are you coming home?" he finally asked, when she didn't sound quite so raw.

"You know, I was going to stay through the summer, but I think it might be good to spend some time at home," she said. "I don't even know what home is, at this point."

"We're your home."

"You are my home."

"WE NEVER HANG OUT, just the three of us. We never get to talk about the things we have to keep secret from everyone else," Celia said.

"What are you going to do?" Bruno asked Tomasi. "About the agon?"

"I'm going to try to stop."

"Stop dating?"

"No, stop being one of the Kind."

"Can you do that?"

"Well, it hasn't been a picnic anyway. First I was told I

had a learning disorder. Then my parents thought I was into black magic and sent me off to my grandfather's labor camp, commonly known as his farm. Now I find out my relationship with my girlfriend is against the rules for Kind and Ambassadors, which sounds pretty ridiculous to me. It just doesn't seem worth it."

"What are you going to do?"

"I'm trying to avoid it all, as much as possible. I've stopped traveling between books. I walk over to Celia's house now. I can't stop seeing books the way I do, but most of the time I can suppress my ability to see the books and letters in people's bags and pockets. I'm not going to try to fulfill any more admonitions."

"Is someone going to get mad or something?"

"I don't know. I didn't fulfill a slew of admonitions at the beginning, and no one came after me—just the next admonition. But right now I don't care. I'm trying out being a normal guy, dating a girl, nothing crazier than that, and so far it feels pretty good."

"Okay," Bruno said. He understood, but he was disappointed. Tomasi wasn't going to be a comrade as Bruno explored being Kind.

He was concerned, too. Deep down, he didn't believe Tomasi and Celia's problem could be solved that easily. If Bruno knew anything, it was that his new life embraced complexity, not the obvious choices or the simplest answers. "I hope it works."

"I hope so, too, but I know what you're thinking, and I wonder the same thing," Celia said. "We're going to try it and see what happens."

"If you ever need help, for any reason, I'll do whatever I

can," Bruno said. "I'm still really new to this, so there's not a lot I can do, but . . ."

"After what happened this week, I wouldn't say that," Tomasi said. "But it means a lot for you to say it. Thank you."

VAN CAME UP TO BRUNO after the last gym class of the year. "Can I talk to you?" he asked, and Bruno nodded. They hung back from the rest of the guys walking out. "I . . . I think I'm going crazy," Van said quietly. "I've been blacking out, and then I can't remember what's happened for ten or fifteen minutes, sometimes longer."

Bruno tried to think of what he could say. "Have you gone to the doctor?"

Van nodded sadly. "They're testing me for a whole bunch of things, but I'm sure they won't find it. Please. You know something. You know what's wrong with me."

"What makes you say that?"

"Because whenever I remember something from this year —and there are so many things I've forgotten, but every once in a while I remember—it's always something I can't explain . . . and it always has something to do with you."

"What are you remembering?"

"Some kind of passageway under the stairs over by the cafeteria. Talking to you at that bookstore, and then *flying*—" Van said the word in disbelief. "Finding myself in a classroom with you and Celia and having no idea how I got there. Did those things happen?"

"I don't think so . . ."

"Don't do this to me!" Van said, and Bruno thought the poor guy might cry. "Everyone else looks at me like I've lost my mind! They want to put me on medication; they think I'm schizophrenic or something! Please, *you know* that's not it—it's something else, isn't it?" Van grabbed Bruno's arm desperately.

No one else was nearby, and Bruno kept his voice low. "Okay. It might be true. Those things might have happened. You may have been given secret power at the beginning of the year, and when you got on the wrong side of some people, your power and all your memories of it were stripped from you. And you may be having flashbacks to those times, which make you black out until they're over. But I don't know how to help you. I don't know if anyone can do anything to make this better."

"Please," Van said again, his voice weak with despair.

Bruno looked him in the eye. "I've heard there are ways to get back, once you've gone to the Unkind side, but I don't know anyone who knows what to do, or how it works. I'm sorry."

In the middle of the empty lobby, Van's eyes filmed over and his face went slack. Staring into the distance, the mono-tonic voice from his trance in the classroom returned, and he said, "A dark wind has been rising toward you from somewhere deep in your future, across years that are still to come. And as it passes, it will level whatever is offered to you at the time, in years no more real than the ones you are living now." Then he walked like a somnambulist in a straight line out the front door and across the street to the field on the far side, never looking back.

BRUNO WAITED UNTIL THE appointed day—a Sunday—was over, and the last new moon before the summer solstice had passed. The deadline given by his admonition was at hand. He knew there wouldn't be any strange new feeling, like a ghost limb felt for the first time. But on several mornings recently he had woken with the remnants of recurring dreams still flowing through his body, and he had a hunch about what to do. He sat down at his desk with a new sheet of drawing paper alongside the smudged plan of Suburban he'd drawn back in the first semester.

On the wall above his desk Bruno had pinned copies of a dozen Piranesi etchings. Many nights he had stared at them so long, he wouldn't have been surprised if they had opened up the way the drawings in the huge *You Are Here* books had, allowing him to step inside. He contemplated them for a long time, preparing himself. The boundary between reality and imagination was as thin as a piece of paper.

Across the top of the blank sheet he carefully wrote *Suburban High School* in block letters. Then he began drawing, first the main hall of the school. "It would be better if the science wing were here," he murmured, drawing the wing branching out in a new place from the main hall. "And the Chancellor Wing should be here." The technology wing, the pool, the gymnasium, the auditorium—Bruno fit each one onto his new plan for the high school in ways that made them easier to navigate, less like a sprawling maze so contorted it made everything even farther away than it actually was. In his bones he thought he could feel the steel and bricks shifting around six miles away.

He did the library last, tucking it into a new space near the center of the plan. Only a front door, no back door. Thick walls on all sides, solid and dark. There were fifteen aisles of bookshelves in the stacks and no more. Bruno wondered whether he was destroying the *You Are Here* volumes in the process, and whether he might come to regret that. But he was resolute. A high school library had to be a place where books were always where they were supposed to be, where the lights reached into the farthest corners, and where people didn't get lost in impenetrable sections that left them scared and despondent—or worse.

Bruno finished his drawing and sat back to look at his work. Suburban was still a large school, but it wasn't a confusing school any longer. He picked up his pencil and drew a few more small rooms at the ends of the main halls. "Janitor's closets. How could I forget?"

Finished, he wandered out of his room and downstairs, where he found his father in the study.

"What's new?" Mr. Perilunas asked, looking up from his paper.

"I wanted to ask you something. When you have time."

"Now's fine. I'm finished with this." He set the paper aside. "What's on your mind?"

Bruno sat down in the wingback chair across from his father. "I wanted to ask you . . . Has there ever been a time when you weren't sure whether you believed in God?"

"Do you feel that way?"

"I don't know. I just don't understand. It's hard to explain. I just don't know what I believe anymore."

His father looked at his hands. "I always thought it would be Sylvio. Sophia is brilliant, but I don't think she spends a lot of time wrestling with stuff like this. When Sylvio started changing his style and listening to strange music, I wondered if it was coming. Who knows what he thinks or believes, but he's never talked to me about it." He shifted in his seat. "I'm not going to be any better at talking about this than you are. Because there's a point where words don't say enough, you know? What you believe, what you know to be true without having proof — or the things you don't believe, the things of which you can't convince yourself—those things can be very hard to describe.

"Faith is such a strange gift. And I think it is a gift. For those of us who receive it, it is the best gift we could ever hope to have, and it is so tempting to assume everyone has it, or to wish it for everyone else. And when we meet someone who has lost it, or maybe never even had it, it's so tempting to say, 'You must ask for this gift, pray for it, because it will comfort you, and help you through your life, the way it comforts me and helps me through mine.' But that's condescending, isn't it? To tell someone they should ask a higher power in which they don't believe to help them to know something of which they are skeptical, and to do it without any tangible proof. It's absurd.

"I believe you can live your life without religion, even without faith, and be a good, strong, upright person. I've seen many people do it. But I also will pray for you, because if you can be at home in your faith, I think your life will be richer, and even more meaningful."

Bruno nodded. "I'm sorry."

"You don't have to apologize for anything!" His father looked at him lovingly. "I will be happy to talk to you about this whenever you want." He stood up when Bruno did, and hugged him close when Bruno stepped into his arms. "I did most of the talking, didn't I? Ministers—we'll preach at the drop of a hat."

IN THE CAR WITH SYLVIO the next morning, Bruno was more nervous than any other time he could remember. Had it worked? Could he really have done such a thing? Was he insane?

From the road he could see the difference. He swallowed

hard and felt his heart swell in his chest. Suburban appeared just as he had redrawn it: Wings had folded back into the building, and the sprawl had been squared off into a shape that was equal in size to the old school but laid out in simpler lines, with shorter distances among all points.

In the lobby he wondered whether this was how architects felt the first time they went into a newly completed building they had designed. He saw his handiwork in three dimensions around him. One thing hadn't changed: To enter Suburban was to agree to its terms, even if they included curses, ghosts, and storm clouds on the ceiling.

As he suspected, no one else seemed to have noticed any difference. Bruno had reordered Suburban, and Suburban had reordered itself in everyone's minds. Just as on every morning since the beginning of the school year, distracted students rushed up and down the halls, in and out of doorways, taking for granted that their destinations awaited them in their expected place, never realizing their expectations had changed.

He looked at Celia and could tell immediately she was as oblivious as the citizens. So he went up to the library to find Lois.

"You did this?" she asked him. "I'm impressed!"

"Thanks! Celia can't see it."

"I'm not surprised. I do think in a lot of ways, Ambassadors are closer to citizens than they are to Kind," Lois said. "Are you disappointed she doesn't know what you've done?"

"I guess not." Bruno looked over at the stacks. "That's weird."

"What?"

"My plan closed off the Ebentwine. But it's still dark back there. I still can't see the back wall."

"I have a hunch the Ebentwine isn't that easily manipulated," Lois said. "That's okay. It must be here for a reason. We probably should see if we can figure that out."

"I guess so," Bruno said. "I have to go to homeroom."

"See you later!"

All day he marveled at the new Suburban he had created. He took detours to each class to explore all the new corners of the school. He saw things on which he could improve even more. Suburban was his now—his to configure and his to protect.

He was passing through the new technology hall when his books went flying out of his arms and into an empty classroom. Bruno almost said *Mariette!* out loud, shaking his head in amusement as he went in to retrieve them. *Is this how it's going to be now?*

But she didn't appear in the classroom while he gathered up his things. Bruno turned to head back out to the hall, when a shower of loose papers fell down around him. He jumped out of the way and looked up.

Tina Moreletii stood upside down on the ceiling, her wavy hair hanging toward the floor. The legs of her pantsuit bunched down toward her knees, revealing her stockings and her high heels planted against the acoustic tiles. She held the empty trashcan, still upended over the place where he had stood. Her wild eyes roamed around the room. "You dropped those!"

"What are you doing here? What are you *doing*?" Bruno wondered if he should run, but she looked as unfocused as a drunk.

"I'm emptying the trash!" She laughed sadly, dropping the plastic bin down to the floor, where it clattered around among the desks. "You're welcome!"

328

"You have to be kidding me." Bruno turned at the sound of Mariette's voice, and there she was, looking up at Ms. More- letii with an annoyed expression. "She's driving me crazy."

"What's wrong with her?" Bruno asked.

"When people arrive on this side, they're never quite the same as they were when they were alive," Mariette said. "And the urge to make mischief seems to be a common quality we pick up along the way." She smiled at Bruno, who smiled back.

Meanwhile, Ms. Moreletii had begun to dance lightly across the ceiling, and the papers she had scattered down on Bruno began to fly up in the air, whirling around her and then peeling away to flutter back down. "You're welcome! You're welcome! You're welcome!" she sang, hands waving back and forth.

"You'd better go. I'll take care of this," Mariette said.

"Thank you." Out in the hall, Bruno laughed and shook his head.

GWENDOLYN WAS CLEANING OUT her locker when Bruno came up to her. She wore a black and white dress and a black ribbon in her blond hair, which now fell halfway down her back, making her look like a shorter, blond version of Celia. She turned to him, and for a moment she looked lost again.

"I wish this had turned out differently," he said.

"In what way?"

"I kind of hoped we'd be friends, way back, before I med- dled in your life."

"You wanted to be my hero," she said quietly. "And you got what you wanted."

"That's not why I did it—to be a hero."

"Why, then?"

He was desperate not to say the wrong thing. "I would have wanted someone to do it for me, if I had been in that position. I wasn't expecting anything. I kind of hoped we'd just put it behind us and move on."

"Don't you hear how that sounds? You wanted to swoop into my life and fix things, and then pretend we were somehow just friends at school?"

"If you want me to apologize for doing what I thought was right—what you know was the right thing to do, I will, but I don't think I should have to. I knew it was none of my business, which is why I've never brought it up again."

She closed her locker. "You know what, forget it. You did a very nice thing, and I fell in love with you, and you didn't love me back, and I'm a fool. Can we just not talk about it?"

"Gwendolyn, I'm sorry. I know what it's like to wish for things that aren't going to happen. Can we . . . I don't know . . . can we come back in the fall and maybe start over? Maybe do things differently?"

Gwendolyn lifted her bag onto her shoulder. "Well, I guess we'll find out when the fall comes. No promises." He watched her walk away.

BRUNO SAT IN CHURCH ON Sunday, the day after Marco and Regine's graduation, marveling that his first year at Suburban was over. It was nothing like he had expected, in too many ways to count. He hoped his summer away from Suburban would be as uneventful as possible. He would have a few months with Marco, and now Sophia, too, before Bruno and Celia had to wade back into the tangle of unanswered questions at the high school.

His father's words brought Bruno back to the chapel. "Recently someone shared with me that he was struggling with his faith." Bruno flushed, sure his father would not betray this confidence, but nervous it would be obvious anyway. He waited to hear what his father would say.

"I've been thinking about it ever since, and I wanted to talk about it here because it scares me. And that made me think it's likely that it scares some of you, too — the idea of losing my faith, of coming unmoored from the beliefs that help me understand why I'm here and what my purpose is. I'll tell you what I told this man when we talked about it: Faith is a gift, and it is one of the ultimate gifts, because there is no way to ask for it, and no way to be sure it will remain with us if we have received it.

"I don't think there is any point in skirting the scary parts of religion. We are asked to believe things that defy logic. We experience moments of pain, of suffering, and even death, knowing they are the things that truly enable us to live, and give our lives meaning. We choose harder roads, longer paths that force us to confront things about ourselves we might prefer to ignore. And we do that because our faith closes the gap between our heads and our hearts, between our bodies and our souls, between our solitary lives and the world around us.

"I told this man I believe it is possible to live an upright life without faith. The great secular humanists have done almost as much to shape the modern church as the great theologians, and we would be foolish to deny it. For each of us, the way we make sense of the world is as unique as our fingerprint. Maybe this is the most important thing I want to say to you today — the same thing I want that man to know: When you close your eyes at night, trusting you will open them again after you have slept, *that is basic faith.* And at times we might have to retreat to an experience of our faith that is as simple, as pure as that. It's an excellent reminder that every day we are given the opportunity to believe amazing, impossible things, and we do. We believe, and because we believe, we live."

Mr. Perilunas sat down, and the pianist began the meditation. Next to him, Bruno noticed a woman cupping her hands together in the same way his father did. He looked around and saw congregants on all sides, their hands curled into nests.

"DID YOU EVER THINK YOUR first year of high school would turn out the way it did?" Celia glanced up at Bruno as she drew him in her sketchbook.

"No, I never would have guessed," he said, trying to look natural but feeling self-conscious.

"Same here. Nobody would believe us if we told them. Any regrets?"

"Maybe. I learned a lot. Maybe I won't make some mistakes again."

"Don't be so hard on yourself. You did some amazing things."

Bruno shrugged and then wondered if he had shifted too much, but Celia didn't seem to notice. She worked in silence for a little, and he was content to sit quietly. He felt the delicious hum of his attraction to her. Knowing they were like magnets—rare elements that combine to form an even rarer compound—didn't really change anything for him. Celia was still the most beautiful girl he'd ever met, and his devotion to her was unchanged.

"Next year, it'll just be Silver and me and you."

"I think Gwendolyn would hang out with us, if we asked her."

"Whatever happened with her?"

"Nothing. She's very nice, and she likes our style. I bet she'd love Diaboliques."

"Well, we should ask her, then, if you think so. That's how it happens: Regine asked me. She asked your brother, too. Marco and I didn't really give you a choice, did we?" Celia smiled at him. "If you think Gwendolyn is a good fit, ask her. This group is yours as much as any of ours."

"I will." Bruno thought back to the first day of school and how graced he had felt by Celia's presence. "There is something I've always wanted to ask you."

"What is it?"

"There's a song you like, by This Mortal Coil. I wonder why you like it so much."

She stopped drawing. "Which song?"

"'Song to the Siren.'"

"I'm not a huge This Mortal Coil fan, though Brenden would kill me for saying that. I like them, but I can't remember which song that is. Which album is it on?"

"*It'll End in Tears*. It's the one where the woman sings, 'I dreamed that you dreamed about me?'"

"Oh, yeah. I'll have to go listen to it again. What made you think I like it?"

"Well, way back before school started, when I had just found the Ebentwine clearing—I didn't even know how it worked—I wound up in your backyard, and I actually thought you lived next door to me, because I didn't understand where it was taking me."

"Is that why you asked me where I lived on the first day of school?"

"Yes. So, I was in your backyard and your window was open, and I heard the song playing—'Song to the Siren'—but I didn't know it then. It took me months to figure out what it was. I couldn't ask you because I didn't want you to think I was some creep lurking around in your backyard, spying on you."

"What makes you sure I'm not thinking that now?" Celia smiled.

"I went back the next night because I couldn't figure it out. You had told me where you lived, so I thought I must have seen someone else. But I was sure it was you, so I went back through the clearing, into your backyard, and you were in your room again. And the same song was playing."

"You know, I think Brenden had just given me that album that week," Celia said. "A couple nights I put it on and listened to it the whole way through. You must have gotten there when that song came on, each time. What a coincidence." She went back to her drawing.

"Wow."

"And the odd thing is, I don't think I've listened to it since. Wait—that's not true. I listened to it one other time, right around New Year's."

Bruno kept quiet about having been listening from the back of her closet that time. The strange bridge that had connected him to her all year through the simple plea—*Do you dream about me?*—crumbled away. Sitting alone with her, as he had wanted since they had met—it was lovely, and hollow, and it felt like the brightness had drained out of the day.

"If it made such an impression on you, then I really want to hear it again. It must be good."

"Oh, you don't need to . . ." He was mortified now. She would hear the lyrics, and even though they had talked about it, had moved past it, all his pathetic little feelings would be laid bare for her.

"I'll never know how you feel," Celia said. "But if you feel it, it's true. And the truth is beautiful, right? Even if it hurts."

"I guess so." He felt his stale crush—his fumbling love —shifting deep inside him, like the foundations of Suburban, to devotion. Some of the sting had gone. This privileged but platonic relationship was the most he would have with her, ever. Still, the hum was there, like power lines or underground trains.

"I'm finished." Celia handed her sketchbook to Bruno. There he was, lifelike on the page. Just as when she had drawn him before, it was a small shock to see, looking back at himself as though from a mirror. "Is that how I look? I mean, my expression?"

"Not all the time. But it's my favorite expression of yours. You look that way when you've told someone you don't know something, but you really do."

Bruno grinned. Something in the background of the drawing caught his eye: a figure standing a distance behind him. "Who is this?"

"It's you."

"No, the girl." Bruno handed the sketchbook back to Celia and pointed out the smaller figure in the background. Her face wasn't clear, but her hair blew dramatically around her head.

"Did I draw that?" Celia squinted at the page. "I didn't even notice. I have no idea who that is. She doesn't look familiar?"

"Not at all," Bruno said.

"That's very strange. I swear to you, I don't remember

drawing her at all." Celia looked concerned. "What could that mean?"

"Maybe someone is coming," Bruno suggested.

"Wouldn't that be interesting."

acknowledgments

My unending gratitude to Zoe Shacham, who ushered me into publishing in such a spectacular way. This book doesn't have your fingerprints on it quite as markedly as *The Suburban Strange*, but it exists because of you nonetheless, and I send you my fondest wishes.

To everyone at Nancy Yost Literary Agency, especially Adrienne Rosado, who was kind/crazy enough to take me on, feed me macaroons, and help me land the plane not once, but twice. I can't wait to find out what story we'll tell next.

To Margaret Raymo, who keeps the bar high and gets me over it every time. I am a stronger writer because of you, and I don't know a better definition of *editor* than that. I am so fortunate to have found my way into your care.

When I wrote the acknowledgments for *The Suburban Strange*, I hadn't yet met some of the other amazing people on the Houghton Mifflin Harcourt team who provided rock star support for that project. I am fortunate to be working with them again this time around, so these thanks are for both books: Christine Krones for keeping an eye on the business details, Roshan Nozari for wrangling the Internet publicity, and the fantastic Rachel Wasdyke for being the best publicity contact an author could ever hope to find. I also salute the Design department for their stellar work on the jackets and layouts—I don't know you by name, but I think of you gratefully every time someone gushes about these covers.

Thanks to all the musicians, authors, artists, and designers to whom I pay tribute in this book. In the same way you enrich my life, you enrich my story, and I hope someday to join your ranks.

Over this past year I have met so many amazing independent booksellers, librarians, and teachers who have gotten behind *The Suburban Strange*. The chance to talk about books, reading, writing, and learning with you and your clients, patrons, and students has been the unexpected blessing of this journey. I have to mention by name LueAnn Brenson, Staci Bumgarner, Rebecca Carr, Suzanne de Gaetano, Megan Graves, Siobhan Loendorf, Marie Murphy, Jennifer Newcome, Kate Schlademan, Jackie Shaw, Josie Whysall, and Autumn Winters. And to Sarah Carr and all at Flyleaf Books in Chapel Hill—I am blown away by your support.

Hats off to some amazing authors I've met this year, whose work inspires me and whose camaraderie has been a joy: Jodi Lynn Anderson and Kristen-Paige Madonia, I've enjoyed our chats immensely. Dennis Mahoney, it's been a blast trading manuscripts with you, and then watching them get up on their legs and out the door.

Some dear friends have been amazing cheerleaders during this crazy adventure, going to incredible lengths on my behalf: Dana Aritonovich and Melanie Russ Rinzel, thank you so much for giving me some brilliant chapters this past year. Kimberly Hirsh, you started by opening doors for me, but I quickly realized the room was much more fun if you came in, too. And Emily Jack, your countless hours and talents are bested only by the number of times we have laughed until we couldn't breathe. Many thanks!

To Amy Carreira, Chris Fellows, and Debbie Meyers: *Troika Forever!*

And now, my Rosary. Alli Cooke, Lisa Schieler Blackman, and Andrea Gangloff Klores — eternal thanks to you for coming along on these adventures; I wouldn't have it any other way. Your insight and love mean the world to me. And Mr. Gates, I am so lucky to be allowed to visit the world inside your photographs.

Finally, to my family. Everything is better when shared with you. Much love.

author's note

When Bruno finally identified the song he'd heard from Celia's window as This Mortal Coil's cover of "Song to the Siren" by Tim Buckley, did you track down the song and listen to it? If you haven't yet, I hope you will. Just as "Second Skin" by the Chameleons was such a beautiful reinforcement of Celia's journey in *The Suburban Strange*, "Song to the Siren" is the perfect underscore for Bruno's experience in *Pull Down the Night*.

For that matter, you could spend some enjoyable time listening to the dark alternative songs that lend their names to the chapter titles in this book. Just a thought . . .

I continue to believe, as Brenden said in *The Suburban Strange*, that life is always better with the right soundtrack. Keep reading, and keep listening.